GABI

GABI

by

George
Hatcher

This book can be purchased at over 40,000 bookstores and libraries including brick and mortar stores, online, in print and digital, including Apple, Kindle,and Audible formats. Casa Hatcher Press books are available at special quantity discounts for bulk purchases, for sales promotions, premiums, and educational use for fund raising.

Casa Hatcher Press is a subsidiary of Pretty Face, Inc. Pasadena, CA 91103

For details, contact:
Casa Hatcher Press.
http://casahatcherpress.com
(818) 519-2976

Book and cover designed by Casa Hatcher Press
Cover photos svittlana @adobestock.com, Subbotina Anna @ adobestock.com, trongnguyen@adobestock.com
©George Hatcher interior art by Tarik Chraiti

Gabi by George J. Hatcher
First Edition August 2020
LCCN 2020942990
ISBN: 978-1-7332351-4-3 (Hardback)
ISBN: 978-1-7332351-5-0 (Paperback)
ISBN: 978-1-7332351-7-4 (E-book)
An earlier revision of this E-book was published
R: 20201107

Dedication

Molly

You are my sun during the
day and my moon at night.

Love forever,

George

Acknowledgements

Tarik thank you for your quick hand and artistic eye. Your artwork enhances these pages.

If it were up to my editor, Allie Bates, this book would still be in edits. I had to pry it out of her grip while she was still marking up. Every pass makes it a little better, she says. Just let me proofread it one more time, she says.

WARNING!

Adult matter

This book is intended for adults. Violence and sexual antics are not intended for minors, sensitive readers, or people living in the real world where there are sexually transmitted diseases which are incurable. Gabi is a work of fiction. The people in the book lived and died only in my imagination. Any resemblance to actual people will be only in your imagination. The story is sheer fantasy, and you can blame it on the pandemic. Unlike Gabi, I am no lawyer. I have not engaged in her professions.

Works by George Hatcher

Ambulance Chaser Series

Mario 1: Woman in Jeopardy

Mario 2: Coming of Age

Mario 3: Risky Business

Mario 4: Free Fall

Mario 5: Afire

Mario 6: Marked

Mario 7: Aftershock

Mario 8: Captivated

Single titles

One Wilshire

Gabi

Coming Soon

Billion Dollar Rainmaker part 1

Billion Dollar Rainmaker part 2

Mario 9

Arabe

Flyboy

Pretty Face

Gabi 2

1972
East Los Angeles
Gabi

I was born in 1964 in Phoenix, Arizona. My mother Cira was a waitress, my father Armand Rana, a bartender. When I was eight, my mother's little sister picked me up and brought me to Los Angeles to live with her. This was after my dad had died drunk in a car accident, and my mother overdosed. My aunt had never been married, and went by her maiden name, Isabel Guerrero. I like the sound of the family name, and my mother's maiden name, Cira Guerrero. I wanted to fit in with my new family, so every chance I got, I gave my last name as Guerrero. I never use the name Gabriella. I hate my name. It's the name you give a girl when you expect to have a boy you want to call Gabriel. Gabi, I can live with. I tell people I am Gabi Guerrero. The warrior. I like the sound of it better than Gabriella Frog.

"Aunt Isabel, who named me?"

"Cira did. Your mom ran away from home when she was sixteen and ended up somewhere in Italy. She came back and married your dad. When you were born, she picked an Italian name. Gabriella is Italian."

More than one time, I said to Isabel, "Maybe my dad wasn't my dad. Maybe my dad isn't dead, and he's in Italy somewhere."

I liked kidding my aunt. She was so crazy serious I couldn't help it. She's super serious but she had a thing for that witch show with that actress Elizabeth Montgomery. She named her boys Darrin and Larry, and her daughter Serena. I would have teased her about it, except I like their names better than mine.

"Hush, *muchacha loca.* Your dad was a good man."

"Which one, the one that died, or the one in Italy?"

My aunt frowned and didn't respond. She never struck me, but sometimes it looked like it was coming.

"I know my dad and mother were good people," I said. I wanted to say 'even though my dad drank himself into a car accident and my mom doped herself to death.' I was a little kid, but not only already understood that we humans have all sorts of problems, but also that my aunt was the kind of person who picked up the pieces her broken sister had left behind. I knew all about picking up the pieces. She and me, we were alike. Two peas in a pod.

At eight years old, it had been hard for me to learn how to live with her, how to be dependent on her, how to trust her. I wasn't used to responsible caregivers. I remember being the responsible one. The first thing I remember in my life is the social worker coming in, and showing my mother how to make the bed, how to clean, what to shop for, how to do all the motherly things she was supposed to be doing. I think I was around three. She was good at being pretty and sweet and kind. She was not good at bed-making, cleaning, shopping and cooking, so I did it for her. I remember making her get out of bed to walk to the store with me. It was a local grocery, just a little mom and pop, and I would push the basket from one end to the other and fill it with everything we needed for the month, while she had a little private meeting with Pop in the back office. The cashiers thought it was so cute to see a six-year old doing the shopping, but by the time I was eight or so, they were used to it. Mommy would come out of the back room, and Pop would check us out. We'd roll the basket all the way down the block to our apartment. When we got home, Mommy would take a shower, and I would put away the groceries, take the basket back, and put our TV dinners in the oven. When I moved in with my auntie, I did not believe somebody was going to make sure I didn't go to bed hungry or cold. After all, I was the one who made sure my Mommy was covered up, even if she had gone to sleep on the floor. I was the one who took off her shoes and socks when she was tired and sick.

Not only did my auntie do all things to run the house, she always noticed everything I did to help, which nobody had ever done before. But my first night there, Aunt Isabel showed me a place to put the clothes from the grocery bag I brought with me. She gave me my own pillow, and when all four of us kids got in the one bed we had to sleep in, she made sure we were all tucked in, even me, even though I wasn't even her kid.

I saw things that my cousins didn't. They were just naïve, and my aunt did her level best to keep them that way. Aunt Isabel showed me that responsibility is a kind of courage, and I respected her for it. I saw how she made sure we kids were fed before she herself ate, how she went without so that we had clothes to wear. I saw the endless darning, stitching, and duct taping that kept her clothes and shoes going long after they should have been consigned to the trash.

Aunt Isabel had three children plus me and there were always more bills than there was money to pay them. We lived on food stamps, plus every public assistance aid my aunt could get her hands on. I didn't quite understand how that worked, but I knew a social worker when I saw one. One came by to inspect us and the house, and even opened our kitchen cupboards to see if we were spending the food stamps on food and not something else.

My aunt was pretty. When we went to the grocery, shopping, or to the flea market, I heard men tell her how beautiful she was. Her three kids paid no attention to this. All they did was fool around and play games with each other no matter where we were. I paid attention. I was curious about my aunt. She didn't look like a mom at all. My memory of my mom would always be how beautiful she was, even when she was bone thin and sick from the drugs she took. I wasn't supposed to know this. I'm not blind. I lived with her. I knew. My aunt was healthy-looking, like my mom was when I was a very little girl.

1979
Los Angeles, California
Isabel

My social worker said, "Our guidelines say to keep public assistance, you must put in three hours of work daily during the week."

"Who is going to hire me for three hours a day?" I asked.

"Try finding something, anything, as long as you get paid by check."

I went to all the businesses in walking distance, but no one was hiring. I looked at some places I could reach by bus, though the cost of transportation would eat up the income.

"No one wants me, Ms. Delavega," I said.

"Isabel, call me Kenya."

"No one wants me, Kenya," I said.

"You ever work before?"

"Yes, if you call it work giving birth to three kids and taking care of them. Oh, and my niece. She's been with me seven years. Raising four kids, Kenya, is that work experience?"

Kenya made a joke by waving off what I said. "I didn't mean that kind of work and you know it."

My social worker was short, heavyset, and had a mop of rebellious curly red-brown hair that hung to her shoulders. She was always quick with a smile or a joke even though she was overworked. "You can break out of the cycle," she said earnestly. "You've got the smarts. I was in your shoes once too. If I can do it, you can do it."

"But I never—"

"It's about time you start." She handed me a card.

I took the card, feeling equal parts inspiration and fear. I read the card and couldn't believe it.

"This is an introduction to the coroner's office? They will hire me for three hours a day?"

"Yes. Make a good impression, and they will put you to work for minimum wage. A job will build your resume. When you get off public assistance, you can get on full-time with the County of Los Angeles. It will change your life."

"Mrs. Delavega, do I have to do this?"

"Only if you want to keep your public assistance. It's either the job in your hand or...."

I looked down at the card and wondered what a minimum wage worker did at the coroner's office. It couldn't be good.

At twenty-nine, I look okay though having three kids in a row when I was sixteen, seventeen and eighteen, and putting up with their drunken father had taken a toll on my body. Their father never married me. He kept getting me pregnant so the welfare checks could get bigger, till I figured out how to get on the pill. He took off about the time I inherited Gabi, never to be seen again. He's probably dead. There was no help in that direction. I only had myself to rely on. I had to do what I had to do.

I put on my best pair of jeans that fit like a second skin, a white button-down shirt that only had a mend in the cuff that no one could see, and an almost new pair of Van tennis shoes that I'd picked up for a song at Goodwill, and walked right into the human resources department at the coroner's office as if I had a right to be there. I felt like they would catch on that I was just me, and they'd kick me out.

"The only opening right now is in the cremation department," Peggy Munch said, reading over something on a clipboard. "Fernando can use the help, says here for three hours a day. Are you afraid of dead people?"

Miss Munch was a hundred years old if she was a day, and her fuzz of sparse hair was an unlikely color red. She had a narrow, yellowed face, and looked at me through a pair of large round glasses that matched her hair. She wore a sedate beige suit that clashed with the huge concentric maroon earrings hanging from her ears, with a string of fat matching beads the size of ping pong balls wound three times around her neck. A dozen thin brass bracelets ringed her right arm and clacked against the desk as she tapped long maroon nails against the desktop.

I looked at this crazy looking lady and said, "In my neighborhood, I'm more afraid of the people who are alive."

Miss Munch smiled as best she could. I got a good look at some horsey yellow teeth that may or may not have been store-bought.

"Good attitude, Miss Guerrero. Go down the hall there, take the elevator to the basement and find Fernando. I'll call and tell him you are going to see him. If he likes you, you got a job."

Fernando was about ten years older than me, around forty.

He had the faded tan of someone who used to be outside frequently, paired with a government worker haircut. There was enough scruff on his face that he was somewhere between interesting and needing a good scrub, only I wasn't interested in finding out the answer. He was from a barrio but not mine. He had a beer belly, but who could blame him, doing the job he did? I am sure he was justified in over-doing whatever vice he might have. I assumed it was drinking.

He showed me around.

"This area has the cremators," he said. "You okay?"

I nodded that I was. "Is that what you call them? Not furnaces?"

"Furnace works, too," he explained. "Some professionals call them incinerators."

"That sounds ugly," I said.

Fernando chuckled a little.

"I have couple questions." I felt comfortable with Fernando.

"Shoot."

"Are the bodies put in a coffin?"

"Sometimes, yes, but not the top of the coffin. I'll explain later about that. The body is put in a container with no steel. That's the rule. They are often wearing the clothes they had on when they died."

I didn't feel sick, but it was possible I could.

After an hour with Fernando, I didn't get sick and that surprised him. I'm not denying it was gross and unsettling.

"If you want the job, you got it. I know they won't pay you much, but I got nothing to do with that part of it."

"I want the job," I said.

I went back to my interviewer, Mrs. Munch. I filled out a bunch of paperwork, and I started the next morning, one hour after my kids went to school.

I took the bus the short distance to the county facility. It was good getting out of the house. The county supplied me with khaki uniforms. Patches on my shirt sleeve said 'County of Los Angeles Coroner's Office.' Of course, I had to supply my own underwear.

I bought a pair of Van tennis shoes. New.

I discovered a thing about riding the bus daily at the exact same time. You run into the same people. They are still strangers, but you start to feel like they are acquaintances. Some of these are people you would prefer not to be acquainted with.

I'd been observing one such fellow from a distance. He was a heavily pomaded man, greased with Vitalis, and strongly scented by cheap aftershave. It appeared to me that he would sit next to an attractive woman, then she would get disturbed over something he'd said, done, or grabbed, and the woman next to him would always change seats before she got where she was going. Inevitably the day came when he sat down next to me.

"What you do for the county?" he asked.

I did not want my friendship with this bus Lothario to get that far, so I cut it short in a creative fashion: I told the truth.

"I cremate people."

"You are jiving?"

"Someone has to do it."

I gave him a big smile. I reached into my big carry-all and pulled out a white-wrapped piece of meat I'd gotten from Ralph's before catching the bus home. "I brought home a piece of one. Do you want to see?"

His eyes got big, and he backed off like I'd just contracted rabies, scabies, and a bad case of dysentery, all in one. He inched away, mumbled something, and took himself off to the farthest seat from me that the bus had.

I laughed to myself all the way home.

At home, I didn't talk about my work. Gabi asked a million questions, and that kid wouldn't ever take 'no' for an answer. So finally, I told her.

"You burn people?"

"No. I burn dead people," I corrected her.

"I'm sick," she said, running to her room.

When she got over it, she told my kids what I did.

Darrin is three years younger than Gabi. He shut himself in his room for an hour and wouldn't come out. He didn't want his mother burning people.

"Gabi, you are miserable," I screamed at my niece. "You got the devil in you."

She stuck her tongue out at me.

"Auntie, we're family. No hiding."

The kids were okay with it by dinner time. Ever since, they have been coming up with ghoulish jokes, and make like we are the Adams family or the Munsters. I walk in the room, and they start singing the Adams Family theme song or instead of Mami, they call me Morticia. Maybe Gabi was right. Why hide?

Mrs. Delavega made her monthly stop.

"How's it going?"

"Want to know how many I cremated so far?"

"No, I don't want to know any such thing."

"Seriously, thanks for the reference. I'm starting to realize there's a whole world outside these doors."

"Good attitude," Mrs. Delavega said. I remembered when the crazy looker, Mrs. Munch, told me that.

Fernando and I got along like corn and beans, except that he was married with four kids. He made good money and fringe benefits. After twenty years on the job, he would be able to retire and draw a pension.

"Someday, maybe I can get a regular job here," I said. Often.

"No reason why you can't," he said.

A regular job would mean I'd make too much for aid. I'd have to give up the aid, maybe even the check I got for Gabi from the government. If the paycheck wasn't enough to live on, or the job didn't work out for one reason or another, it would take forever to get the aid back. It was too risky.

"When my kids are older," I said.

It was Fernando and me from nine till noon. When we only had one body to do, we had time to talk. Fernando had to do paperwork, but his boss worked another shift. One day he said, "Those jeans were made for that fine ass, Isabel. Don't get pissed. I had to tell you."

"I'm not pissed. Aren't you getting any at home?"

"I get enough," he said.

The next time we had time to burn, he did it to me in his office. I bent over his desk, my work pants around my ankles. The whole floor was quiet, but the desk squeaked really loud. Nobody was around, but he turned on the radio to the local rock station to try to cover it up.

"Not bad, Fernando," I said afterwards. "At least ten minutes."

"You're making fun," he said.

"Not a chance. The father of my kids came in two minutes. This time, so did I."

I kissed Fernando. It been a long time since I'd been with a man.

1978
Los Angeles, California
Gabi

At fourteen, I asked my school counselor to give me a work permit, but she told me no way. I had to be fifteen, plus so many months. I wasn't going to take no for an answer, so I hit on the manager at the McDonalds three blocks from the house. His name was Ramirez. He was twenty-one, a good dude from the barrio. He had a cute laugh.

"Put me down for three or four hours a day," I said. "Please."

He said, "Sure thing kiddo. I need a work permit and a social security number."

The social security number was easy. My aunt had my card. Without a social security card for each kid, she couldn't get aid. I went back to Ramirez and gave him the social security number.

When I returned, he took me in his office.

"Come back when you get the work permit, and then come back when you're eighteen so I can get some of that booty."

"Oh, you like my booty?"

I didn't hesitate to use that as bribery. "Give me a job and you don't have to wait. I dare you."

Ramirez turned red as a tomato. His face clashed horribly with his yellow and orange getup. "I'm out of here, jailbait," he said, shooting out of his office at a run, leaving me there alone.

I knew my body was okay, but I was low key about it. I knew I was pretty. I surprised myself when I looked in the mirror. My mom had been pretty, but I couldn't see much of her in me, or my father either. Maybe I did have a father in Italy whose looks I had inherited. I had no zits and didn't need makeup for my eyes. My brows were naturally dark, and my lashes were long and thick without any help.

"Good thing you go natural," my aunt would say. "You are way too young to fool around with makeup. It would ruin your pretty skin."

"Auntie, you put makeup on yourself to go burn dead people. Why shouldn't I do it for live ones?"

"Don't sass me girl. If your mother was alive, she'd slap you silly."

"Sorry, Auntie, I didn't mean it the way it came out. I mean, about the make-up. I noticed you started wearing it, so I've been wondering if you got a boyfriend."

"I'm an old lady of twenty-nine. What would I even do with a boyfriend? And when? All my awake hours are accounted for."

"Okay, Auntie. I just wondered."

I wondered if she was lonely. She never did anything except put on make-up for her job to look pretty for the dead people, and then, come home and wash it off. I didn't see the point, but I guess that was up to her. She never brought a man home.

Months went by. I went to McDonalds regularly where Ramirez noticed me. His dark, hungry eyes would follow me around like he wanted to ketchup my fries. He remembered my name. He came up to my table whenever he saw me hanging out and handed over a large fry. He chatted me up like the boys at school did. He asked if I was hungry, or he gave me a soda. If I said I was hungry, I ate for free. I loved teasing him. If I flirted the least little bit, he got all shaky and nervous. I'd whisper dirty to him.

"You're jailbait," he said.

I laughed. "I'm just trying to pay you back for the drinks and food you give me."

Ramirez never let me follow up that kind of talk. I figured he was waiting till I was no longer jailbait. Just a matter of time.

When I turned fifteen in 1979, I put on makeup and did my hair. It made me look at least eighteen. I even padded my bra. A little sock goes a long way in a bra. I hit Ramirez up again for a job.

He said, "As soon as you get the permit from school, you're in."

He showed me he still had my application in his desk.

My lady counselor was history. Mr. Snow, the guy I was assigned to was always busy. He never looked up.

The first meeting we had, he pretty much talked me into taking a drivers ed class that ended with everybody taking the test and getting a permit. Like, how could I ever have a car? But I did it. Why the hell not? It was an easy elective. Everyone who had him said he was nutty. He never paid any attention to students but was very involved with the papers on his desk.

He could listen when he needed to. I tested him. I had to get all full of drama.

"Things are bad at home. I need to help out. We ran out of

milk this morning and there is no money to buy more. Mr. Snow, I need a job permit."

Breakfast was a big deal at home, whether it was just cereal, bananas and milk, tortillas rolled up around scrambled eggs, or whatever. May Aunt Isabel forgive me. She had just this morning stuffed me full of pancakes before she went to work. Pancakes are cheap, yummy, and don't leave you feeling empty. She made sure everybody ate, even when she didn't. She said she'd have coffee at the office.

"We are near starvation at my house," I said.

He looked at me. I couldn't read his expression, but the fact is that he looked up. His eyes, I noticed, were light gray. He had a shock of white hair on top of his head like a troll doll and wore a white turtleneck, come rain or shine.

"McDonalds will hire me if I have a permit."

He pulled my file, took a fast look, and put the file back.

"You need another eight months," he said.

"Mr. Snow, how about you make an exception? My family is in trouble."

My aunt would have kicked my ass for telling the counselor this. With five mouths to feed, how could we not be hurting? She went without more often than not but we kids never did. We had lots of bread, rice, potatoes, tortillas, and my two boy cousins put food away like they were in an eating competition.

I had two sets of underwear, one pair of worn out jeans, two skirts, three blouses, and two shirts. They were all bought cheap from the Salvation Army or Goodwill. My one pair of shoes were from Goodwill. Serena was a couple years younger but had bigger feet and had worn them first. They barely fit. I had four pairs of socks that I guarded like a hawk. I made what I wore look good, clean and ironed, fresh, but I had to wash and iron every day. There was no money for the laundromat, and even if there was, my aunt wasn't going to let me machine wash my clothes every

day. I washed my clothes in the bathroom sink. I hung them outside if the weather was right or on the curtain rod in the bathroom. My cousins always made fun of my panties and bra always
hanging in the bathroom.

Snowman looked up a second time. He stared like he was studying me. Maybe he realized how pretty I was. Fuck, am I con-
ceited or what? Whatever it was, a miracle happened.

"Are you telling me the truth?"

Maybe going without breakfast wasn't true, but if anybody
was in money trouble, it was us.

Ten minutes later, I walked out of his office with the permit.
I came straight from school to show Ramirez. The next day, I went
to work at McDonalds. I got to eat free, though thanks to Ramirez, I'd already been doing that for a long time.

The second day at work, I gave Ramirez a hand job in his office. It took him less than three minutes to finish. It was my first
sexual experience. All that talk about jailbait. When the time
came, he took it out, then freaked out when I put my hand
around it and pumped it. I'd never done anything of the kind before—but I sleep in a room with two boys. Serena and me, we are
excellent at pretending to sleep through anything.

"Ramirez," I said. "We're even."

"This never happened," he said.

Two weeks later, Ramirez cashed my first check. I gave half to
my aunt. She cried.

"Promise you won't quit school. You go all the way and graduate."

"I promise," I said. I meant it. I wanted to go to college.

It wasn't just that I liked school. I had a knack for learning. I
was good in math and very good in English. I liked gym class. I
heard the gym coach tell another teacher that I could climb rope
better than the boys. I did push-ups and sit-ups like crazy, and at
home I'd work out. I restacked boxes in the refrigerated store-

room so often that Ramirez, who was standing in the corner eating fries and watching me, started calling me Rocky. I jogged to
and from work. If I had owned a bike, I would have used it,
though in my neighborhood, no one rode bikes for exercise.
Joggers were also rare. At school I ran track. A good workout
made me sweat like crazy.

"You have to wear panties under those gym shorts, or you'll
get an infection," my aunt said when I came in from a run, pointing how the material pressed up to my skin down there. A girl at
school called it a camel toe. I was daring, and I got worked up
flashing. I teased, then pretended to be pissed when something
nasty was said to me. The lady coach scolded like my aunt, but the
men coaches watched me the way Ramirez did, like I was a bowl
of strawberries and honey, and they hadn't eaten for a week.

Rumor was that the coaches spied on the locker room. We
found a hole in the wall behind one of the lockers that backed up
to the janitor's supply closet, but we never managed to catch anybody inside there. There was also an air vent in the middle of the
wall, that we could look through into the boy's locker room, but
we never caught anyone in there either. Not in the act, anyway.

The four of us kids had been sleeping in one bed for as long as
I could remember, Serena and me on one side, and Darrin and
Larry on the other. After a couple of paychecks, I went and
bought two sets of almost-new bunk beds from Goodwill. Ramirez brought it over in his truck and helped me set it up. I lay claim
to one of the bottom bunks. My aunt found us sets of white sheets
from somewhere, and they looked brand new. I was a little scared
they had come from her work and never worked up the nerve to
ask.

At the end of a month, from my aunt's side of things, there
wasn't more money than there was before she worked at the coroner's office. The only one who benefited from her job was the
government. They used her check to reduce the amount of money

they'd let her have. The little bit I made was the only extra, so it made a huge difference. Yeah, my check was tiny, but it was better than no paycheck. And no one was telling that I had a job, and my aunt wasn't telling Mrs. Delavega that I gave her half my paycheck. My cousins weren't about to tell anybody how many cold McDonalds hamburgers they had for breakfast. See, an all-night McDonalds like the one in my neighborhood tosses food after it's been out for too long.

I always snagged it to bring home: paper bags full of biscuits, burgers, apple pies, English muffins, jelly, and ketchup packets. Once I scored a big toilet paper roll that lasted us a month and a half. No one at work gave a shit. Darrin, who was almost mechanically inclined, hung a broomstick between the bathroom sink and the tub and hung the giant roll on there.

1981
Los Angeles, California

The free bus ran all summer to the beach taking kids there and back after eight hours on the sand. I wasn't on that bus. I worked long hours, continued to give my aunt half my earnings and saved most of the rest for tuition and stuff at ELA Junior College. I had told Ramirez that his jollies with me were a one-time thing, but it wasn't true. When I needed a special favor, like a raise or something important, he was up for it, and so was I. He never went long. I got the hang of how to do it so it would go faster. Eventually, Ramirez got promoted and moved on. I got a microscopic raise or two. At seventeen, I was still too young for the assistant manager job, but by then, I had two years on the job. At least, seniority allowed me to pick my hours. I took split shifts and all kinds of hours not available to a minor, but no one was looking. It wasn't like we served alcohol.

I knew that for college, I would need clothes and supplies. Many of my friends used school to look for a man to hang with, to have kids with, and make a life together. I wasn't going for that. I craved sex and a future as much as any other girl, and hearing other girls talk worked me up, but I knew the truth. Like Ramirez, guys just move on.

I didn't get along with everyone. I guess my looks and the way I flashed and flirted bothered some of the girls. I didn't take shit from anybody. That resulted in a number of fights, two of them with lots of blood. We had no snitches at our school, so nothing ever happened to me or the others that I had it out with. The vice principal never had words with me. Whatever I did, I got away with it.

Everybody else was calling him Mr. Snow, but I called him Snowman, my little nickname. He'd summon me to his office just to ask if I was doing okay. When I went in to see him, he stopped working.

Sometimes he had to move a pile of files to the side in order to see me. He had been attentive ever since giving me the work permit. He pumped me up about my grades and tossed professions at me about what I should shoot for. We talked about our favorite TV shows. He liked Star Trek, The Next Generation. I kidded him about being a Trekkie. I admitted I like lawyer shows, all of them, like Petrocelli, Paper Chase, Judd for the Defense, Owen Marshall, The Defenders, even old Perry Mason. Instead of kidding me about it, he used it to lever me to talk about what I saw in my future. Sure, I had dreams, but his making me talk about them made them seem like they could be real, and not just a fairy story.

He said, "Fight using the law instead of your fists."

I was embarrassed that he knew. I didn't know a lot of guys I respected—maybe my cousins because they talk protective of me. Snowman believes there's more to me than a pretty face and a hot body.

"I'm sorry Snowman. I didn't know you knew."

He shook his head and looked sorrowful for a second.

"You could be a lawyer," he said.

"You think I'm smart enough for that profession?" I tried to picture myself as one of the characters. Their lives seemed very far away from mine.

"Yes."

"I'll think about it," I said.

"Gabriella, I don't want to see you in the vice principal's office where I won't be able to help you."

"Thank you, Mr. Snowman."

I walked around his desk and gave him a tiny kiss on the cheek. We were tight. I thought about giving him a wank job, but that would get us both in trouble if we got caught. It was like the best thing I could do for him is live up to my potential, whatever that meant. A good part of it would be graduating from high school and finishing college.

I was walking home from work and noticed the driver following me. I'd seen the car before, a VW convertible, old and dented. I was surprised that a guy not from our barrio cruised along like he had a free pass from seven (at least!) gangs that called my neighborhood their turf. I was almost home when he pulled up just ahead of me, lifted his sunglasses and waited till I was passing to offer me a lift.

I looked over, recognized him, and kept walking.

"Thanks. I'm almost home, then off to work. Running late."

He followed and repeated the maneuver, pulling up ahead of me and asking again when I was abreast of his car.

This time I shined him on. Eventually, he drove off.

I got home, took a quick shower, jumped in my uniform and left the house to make the short walk to McDonalds. He was back. He pulled alongside parked cars driving at my speed as I walked on the sidewalk.

"My name is Alex Rose. What's your name?"

"I don't know you, Alex Rose."

"Let's meet."

It was my bad luck that he was good looking and charming, and I was just seventeen. It took a little while for him to convince me to go on a date. He was persistent, plus he had a dimple on his chin. A week or so later, he took me to Hollywood. I had only been to the Egyptian Theater once and couldn't even remember what movie I'd gone to see with my aunt and her kids.

Alex was beyond handsome. He had great hair, and a smooth manner. He was twenty-six, an age that sounded exotic and important to my seventeen-year-old self. He was a white guy but that didn't matter to me. I am just as white, color-wise, but I am Hispanic by culture.

"You're beautiful."

He didn't say it once. He said it practically every time he looked at me or opened his mouth. He took my hand again and told me I was beautiful. If he had asked me to do it with him, I would have if there had been someplace to do it in the theater.

1981
Los Angeles, California
Isabel

This is the third time that man has gone out with her. I've told her I don't like him, but that doesn't matter to her. She's as stubborn, obnoxious, and belligerent as Cira was, may she rest in peace. It didn't do any good to say anything to her either. She did what she wanted to do.

"Why doesn't he bring his skanky ass in, and let me meet him?" I asked Gabi. "A shifty man is a no-good man. I know what I am talking about. He is too old for you, and he is up to no good."

She laughed at me.

"Auntie, he's not my boyfriend. Don't be so old fashioned."

"I got a good look at him. He's way too old for you."

"He's twenty-six."

"And you're barely seventeen! I don't like him."

"Chill, Auntie."

Gabi sighed at me like I was such a burden and closed herself in the bedroom.

Even when she's ticked off at my being such a busybody, Gabi is always responsible to our family. I just wish she understood that I am trying to look out for her. I can see ten miles down the road what happens if she keeps it up with that bad boy, and it's a path that doesn't look good.

Before we were eating lunch in the break room, Fernando had taken off his lab coat. I tried not to be obvious about it, but I couldn't help admiring his biceps. He's been working out lately. I brought in a sack of McDonald's hamburgers that Gabi brings us an abundance of. The freezer is full of them, but that's okay. The boys put them away like they are going out of style. The burgers heat up pretty well in the microwave if you wrap them in a moist paper towel. Fernando likes them as much as my sons do.

"Isabel, there's an opening in the field," Fernando said, surprising me. "Driving, picking up corpses, and bringing them to the facility. When there is something for cremation, you bring them here. It's not huge pay, but it is a living wage, more than you are making now."

"I'd have to give up all my public assistance. Are you sure it is enough to support five people? How do you know I can get the job?"

Fernando was my friend by then, not only my fucking friend, either.

"You'll have the recommendation from the chief here. I talked to him. You'll have my vote too, of course."

"You mean your boss?"

"Yeah, he likes you."

"He's barely seen me a couple times."

"Isabel, you want this or not?"

"What about my kids?"

"The baby is thirteen, right? That's old enough to babysit somebody else. I'm betting he'll love the independence of being a latchkey kid. And he'll only be alone a couple of hours. Drivers keep banker's hours. You'd be done by four at the latest. You've got some experience in the department, and it is a couple of steps up. You should grab this. It's a good job. You can come back here someday and make as much money as I do. You have the experience now."

Gabi works hard, then gives me half of her check. I wouldn't have to take it if I made enough on my own. She needs to save for college.

At home, I told Gabi first about my decision to apply for the job. I got a big hug and kiss, and plenty of encouragement.

"Congratulations," she said. "Chauffeuring corpses, is that a move up? I know you can do it."

"Thank you," I said.

"Won't you be afraid driving around with dead people alone?"

"That's nothing to what I do now," I said.

At work, I wheeled around bodies and helped move them into cartons if there was no coffin in order to put them in the cremator. I wouldn't miss that part of the job, but I would miss Fernando.

I got the job. All I had to do was apply. After I was hired, I made arrangements with Miss Delavega to drop me from my benefits, but the small check I got for taking care of Gabi would continue until her eighteenth birthday which was just a few months away. It could continue longer if she was in school and living with me. I told Gabi about it. The month's bills were paid, and that was a good thing, because I would be working a month before I saw my first paycheck. I filled up our little refrigerator, and our pantry. At the end of the month, we might be on beans and rice, but at least we'd have plenty of burgers.

"I didn't even know you got a check for me," she said.

"I told you a long time ago. It's only a couple hundred a month, your parents' social security benefits. You can have that now. Maybe you don't have to work so many hours. Maybe we can put it in your college fund?"

"I like the idea I can keep my whole paycheck. Auntie, are you sure?"

"I'm sure. I did the math."

I wanted to tell her that she should stop seeing that man, but I kept my mouth shut to keep the peace. I had terrible feelings about him. He's bad news. I went from not liking him to having nightmares about him. I fear she will be raped or worse.

1981
Los Angeles, California
Gabi

I told Alex to pick me up at McDonalds and not at the house from then on. I knew how she felt about him, so there was no need to rub her face in his re-occurring presence. On our fifth date, he took me to a Sunset Boulevard motel that rented rooms by the hour. He paid for two hours.

"Is she old enough?" the clerk asked Alex.

"I wouldn't mess with a minor."

He knew I was seventeen, but neither one of us was going to tell the desk clerk who didn't care anyway.

"Why don't we use your apartment? Don't you live over here?"

"I have two roommates," he said. "I don't want them making eyes at you."

"What do you do for work?" I asked.

"This and that. I'm between jobs."

I would have asked him another question, but he kissed me. I loved the way he kissed me. One minute we were kissing, the next we were necking, and before I had a thought in my head, he was making love to me. We went all the way. It hurt, but I am strong. I worried more about the blood on the sheet than the pain I felt.

"Oh, you are so tight. I didn't know you were a virgin. Man."

"I'm not a man," I joked.

I was expecting three minutes like Ramirez lasted when I wanked his thing. Alex went long enough for me to ask him to hurry up. It hurt. He pulled out and didn't finish inside of me. I liked that he was being careful, though now I know that pulling out isn't protection from pregnancy. What can I say? I was naïve at seventeen.

"I'm going to junior college when I graduate. I can't afford to get pregnant," I said.

"College, right," he said, sounding dubious, like I'd said I was flying to the moon or running for president.

"If we're going to do this again, I need to get pills, or you need to buy something."

"Yeah, yeah, for sure," he said. "I don't like having to pull out when I'm ready to explode. Babe, you're really good. Thanks."

Thanks? I felt a let down. I wasn't expecting him to say he loved me, but still...thanks?

Alex Rose never called at home. I never gave him my home phone.

"It's my aunt's phone. She gets crazy if anyone calls me. Call me at work. It's okay," I told him. I hated lying about my aunt. It was half true. Anybody else could call me, but not Alex Rose. Alex

Rose made her crazy upset.

Alex got me the pills and I started taking them. He knew my work hours, and usually managed to time his calls to catch me. We went out a lot. It takes a couple of weeks before it is safe to make love, but we were fooling around every night I had time off. He was wearing protection. I got familiar with his car's tiny back seat. Sometimes we did it while pulled into a parking lot, not McDonalds, because the McDonalds lot was too brightly lit. There was an alley back behind the building that was secluded. Sometimes we returned to the dumpy motel room on Sunset Boulevard. It was the kind of place you never take your socks off. The king bed was squeaky, and the room smelled funny, like the inside of a damp closet. Flyspecked flowered wallpaper went half-way up one wall, and there were some fly-specked beach prints on the wall behind the bed. The navy-blue flowered spread had seen better days. The flowers made a brave try at being cheerful and vibrant, but they were faded in places and none too clean. We'd toss it on the floor, and just go for it on top of the sheets. They were mostly white and seemed mostly laundered. I didn't want to think about the other people who might have used the bed and those sheets, or if they'd been washed recently. We did it, and then afterwards, he wanted to talk. He sat up with his legs hanging over the side of the bed and started playing with his wallet. He pulled out fifty dollars and gestured with it while he was talking.

"How long do you have to work to make fifty dollars?"

"Net or gross?" I asked. I had a brush in my purse and started getting the knots out of my hair. I pulled it back into the ponytail I usually wore to work. I still smelled like French fries.

"Net."

"Not quite twenty hours. Why?" If I got in a forty-hour week, I could take home a hundred dollars. More than forty hours was time and a half, but McDonalds watched our hours like hawks, and frowned on overtime.

He tapped out a cigarette on the bedside table and lit it. He held it out to me. I coughed and shoved his hand away.

"Would you be game to make fifty for, let's say, less than thirty minutes?"

I wasn't stupid. I hopped up out of the bed, naked except for my socks. The closet by the door had a single permanent hanger that wouldn't come off the rod, and my McDonalds uniform was hanging on it. I stepped into my underwear and put on the uniform while Alex was explaining himself. I would have to shower, but just looking into the bathroom gave me hives.

"I'd have to fuck some creep," I said.

"Not a creep. Give me a break."

I was confused but only for a second.

"Bottom line, Alex," I said. I was only seventeen, but my brain worked faster than Alex Rose's, and I'm a realist. He was never going to be the candy and flowers type. I didn't need a telegram to tell me that a guy who worshipped the ground I walked on wasn't going to suggest I fuck other guys for money.

"I'm out here in Hollywood. All I have to do is flash one picture of you, your face, and bang, the guy is sold."

He turned to me with a big satisfied smile like he just hadn't insulted the hell out of me.

I was dressed. I just gave him a look, like *Are you serious, man?* and walked out of the dumpy room, down the dumpy hall, out into the street. He came running down the hall after me but hadn't put his clothes on yet. Had to go back and get dressed. Bastard.

"Wait, I'll drive you home, Gabi. I wasn't serious."

I was on Sunset Boulevard walking in the general direction of home (I hoped), looking for a bus stop. I knew the way if I was driving or walking in daylight. But it was night, and I had no idea how to get home from Hollywood on the bus. Maybe the bus driver would tell me.

I hadn't walked far enough fast enough. He got out of his car and ran to catch up to me. Put his arm around me. The skank. I didn't want anything to do with him, but I wanted to go home.

"You take me home," I said.

He drove me back to McDonalds.

We never said a word to each other the whole ride back. I did not say a word to him when I got out of the car.

It's a short walk from work to home, and Alex was long gone. I stood outside the door for a couple of minutes, wondering if I looked any different. I felt different, but why should I? It's not like I loved Alex Rose. The sex was sex. It was good because sex was new to me.

My aunt and my cousins were watching television in the living room.

"Where were you?"

"Out," I said, hoping the uniform I was wearing would speak for itself. I walked into the bedroom.

My aunt had the smaller one all to herself.

All I had was my own bed. The rule was that no one, absolutely no one, could sit or lie down on my bed. We all had our own spaces now. I guess my cousins hated sharing the same bed as much as I had. We were all possessive about our new private spaces. I had inspired my oldest cousin to work too. She was no genius, but her heart was in the right place. The babysitting Serena did around the neighborhood didn't pay a whole lot, but it was something. It helped take the load off of Aunt Isabel. Lots of our neighbors had as little money as we did, but they always needed someone to watch their kids. At least there was plenty of food in the house, and the utilities were paid.

At an auction, my aunt's friend Fernando had gotten one of those TVs like they have at the hospital. It was mounted on the ceiling so we could be in bed and watch. I turned it on and went through the channels. The only thing that caught my eye was a movie of the week where some guy went after his son's killer when the son's killer was set free. I turned the TV off and thought of the story, how there was justice, and there was law, and maybe they weren't always the same thing. Snowman kept saying my liking lawyer shows meant that I should consider becoming a lawyer. It seemed like a really complicated business, but I knew two things for sure. It paid better than flipping burgers, and people respected lawyers more than they did hookers.

Snowman always rooted for me to have a big life, to have confidence in myself, and to go for it.

Alex Rose was his opposite, and I had fucked up by getting in bed with him. What a prick. I didn't see that coming. Aunt Isabel was right all along. Alex Rose had been working me, so I'd agree to have him sell my body on Hollywood Fucking Boulevard. He got all lovey-dovey with me, not because he gave a shit, but because he wanted to sell my pussy.

Fucker.

Fifty dollars. Is that what I am worth?

I wondered if the streetwalkers over there got fifty for doing it. Who knows? How would I have a clue what streetwalkers were paid? Would I do it for fifty? If I did, it would have to be my idea and not someone else's idea.

I worked every day after that. Keeping busy helped. A week passed. Then another. I answered the work phone one day, and it was him. I told him not to call me and hung up. After that, I just didn't answer the phone. If he called for me, the girls knew to tell him I was busy with customers. The new manager, Ricky, didn't know, but we weren't that close. I didn't know him that well. The girls were different—we'd sit in the corner booth when there weren't any customers, and everyone would talk about their love lives and their rotten or glorious boyfriends—usually the same guy in both cases. At least now I had something to talk about. I didn't let on that he wanted me to hook for him! I just made it clear he was rotten to the core and then some.

Then he showed up, bought a coffee, and sat down with a magazine in his hand.

He looked good. I wish he hadn't looked so good. He didn't come my way, or anything. After a while I went to the booth where he was, and just stood there. He wasn't wearing anything special, just jeans and some band tee shirt. His shirtsleeve was folded back, and a pack of cigarettes was stuck in the fold. He'd gotten some sun since I'd seen him last and looked healthier. Being a skank didn't show.

"I know we can't talk here," he said. "I'm just here to scope you out. I miss you. I gotta see you." He put his hand out to touch my hand. My skin jumped at his touch. It was like he'd caressed me inside. I practically came just from the expression on his face. I could fight him all I wanted, but I couldn't fight my own hormones. I didn't even hold out for an apology. I'm so stupid. I saw him, and my horny hoo-ha nerve endings felt him all over my goose-bumpy body with sex-colored glasses.

"Pick me up tomorrow if you want," I said.

It was just getting dark when Alex left. I could see him from the counter, but what I couldn't see is that his car was on its side. I moved up close to the parking lot window and saw four dudes. I didn't know them, but they looked familiar. They were tattooed, long-haired, wearing gang colors, gang signs, the type of guys I usually avoid because I've seen what these guys can do when they're riled. They were laughing. If the situation had not been so serious, it would have been funny. I saw this kind of thing at school. Jocks or teachers that drove small cars like the VW sometimes came out to find their car propped up on benches or on its side like this one. Guys can be such wankers.

Alex was not laughing.

Alex walked over to his sideways car. He came back carrying

a baseball bat, running double-time to where the vatos were making fun of him. They all ran off except for one that Alex managed to corner. The bat caught him on the side of the head, knocking him to the ground. He hit him and kept hitting him.

I ran outside.

"Alex, stop, stop! You'll kill him."

"He may be dead already. I can only hope."

"Alex, the gang will kill you. Stop."

He was flailing wildly with the bat. I almost got hit. I got close and wrapped my arms around him.

"Alex, your car's not hurt. It's just sideways. It's a thing they do."

I managed to get Alex distracted. He stopped whaling on the guy for a second while I tried to reason with him. But now the other gang guys were back with bats of their own, chains, and who knows what else. They would have killed Alex if they'd caught him. Rick came out and talked them into disappearing before the ambulance and police arrived. We could hear the sirens already.

"You dead, motherfucker," one of them yelled at Alex.

Alex still had his bat in hand, unafraid, or so it seemed. He raised it high and shook it in their direction.

The guys ran off.

Ricky, two cooks and Alex tipped the car upright. It barely took a minute. Alex got in and started it. Through the driver's window, Ricky told him not to come back. The ambulance came and took the banged-up kid to the hospital. He wasn't looking too good. His head was shaped all wrong, and his features were a bloody mess. I felt queasy and went into the bathroom to throw up until my stomach was empty. I rinsed my mouth out with water and washed my face. I stared in the mirror for a long time, wondering how things could have come to this. I'd seen people come unglued before, but it was never someone I'd been close to. Alex was a real psycho. It took me a while to collect myself to be able to come out. When I did, Ricky asked me to join him in his office.

"I got to let you go," he said.

I stared at him like he was suddenly speaking Martian or something.

"Excuse me?"

"McDonalds can get sued for something like this," he said.

"Ricky, I need this job," I pleaded.

"Gabi, I promise that if it blows over and nothing happens in a couple weeks, I'll put you back on the payroll. I have to take action now. What are you doing with a punk like that? He's a fucking fool."

"Ricky, it's not fair. I didn't invite him here. Why are you holding me responsible for his violence and stupidity?"

Ricky shrugged. "He was here because of you. Gabi, I'm sorry."

I was stunned. I'd already been through too much that night. He had been swinging the bat like he was crazed. I'd seen many fights in school, outside of school at local parks. I had so many fights I couldn't count how many. A fight was always ugly, and this one, uglier than most.

I was on my way home, and the gang guys that ran from the cops were lying in wait. They stopped me.

"Look, I just got fired," I said, crying on their shoulders. "I'm sorry about your friend. I hate this bastard. I need that job."

One of the guys knew me from school.

"Gabi, that motherfucker comes back to the hood, he's dead. Don't get in the crossfire."

"Beat his ass for me," I said. I nodded in agreement, and we fisted.

"Is your friend named Gus?" I asked as they started to walk away.

"Yeah," one guy replied.

"I thought so. I know him. Let me know how he comes out."

I walked home. If something happened to Gus, it would not be good for me, no matter how tight I was with everyone in the barrio.

In the morning on my way to school, I stopped at a pay phone and called Alex's number. I had never called him before.

"Alex, you can't come back to this neighborhood. They will kill you."

I heard his laugh. It sounded loco to me.

"Your bat has no chance against guns, Alex."

"How am I going to see you?"

I didn't know. I didn't care if I ever saw him again.

"I got fired." I ached but refused to cry. My job meant so much to me, and so much to my family.

Alex laughed again.

"You think it's funny? Are you high or something?" I was furious.

"Good timing, Gabi. Let me work on what I told you."

"Fucking asshole," I said. I slammed the phone so hard it broke. I left it hanging, the mouthpiece hanging by a thin red wire to the floor of the phone booth.

I heard at school that Gus was recuperating at home, and he was going to recover. I was surprised and happy. Alex had clubbed him so hard. And it meant that if the police put two and two together, Alex wasn't facing a murder charge.

Monday night, four days after my phone call to him, I woke with him in my bed. At first, I thought I must have been dreaming, but he was there in person.

"I miss you, Gabi," Alex said.

I woke up as groggy and disoriented as one can be when waked up in the middle of the night. Our room had foil on the window, and blackout curtains over that. It helped keep the temperature, but I couldn't see him lying next to me in my small bed. My cousins were sound asleep, or so I hoped. He put his hand over my mouth. I couldn't see him at all.

"Shh."

It took about three minutes of his caresses and kisses to get me soaked. I caved like a stupid fool. I turned to my side facing the wall, let him fuck me. He moved slow and neither of us uttered a word, a sigh, a groan, nothing. I was trembling with heat when he exploded inside me.

"Call me, I'm always home," he said. "If you don't call, I'll just be back."

And he was gone.

I got up and walked around in the house and found the back door was unlocked. The windows were open, but they had wrought iron bars. I did not hear a car start up. It was after three in the morning.

I went back to bed and silently cried myself to sleep, hoping my cousins had slept through everything.

"Ricky, it's been two weeks and two days. Nothing has happened. Hire me back."

He gave me a rash of bullshit. He did not put me back on the schedule. It was too soon.

I got out of school at two in the afternoon. I didn't think about it, just took a bus that went downtown where I transferred to a bus that took me to Hollywood. I went to his apartment.

"You waste over an hour on that bus," Alex complained as he opened the door. "I can pick you up."

"I don't want to be in the crossfire when the gang shoots you down."

"I'll kill those punks. They not the only ones packing heavy."

With Alex, everything was an argument. "What are you on? You weren't like this before."

"I always been like this," he said, all cocky talk and grins.

Alex's apartment was the size of my aunt's house. He had no roommates like he said. It was like a junk drawer. Nothing matched, and everything was on the used up-side of used, like the first half-dozen people who'd owned all the stuff had done a pretty good job of getting their money's worth. Like all the social workers I ever knew, I checked inside the kitchen. It's funny how much that tells about a person. He had nothing in the closet but cereal and about a hundred kinds of half-eaten bags of potato chips. The refrigerator had beer in it. That's all. Mrs. Delavega would have had a cow.

The couch was plaid Herculon, a brown and white coarse weave, and if you ignored the stains and cigarette burns, it looked okay. It was ok that the springs were shot because somebody had put a piece of plywood underneath, so you didn't fall through. I learned the hard way when I flopped down on it, and it seesawed a ratty pillow on the other side of the couch up in the air like a reverse high-wire act. When I returned the seat cushions to the frame, I noticed the plywood. He could have warned me, but no, all he did was laugh. Bastard.

"I don't know why I'm here," I said. "I'm leaving."

I turned to go, and he wheeled me around before I hit the door, like we were in some kind of dance contest.

"Because you want sex," he said, his hands all over me.

I wasn't prepared to fend off his international attack—what Serena called Russian hands and Roman fingers. We used the couch. It wasn't much better for sex than it was for sitting, but I didn't notice for the first five minutes.

He left. I sat there alone in the apartment, and almost walked out the door a dozen times. I didn't really want to go through with it. I'd only been with Alex. I didn't want to be up close and personal with a stranger, have their breath on me, their strange

hands on me, but it was all theoretical. It was like it hadn't happened yet, so I didn't really expect it would ever happen. I was
just sort of swept into it. It was how, like for my aunt, I had fulfilled her expectations by staying in school, going to work, planning college. Like for Snowman, the college plans. Did I always
live up to what people expected of me? The clock ticked, and I sat
there, waiting, like a trained hound, telling myself this was my
idea.

The door opened, and the stranger walked in first. Alex followed.

The guy was thirty or so, a tourist from the mid-west, he said,
without identifying what state.

"She looks just like the pictures," he said with some amaze-
ment.

"I told you, man," Alex said with that grin. "You got twenty
minutes."

I sat up on the bed. "Hey wait. Where's the bread?"

"I got it," Alex said, showing me some bills. "Fifty."

Midwest and I, we walked into the bedroom. I took off my
pants and lay down in a bra and tee shirt. He didn't take off anything, but he unzipped his jeans, then locked the bedroom door.

Midwest got on top of me, pushed my shirt up, squeezed my
boobs inside my bra. He was hard and took three minutes to finish. I stared at a stain on the ceiling and lay there. He did all the
work. He didn't say anything. Afterward, he used the bathroom.
He came out and looked at his watch. He stood around for
another thirteen minutes. "Can I smoke?" he asked politely. He
seemed young for his age and was very clean. He smelled like soap.
He smelled better than Alex. His hair was cut very short. I wondered if he was in the military.

"Make yourself at home, captain," I said.

He blushed again. "Private first class," he said.

He lit up and offered me one.

"No thanks," I said, coughing a little.

"Excuse me," he apologized, and put it out. He opened the bathroom door and turned on the fan.

"Thanks," I said.

"Don't mention it."

I heard Alex yell, "Time's up."

Midwest blushed again and walked toward the door.

"Fuck him," I said. I yelled at the door, "Wait a minute, we're not done."

I started moaning and carrying on, bouncing on the bed. I patted the bed next to me, and Midwest sat down by me, and started bouncing along, moaning along like we were doing it. We rocked the hell out of those bedsprings.

"You're so pretty," he said, whispering. Then he moaned really loud like he was done, and we stopped bouncing. When I unlocked the door, I had my pants back on. Alex was pissed at the extra time spent. Midwest pulled out another ten bucks, mumbled an apology for taking too long, and started to hand it to me. I pointed at Alex. Midwest smiled at me and said it began good, and how the last part was the best.

I did two more guys that day, in a few hours. It always took less time than promised. I lucked out on the first guy. The next two weren't as shy, nice, young, polite, or clean. But by the time they were done, I knew I was tough enough to handle it, and never whine about lying down in the bed I made for myself. To me, it had already turned into a job. I didn't want to come home to my aunt empty-handed, even though she said I could keep my paycheck. I felt like if I quit bringing home burgers, my cousins would eat my aunt out of house and home. And I know Serena pretended not to, but she really loved those fried apple pies. I sure hated to disappoint her.

After the third one left, I attacked Alex's bathroom with a

sponge and a bottle of bleach. It hadn't been cleaned while he'd been living there, I felt sure. I took a shower and made plans to bring more cleaning supplies, plus some of my own favorite shampoo, soap and bubble bath for the next time. I needed to bring extra underwear for the next time...I was planning on continuing this? I don't know when it happened, but some time during the evening, I'd gotten aboard.

"Gabi, come out of there," Alex thumped on the bathroom door till I opened it. I was in my underwear, with my hair in his dubiously-clean towel.

I was rubbing my hair in the towel. I dressed, aimed the box fan in my direction, sat carefully on the couch, and began brushing my hair dry.

"How did you get these dudes?"

"I told you, your picture. I didn't use the nudes I took, just your face."

"Bullshit," I said.

"Okay, Bullshit."

"What's the split?" I asked.

"Half and half," Alex said, counting out the cash. "Here's sixty." He handed the bills to me.

"Half is eighty."

"One didn't pay the fifty."

"Midwest gave you ten extra. Alex, this fucked-up business is your idea. Don't screw with me."

"I was kidding," he said, handling me the missing twenty.

"If you pay the gas, I can take you," he said.

"You got nerve, Alex," I said.

Even though I wouldn't let him give me a ride back to the neighborhood, he was being a prick to ask for gas money. I took the bus then transferred and got home at eight that evening. On the bus ride home, I couldn't get the experience out of my head.

I had covered my bases by telling my aunt I got laid off because there wasn't enough work for all the people working at McDonalds.

"Where have you been?"

My aunt didn't look mad, but I was totally wound up.

"I got a job at a restaurant in Hollywood," I lied. "Alex helped me get it."

"I don't like that man. I told you."

"I need to work and make my own money," I said. "I don't mind taking the bus. I'm making more money too. I can give you like before."

"I already told you, we can make it without you doing that. Use the money on yourself and save for college. Buy clothes. You deserve it." She hugged me and I hugged her back.

"Please don't get in trouble," she told me.

"Auntie, trouble? I'm just waitressing."

"I don't want you to quit school, *mi hijita*."

She started crying.

This was my rescuer, the woman who had taken care of me ever since my parents died. I hugged her. "I'm not going to quit school. I'm going to graduate before you know it."

The next day, I wore jeans and an untucked shirt and rode the bus back to Hollywood. On the way, I stopped and shopped for an extra change of clothes. That way I could hang up the clothes I arrived in, and they'd be fresh enough when I wore them home.

In school we learned about sexually transmitted diseases. I hoped that I wouldn't become a victim. I didn't want to get pregnant either. I had no choice but to trust the pill I took. You'd think that the guys Alex brought to me would want to use a condom to protect themselves but that wasn't the case. If I had any sense, I would insist on the condom. I wanted the guys to pay him in front of me. He could hold on to the money but that's how it had to be. Alex didn't argue.

"You should stay. I can go out and get another one," Alex said after I went through four.

I took a hundred home.

"How are the dead people at work?"

"Oh, that mouth. You are just like your mother!"

"Kidding, Auntie. How's work?"

"I'm going to be good at it. I'm using a van. Sometimes I have to use a bigger vehicle. I need to get used to the driving. The rest is fine."

"Are you sure you don't need any money?"

"No, don't need it."

I was getting used to the money. A hundred dollars a day for a couple of hours is very different from fifty dollars a week. I could save most of it, and still have plenty of spending money.

Alex and I got along okay. No one ever did a U-turn and left. I have to give that point to Alex.

"If you can spend a night, we could score dudes who will pay more," Alex said.

"I'll work on it."

Schedules were a challenge. I had to deal with my aunt who worked days, and I had to show for school. I wasn't worried about falling behind.

"After I graduate, I'll have some time off until I start Junior College."

"We can make good bread together."

I hung up my clothes on the rack in Alex's bathroom, and was about to put on the new jeans and top.

"Go get me some customers. I'm ready to knock them dead," I said.

Alex had other ideas. He maneuvered me to the bed.

"Let me get some while you're nice and clean," he said, dropping his sweatpants and underwear. I noticed some spots on his arms. I'd seen track marks on a whole lot of vatos at school who fucked their life up early on by getting hooked on heroin. It was hard for me to stay quiet, but I wasn't his mama. I wasn't his counselor. I wasn't anything to him. We were business partners and once in a while, bed partners.

Every word out of his mouth showed him out to be more of a jerk, but I was still seventeen and stupid. A minute later I was on all fours. He fucked my pussy hard and noisy. I went down flat, and he stayed on top of me, my face pushed into the pillow.

Then he headed out and started finding men.

I worked for ten hours.

My cut was two hundred twenty dollars. Between guys, I hit the bathroom. I cleaned the bathroom and myself, and douched, getting a little OCD about it. I was a freak about being clean. I had cleaned up the bathroom, so that being in there was my breathing space, down time between jobs, so to speak. I was running through cleaning supplies pretty fast. Bleach had taken the mold off of the old bathroom tiles and erased a lot of grime. I threw out Alex's grimy old towels and cleaned out the space under the bathroom sink. It's amazing how much nicer the bathroom was after I got all of Alex's crap and grime out of there. It's a shame cleaning pays less than fucking.

I told my aunt that I was staying in Hollywood for the night. She wasn't happy. She was not happy when I ignored her question about where I was going to stay the night either. She had to know I was staying with Alex, but I managed to get out of the phone call before she actually said his name.

We went out to eat at a Chinese restaurant. Alex paid the bill. Last time we went to eat fast food, he stiffed me with the bill so maybe this was an improvement.

We stopped at the store. I bought more cleaning supplies, paper towels, four bath towels, body wash, shampoo, a bathmat, bubble bath, and an inflatable bath pillow.

"Give me half. I spent eighty bucks in there."

To my surprise, he complied. He gave me two twenties and carried the two bags up to his place. I put everything out, including a couple of decorative candles, and some sachets, a colorful shower curtain and other little touches I didn't expect anybody to notice.

He whistled when he saw it. "Where am I? Is this the fucking Taj Mahal, or what? This must be the Hilton, cause it sure ain't my place. I moved uptown and never changed my address. You done good, kid," he said.

He liked the changes to his bathroom. He stripped down and took a bath, even used some of the bubble bath. He made a wreck of the room, though. I made note that he needed to get a hamper. I picked up after him, rehung the towels to dry, and hid his dirty clothes in the floor of his bedroom closet because I wanted to keep the sanctuary nice. Still, he was acting more human. Maybe the tracks were not from heroin.

I was a natural getting caught up in school. I took two tests that were late. The teacher slapped me down for missing class and shamed the rest of the class for me being the only one to get an A on both.

I got to Hollywood at two and worked until ten. I would have given anything to watch how Alex got the clients. I know what he told me, but he was such a liar. What's the difference? How would I get the business without him?

I averaged a hundred or more a day. There were good days, too.

It went like this: Alex brought the client to meet me. The

client saw me on the bed and paid Alex. Alex would walk out of the apartment and wait outside the door on a chair he kept in the hallway. When the client left, Alex went off on his hunt for more clients. After I got the bathroom up to speed, I tried sprucing the bedroom up a little. Alex left a lot of his crap around. I tossed it in a box and shoved it in a closet. And one time, I went off to Goodwill, and found a really nice duvet and some new-looking sheets. It classed up the place more than the ratty spread he'd been using.

Nobody was paying me to be a maid and decorator, but it was more about presenting the whole package, you know? I felt like I was coming into my own. And by my computation, my own didn't include a cigarette-burned polyester spread that had seen better days, or sweaty socks, dirty magazines, last week's beer cans and TV dinner trays.

"You got to pay half the rent," Alex said when it came due.

"Yeah, but you live here full time, and I'm not even on the lease."

I caved. I agreed to pay my share of the rent, two fifty.

He tried to have sex with me in the afternoon. After sex, he would get placid. If it was morning, we did it, and it was good. My street brain told me he was shooting up, but I never saw any shooting-up gear, or any physical evidence of it other than the scars. Maybe he didn't take much. When we had sex, it was good. I liked his looks. I liked going out to dinner with him on the nights I stayed over. Out in public, ladies looked at him just as men eyed me. We made a hot couple, but I didn't love Alex. I'm a realist. I knew he was a jerk, and if he'd given half a shit about me, he wouldn't be farming me out like meat. If he wasn't around, I'd miss him. Maybe.

There is no lying to myself about what I'm doing for a living.

The good thing is that soap and water washes it away. I spend hours in the bathroom washing it away. Sometimes I'd soak in the hot water and think about Lady MacBeth who we were studying in school.

"Out, damned spot!" That was me in the bathroom.

"I want to fuck your ass. Alex said I could."

The guy flipped me over on my stomach. At first, I didn't do anything except protest. He was just an average guy, not too tall, no musculature to speak of, skinny but with a round belly like he swallowed an entire melon whole, and it had migrated to his trunk. Light brown hair, a little long, and he wore his facial hair cut with mutton chops in a way that said, 'HEY NOTICE MY WEIRD HAIR.' He'd said he was a student at Berkeley.

"No anal, buddy. Sorry," I said.

He didn't want to take no for an answer. He got rough. I rolled on my back, planted my foot in his chest, and launched him off the bed, screaming for Alex. The guy came at me, caught me by my hair, and turned me over. I elbowed him hard on the face while he had me pinned down, and I was steady calling for Alex.

Alex ran in with his baseball bat and yanked Berkeley off the bed.

"I'm not done yet," he complained.

"Yeah you are," Alex told him.

I ran to the bathroom but caught sight of Alex poking Berkeley's back hard with the bat.

Berkeley screamed in agony and cussed at Alex before running out, stumbling.

Alex looked furious.

"I'm not giving up my ass," I said.

"Your call," Alex said.

When the next guy was doing me, I thought about how much I would charge to let them in there.

I guess there's a price for everything.

Once there was this guy Alex brought in. I think he was a construction worker straight off the job. He sure smelled that way. He was in a tar-stained tee shirt, canvas pants, empty work belt. He looked okay, but when I got close, I had to call it off. Alex was standing there with his hand out, and I put an end to it.

I took the cash out of Alex's fist and gave it back to Mr. Construction.

"Come back when you've taken a bath."

To his credit, he didn't put up a fuss. He got a little red in the face and took off.

Alex was pissed off, though.

"Took me twenty minutes to get that guy. You are being too fucking fussy."

"I got an idea," I said. "You let him fuck you."

Alex came at me, but I stood there on the side of the bed, totally naked, my chin out, arms crossed.

"Don't even think about hitting me," I said. "You put one bruise on me, and I quit. Want me to work? Get your ass back on the Boulevard."

Alex went from Doberman to lapdog in two seconds flat.

He came back with a black guy who pulled out a big roll of money. He paid the fifty.

"I'm Elmer," he said.

"I don't usually exchange names," I said. "But hello, Elmer. Nice to meet you. I'm Gabi."

I sat on the bed naked, watching him take off and fold his clothes and put them on the easy chair in the corner of the room. It took him a full ten minutes to get his clothes the way he wanted them. He came across as classy, but it was more than his small fine features, or that he was good looking. It was how he carried himself, and the way he talked. I wondered why he was paying for sex.

After that dirty mess I'd just thrown out, he was a welcome change.

By the time he got in bed, his dick was immense.

Alex started knocking on the door after twenty minutes. I would have let him stay longer, no charge.

"You need to pay Alex another fifty if you want another twenty minutes," I said. "I'm sorry. He won't stop beating on the door until you give it up."

Elmer walked to his folded clothes and retrieved the cash, handed the money through the cracked door to Alex, and locked it again. The interruption had not affected his hardness. When he was done, I went down on him, and he finished again. Sometimes part of the job was giving head. This time, I'd volunteered.

When he got dressed, he handed me a fifty and put his finger in front of his lips.

"Shh..."

He winked. I gave him a high five.

When I came out of the bathroom after my cleaning ritual, Elmer was gone. I handed the fifty to Alex.

"Be sure you're as honest with me," I said.

"I'm way honest," he said.

I smiled and hugged him. It was rare that we hugged or kissed. There was no romance. Fucking was not romance.

I bought three killer panties to keep at Alex's. If I took them home, my aunt would go bananas with questions, for sure. I imagined what the cousins would say if they saw them hanging on the shower curtain rod with my other laundry.

I was dying for school to finish so I could work longer. I wanted a car and a new wardrobe. My cousins were sporting clothes that my aunt got new on sale instead of from Goodwill or the Salvation Army. The cupboards and fridge were full to the brim. I mean, to the point you had to check the balance of the stuff in the rattle-trap old fridge so the next time it was opened, the piles of stuff didn't come rolling out. We were stockpiled for the next great national disaster.

After getting the refrigerator shut on the third try, I made a suggestion. "Maybe you can cut back on the grocery shopping. You don't have to make up for lost time."

"I enjoy it," she said. "It's nice to have rather than have-not."

"You got it covered, Auntie. You're doing great. We're all doing great."

"I'm so happy, *hijita*. Thank you."

I gave her no money anymore, but she was still thanking me from before. She thanked me every time she saw me.

I spent more time, more nights in Hollywood. I was close to graduation and totally fucking up my classes with poor attendance. I was lucky to have a natural ability to read an assignment and get through the tests with flying colors. I don't know where my smarts came from.

After a test, I got out of school early. I wasn't supposed to show until two, and I got there before eleven in the morning after stopping off to get a bag of fast food. The front door was unlocked, and I walked in on a chick about my age watching Alex inject himself. She had long straight hair, a school uniform like maybe a catholic school because there was a vest with initials on the pocket. Plaid skirt, saddle oxfords, knee socks.

He saw me. She saw me and got her bony ass up. You'd think that Alex would have jumped up too, but he was busy with the needle in his arm.

I went straight to the bedroom, ignoring them both.

"I didn't expect you until this afternoon," Alex called out.

I heard the door slam. Probably the girl leaving.

I took a bubble bath to calm myself and put on my 'work'

clothes, a pair of killer panties, camisole, and sandals. I forced myself to stop thinking about the drugs.

When I came out, he was in the bedroom.

"Sorry you had to see that," he said. "It's hard to quit."

He seemed sincere. Of course, he did. He'd just had a fix. "It's your life."

I got on the bed. I kicked my sandals off.

"Are you going out, or are we going to sit around here and chat?"

"I'll be back before you know it," he said. He was all smiles.

"Alex, wait. Lately, you haven't changed clothes. I know you shower. You're looking shabby." Soon as I said it, I wish I hadn't.

"You're right. If I look shabby, I can't get close to the prospects as good. I'll buy me some new sweats."

Then he was out the door.

All I knew about drugs was what I'd seen in my neighborhood, but I knew nothing firsthand. I wasn't friends with any junkies that I knew of. Thank God I wasn't in love with Alex. If I cared, I'd be torn apart after seeing what I did. I felt bad, but I wasn't torn apart. I didn't care.

Alex came back with a guy. Jeans and shirt, socks and flipflops, always a bad combo. The guy was a little drunk, I guess, but Alex was wasted. I'd seen dudes that were high that way. I think that after an injection, you nod out for a while or get wound up or something. I guess it depends on what the needle is delivering. I didn't care. Alex went out after the client paid him. I figured he'd fall asleep sitting on his chair. I hope I wasn't going to need his services as a bouncer, because I'm betting that he was down for the count.

"Are you an ass girl?" the thirtyish guy said.

"What's that?"

"I like tight ass. Yours tight?"

"Virgin tight," I said. He didn't give me a name, so I dubbed him Tight-ass. I'm always naming clients like that, and this guy sure looked the part.

"Two hundred," he said.

"Not for two hundred," I said, shaking my head.

"How much?"

I rocked my head to the side slowly a couple times like I was thinking. Okay, I was thinking.

"Five hundred."

"I give you three."

"I'll take six."

"Where the hell did you learn to negotiate?"

"It's going up to seven," I said.

"Six. I'll pay you six. That's my whole paycheck plus overtime. You better be worth my whole paycheck."

"Okay but you better not hurt me."

The door to the living room was open so I could see the front door when I was in bed. I had him shut the door. He shucked off his clothes and tossed his pants on the floor. I was having second thoughts. Every time I had a second thought about how big he was, I had a third thought about all that money. That was a whole month of working at McDonalds, and then some. How does any rational person set aside getting paid a whole month of work for a couple minutes of blood, sweat, and tears? Besides, whatever doesn't kill you, makes you stronger, right?

"Your thing is too big," I said, though Alex had showed me a video of a bigger guy doing anal to a girl.

He bent down, got the money from his pants, and handed it over.

"Maybe this will convince you."

He clung to the dollars as I pried them out of his grip. I put it in the top drawer of the nightstand and closed the drawer firmly.

We kept sex jelly on hand, so I pumped it and applied it to

the spot. It felt wrong. I pumped some more, and put it on me again, then I put it on his thing.

At least he smelled clean.

"How do you want me?" I figured I would be on my stomach, facing down. But no, he wanted a fucking gymnast. I lay on my back. He fiddled with some pillows and my leg position, and I spread for him. His finger worked the jelly in me, first one finger then fingers. I watched the bead of sweat on his forehead. He was excited. I found myself in an awkward position and took hold of his thing to guide him.

He moved my hand aside. He was going to do it himself. I closed my eyes and felt his penis enter me. I knew I was going to live through it, but I earned every penny of that six hundred.

When he was done, he kissed me lightly on my forehead. He got dressed and handed me a card.

"If you ever get away from this creep, call me. Here's my cell number. I do carpenter work."

I laughed to myself. All he saw was a smile. Elmer had given me his card, too.

I read about a new portable phone by Motorola called the DynaTAC, amazed by the technology. It was nicknamed the brick for its weight and shape. The problem was not just that it was going to cost from three to six thousand dollars, but it wasn't coming out for two more years. No way. The minute I had some cash saved up, I was looking for a car. Fuck the brick.

Riding the bus was wearing me out. City Terrace to Hollywood was okay but going home after hours of sex, running to school, attending a class then ditching the rest of the day was insane. Had it not been for Snowman, my promise to my aunt that I would graduate would be in danger. I kept thinking that the roll I was on with Alex might not last. He was not the most reliable of men.

But I had some popularity. Sometimes I'd finish, and Alex

would tell me some guy who had been there before waited for me
to become available.

"I worry about the cops," I said. "Nothing lasts forever."
Someone told me that.

"We never going to get busted," Alex said with a cocky grin.
"I know how to do it."

Alex and me, we were all business now. When we tried sex
now, he couldn't get it up. If he couldn't make it and I needed it,
I'd get myself off. At school a savvy friend said shooting heroin
keeps you with a boner all day long. Alex didn't walk around with
a boner. Orgasm-wise, I hoped that at least one dude daily that
Alex brought me would turn out to be a good lay.

In the mornings, it was not uncommon for Alex to nod out
in the chair. I shook him awake.

"Alex, time to get to work."

"I'm out of here," he said and weaved, yawning down the hallway to the exit.

He came back with a man and woman. She was probably forty
with a fine figure. I hope I look that good when I hit that age. The
guy was about the same age. He wasn't fat or skinny, medium
build, probably had a desk job, like accountant. His hands were
ink-stained instead of calloused. He was pale rather than out-
doorsy, and in Sears brand slacks instead of jeans.

Alex walked in with them while I was on the bed wearing my
work panties.

She said to her partner, "She's beautiful."

"She is beautiful."

I was like, "You guys, I'm right here. You can talk to me."

"They want a threesome," Alex said. "Two hundred."

"No way," I said. "Three hundred and you get an hour."

Alex looked like he would protest, but then the guy jumped

in.

He said, "Deal."

Hygiene is so important. If I was starving, I'd have trouble bedding a smelly human being. Ugly, okay, but they got to be clean. Normal wear and tear, okay. This couple were clean. Maybe they came to Hollywood right after a bath or a shower.

Alex got the three hundred. Three hundred was good bread.

This was not the couple's first threesome, but it was mine. He put my legs over his shoulders and pushed his mouth on me, then his tongue went to work down there. She worked my breasts. They weren't tiny, but they weren't big either. She nibbled on my nipples. I became relaxed. I did to her breasts what she had done to mine. Her partner penetrated me from behind while I went down on her. The couple stayed for two hours, and we all changed positions a couple of times. She was like my teacher, doing first, then I copied what she was doing. I sort of lost track of what was going where, but it was a groundbreaking experience for me.

We made six hundred dollars. It may be ages before that could happen again.

"We went from fifty to six hundred," I said with some glee to Alex.

He looked wasted.

As my date of graduation drew near, I turned down at least five invites for the prom. I couldn't spare the time for kid stuff.

"I need to leave early," I told Alex. "I want the diploma. I have to show up for practice on how we march on to the stage."

Alex turned red.

"I planned on a full day," he said.

He went out. I watched television until he got back, like every day. Between clients, I washed up, and watched television till the next one.

In the afternoon, I said, "If you get back here by half past three, I can handle one more. I need to leave at four."

He looked crazy. He started to walk away but stopped and slapped me so hard it threw me on the bed. I got right up to his face and hit him in the face with the cast iron lamp off the nightstand. The blood gushing out of his nose caught him off guard. He swung at me and missed. I grabbed my bag with the clothes in it and ran out the front door, bare ass naked. I pulled my sun dress over my head in the hallway and ran towards Hollywood Boulevard. I didn't even put on my scuffs till I was at the bus stop.

On my way home, I was pissed that he had slapped me. I had not gotten my cut for the business that day. That motherfucker. In the bus, I checked out my reflection in my compact, and played at putting on powder. The area was red and tender. I hoped it wouldn't bruise. Now that my heart had slowed to normal and he wasn't after me, I was feeling more confident.

I had punched him and defended myself. Fucking sissy. Without his bat, he was nothing to worry about. I used to think he was so handsome, but he was wasting away. He was mean. The way he'd beaten Gus in the McDonalds parking lot, I don't think he would have stopped hitting him with the bat if I hadn't stopped him. That's mean, right? He would have gone to prison for murder, and I wouldn't be a hooker today.

What a sicko he was. I was my own kind of sicko, turning eighteen after I'd been selling my body for almost a year. I made it to school on time for the rehearsal and split for home. I was exhausted and happy that I didn't have a bruise on my face. I hoped I broke his nose.

I went to bed early. I never heard my cousins come to bed. I was sound asleep when I woke up with a jolt, his hand on my mouth, his lips on my ear.

"It's only me," Alex said.

I twisted but the bed was small, and he took up most of it. I was up against the wall.

"I will never touch your body again, not without your say so," he said. "I swear on everything that is holy to me."

Asshole had nothing holy. Fucking con man.

"Only a coward hits a woman." I said. "Fucking wimp is what you are. And you owe me four hundred. You give me my four hundred, and I'll consider it."

I heard him fumble in the dark, and me pushed a wad of cash into my hand. I stuffed it in my pillowcase, feeling slightly more open to listening to him beg.

"It's all I got," he said. "You got even, and I deserve it. You broke my nose. Forgive me, please. We have something good going. Don't mess it up."

Months of fucking for money had made me sex starved. Alex had me boxed in a love-hate relationship. I should have booted him out.

"Let me try and make love to you," he whispered. "I think it might work right now."

My head was pissed off at him. My head heard his con and knew it for what it was, but it was my hormones that answered.

I went for it.

I moved on top of him. He was hard and I rode him through two orgasms. In the dark, I pretended he was Elmer. I needed a real man in my head. Alex left my body relieved that night when he took off. My head? Not so much.

I always thought that I was smart. Anyone who knew me at school, boy or girl, would say that I take no shit from anyone. Taking on someone like Alex and making him bleed was something I'd done before. Anyone who gave me any shit got an earful, and if that didn't fix it, it was war. That was twice he had snuck in the house and into my bed. I was not afraid of him, and I knew that he wanted me afraid.

In the morning, I was all set for repercussions at the breakfast table. No one said anything, so I figured I was home clear. I went in the shower to clean up for my big night. I had put the stopper in the tub and ran hot water with lots of bubbles. Serena knocked at the door. I let her in, because when there's only one bathroom in the house, you can't hog it. I got in the tub and pulled the shower curtain closed for Serena's sake more than mine.

"We gotta talk," she said.

For all time, those words have struck fear in peoples' hearts. I am no exception.

"I heard your boyfriend last night," she said. "You're in the clear. Nobody was awake but me. I ain't gonna rat you out."

"No kidding," I said cautiously. "Thanks. I didn't want him to come over, and he snuck in. He gets crazy after we have an argument."

"Yeah, well," she said, looking down. "I gotta go work this afternoon, but I can take a spit bath here at the sink. I might be late to your graduation." She shucked off her shirt, plugged the sink, and ran some water.

Her work was babysitting. I was surprised she'd wash her hair for that. The babies were always spitting up on her. The bath, I would think, would be more important afterward than before.

"You been working out? Or is it from carrying around all those babies you watch?" I asked and squirted some shampoo on my hair. She was standing not three feet away in her bra and panties, and it seemed to me like she'd built up some muscles in her shoulders and had lost some baby fat in her waist. She dunked her head in the water, and stood up, water streaming everywhere. Serena was the closest to my own age. She was two years younger than me.

I handed her the shampoo bottle, and she put some on her head and started soaping up. She turned to look at herself in the mirror over the sink, splashed water on it to clear off the fog, and then did the muscle pose, like one of those muscle guy competitors.

She laughed when her muscles flexed a little. She wasn't musclebound or anything, but she looked strong as hell. She faced me with a big grin on her face. "You're not the only one with a secret. I been working nights at La Taberna as a waitress since my last birthday. I guess carrying around those crates of beer make a difference. I couldn't let you outdo me." She flexed at herself in the mirror, and then bumped her hip at her reflection. We both laughed.

"At first it wasn't much, but now I make like fifty or sixty a night. It's just a beer bar, but it pays more than babysitting. I been putting half my pay in Mama's sock drawer. She'd pitch a fit if she knew I was working in a bar."

"I bet she thinks that extra money is from me. Oh, and I was thinking you were such a goody two shoes," I said.

"Me? That's what I thought about you and that fancy restaurant job you got, till you sneak in and screw your boyfriend in our bedroom with me, Larry, and Darrin in it! You got balls like grapefruit, cousin."

I stood up out of the water and we hugged and giggled. I came this close to telling her what was really going on between Alex and me.

She rinsed her hair off, wrapped it in a towel, and sat on the toilet. "I haven't figured out how to tell Mama I have this job she wouldn't approve of."

Maybe I'm not one who should be handing out advice, but I was just thinking, working in a bar was going to be a whole lot easier to explain than what I was doing. "Maybe you can tell her when you hit eighteen," I said. "I bet she might not mind as much as you think."

"I promise I'll make your graduation," Serena said.

Once I had my clothes on, I sneaked in Auntie's room and rolled up an extra hundred into one of her socks. Serena caught me doing it and flashed me the victory sign.

I graduated from high school.

My family, including Serena, was there in the audience clapping. We all went out for dinner afterwards. It's the first time I ever noticed Serena wearing lipstick.

Before we split, I found Snowman in the crowd and gave him a big hug.

"Thank you, friend," I told him. "There is nothing I won't do for you," I said.

I meant it.

"I'm eighteen now. That makes me legal."

I kissed him again, first time ever smack dab on the lips, and split.

I would have loved to stick around for his reaction, but Fernando, Aunt Isabel and my cousins were waiting. We were going to the PDC, a big deal for us.

I enrolled at ELA Junior College. In a month, classes would begin. Cash—over two thousand dollars—was stockpiled in my mattress. There had been more, but I'd spent some already on the first semester's tuition and the car.

My aunt took me to the car dealer she'd gotten her car from. He was a soft looking person with dark eyebrows and hair, slightly overweight, and, frankly, I wasn't sure if it was a masculine woman or a feminine man in that suit and tie. Aunt Isabel sat around and monitored the entire deal, but she let me do the talking. The asking price was eighteen hundred. I got it down to twelve hundred with the guarantee they would take it back for sixty days if anything happened to the car.

"I don't want credit. I have the cash. Let's do this."

The salesperson left the room twice to get okays, came back twice with counter offers, but I held fast to my position and my cash.

The third time, the salesperson was gone a long time.

"Boss says we have a deal."

Paperwork took a long time, especially long for me since it hadn't been long since I'd had all my final exams. At last I got the keys and kissed my aunt goodbye.

The barrio insurance agent got me a year of full coverage for two hundred and forty dollars.

"I got a car," I told Alex on the phone. "Want to work today or wait until tomorrow?"

"Come on down. We can both use the bread."

I never asked what he did with his money. I supposed he used it on drugs. I had no idea what it cost. I had to get my cash from him. He owed me for my last day's gig. I drove to Hollywood, took Brooklyn Avenue through downtown and Sunset Boulevard all the way to Hollywood. I wasn't up to using the freeway on my first drive. It was a mess finding a spot to park near Alex's dump.

There is wisdom in using public transportation as I had been doing. Alex's VW, with a blown engine, was sitting in the only parking spot he got with the apartment. I had to park in the street two blocks away. I figured I was paying half the rent; I might ask him to get rid of that piece of shit so I could use it when I came to work. I looked back to check my car, feeling proud. My car, all paid for.

A Porsche too nice for this neighborhood slowed. The top was down, so I could see the driver as he followed alongside me.

"Need a ride?"

"No thanks," I said. The conversation reminded me of my first time seeing Alex.

"You got anything going?" the man asked.

I stopped. He stopped.

"Are you a cop?"

"I'm not a cop."

He looked like a cop. I walked between two parked cars to the passenger side of his ride.

"Are you looking for something special?" I asked.

"You are one fine lady," he said.

"Are you a cop?" I asked again.

"Do cops drive around in sport cars like this?"

"Cops drive around in all sorts of confiscated cars, so yeah."

"I'm not a cop," he repeated. "How much?"

"What's your name?"

"They call me Macho. How much?"

I looked at him and felt like he was being truthful. He was pure white, *Gabacho* for sure. That was okay. Alex was white, and so were most of the customers he brought to me.

"Hundred for half hour," I said, hoping he'd bite.

"I need at least an hour with a gal as fine as you. Maybe two."

"Show me the green," I said. My face was three inches from his. He smelled nice.

"Two hundred for two hours," he said.

I turned around and began walking toward Alex's.

"Wait. How much? I'm the real thing."

I was back to this car in a flash. I stopped with my face only a few inches from his. He was at least forty and packed a few extra pounds. Light blue eyes, brownish hair, not pretty but clean-shaven. It's not like I have radar about guys, but he didn't strike me like he was a weasel the way Alex always had, in spite of his looks. Snarly face. His skin was really pale for a guy who drove a convertible in the California sun. He was more muscled than Alex, but then so was my cousin Serena. Macho looked like an enforcer in a movie. He made no effort to smile but he was mellow.

"Two hours, three hundred. For that, I'll throw in anal if you like that kind of thing. Up to you. It's like brand new. I only used it once." I made a face at him.

Macho laughed. I didn't think he could laugh.

"Something funny?"

"You got it," he said. "Do you have a place?"

Alex was waiting for me, but I wasn't giving up three hundred bucks.

I said, "It has to be your place."

"Get in. I'll rent a room."

I put my hand out. "The green please."

He reached in his pocket and came up with a roll of bills. He put three hundred-dollar bills in my hand. I was so excited I almost peed in my panties.

Now that I had a car, I paid attention to the route. Macho drove us a few blocks to Hollywood Boulevard, and from there to the Roosevelt Hotel. I had taken a shower that morning, but I liked the looks of the bathroom, so I made him wait while I showered again. I sprayed a wisp of fragrance in the air and walked through it before I came out of the bathroom naked. Macho was sitting up in bed watching an X-rated movie on pay television.

"Looks like you're all ready," I said.

His thing wasn't huge, better than some, and it was hard as a rock.

"I'm dying here waiting," he said with a grin. He curled his finger at me, beckoning me to bed.

A lot about Macho was unique. He had a mean look, but I was not taken aback by it. He was rugged. He had absolutely no hair on his body and was as white as a Sears Kenmore refrigerator. Early on, I quit kissing the customers, but Macho's breath smelled good. He wasn't anything like the guys I'd been fucking under Alex's direction. I kissed him. He embraced me.

We did it with him on top.

"Macho, you are good," I said. It wasn't that great, but it was exciting: the nice room, the air conditioning, the X-rated movie in the background. He was rapid fire. I heard his balls slapping a fast tattoo against my ass and lasted about ten minutes.

When he was finished, he slid down my body and went down on me.

"Are you sure you want to do that?"

He didn't reply. He just went right to it. Since the threesome, no one had gone down on me. No one had ever done it with the intention of making me come. Macho knew exactly where, when, and how to move his tongue. It was the kind of stroking I did to myself with my fingers when I need to get off. He went for it with obvious gusto. He found some place inside that only my fingers knew, and I had a series of uncontrollable orgasms, explosions that I didn't have anything to compare to. There was an hour left on the clock, and I did my best to return the favor.

He took me back and dropped me at my car.

"Here's my business card. Call me when you want to spring forward."

The card read, Macho Flores, Beverly Hills Model Agency.

"Funny, you don't look Mexican," I said in Spanish. "Flores?"

"Long story," he said. "Puedo hablar Espanol mejor que tu, estoy seguro."[1] He smiled.

"You've got no accent at all," I said. Thanks to my aunt, my Spanish was the real stuff, no accent and fluent. I didn't tell him my Spanish was better than his.

I looked down at the classy-looking business card. "I figure you're a pimp working as a modeling agency. Is that about, right?"

"I hate that handle," he said. "Such an ugly word. I'm an agent. A manager. I have a few models I keep busy. When I spotted you today, I knew you were special. I hope I didn't just have sex with a minor."

"Nope, just turned 18."

---

1 I can speak Spanish better than you, I am sure.

"You have a beautiful face."

"That's all?"

Macho laughed. "You're beautiful. I'd love to represent you."

"Is the pay good?"

"Pay is over the top," he said.

"I'm impressed, Macho, believe me. I will call you."

"Gabi be careful. Don't get hooked up with a pimp. It can be dangerous, especially here in Hollywood."

"Thanks for the advice." If he only knew my pimp is an addict.

"I'm just saying be careful," he said.

I nodded, "Thanks again. It was fun."

I had planned to walk down the hill to Alex's place, but I got in my car and drove toward home. I saw a row of phone booths on Santa Monica Boulevard and parked alongside the curb. I looked back and smiled at how I had parked perfectly. I called Alex.

"Just got this miserable car and already having car problems," I lied. I thought about saying I'd just had a wonderful time getting fucked and my pussy ached from the licking and sucking I'd gotten.

"Why did you wait all this time to call me?"

I could tell he was angry.

"I've been battling with the tow truck and talking to the dealer on the phone about getting me a new battery. It's frustrating." I was so bad at lying. "You're right, I should have called you."

"Damn right you should have called. I had customers waiting."

"Oh, you did not," I said merrily, trying to tone him down.

"I did bitch."

"Now don't get mean," I warned, not so merrily.

There was silence before he said, "Sorry."

"I'll see you tomorrow, even if I have to take the bus. I'll be there."

"Alright," he said after a pause. There was something iffy about his voice.

That night when I was sound asleep, he did it again. I should have been used to it, but I was startled when I felt a hand over my mouth. I struggled but not nearly as much as I should have.

"You were in Hollywood today," he whispered in my ear. "Why didn't you come to work?"

There was no way he knew I had been to Hollywood. He was bluffing. He took his hand from my mouth. I sat up, my head inches from the top bunk. He remained lying down. There was enough light coming from the crack under the door that I could make out his shape. I heard a thump from the top bunk. I realized Serena must be awake.

"Alex, if you ever come back like this again, I will vanish, and you will never find me."

"Oh, I see," he said in a low voice. "Threats. You think you can—"

That's when I saw the glint of the baseball bat on the beside him. His hand was on it.

I interrupted him. "What I say is for real," I said.

He pulled me roughly against him. I was face down on him. "You vanish, and I come back here, and I kill everyone in this house with this bat, then I go hunting for you."

"You miserable bastard. Get the fuck out of this house before I start screaming." It was a whisper, but it came out more like a hiss.

He started laughing, he pushed me to the side, and got out of the bed.

"I don't ever want to see you again," I said, almost in a normal voice. "I must have been blind not to see through you, you evil bastard."

I climbed out of bed. I could feel his breath on my skin. I knew he was doped up. Alex had crossed the line again. Slapping me that one time was bad enough, but threatening my aunt and cousins was going too far. I felt the slam of the bat on my stomach. I bent over and threw up all over him.

"Oh, you dirty whore!"

He dropped the bat and wiped at his clothes with whatever he could find. I couldn't breathe, and my lungs felt crushed, but I snatched up that bat. He was too busy dealing with puke and wasn't paying attention to me. I stepped back and managed to raise the bat. I swung with all my might. I heard the crack and his scream of pain, once, and then again when the bat struck him the second time. He flung his hand back trying to cover himself, knocking the bat into my chin, and the pain in my chest and stomach spread to my head. I collapsed and saw my aunt in the door she must have opened. The light went on. Alex was on the floor next to me, moaning, blood gushing from his head, nose and mouth. I saw Serena's shocked face peering down from the top bunk. The boys were asleep. They sleep like the dead. And thank God that they do. I woke up in an ambulance, moving fast, but I didn't hear a siren. They were trying to put a mask over my face. I felt like I was suffocating. I went out again.

1981
Los Angeles, California
Isabel

As the paramedics checked Gabi, I felt like a train had slammed into me. Serena climbed off the top bunk, put on a robe, and stood silently by my side as they put Gabi on a gurney. A pair of cops from Hollenbeck were in the house, and they warned us not to touch anything until the detectives arrived. Serena bundled off her brothers into my bedroom to sleep the rest of the night so they wouldn't get in the way.

Two paramedics had responded to my call. I addressed the one that seemed closest to my age. I figured he worked for the county, too.

"Hey, Kildare," I read the name on his badge. "I work at the county coroner's office. I need a big favor."

"What is it?"

"I can't leave here till the cops are finished. Can you please call me here at home and tell me her condition when you get to the hospital?" I wrote my number on a pad I carry for work and tore off the page and handed it to hm.

"You got it."

"I owe you bigtime," I said, "My name is Isabel Guerrero. Is she going to be okay?"

"I think it's her ribs," he said. "Got to be careful with her lungs. I'll call you."

Serena had worked magic with her brothers, getting them moved without them realizing anything was going on. As for her, there were no questions, nothing, not even when the paramedics called in that the intruder was dead. Maybe it was weak of me, but it was good to have her by my side.

At least I knew how that worked. Soon the coroner would arrive. I knew most of them by name, but not like I knew Fernando.

I was worried about Gabi. I wanted to spring out of here to the hospital, but I knew it would take a long time to clear the house, especially the bedroom where the bastard was killed. I recognized him. I thought Gabi had broken it off with him. What was he doing in the house? How did he get in? All that I knew was that the baseball bat wasn't Gabi's. He must have brought it with him.

Kildare called to say Gabi was in the ER. Her vitals were okay. She was having breathing problems, but he figured it was a rib or ribs pushing against a lung. The doctor would let me know.

"The charge nurse is Sally," Kildare said. "I know her. I'll give you her direct number and let her know you'll be in touch with her for updates. That way you can eliminate the switchboard."

"Boy, do I owe you," I said. "I hope I can return a favor some time."

Sally turned out to be a peach and kept in touch with me all through her eight-hour shift. Gabi was not out of the woods. A rib had come close to rupturing her left lung.

I knew my niece went out with him and that he lived in Hollywood, but I told the two detectives on the scene that I had never met this man. "He must have identification," I said.

One of them found an expired out-of-state driver's license and a wallet with some cash.

"His name is Alex Rose," one of them said.

They asked their questions. I wasn't much help.

I didn't know how he got into the house. I didn't know why he was in the house, or why he would have attacked Gabi, prompting her to defend herself. She's a pretty girl. They suggested he might have intended rape.

"I've never seen the bat before. We don't even have a bat in the house. He must have come with it."

The coroner driver appeared and did the job I currently do. He put the body on a gurney with the help of his helper, and then surprised me when they cleaned up all the blood on the floor. The sheets, blankets and pillow from Gabi's bed were bagged and taken by the cops. When they left, I got my mop out, went over the floor again with Lysol, and wiped down everything in the room. At least there was no carpet to get stained.

Serena said we didn't need her, but my neighbor Blanche came over to help. She used my sofa as a bed.

"I can get us all up for school," Serena said. She couldn't sleep in her room because the cops were still in there, and she didn't want to get on my bed with the boys. She got on the old creaky recliner and promised me she would try to get some sleep.

"Maybe you can just get yourself up in the morning. You know how hard it is to get the boys moving," I said.

"I don't like the idea of staying here alone in a house where a dude was just killed," Blanche said.

"I don't like leaving the kids alone in a house where a dude was just killed, so we're even," I told her. "I'll give you some money."

"Okay, money makes me feel better, Isabel. Are you going to tell me what happened?"

"I will do that when I find out," I said. "I got to go to the hospital. Be sure the kids are up and out for school on time."

"I can get myself up," Serena said from the recliner. "You get the boys up. Don't you worry about me."

"Worry not," Blanche said. "I'll just close my eyes for a couple hours."

1981
Los Angeles, California
Gabi

I woke up in the hospital with my aunt in a chair next to my bed.

"What happened, Auntie?"

Auntie started crying.

"I told you I didn't like that man."

I remembered then. He had hit me with the bat. I touched my stomach. I couldn't feel anything. My skin felt a foot thick and numb. I think I was drooling.

"Did he die?"

My aunt nodded. "Yes, he died."

I still didn't feel anything. My heart felt a foot thick and numb. I was still drooling.

"I'm sorry, Auntie."

"You lost the baby, Hijita. I'm so sorry."

"What are you talking about?" I could not keep my eyes from closing.

My aunt moved up close to me. I caught a squinty glimpse of her looking confused.

"You had to know."

"I wasn't pregnant," I said, feeling nausea.

A female voice said, "She's sedated. Figure another five hours for her to come to. Go home and come back."

"Will she be fine?"

"She's a youngster. She will be perfect. Don't you worry. We will see to her."

When I woke again, my aunt was gone, and a doctor was there reading my chart. He had coffee colored hair and eyes. His skin was about the color of a good croissant, and his tie was the color of scrambled eggs. Or maybe I was just feeling hungry.

"Does that say anything worth reading?" I asked.

"My name is Dr. Rodriguez."

"I'm Gabi," I said in a small voice. "Am I going to live? Why is it so hard to breathe?"

"You had several broken ribs. One of them was causing problems with your right lung. You had a condition known as pneumothorax—"

I interrupted him. Like I was in school, my hand went up.

"English please, Doctor. Please use words I understand. Little words, not those ten-dollar college words. Am I going to be okay?"

For three days I walked the hallways with a nurse, and then without the nurse, which made it my graduation day. I got discharged, and my aunt picked me up in my car. At home, I got in my tiny bed on new sheets. I turned on the television, planning to rest like the doctor had told me to. I remembered the blood on the floor.

"Who cleaned up the mess?"

"The coroner driver and his assistant. When he found out the four of you slept in that room, he went out to the van and came back with cleaning solutions and disinfectants. I washed up after they were done, for good measure. You have a new mattress, sheets and a pillow. I promise they didn't come from work. I put the money you had in the mattress in that shoebox for you."

"Auntie, thanks. I guess I'm lucky the police didn't take it with them. I'm sorry this happened here. I mean, I'm sorry it happened, period but I wish it had not happened here. I think Serena woke up. She might have seen it all."

"I think she did, but she told the police she slept through it. The boys slept through it, but they know about it from the neighbors."

"Was it in the newspaper?" I asked.

"Nah, no one pays attention to us folks out here in East Los Angeles."

Laughing hurt and felt good at the same time. "I'm glad it didn't make the news."

"It made Bettina Chavez's front stoop, which was close enough."

My aunt was looking down at me as I lay there on the bed. She seemed anxious, and finally said what was on her mind.

"You have to meet with the detectives. They been decent not bothering you at the hospital."

I agreed to meet with the head detective handling the case. He brought along a guy named Gary Hoover, a Deputy District Attorney. We sat at the kitchen dining table. I gave a recorded statement.

I knew I might be getting myself into a jam that could send me to jail for prostitution, but it was better than getting charged with murder or manslaughter. I told them I wasn't going to talk with my aunt around, so they came when she was at work.

"I started hooking a little over a year ago. I was seventeen," I said.

Gary Hoover was friendly when we talked with the recorder on. When it was off, he told me to tell the truth or else. It took me over thirty minutes to go through the details, including Alex's previous unwanted visits.

"Did you fear for your life once he struck you with the bat?" the detective asked.

"Absolutely. I was afraid for my life as soon as I saw the bat. I've seen him use it before. When he hit me, I thought I was dead. He hit me so hard I puked on him, and he dropped the bat."

"Did you intend to kill him?" asked the DA.

"I didn't think. There was no thinking involved. It was fast. He dropped the bat, and I grabbed it. It was too fast for me to think."

Three weeks later, the detective let me know the outcome. He came and talked to me in the kitchen.

"The DA is not pressing charges, Gabi. Go get a job doing something legal. You may not make as much money, but..."

I was lucky to end that chapter of my life without getting jail time, or a record. I wasn't stupid enough to ask about the prostitution I had admitted to. I thanked the detective and he left. I came face to face with my aunt in the den. I didn't know when she'd gotten home and felt a little uneasy.

1981
Los Angeles, California
Isabel

When I pulled up, there was a black car parked at my house. An unmarked car. I wondered what was going on, and rushed into the house, tossed my keys in the bowl in the den. I heard a man going on and on, with Gabi breaking in every so often. Like before, she and the detective—just one this time—were at the kitchen table. It seemed she was handling it without me. I stopped at the door, and it took me a second to register what the detective was talking about. Telling her she didn't need to hook any more, that Alex was dead, and she could leave that life behind even if she had been doing it since she was seventeen.

I wanted to scream in disgust when I heard her admit she was doing tricks with men that bastard hustled. I was enraged and upset. I wanted to kill that bastard Alex all over again for taking my little Gabi down that path. Then I realized I had let her down, drawing aid from every source available instead of getting off my ass like I am now and working for a living, so that my little girl didn't feel like she had to work and give me part of her paycheck. Who am I to tell her what to do? I had three babies by a man I wasn't married to by the time I was eighteen. Her mother Cira had been wild too, running off to Italy, and marrying that no-ac-count Armand Rana as soon as she was back in the States. Maybe it's in the blood.

B ut no, I know it isn't. I knew one good thing. Alex was dead. It's possible he threatened her to do what she was doing. Maybe she resisted and he came to kill her that night. Even at a distance, the only way I had seen him, I knew he was evil, no good. I sat down heavily in the den with my head in my hands. The detective was giving her the kind of talking to her that I wished I had done. It went on for a few more minutes. I had no idea how long he'd been talking to her. I heard the kitchen door slam, looked up, and Gabi was standing in the doorway looking at me.

"How long you been home, auntie?"

"Long enough."

"I need to move out, get a place of my own," she said.

"You only graduated a short time ago. Why move out now? Stay. Let me handle the rent. You can save up some more money."

"Auntie, I need a place of my own. I have to move. I'm sorry to leave you with the terrible memory of what happened in this house."

"This is nothing. Hijita, I work with the dead ones eight hours a day." I got a smile out for Gabi.

"I wish you would move from here Auntie."

"I will when I get a couple more raises."

"Good, Tia, good. When I start making money, I can help you."

"No need, mi hijita. Where are you going to work?"

"Not sure yet."

"Hijita, I heard you and the detective." I couldn't say any more. It was too terrible.

"Tia, please don't worry about me. I'm going to get a job and go to college."

Gabi smiled at me.

I kept smiling back. It was not easy.

1981
Los Angeles, California
Gabi

I went outside, got in my car for the first time since my aunt drove me home, and I drove around the neighborhood. I got on the freeway and got off on Hollywood Boulevard. I went past the apartment building where Alex used to live. I kept driving.

I parked my car in the neighborhood and walked down to the boulevard to get something to drink. I ordered a coke at a burger joint and took out the business card Macho had given me.

I called him.

"Hey, remember me? Take a guess."

"I know the voice. It's Gabi."

"Wanna fuck?" I got right down to business.

I heard him laugh. "I want you to work for me. That's what I want."

"Are you turning me down?" I asked, pretending to be offended.

"Where are you?"

"In Hollywood."

"Where you been?"

"Long story."

"I'll come get you," Macho said. "You woke me. I sleep days, work nights. Give me a few minutes to get dressed."

"I have a car. Give me directions unless you don't want me to come over."

"Oh, good. I'll tell you how to get here. Tell me exactly where you are in Hollywood."

It was a fifteen-minute walk to my car. As I was driving, I pictured Macho. He was the only person who had ever given me a ride in a Porsche.

That day I met him in his apartment, we made a deal. Macho made it clear that he never had sex with the girls he managed. He hated the word pimp. He had a two page contract for me to sign.

"I'm your agent or your manager. I get you bookings for sessions mostly with customers I've done business with before. What you do in that session is up to you. I make sure you are protected. You never have to worry about entrapment with the cops. I negotiate for your price ahead of time and get a percentage of what the client pays. I don't take anything out of your tips."

In the contract, I agreed to give a hundred-twenty day-notice when I no longer wanted him to represent me.

"Are you going to sue me if I violate the agreement?"

"You won't do that. You will love the money." He wasn't angry but he had a look I would have to get used to.

"Are you serious?"

"I'm building a high-end clientele. You will love it."

"You will love me, too," I said.

He handed me a stack of bills.

"I'll help you get an apartment. See Gina at this address. She leases executive apartments by the month. Move out of your aunt's house, give Gina fifteen hundred for the first month's rent. She won't charge a deposit. The apartments are furnished and very nice, two blocks from Pacific Coast Highway, the beach. Use a thousand for clothes. Keep five hundred for personal expenses."

"I'll pay you back."

"You will owe me more before we get you set up. You will pay me back as you begin to make money. I know you will be an earner."

"For us both, Macho, is there anything I can do for you right now?"

"Gabi, you and me, we are never going to have sex, unless I fire you or you quit."

I shrugged. "You're the boss," I said.

"I'm your agent, or manager, just like the contract reads. I'm not your boss."

"Understood, Macho. I'm so excited that I feel like spinning."

He got up from the sofa and I did too. He hugged me.

"I'm going to look out for you," he said. "All you need to do is listen and do as I say."

With three thousand dollars, I left his house for Gina's apartment building in Santa Monica. I heard somewhere that he had ten girls that he kept busy. Right off, he kept me working every day except for that time of the month.

I nixed my enrollment at ELA Junior College, and I enrolled at Santa Monica Junior College close to the apartment I rented.

Two years later in 1983, I transferred to UCLA. Tests were still easy for me. Studying was no big deal. My brain was a sponge. Whatever I read, I retained.

Business was at night. I had all day to go to school, study, or kill time. Somewhere in there, I squeezed in four or six hours of sleep, usually cat naps.

In 1983 Macho bought a condo in Westwood and I rented an apartment less than two blocks away from him. I stayed in touch with my aunt by phone. She never asked me about my job, not once, but I wasn't forgetting that she heard the detective and me the day I left her house.

When I got accepted to UCLA, she was overjoyed. I met her and the cousins at Barragan's Mexican Restaurant in Echo Park for dinner. Aunt Isabel was dressed like I'd never seen her. She was wearing a tight skirt and a cool blouse that showed off her boobs. I wanted to tease her that with a body like hers, she could be making some serious bread, but I knew how well-received that joke would be.

"You look great, Tia. Must have a boyfriend."

"She has a boyfriend," Serena said, laughing. "Tell her, mom."

I was laughing with joy. I loved my aunt. I loved my cousins. I had missed them.

Auntie didn't give up any details, but Serena did.

"The boyfriend, it's Frederick, the guy she works with."

"Next family dinner we have, you have to bring him," I said.

My aunt blushed like a kid.

I wasn't surprised. How could he work side-by-side with her and resist? I was glad my aunt had a job with surprise fringe benefits, especially after being alone so long. My aunt blushed and her cheeks got rosy. It seemed like my aunt was getting prettier as time passed.

"Two years of UCLA, then what?" Serena asked.

"I don't know yet. Maybe go for a law degree."

"You always loved lawyer shows," Darrin said.

"I still do," I said.

"I don't like them," Larry said. "I remember you never missed Petrocelli, Owen Marshall or Perry Mason. Made us watch them too."

All of us laughed. Serena was sitting next to Larry and gave him a pretend knock on his head.

"Cool it, sis, or I'll sue," he said, laughing.

"A lawyer in the family would be wonderful," Aunt Isabel said.

April 1983
Los Angeles

It was that time of the month. I was off for a week and Macho wanted me to come over to check out the condo he had just finished furnishing, and to talk to me about going to Cannes the following month in May.

His condo was great. He indulged me and let me boss the movers around, rearranging everything.

"I have a friend that does the same in Cannes as I do here. He doesn't do that much during the rest of the year but makes up for it during the Cannes Festival. He's very connected with high-end clients who pay top dollar for company."

"Did you send anyone last year?"

"I did not. My man there is Guillermo. We call him G. He's pushing me to send someone this year. He wants me to send two or three girls, but I'm too busy here. Are you game?"

"Maybe."

"I figure you can go there," he said. "Make a killing in twelve days, and come home."

"How much does G get?"

"I get my usual twenty percent, and you give G ten."

"I'm in but let me tell you for sure in a couple days. I want to check on the hotels."

"No need. G handles it."

"I'm not going to a strange country and not know in advance where I'm staying."

Macho flung his hands in the air and let me have my way.

Two days later, I called Macho.

"I want to stay at the Carlton. It's expensive. The travel agent told me it is booked solid."

"If you don't stay at a hotel G wants you in, you have to pay the fare."

"If I'm going to make big money, it doesn't matter. I'm going alone. I need to be in a safe spot and not some dump."

"G is not going to put you up in a dump. He runs a high-class operation. And I won't let it happen."

"In that case, tell him to get me a room at the Carlton. I'll reimburse him."

Macho let me know that G had gone through hell getting the reservation. It was going to cost me five hundred a night.

"I saw pictures of the place. Five hundred is okay."

"G says you'll never use your room for the dates he gets you, so it shouldn't matter where you stay."

"Macho, I love you but I'm at the Carlton or I'm not going. I do good right here with you."

"For twelve days, you will make double or more over there," Macho said. "Do you have a passport?"

"I can get it on a rush in forty-eight hours, once I have a plane ticket. I'm not paying airfare and transportation."

"You should go for law," Macho said.

"Let me tell you, I'm seriously thinking about it."

Cannes
May 1983

I checked on the weather. The South of France was chilly in the evenings. I had all the clothes I needed for a gig like this, but I didn't have a mink coat. I went as far as to call the concierge at the Carlton to ask about the weather.

"I'm going to be there for twelve days or so. Will I need a coat in the evenings? Do I need to bring my mink?"

"Madam, by all means, bring your mink. Nights are rather cold if you are out and about."

A furrier advertised in the Yellow Pages that every day of the year was a sale date. He was in downtown Los Angeles. From him, I bought a beautiful full-length mink for forty-five hundred in green cash. He gave me fifteen hundred off the regular price because I paid in cash and because I didn't need a receipt. It was beautiful. In Los Angeles, I would never need it.

I bought two TUMI suitcases and packed them with day and night outfits. I figured if I lost my luggage, I'd be flushing more than thirty thousand dollars. I owned nothing fake.

If I did well in Cannes, I would try for an upgrade to first class. Economy was the pits, but I got an aisle seat and got up a lot to walk off the stiffness. I totally tripped out when the overhead lights were out, flying at night.

In Paris I caught a connecting flight to Nice. That leg of the trip was fast.

I took a taxi from Nice to the Carlton in Cannes.

My room was great. I had a king size bed just like I had at home only this had fancy expensive bedding and six pillows, not counting the shams. The view from my bedroom window, I could see more boats than sea. I opened the window during the day. It wasn't cool at all. It was wonderful. It was two in the afternoon.

I called G and introduced myself. He was a grump like Macho.

"I'm happy you made it," he said. "In the future, don't call me before six in the afternoon. I work all night."

"Sorry, G. My bad. Blame it on jet lag. Go back to sleep."

I hung up.

Five minutes later, the phone rang in my room. It was G.

"You hung up on me," he said, then laughed, kind of a crazy laugh.

"Oh no, I was embarrassed. I wanted you to get back to sleep," I lied.

"It's okay. Want to work tonight or start tomorrow?"

"I'm going to sleep for a few hours, then I'm ready."

"Good girl. I have your pictures. You are beautiful."

"Thanks. You think I'll do well here?"

"I promise, you will do wonderful. Macho has told me how good you work. After he sent me your pictures, I can see why he keeps you busy."

"Thanks, G."

I undressed to bare skin, didn't bother with a shower, went right to bed. I put on the blackout mask they had given us on the plane and left the windows open, light streaming in.

The phone woke me. I fumbled around until I remembered what side of the bed the phone was on. I took off the mask. It was dark but not pitch black. I was on the 3rd floor. There was enough light to navigate without turning on the lamp.

"It's G," the voice said. "I got something for you."

"What time is it?"

"It's eight. Date at ten. Can you do it?"

"Damn right. Give me details."

I was to meet in the lobby of the JW Marriott. I had to taxi it there.

"Three hundred an hour, four hours," he said.

"I make that back home," I said.

I heard his crazy laugh.

"Relax. The festival officially starts tomorrow."

"Got it," I said. "Sorry. I just woke up."

"It's okay. When you're done, call and confirm he paid the agreed amount. The tip is your business. Tomorrow I'll send a runner to pick up my cut. You hold Macho's cut until you get home."

"Perfect," I said, "Thanks, G."

"How long you been with Macho?"

"Couple years. Couple busy years."

The laugh again.

"I am happy you are in Cannes. I will have to meet you."

"Love to meet you," I said.

Thirteen days after I arrived in Cannes, I boarded a plane to Los Angeles. An upgrade was available for a thousand dollars. I happily paid. My seat was heavenly. I got a window, only one seat next to me on the aisle and no one occupied it to London, and no one occupied it from London to Los Angeles. It wouldn't have mattered. I had my own space. I was happy. I had done the math. After paying for my room and charges at the hotel, paying G's cut and the twenty percent to Macho, I cleared sixty-four thousand dollars, an enormous amount of money for me, all cash.

Yes, I worked my ass off, I was never lazy, and when G called, I never said I was too tired. I'd often finish a four-hour session and go out on another session for two hours or more. It was a bitch. It was worth it.

The smallest tip I received was a thousand dollars. The most I received for a session was ten thousand dollars, five thousand of which was a tip from a couple. That couple loved me. I loved them, too.

G came to see me two or three times. He was a big black man, good looking. I would have done him, but he made no moves.

Four Seasons Hotel, New York City

The client's name is Albert. He lives in Moscow, but his English isn't bad. I've had two sessions with him in the past. His Russian accent and deep voice can be pretty sexy. Earlier on the flight from Los Angeles in his jet, we had a thirty-minute session that he called a quickie. Then we were in a boss penthouse suite in New York, and he was on top, driving into me like a jackhammer while I lay spread-eagle on the king-size bed. Albert prefers this position. If I wrap my legs around him, he says it messes up his rhythm. He's sixty-seven. Fucks like seventeen.

Providing all goes perfectly, I'll graduate from UCLA in two months. My ass was getting a pounding in this hotel bed, but my brain was miles away, engaged in finishing an upcoming paper. Some people pay for school by working in the cafeteria. I have my own financial plan independent of federal student aid, and Albert is one small part of it. Macho has brought me a long-long way from where I was four years ago. I love that grumpy man.

"I don't hear you moaning," Albert said.

I started moaning. He doesn't like to be squeezed. I rested my hands on his ass as he pumped and gyrated. I moaned louder. Spacing out during my business with him is not part of the menu. I mentally put away the dissertation and concentrated on the now. Afterward, he took me out to dinner. Our table butted up against an elegant wood railing two floors above a strip club's stage and sitting area. We had a perfect view of the action below: dancers on stage, customers getting lap dances, etc. We'd started off downstairs but not with the hoi polloi. We'd been in a private area. His voice was always cranked to high volume almost like he was angry, but he wasn't. This was just him. Maybe he is going deaf. Once we were up here, he claimed he'd forgotten his glasses and had me read aloud portions of the menu so we could order. I'm thinking he can speak it okay but can't read English. His accent is Russian, and he has hugely bushy gray eyebrows that I'd love to be able to trim, and a mole on one side of his face, but I am not ashamed to be seen with him. He dresses fancy, a little flashier than your run-of-the-mill businessman back in Los Angeles. When the waitress came to take our order, his volume when ordering made people look. People at their tables glanced in his direction, put their noses in the air, and looked appalled. I think they had a lot of nerve to be snooty here. It's highbrow but still just a strip club. With the loud music, you do need to speak loudly.

"Gabi, your body is better than any bitch down there," he said and chewed on his steak.

If he thought I looked that good, why were we here and not back at the suite having room service? Why did we sit for an hour downstairs while two girls danced on his lap, song after song before we came up here to eat? Steak is great, a loaded baked potato is even better, but keeping me financially solid beats it all. For him, I guess being in public is part of the thrill. He was the one who wanted me to fly to New York City, for some reason. I wasn't here for the food. I was here for him. I was busy with the loaded baked potato but kept my attention on him.

"You're too good to me, Albert. I like being with you." I chewed delicately, my eyes on his face so when he looked my way, he noticed that my attention was all on him.

When he was done eating, we went back down to the first-floor sofa reserved for him in a private area with a view of the stage. This time, one girl danced on his lap. I sat beside him, sipped wine, and kept a smile on my face. The blonde was beautiful, face and body. I am straight, but girl on girl is not taboo.

The club rules were that a customer could not manhandle the dancer. He could touch her hips, legs, and face but couldn't get personal. No serious kissing. The girls were their own enforcers. I suppose that if they broke the rules, they were gone. I could see how tips from guys like Albert were much too good to risk losing. Albert liked to stroke the dancer and laugh while she danced on him, but I give Albert credit. He didn't go beyond fresh. Every so often, he leaned my way, and our lips would meet in a wet kiss. When he did, I reached under the dancer's ass to tease the erect ridge pushing against his pants.

Albert can drink and so can I, but I don't get crazy with a client. I sip and play the part of being high when the client expects it. Albert has no such requirement. He has lots of other requirements, like no coke, and though alcohol and weed are okay by him, with Albert, I do neither. I want him to keep calling Macho and requesting me when he's in town.

By the time his hired driver delivered us to the hotel, Albert was ready for bed. I helped him undress. He lay on the bed, half asleep, laughing as I pulled his shoes off, then his socks, and down the list of his clothes till I'd peeled my way down to his naked body, the way he liked to sleep.

He was awake enough to move himself under the covers and roll on his side. I cuddled him from behind, kissing his neck, rubbing his hairy chest, and fondling his soft penis that was drifting to sleep just as he was. He was fit for a graybeard, no fat on him. I knew he must lift weights like a demon. It didn't show so much now while he was relaxed, but I've seen him pumped up. His muscles don't match the gray in his hair. Of course, he's relaxed in bed. I heard a soft, rumbling snore, and made sure he was covered up when I escaped to one of the bathrooms. The hotel bathroom was impressive, roomy with a glass view of the New York skyscape so different from California. We were up high enough that the streets below looked unreal, like toy cars playing stop and go at streetlights. The water pressure was impressive too, much to my delight. I filled the tub with a hard blast of steaming water, augmented with the whole bottle of hotel brand bubble soap. The bubbles kept getting higher, standing over the rim of the tub in bubbly abandon, wetly sagging over the edge like the head of a giant sloppy beer. I love taking bubble baths. I can't have too many bubbles, and I wasn't going to be satisfied with this one until the bubbles were wild and overflowed to the floor. This marble palace was nothing like my aunt's creaky bathroom with five of us sharing the tiny mildewed low-ceilinged space, decorated with my squeeze-dried underwear draped over the curtain-rod to drip dry into the rust-stained tub.

I turned off the water and started to get in but caught sight of the reflection of my bruised ass. I turned to the three-pane mirror that looked like something in a magazine or a runway showroom, all gold-framed and baroque like its first life was spent in a millionaire's castle. Albert had left bruises on my ass where he squeezed as he pounded me. I don't mind my ass being squeezed, but Albert is extreme. He does it for as long as he's fucking me, and he can go for a very long time before he finishes. It didn't hurt then or now, but I don't like bruises.

Albert is not gentle at anything. When there is foreplay, not often, he is a finger person. He fingered my anus like it couldn't be uncomfortable for me. I'm not thinking badly of him. He's a saint. Some guys think because they have money, they have license to do what they want. Albert is generous. His kind-heartedness goes a long way to soothe the discomfort of anything he does.

February 1985
Four Seasons Hotel, New York City

The bedside clock said ten past eleven. Albert was missing, and the space where he'd been was cold. The room was so dark that I didn't know if it was night or day. I slipped out of bed, pulled aside the blackout drapes and revealed the wall of glass. Nighttime in the room, daytime outside. I pushed the illuminated drapery button on my end table. Spectacularly, the blackout drapes drew open, revealing drapery sheers lush enough to be a theater back-drop. The daylight was dazzling, but it was cloudy. On Albert's side of the bed was a note, probably written by his trained-to-be-invisible bodyguard. Judging by his menu performance last night, I think Albert can't write English. I sat on the edge of the bed to read.

You looked like an angel sleeping. I did not have heart to wake you. Thank you for wonderful time.

Albert

I saw the stack of bills he left me, and fell on my back, squealing aloud, clutching the money to my chest, my legs in the air. I make good money, but still, six big ones all at once is a red-letter day. Macho charged him five thousand, the extra thousand was a tip. It was sweet. I'd fly back coach, pay my agent his twenty percent. The balance plus the tip was all mine. Eventually I got in control of my emotions, though it took a shower to do it. I called the front desk.

"What time do I need to be out of here?"

"You have a late check out. Four p.m. ma'am. Do you need more time?"

"No, that's perfect. Thanks."

I put on the hotel bathrobe, ordered room service, then called United Airlines to reserve my return flight home. I gave my agent a heads-up.

"How did you do?" Macho sounded like I just woke him up. He's such a night owl.

"All good. I'll be in town by seven. Got anything going for me?"

"I will by the time you land."

"Keep it local, I have—"

"I know, you have classes tomorrow."

"I love you, Macho. You know me."

I'm twenty-two but look younger as a blonde. Macho found me in the gutter. He taught me how to apply makeup, how to sit with the client if we went out, how to handle the flatware when it was time to eat. I'd been hit on as far back as I could remember. I had fights with girls at school after their boyfriends stared or made passes at me. I lost count of the times I had to defend myself from male classmates in high school who couldn't keep their hands to themselves, even more of them once I started dying my hair blonde.

Macho prefers me as a blonde and manages me like an agent handling a high-class model, just like our contract says he will. If a guy is hooked up with Macho and wants a date at his home, the guy and his crib both have to pass Macho's guidelines. I didn't know it until a year or so after I hooked up with him that he was once with the DEA. To me, that explained a lot about his actions. He was like something out of a military movie.

I keep my two-bedroom high-rise in top notch shape. It's right out of a magazine. I only conduct business in one bedroom. The other is my real bedroom. Macho keeps a photo album of me in a bunch of poses with just enough erotic edge to hook new customers. It was hard not to remember Alex Rose using my picture out on Hollywood Boulevard to hook a sex-hungry dude to come back to the apartment where I was waiting to do what was necessary to get paid as much as possible.

It is a rare occasion when a client requests a session in my apartment, and that's fine with me. The fewer people know where I live, the better for me.

Macho insists on a vinegar douche once a week. He believes a weekly vinegar douche keeps a pussy tight. My daily douches kept me fresh. If I was pliable like a gymnast, I would eat my own pussy. That's how clean and fresh I am.

Macho is connected and has been from the beginning. If he sent me to a hotel for a half hour, the customer paid two hundred, Macho got fifty, and I kept the difference. Compared to that motherfucker Alex Rose, it was like hitting a gold mine. Then again, given time, conditions, and what the traffic will bear, for working out of a cheap apartment in Hollywood, fifty dollars for thirty minutes was great. It wasn't that long ago.

Macho is connected with VIP internationals like Albert. One time, I was included in a group of girls that entertained a Saudi prince at the Century Plaza Hotel. He was a handsome dude, like right out of a magazine. All the girls got to choose gifts from a big basket of goodies. I didn't get laid by the prince, but I did get a passionate kiss, a Rolex, and ten thousand dollars. The prince was loaded. In the Saudi royal family, there are over a thousand princes just like him.

If Albert had kept me one day in Los Angeles, it would have cost him two grand, but when he decided we were going to New York, Macho got me five. When I started with him, I felt twenty-five was too much so his cut is twenty percent. Now that I make so much more than before, twenty-five would have been cool. I was not going to suggest changing the cut up to a quarter.

I meet up with one or more of Macho's girls if the customer requests it. We make good money, but much of it gets spent on clothes. Our purses and shoes have to be designer. He checks his girls' closets.

"If it's fake, don't wear it." That's what he says.

I have two watches, a Rolex, a gift from the prince. The other is Cartier, a gift from myself to me.

Here's the thing: Macho is not my agent or in the real world, my pimp. He's my friend. We are both opportunists and take advantage of each other.

I have a student uniform. When I go to school, I'm in jeans and a shirt. Nothing fancy. If there's a test with a particularly conservative teacher, I show up looking like a conservative secretary. None of that wardrobe flew with me to New York. Albert liked to see me as a hot sophisticate, so that's all I had. I put on the plainest thing I'd brought with me: a long-sleeved dress, bright lavender, the best color for a blonde. It doesn't have a scrap of decoration but fits like a second skin, and is so finely knit, it looks like it is sheer—it isn't, really, thanks to a flesh-toned under-slip. I always feel glamorous putting it on, even though I didn't supplement it with any jewelry. Lavender hose, though.

The dress was mostly covered up by my short and swingy winter coat. New York is cold in February. I wore stilettos to the airport, but only because that's all I brought with me. No harm done. It's not like I'll walk through acres of snow between the taxi and the entrance.

When I checked in at Kennedy Airport, I was offered an upgrade to first class.

"No thanks."

The ticket person was on the short side, dressed in the standard airline-type uniform with a military cut. She was close to my age. She didn't look at all military though. Her hair reminded me of a standardbred poodle. She had straight up curls with strange Lyle Lovett-styled bangs. She printed my ticket and handed it to me. I looked at it.

"What seat do I have, window, aisle or middle?"

"Middle."

I returned the ticket to her. "I have a paper to write. Any chance I can get a window?"

Poodle lady didn't even look. "I'm sorry."

"Okay, I'll take the upgrade if it is on the window." I put one hundred twenty-five dollars on the counter. Poodle smiled and printed me a new ticket.

"You got a window," she said to me with a plastic smile.

"Very cool," I said and handed her a five. She almost didn't take it.

I figured I could write all the way to LA. With any luck, I'd finish the damn paper by the time I got to LAX, then all I'd have to do when I got home is type it out. I didn't have twelve hundred dollars to spend on a portable computer.

I took off my coat and carried it on board. I was glad I'd worn something long enough that I didn't have to worry about modesty. I was able to focus on my work. I passed on dinner and snacks but kept the stewardess busy bringing me diet cokes. The man sitting next to me was probably sixty, probably a lawyer, a little chubby, but he wore an expensive dress shirt and cufflinks. The pants to his suit were designer or custom, and his shoes in the same league as the Rolex he wore. I smiled. He smiled. When I passed on dinner, he passed on dinner too. Every time I got a coke, he asked for wine, then switched to Chivas on the rocks.

At least ten times between the Atlantic and the Pacific, he said, "You're a busy young lady."

Each time, I looked away from my legal pad and smiled.

I chugged too much diet Coke and had to use the restroom. There was space for me to walk in front of him, but he got up when I left, and again when I returned. That was about the extent of our interaction, but at times, I had the feeling he was aware of me.

As we were descending, the flight attendant brought our coats. He got up and put his on. I stowed my writing stuff in my briefcase, and he caught me looking at him. I caught him looking at me, too.

"Name is Ed Homer." He extended his hand.

"Gabi," I said. We shook hands. "Pleased to meet you."

"The pleasure is mine," he said.

February 1985
Los Angeles, California
Homer

For the entire flight, I tried to figure her out. I read enough on her writing pad to know she's a student writing a paper and not a love letter. With that get-up she was wearing, rich parents. In the old days, I'd have just hit on her. Hit on her while sitting in first class filled to capacity? I look like her father. Maybe not.

She finally put that damn legal pad away.

She's gorgeous. Her coloring is striking. She's very fair, deep, dark brown eyes that I could just fall into. She has very blonde hair, a kissable mouth and her skin looks touchable. I thought about kissing it for a couple hundred miles. That purple dress she was in looked like she was naked underneath. I kept reminding myself that she's a student. She might have been dressed to tease, but she was writing a school paper.

I took a business card out of my jacket pocket and wrote on the back.

"This is stupid. Here goes. Can I buy you a drink?"

I handed her the card. She read it, looked up at me.

She opened her designer purse and took out a pen. She's right-handed. She wrote on the palm of her left hand. $500 1 hour. $2500 night.

I felt this big grin emerge on my face.

She smiled and looked out of the window as the plane was descending.

1985
Los Angeles, California
Gabi

We walked out of the plane. I had my Louis Vuitton carryon, purse, and my briefcase, and was wearing my Louis Vuitton padlock peep toe stilettos. I could feel the little gold padlocks on the heel swing with each step. They don't really do anything, but they pack a message. Homer had a small carryon and a briefcase. He offered to help carry something for me.

"I got it," I said. "I'm used to this. Thank you."

We exited side-by-side. He's much taller than me.

"Are we doing this?"

"I'm game," I said. "Which option?"

"All night," he said.

We were both looking ahead. So many people at LAX.

"Do you have a car here?"

"No car," I said. I had been planning to hail a taxi.

"My driver is out front."

Cars don't impress me. Most of the ones I see are hired. Homer's Rolls Royce is his, and so is his driver.

"This is Archie," Homer introduced us.

Archie smiled. I felt an instant connection with him. There's something engaging about his smile. It's like a hug. Archie was a big, tall guy, wearing a crisp uniform and chauffeur's hat. He was a shade or two darker than his driving suit, though the clothes lean toward navy-blue and Archie's skin tone leaned more toward mahogany. He had perfect teeth. His face was angular, strong, his hair close-cut. His cheekbones were well defined. He bowed and snapped his heels. The gesture made Homer laugh. He had a physique too, could have been a bouncer, a bodyguard, a wrestler.

"Get over yourself," Homer said, laughing.

Archie laughed too. I didn't feel any social distance between them, which made me like Homer more as a guy who doesn't stand on ceremony. A minute later, we were in the flow of traffic getting out of LAX.

"I have diet coke," Homer said. His car was equipped with a bar.

"I had enough diet coke for one day. I'll have what you're having," I pointed to his chilled bottle of white. "Where are we going?"

"My house if that's okay. I'm in Holmby Hills."

"That works," I said, sipping from my glass.

"Where do you live?"

"Brentwood, on Wilshire," I said.

"Neither of us ate," Homer said.

"You want to stop for something?" I put my glass in the tray, and my right hand on his thigh.

"If you don't mind, I have a good cook at home. He'll fix up anything you feel like eating."

"Deal," I said with a little laugh. "Do you live alone?"

"Yes. My wife died two years ago."

I reached out and held his hand.

"I have four cats, three dogs, and an aviary filled with birds."

"Neat," I said.

"I think you will like my house. A big house." He took a drink. "A lonely house that echoes with memories."

I have met many men who talked like Homer. They have lost their wives (or said they did) and talked about how lonely they were. Only two took me to their homes, and they were not in Holmby Hills, or anywhere close to that altitude.

"I can pay you soon as we get to the house," he said.

"I'm not worried."

I knew this guy was money, but I never would have guessed that he owned anything like the house I entered. Streetlight highlighted tall gates and nothing else, so once we were inside the gates, the size of the house was a surprise. We turned in the driveway, and I was led inside. It looked more like a public building than a residence.

Archie the chauffeur is also the cook. Homer introduced Carmen and Ignazio as they served us snacks when we sat in the den. A den. A house this size probably has more than one. Soft tacos of cheese, chicken, or beef were provided on trays.

"This is dinner. I'm good with just this," I said.

"Let Archie cook up a real meal for us," Homer said.

Wine again. The serving couple was all over us. More drinks, more tacos. Both wore white chef jackets matching what Archie was wearing when he came to find out what we wanted to eat. Maybe he had a changing closet in the kitchen.

"We have everything. What's your pleasure?" Archie asked.

"Homer, whatever you order is fine with me."

"Judge, no one else calls you Homer." Archie laughed.

Judge? I wondered.

His suit coat came off, then his tie. His cufflinks were gone. He rolled up his sleeves.

"I'll give you time to decide," Archie said.

The couple and Archie disappeared. We were alone side-by-side on a suede sofa. I don't know furniture or cars, but I bet it cost as much as a Lamborghini. I smelled real suede and saw dragons and fanciful animals carved into the wood. The legs had dragon feet, or at least the feet dragons would have if they were real. Giant lizardy claws, with scales, all carved in fine detail.

"If you don't go by Homer, tell me what I should be calling you."

"Homer is fine."

"Homer, what made you hit on me?"

"I just asked if you wanted to go for a drink."

"Is there something in my look that says, hey, you can rent me? Someday I'm not going to be doing this. I don't want to look like this is what I do."

"You are always going to be hit on. Just look at you. You're beautiful. The question you should be asking is how can any man not hit on you?"

"Thanks."

"If I can ask a personal question, how are you set financially? Do you make a lot of money?"

I took a sip of wine so I could delay the answer.

"I do okay." I felt my face get hot. He patted my hand.

"You're blushing," Homer said. "I'm glad you're here." Homer refilled my glass.

"I don't have to drink. I don't drink when I'm working."

"I don't have a problem if you drink or not. I'd like very much for you to please yourself."

We clicked glasses, but I put the glass down.

"I like you. I'm glad you wrote me that note," I said.

"I'm glad you wrote me back."

More wine. More laughter.

Archie returned.

I asked for a club sandwich. Homer wanted a grilled cheese.

"Humble food," Homer said.

He sipped. I touched the glass to my lips. No sip.

Last night's dinner, Albert had had chateaubriand, snails, baked Alaska. I'd had mostly potato. It's hard to beat a loaded baked potato.

"I love this kind of food," I said.

Archie brought out the food plus French fries, onion rings, fried mozzarella.

"Delicious," I said with gusto.

Archie smiled. His lips were the color of the burgundy he poured in Homer's glass. I figured he might be thirty.

We ate in the family room where Homer had a huge party bar with a dozen fancy stools and lots of seating. The room had the kind of lived-in comfy clutter that made it feel like a whole family lived there. It was interactive, a place where groups could sit together and chat, or listen to music and party. I pictured the action. Homer and his people made me feel right at home. Homer opened up about his life while I ate everything in front of me.

"I'm a retired federal court judge. Before that, I was in private practice defending criminals."

Now I understood why Archie had called him judge.

"What were you doing in New York?"

"I went to visit my daughter and grandchildren."

"How old are the grandchildren?"

We chatted about his daughter and her six and seven-year-old kids who were growing up fatherless because daddy had had a fatal accident while driving under the influence in New Jersey.

"I'm sorry," I said.

"She's going to be fine. She's an executive with a news organization. Keeps her busy. Her mother-in-law and father-in-law moved to New York to be close to the grandchildren."

The food disappeared. The table was cleared. The conversation continued. I said no to wine, and yes to a diet coke. Leonard Cohen was singing in the background somewhere in the big room.

He tilted his head a little when he talked to me, a quirk I found endearing. I noticed many pictures of his wife and family on the wall. It was a family gallery that hinted how full their life together had been. The whole family had traveled together to exotic places. I realized how much we resembled each other. His wife had dark eyes like mine, and fair skin. Her hair was the color mine would have been if I didn't get it colored regularly. I felt my throat well up in sympathy for him. I wanted to ask her name, but it didn't seem the right time.

"What were you doing in New York?" he asked.

I sipped the diet coke and thought exactly how to phrase it.

"I was there on business."

"Interesting," he said, giving me a sharp glance.

I had the feeling that not much got past Homer. He proved it with his next sentence.

"I got a glimpse at the paper you were writing and figured you for a student."

"I'm at UCLA. With any luck, only two more months."

Homer smiled big. "And then what?"

"I don't know. Maybe go work in something to do with my major."

"What's your major?"

"Business."

"That works for law school," he said.

"It does." Law school is a big step. I sure wasn't going to think about it now. I changed the subject. "What's the plan tonight?"

Homer had to be feeling the drinks. He'd been drinking steadily on the plane, maybe even before he got on the plane, all the way home, and ever since we'd arrived, even straight through dinner. He knew how to hold his liquor.

"I like to watch," Homer stated baldly. Our eyes met.

I had no question about what he meant.

"Is that a problem?"

"No problem," I said. I pushed my seat back and got to my feet. "If you're ready, I'm ready. Except I need to shower first, Homer," I said as he led me to his bedroom.

The bedroom was what you expect in a great big house, grander and bigger than the suite at the Four Seasons in New York. It felt less homey than the den, and more decorated. I mean, there was a cover, shams, and curtains that all matched. The carpet and walls were color coordinated in hues of brown and gold. It was a masculine room that had no frills, but there was a large oil portrait of his wife on one wall.

"Your choice," he said, pointing to two ensuite bathrooms.

I slipped off my heels, turned on the shower, and sat on the throne, looking around at my surroundings. Everything in the bathroom was either marble, glass, or gold. It was stunning, from the teardrop chandelier to the pattern of marble on the shower wall, floor, and sink, to the hammered gold cup beside the faucet. Even the little soaps were marbled with streaks of gold. The tub looked amazing, deep, wide, and I bet the water pressure was splendid. I could just imagine the head of foam it could create. Too bad I hadn't asked for a bubble bath.

I picked up a house phone in the bathroom and dialed Macho.

"I'm on a job in Holmby Hills. Met on the plane, will explain tomorrow, it's an overnight."

"Should have called earlier," Macho said.

"Don't be mad. I got you covered. You know that."

"Stay in touch," Macho said.

I showered and came out of the bathroom in a thick white robe I found hanging on a hook. It was long on me, a man's robe,

soft and luxurious, and the initials EH had been elaborately embroidered, white on white, on the left side over the heart.

The bedroom was lit, but it took a moment for my eyes to adjust. The lights were dimmed. The bed was turned down. Archie
was in the middle of the bed, bare ass naked. He was sitting up, a
big smile on his face. His teeth were very white.

"Where is Homer?" I asked, hanging back a little bit.

"He likes to watch."

He beckoned me to come to the bed. I undid the robe and
dropped it where I stood. I walked to him as naked as the day I
was born.

"Girl, you are one fine, fine, lady."

I smiled at him, very aware that Homer was watching but not
knowing where he was watching from. I got in bed beside Archie.
The mattress was firm. I should have been nervous, but I wasn't.
This night was different from anything I'd experienced.

"Where is he?"

"The judge is watching. I promise," Archie said. He reached
over to the bedside lamp and switched it on. The crystal candela-
bra centered over the bed was ablaze. He lay down, and I lay beside him wondering what to expect.

"Chauffeur. Cook. Cock. What other jobs do you do?" I asked
mockingly but soft.

"I'm going to fuck you like you never been fucked before," he
said, lying back, letting me get on top.

Homer must not care for foreplay because Archie went right
to it. His manhood filled my pussy. I had an orgasm almost in-
stantly as he entered. Archie knew when I orgasmed. It wasn't
like I kept it a secret.

He said, "That's the best lubricant."

I can't think of a position we didn't do. He kept repositioning
me, almost like setting a shot for a photo shoot. I was almost mesmerized, not just at what Archie was doing to my body, but also

what Homer was doing. His watching played tricks on my mind. I could practically feel his pleasure as he feasted on our every move. Archie's body was firm and well-muscled, and before long he was slick with sweat, strain and excitement coloring his expression. I could not tell if there was a particular place that Archie was performing to, a camera or peep hole. Because I did not know, it felt like Homer was everywhere, not just somewhere behind a wall, but in every corner, on the ceiling, and in the bed with us. I gave up and just went along with the flow. It went on and on, for at least two hours until the phone rang at the bedside table

"That's the judge," Archie said, without answering it.

We were done. I'd been fucked that thoroughly before, but I couldn't say when.

I showered, towel-dried my hair, and ran a comb through it. I checked myself in the mirror, relieved that the marks from last light had not turned into bruises. When I emerged naked from the brightly lit bathroom, I realized the lights had been dimmed. I could hear the buzzing of the dimmers.

"Archie?" I stood in the bathroom door, looking out, unable to make out Archie where I'd left him.

"Archie's gone. Don't be alarmed." I heard Homer's voice. "I'm in bed."

I climbed on top of him, kissed him. He was a distinctly different physical type, less muscular, with a less athletic frame.

"Archie was something else."

"You were something else," he said, hugging me against him.

"Can I take care of you now?" I asked.

Homer chuckled. "Gabi, I'm plumb dry. Nothing left. Thanks for offering, though."

"I have to do something for you."

"You have. Archie will take you home. He has an envelope with what we agreed on. Please leave him your phone number."

"Are you sure? I mean, you're paying me for the whole night.

Maybe in the morning you will be ready for a go?"

It didn't seem quite fair to be leaving him without seeing to his satisfaction. I could not change his mind, though. By the time I dressed and returned to kiss him goodbye, Homer was asleep.

I kissed him. A gray curl hung down on his forehead giving him a roguish look. I smoothed it back.

"I like you, Homer. Sleep well," I whispered.

I walked out of the bedroom and found Archie, dressed again in navy black with a little hat, just as he'd been the first time that I'd seen him. I wondered if he liked playing dress up. He wore a lot of suits for Homer. He did the sharp bow again, and the heel click, making me laugh, and with a flourish, handed me the envelope. I put it in my purse and followed him down the circular stairs, through the ground level floor and outside.

I didn't feel like talking, so I was glad Archie kept the divider window closed. Conversation between us would have been awkward, anyway. I could still feel him pistoning inside of me. It was a short drive to the address I had given him on Wilshire Boulevard.

After all the showers, I didn't shower again, but I washed my face to make sure there was no makeup lingering and got into a soft white tee shirt and panties, what I usually sleep in when I'm alone. I save the frilly stuff for the date who wants that kind of thing. At three something in the morning, I tossed the shams on the chaise, folded back my floral comforter to reveal the delicate flowers on my Laura Ashley percale sheets, and slid underneath. My night was not done until I checked in, so I called Macho. No problem with the hour for him. For Macho, this was the middle of a business day.

"I'm done," I told him. "I didn't have to stay the night. I'll be by to see you tomorrow with your end."

"Good girl," he said. "I don't suppose you feel like doing an hour at the Ambassador downtown?"

"I'll do it if you want me to."

"It's five hundred. I can get it covered."

"I'll do it. I need an hour and change to get there."

Macho said, "Okay. The client already paid by credit card."

"Got it," I said, and wrote down the date's name—Gilbert—and room number. I flipped down the comforter, tossed the shams back on the bed, and put on a fresh outfit.

It was six in the morning when I got back home from the Ambassador downtown. The client gave me a two-hundred-dollar tip. I ran a tub of hot water, poured in my favorite jasmine and lavender soap. The hot water performed its magic on me, and I called Macho from the tub to tell him Gilbert was done, and that when I got home from school at three, I was done, out of circulation until I let him know I'd rejoined the living.

I don't know how I managed to stay awake through school long enough to make it to the bedroom and set the alarm clock. It felt more like crossing the uphill deck of a rolling ship than four steps across my white shag carpet.

It had been a long twenty-four hours. I'd started with Albert in Los Angeles then overnight in New York, then back to LA and Homer, then the guy named Gilbert, then school. I shut my eyes. I crashed on my bed to sleep my fill. Sleep was immediate and dreamless.

My phone rang several times while I slept, but I didn't bother with it. The only calls that ever mattered were Macho's. I don't know why I shared my phone number with Homer. I never gave out my number—Macho handled that. If I did any business with him, I'd give Macho his cut. That was the deal. Macho took care of me like family, not that I had any family that took care of me any longer.

No, that's not fair. My aunt cares deeply about me. She had begged me to move back in under her roof. She'd done her best to provide for me from the minute I lived under her roof. We're not tight but we talk on the phone often. I stay in touch with my cousin Serena and once in a while I hear from my two cousins, Darrin and Larry who are still living with my aunt. I avoid visiting because I'm busy with everything I have going and especially because in person, my aunt has too much opportunity to ask me what I'm doing for a living.

It will be years before my college degree gives me the caliber of income I have with Macho, and that won't happen if I settle for the bachelor's degree and stop attending school. I struggled through the four years of college, not because the academics were challenging, but managing the money and time was practically impossible. I'd promised my aunt I would graduate, but also, I needed to prove to myself that I had the grit to get it done.

That's me.

I've had countless pretty women, but Gabi strikes me as a hundred on a scale of ten. She's not the first woman to come along that I've rated high, but she is definitely special. She fits right in. It's her smarts. There was Liz who was also a student, beautiful, intelligent. She fit in, not as fast as Gabi the other night but she managed to make me feel extremely special. She hung out here six months. I didn't show her the door. She showed herself out. I've been alone for the past two years, since Becky died, but I've been fooling around all my life.

In the short time Gabi was here, I felt energized. Her performance with Archie was off the charts. I need her to stick around for a while. I need to learn more about her. I want her to need me. Next time, I want her to spend the night even if I fall in a deep sleep. I want to wake up to her. Yes, I have to do that.

Damn, when did I get so old?

Women come and go. Why this one? Maybe I'm growing soft. She's not my wife, Becky for sure. I'm not looking for a Becky. I'm living in the moment. Gabi is a winner. Eventually I will tire of her. It's the way I am.

It had been about a week since I'd been to Homer's house. Archie called.

"Judge wants to know when you're available?"

"Geez, Archie, no hello? No hi? No nothing?" I laughed.

"I'm sorry. I don't mean to be short with you."

"No sweat, Archie. I'm kidding. What's he looking for? How much time?"

"Same as before."

I called Macho and told him I got the call direct.

"I'm thinking I shouldn't have charged him as much as I did the last time."

"Gabi charge him what's okay with you and him. I'm okay with that."

I drove myself. I pulled up to the intercom mounted on a steel post outside the gates. I pressed the button. A woman's voice came over the speaker. I assumed it was Carmen.

"It's Gabi."

"Yes, Miss Gabi, please drive in. I open gates."

I pulled up to the front of the house as it was just getting dark.

The space between the gates and the house was like a beautiful manicured forest. It was twilight, but I could see the house a lot better than before. It was huge, and the kind of thing you might see in a magazine devoted to architecture. It was an old beautiful house.

Archie answered the door. I kissed his cheeks European-style, and then Homer came into view.

"Gabi, you look gorgeous," Homer said. When he hugged me, I kissed him on the lips.

"What's it going to be, Homer or Judge?" I asked.

"Homer," he said.

We sat in the cluttered family room where we had dined the first night I was there. We sat across from each other on wide leather chairs. The chairs were wide, but not wide enough for two.

"You should sit next to me," I said. "I don't bite."

Archie laughed. "I'd be careful, Judge."

Archie's mood, before he left the room, seemed light and happy in front of Homer. I had the impression that Archie tended to be serious.

"Are you sure you want me to drink wine?" I asked Homer.

"Not unless you want diet coke?" Homer said. "Yes, drink, enjoy."

"Homer, last time we did this, you paid me what I asked for. I feel bad about it. I didn't stay the night as you know."

"Gabi, let's not talk about finances."

"I thought I'd drop it by one thousand. Fifteen hundred for the night? Is that okay?"

Homer ignored my question. He reached across the table and held his wine out stubbornly until I reached to click his glass.

"You're beautiful, Gabi."

"So are you, Homer." He laughed at me, but I was telling the truth. He did seem beautiful to me, especially when the lean planes of his face creased into a smile. His gray hair streaked with black was distinguished, but that smile off-set the gravity with a hint of mischief. His eyes in this light were more silver than gray, bright, brimming with secrets.

We had dinner, drank, and danced to Leonard Cohen. I guess you could call it dancing. Homer was not a dancer, but he was a good sport. He drank heavily and continuously of wine but seemed sober as a judge. I pictured him holding state in his courtroom in his regal black robe with a gavel at his right hand. He swung me around, laughing. We weren't going to win any dance contests, but I don't know when I ever laughed so hard. His voice was deep and gentle, and I found myself thrilling to the sound of it. I was excited about what might be coming next. I don't know if I was anticipating Homer or Archie, but either way, it would be an adventure.

"Are you going to fuck me tonight, Homer?" I whispered.

By the startled look on his face, I knew I caught him off guard with the question. He didn't flinch, or evade, or change the subject.

"I can do that," he said.

Once we were in bed, I got him hard and ready. The foreplay was hardly necessary. There was absolutely nothing wrong with his hardware. I guess I'd thought there might be issues, that his preference for watching was the result of a problem. I mounted him, and he pulled me down against him. He kissed me as our bodies danced the horizontal dance in earnest. When I thought he was going to finish, he rolled us over, so I was on the bottom. I wrapped my legs around him, and pulled him towards me, making him go deep. That's when he gave it up and exploded inside of me.

He rolled over to his back, breathing heavily. I turned on my side, my face close to his.

"Gabi, I needed that. Thank you."

"Don't thank me, Homer." I stopped myself from saying *you're paying me. No thanks needed.*

I excused myself and went to shower. I washed my hair, squeezed it half-dry in a towel and combed through it. A robe, maybe the one I wore before, was waiting for me. When I came out of the bathroom wearing it, Archie and Homer were sitting on chairs. Homer was sipping something on the rocks. Archie had nothing to drink.

I looked them both in the eyes, a very intense moment. Homer flicked his head toward the bed, and I felt an unexpected sexual jolt from his air of command. We got in the bed. Archie pulled me on top of him and filled me. Homer lay naked next to us. I was so wrapped up in what was happening that when Homer started licking me from behind, I was taken by surprise. In this business, nothing should surprise me. The sensations these two were evoking were thrilling. Archie knew what to do with his big dick, and Homer knew how to play every nerve in a woman's body. The sex went on for a long time and ended in another shower. Last time he sent me home instead of having me stay through the night.

This time, he said, "Gabi, come lie here with me."

I cuddled up next to him. He buried his nose in my just-washed hair—washed for at least the third time that day.

"I love the way you smell."

Crazy me. I got chill when he said that.

It was my second time there. I felt at ease.

He turned on to his side to face me. I kissed him on the lips, tasting Chivas, the dregs of which were in a glass on the night-stand. I reached down and fondled him, kissed my way to his thing, and brought him to another release that put him to sleep with a smile on his face.

I smelled morning before I opened my eyes. I woke to the scent of a breakfast buffet. Well, it wasn't a buffet, but it might as well have been one. Ham, bacon, toast, coffee, all sorts of goodies. I turned over, opened my eyes, and there was Archie with a huge bed tray that was wide enough for two people to use. I kissed Homer who was already awake. We both sat up. Archie centered the tray on the bed in front of us and left.

"Did Archie ever go to bed?"

Homer laughed, coffee mug in his hand, the other hand on my bare thigh under the comforter. "He gets plenty of rest."

"We should maybe skip breakfast and do a morning thing," I said.

"I'd take you up on it, but I have a meeting at eleven."

"Okay," I said. "Your loss."

I focused on the food, drank the coffee black as Homer did. I showered again, dressed, and when I came out, found Archie alone in the bedroom.

"Good Morning," I said. "You left so quickly this morning that I didn't have a chance to thank you for the great breakfast. You are amazing. Do you ever sleep?"

"Judge wants to know if we can do something for him."

I didn't need to ask what it was.

"Let's do it." I put my purse on the bed and followed Archie into the other bathroom where Homer was showering.

It was bigger than the bathroom I had used. The shower was larger, and there was twice as much floorspace, even with the massive double vanity against one wall.

Archie was the stage director. He positioned me against a granite wall by the shower. My slacks and panties were bunched up at my ankles, my blouse untouched, my arms were up like he had told me to keep them. Archie dropped his jeans and entered me from behind. My right cheek was against the wall, my eyes facing the glass enclosure where Homer was watching as the water cascaded down on him. In five minutes with Archie, I orgasmed twice.

When it was over, it wasn't over. Archie left us. Homer beckoned me. I took off the rest of my clothes and joined him in the shower.

An hour later, I was in my car with an envelope that Archie gave me when he walked me to the front door.

He put his arm around my waist and kissed me hard on the lips.

"You're a fire pit, Gabi," he said.

I drove home. With all the sex in my life, I don't reflect on my dates. But I kept remembering and reliving the hours I spent at Homer's house, especially the threesome and the bathroom scene. There was no doubt that Homer was a voyeur. Still, I had good vibes about him. I think he likes me.

At home I counted the money. I called Macho.

"I got three thousand. I told him only fifteen hundred."

"Are you surprised?"

Macho sounded grouchy. He is not a morning person. I hung up and got ready for school. I was at school by eleven, my brain drifting elsewhere, still floating high on a cloud of sex. Archie sex. He was such a hunk, and Homer was special like no one I could readily remember. By special, I mean that he was beyond nice.

Macho lived in Brentwood, less than two blocks away from me in his condominium on the twenty-third floor. He had valet service and doorman service in a high security building. The building where I lived was just as nice, only I rented. I only had one credit card, and a bank account with a couple thousand dollars at any given time. Qualifying for a real estate loan would never happen unless I would be able to report earnings. I had a safe at home that came with the unit, built in the wall of my bedroom closet. I kept $20,000 in cash, half of in small bills. In an emergency, like an earthquake, I would need cash and big bills might be a problem. In my safe deposit box at the bank where I had the tiny balance in checking, I had over a hundred thousand dollars. I could afford tuition if I decided to continue beyond my Bachelors. Law School would eat up what I had stashed, and no doubt I'd come up short before I was done unless I kept working.

With the Alex Rose nightmare hanging over me, I wondered if the bar association would shut the door on me. I had not been arrested, but I had killed a human being. The cops and the district attorney had concluded that it was self-defense. Would the state bar make the same conclusion? I had had no arrests since I started as a working girl. If I got busted while in school, I could say goodbye to a license to practice law, for sure.

What the fuck to do?

At least soon I'd be handed my BS Diploma to hang up on a wall. What would be important to me is a profession I loved and made big money on so I could retire from my present career. I am not always going to look like I do.

It was dark, almost ten when I drove my two-year-old Corvette two blocks to Macho's. Brentwood is safe, but I don't like walking on Wilshire Boulevard at night. The doorman announced me to Macho, and I was allowed in the elevator.

I got the bear hug reserved for me and handed him the envelope. Inside was an index card with the accounting of the money I had enclosed, including giving myself credit for two tricks I'd done that Macho got paid by credit card. Macho was lucky that not all his income was green cash. He had credit to burn and could get whatever he wanted like his fabulous four-bedroom condominium. I guess he ran all the income through the modeling agency. He never talked about his personal business with me.

I drank a glass of red wine that I served myself at his bar and brought Macho a diet Coke. I stood facing the view from his living room. The floor to ceiling glass wall provided a fantastic view. At home, my view faced South. He faced North. South was cheaper than North.

Normally by ten, Macho would be on the phone. Tonight, action started later than ten, though somewhere in the world, it is always ten.

I told him about Judge Homer.

"Sounds like you have a regular," he said.

"We have a regular."

"I'm curious about this guy. I'll have Tension check him out."

Tension was a private investigator, a retired cop.

"He's a retired judge whose wife died two years ago. There's nothing to check out."

"I'm curious," Macho said. "That name sounds familiar."

"Homer is just an unusual name," I said. "But okay chief, you know best."

He looked at his watch and pulled the phone near him. "Time to get the night rolling."

I got up. "Speaking of rolling time, why don't we meet up again over at the Roosevelt Hotel? Or here. Here would be fine."

"Four years ago, that was the first and last time," he said.

I stuck my tongue out, walked over to him, kissed him and headed for the door.

"I love you, Macho."

"I love you, too."

I was lying on my bed with a heating pad against my stomach. I had one of those sleep masks over my eyes because it was daylight and my body wanted it to be night. I took this week off every month. I tend not to get out of the house.

The phone rang. I really didn't want to answer. I knocked over my lamp but got the phone. The huge rotary was hard to miss, even with a mask on.

It was Archie so I was glad I picked up.

"Gabi, hope you are well."

"How are you?"

"I'm good. Thanks for asking. It's been a long time," Archie said.

It had been five days since my last visit.

"Judge wants to know when you will be free."

"Darn," I said. "I'm off duty. It's that time."

"I'll tell him. Call me when you are back to work."

"Archie, thank you. Give Homer a hug from me."

I hung up, tossed the heating pad on the bed, and went to my kitchen to fetch a cup of tea.

The phone rang again. It was Homer.

"If you aren't doing anything, come over for a few days and we'll keep each other company."

"I can't believe you called me yourself," I said.

"No sex. Relax, eat, watch movies, sleep, then do it all over again the next day. What do you say?"

I absolutely never go out on a session during my off week. Macho would never book me. The disadvantage now is that Archie and Homer did not go through Macho. I was called direct. I had to tell them it was that time of the month and that should have been the end of it. But it wasn't. Homer wanted me to come over.

I accepted.

The next day I drove to Homer's. At high noon, we sat out on the patio next to the pool having lunch. We watched two movies in his media room—a new room for me since I hadn't seen it before. There were nine recliner chairs tiered in threes, each row slightly elevated. The movies played on a projector and were shown on a big screen that came down from the ceiling against one wall. It was a mini movie theater but totally neat, and cozy. The big screen was a killer. It was like we were right in the movie.

Homer drank cokes and ate popcorn. I did the same, except I had diet Coke.

The Jerry Lewis movie was old but fun. He asked me twice if the movie was okay.

I laughed but Homer laughed so hard during some scenes, he cried. It was a new side of Homer. I mean, he cried laughing at an old movie he'd seen many times before. It wasn't like he was sad or anything.

A couple of times, I got out of my chair and sat on his lap and hugged him and made a fuss with all the kisses I gave him. He giggled like a teenager, hugged me. Then the movie came out of pause mode, and I went back to my seat.

I felt like I was manipulating him. That's what I did for a living. I made men feel good. I decided to tone it down. I didn't want him to think I was doing all that because I expected to get paid for spending time with him.

Four days after I arrived, I went home. Homer, not Archie handed me an envelope.

"I'm not taking that. I had a good time. You were a lovely host. I had a blast. This was on me."

"Gabi, take the money. Consider it a gift, please," Homer said.

"No," I said softly.

I kissed Homer and saw myself out. Before I got my car in gear, Archie walked to the driver side of my car. My window was open. I stuck my head out, my lips pursed for a kiss. He tapped them with his.

"You were leaving without saying goodbye," he said.

"I'm sorry, I didn't see you."

Archie handed me the envelope. I shook my head.

"Gabi, this is the way he wants it. Don't argue."

I took the envelope, stuck my head through the open window and puckered my lips for him to kiss me again.

He did.

When I got home, I counted it. Homer gave me ten grand. I was going to call him and complain.

Complain? Silly me.

"I have two g for you," I told Macho on the phone.

"I thought this was your week."

"It is."

I told him the story.

Macho laughed. "When I see you, I'll tell you about him. Tension checked him out."

"Really?"

"Get over your thing. Next time I see you, then we can talk," Macho said.

Two days later when I was ready to go back to work, I took the $2,000 to Macho. He opened the door without greeting me, yawned in my face, and walked back to his couch.

"Aren't you cold?" I asked, wishing I'd worn a sweater. March isn't bad weather in LA, but it was December behind Macho's door. He likes to keep it cold when he's sleeping. He ignored me.

Daylight is Macho's sleep-time, and he was nesting in boxers and a tee shirt and socks, laid out like broccoli in his den in front of the television. The TV was off, and the air conditioning on full blast. The balcony curtains were half-closed. I walked over and closed them the rest of the way.

A bowl of potato chips and some onion dip were on his coffee table. He scooped a blob of dip and offered it to me.

"Breakfast?"

"No thanks. I think I'll pass. Tell me what Tension told you."

He ate the chip and dipped a second one.

"Homer was a mob lawyer."

"Excuse me?"

"When he was in private practice, he represented mob bosses, drug lords, money launderers and white collar criminals with deep pockets. He was one of the top criminal attorneys in the country. His wife, Becky Rogers, was the sole heiress of her father Don Rogers."

"Where do I know that name from?"

"Her father founded the worldwide hotel chain. Back to Homer. He was appointed to the federal bench by Ronald Reagan. His wife had lobbied to get him the presidential nomination. He resigned last year for personal reasons. When she died, the lion share of her estate went to her daughter in New York. The judge inherited a measly billion bucks."

"He's worth that much?"

"Probably more than that. He had very high-profile clients."

"He doesn't act that rich. He travels commercial. That's how I met him."

"Tension says there are two executive planes registered in his name."

The news of his wealth painted a better forecast for my accepting his big cash. The ten grand he insisted I take was petty cash for him. I felt a lot better about keeping it.

"I'm glad you looked him up. I feel like I know better where he's coming from." I sat on a chair across from the couch and watched Macho scooping dip with his eyes closed. "I spent four delicious no-sex days with him."

Macho's eyes popped open and he stared at me, sleep in the corners of his eyes.

"I don't want to see you hurt, Gabi. He's too old for you. He's probably playing you. As long as you know it can end from one minute to the next, wonderful."

"Macho, back it up. You sound like I'm going to fall in love with him."

"Stranger things have happened," Macho said.

"I don't believe in blue sky, my friend. I believe the storm is always coming."

He had another huge yawn. I flicked off the light in his bedroom, pulled him to his feet, whipped the pillow and sheet off the couch and put them in his arms before shoving him in the direction of his bedroom. He walked ahead like a zombie, waving goodbye to me without turning around. He said something in the middle of the yawn. It was either "You can let yourself out," or "Pickles give you gout."

I dumped the chips and dip in the kitchen trash compactor and headed back home.

Macho called me at ten something that night with a date. Not bad for a Thursday night.

"I can get you two thousand for a night in Vegas. He's got the jet in Van Nuys."

"Do I know him?"

"Nope."

"Sure," I replied.

It took me fifteen minutes to be out of the house. I was on standby like a doctor, with the only decision being where I was going in order to decide what to wear. I packed a Vegas overnight bag. It took an hour to get to the executive airport in Van Nuys. Even at eleven, traffic was miserable. Rich men who hired me wanted company from the time they took off. It helped that the buzz was Macho had the hottest models around.

A valet took my car. I walked into the terminal with my Louis V carryon, and then out on the tarmac and into the plane. We didn't take off right away. He introduced himself as Waldo. Whether his name was real or not, we made up some game called Where's Waldo that had nothing in common with the book series. Waldo was a very energetic man for his age. We landed at eleven in the morning, and I was home before one Friday afternoon. I'd had no sleep at all. I took a sleeping pill and crashed.

When I woke up Friday night, I found nothing in my refrigerator. I picked up the phone and called the deli.

"Club sandwich and fries. Don, get Jerry to hurry, I'm starved."

I piped Madonna through my apartment, took a bath and did

my accounting. Vegas gave me a five-hundred-dollar tip which I set aside. Macho doesn't get a cut of tips. I put Macho's percentage from last night—four hundred—in an envelope and the rest in my safe. My security guard called from the lobby to say that Miss Kim had arrived. I wore a red silk kimono while Miss Kim took an hour perfecting my pedicure and manicure. I picked a color called Back to the Fuchsia.

"I like your new cut," she said. "It's flattering."

"Easy care. I can be out the door in four minutes with this hair," I said. "Macho says I look like I was scalped by wild Indians."

She laughed. Miss Kim has gorgeous straight black hair down to her hips, but she keeps it in a ponytail most of the time.

At midnight, the doorman at the Century Plaza Hotel handed me a ticket in exchange for my car keys. I went straight to the elevators and rode alone to the tenth floor, room 1015. His name was Jay.

"You're beautiful," Jay said.

Jay was forty years younger than Mister Vegas from the night before.

"You're beautiful, too," I said.

"Thanks," he said. "Want money now?"

"After is fine," I said. A five-hundred-dollar date would be fast. Jay finished, still breathing heavily, pawing me, and kissing my body. Then he lost interest.

"Is it okay if I take a shower?"

"Sure, make yourself at home. Want room service?"

I kissed him, told him how good the sex had been and no, I didn't want room service.

I called Macho from the lobby.

"Should I go home?"

"I got one like Jay. Five hundred in Beverly Hills."

"Yep. I'm all douched and ready," I said.

"Gabi, you don't need to tell me that. Disgusting."

I laughed. I loved to mess with Macho, especially during his work hours.

"Would you want me in Beverly Hills with Jay in my pussy?"

"You are horrible, Gabi."

Macho cringed when I brought up personal grooming, and I only brought it up to joke around with him. When I started working with him, he's the one that counseled me on the vinegar douche, and he wasn't so fussy back then about women stuff. He never wanted to hear that I was on my period or that I was headed for a bloody week. I'd say it's that time of the month.

That's what he had become.

"Okay, I'll stop. Give me the scoop. I'm in the lobby of the Century Plaza."

I drove to the Hilton hotel in Beverly Hills, took care of the client, then went straight home. I was in my bed before four in the morning.

May 1985

UCLA gave me four invitations for my graduation. I loved my aunt and cousins, but I wasn't up to a meet. I didn't want to explain in person where I get so much money to send my aunt and cousins money orders every couple months. I think Serena knows. I didn't want to lie to their faces. I told my aunt they were short of invitations, and I couldn't get enough for everyone. I promised we would get together in the near future. Afterwards, I felt bad that I lied.

I was a weekly regular at Homer's. It was almost like a family thing. It was embarrassing to keep taking money for getting together with him and Archie. I didn't tell anyone about my graduation. Like my aunt, Homer knew I was going to graduate from

UCLA, but he didn't have the date, never asked, and I didn't volunteer.

I told myself it was no big deal. They could come to my next big graduation if law school ever happened. I had no one in the audience when I was given my hard-earned bachelors diploma. I didn't feel that bad. I split right after the ceremony, got in my car and drove to my apartment.

It started as the graduation date approached. It's like something had snapped. I was undecided about stopping or continuing my education. I was a train wreck when I thought about it.

At home, I examined my diploma and kissed it lightly, and not just once. The next day, I drove to the Westwood Village a short distance away and I waited while the man in the frame shop did his thing with my thing. I wanted to cry when he showed it to me. I didn't cry. I paid him and gave him a five-dollar tip. I went home. Now what? More school? Should I go someplace on vacation?

At three in the afternoon, I was ready to work but Macho was asleep. I called Hilda my masseuse. She's a large Germanic woman and very good at her profession. I put on my rose kimono and piped the soft rock station through the apartment.

Hilda arrived looking like she was moving in, with a couple of rolling suitcases equipped with her portable massage table, linens, and all sorts of oil. She was extremely strong and handled all of the equipment she brought with ease. Six feet tall in her stockinged feet, she had to weigh at least two hundred pounds, most of it muscle. Her white-blond hair was weaved into a complicated French braid that streamed down her back.

"You worked out before I got here?"

"Yes ma'am," I said. "I haven't forgotten you told me that weights or exercise should be before the massage, and yoga or stretching afterwards."

"Want a straight massage or nasty?"

"I'll tell you at half time," I replied. "We can play it by ear."

Hilda lit candles and put some oils in front of me to choose from.

"Want me to talk or keep quiet?"

"Suit yourself," I said. Even if I told her to be quiet, she'd start talking sooner or later.

I tossed the kimono over the back of a chair, relaxed naked on the table, and Hilda went to work. As she worked, I realized how tense I had been, and wondered why I didn't do this more often. I loved to have hands on me. Of course, Hilda was a great physical therapist.

"I can't get over your biceps," I said. "You got more definition than last time you were here."

"Doing curls. I don't want to get too crazy and look mannish. Thanks for the compliment."

"You look good, Hilda," I said, not that I could see her while I was face down on her table.

Hilda had set up the massage table in the living room. The hideaway shades were down. Except for two candles, the room was dark. At the one-hour mark, I told her to go another hour if she had the energy.

"I got the energy and the time for as many hours as you want, girl."

My phone rang. No one called the house phone except lobby reception. It rang again. Hilda paused.

"Hilda, get that for me."

Hilda relayed the message. "You got a flower delivery. Is it okay to come up?"

"Flowers? No one sends me flowers, ever," I said.

Maybe Homer?

"Yes or no?" Hilda asked. "He's waiting."

"Okay." I wondered again who might be sending me flowers.

"Lucky you," Hilda said. "Maybe you have a secret admirer."

"Highly unlikely," I said. I closed my eyes and fell into the massage so deeply that I was startled when my doorbell chimed.

"That would be your delivery," Hilda said. "Do you want a towel?"

"No need. You can handle the delivery. Turn on the light if you want."

"I'm good," Hilda said. "I'm going to savor the moment, even if the bouquet is for you."

I turned on my side looking toward the front door. Light flooded the room when Hilda opened the door.

I saw a man with a bouquet of flowers. The arrangement was nothing spectacular, but it was nice that someone was sending me flowers. The delivery man moved in my direction, and I saw his face.

I sat up quick. It was Alex Rose. Impossible! Before I could make heads or tails of what I was watching, he punched Hilda, who fell on her back. He dropped the flowers on the floor, kicking Hilda as he walked past her. I heard the hard thud of impact. She moaned. The entry door closed. The only light came from the candles.

I swung my legs off the table to face the man on my feet. His eyes were cold, hard, his hair shaggy. He had a prison style tattoo on one arm that looked like it had been drawn by a ball point pen. This guy was not Alex Rose. He could be his twin, though, Alex Rose, Hell version. There were subtle differences. This guy had coarser features and was less groomed, and the extreme lighting of the candles gave him the macabre look of a horror movie creature. He had more than a touch of gray in the bristle on his face, and a scar across his lip. He was carrying something, a knife, maybe. It looked big for a knife.

"Motherfucker!" I said, looking for something to hit the bastard with. It wasn't a knife he had but a billy-club. I'd seen plenty of those in my barrio.

I grabbed a tall brass lamp but before I could swing it, I felt a blow on my neck, then my shoulder, and dropped the lamp.

"Whore bitch. I'm going to waste you."

I grabbed for the lamp. He swung wildly at me and tried to kick, but only managed a glancing blow. I had the lamp in hand, and Hilda appeared behind him. Blood was streaming from her face. She kneed him from behind and he fell to his knees. She was so tall.

"Bastard," she said, giving him a kick as he had kicked her. I got the lamp and staggered to my feet. His head was about the level of a perfect tennis ball. The electric cord was swinging around as I hit him on the head. I didn't aim well and whacked him on the ear. Blood streamed from the side of his head. I saw Hilda fall back against the couch.

"Die motherfucker, whoever the hell you are," I said.

The intruder screamed in pain.

"You killed my brother. I'm going to return the favor!" he yelled, putting a hand up to his ear.

I don't know where the billy-club went. Somewhere on the floor. It was too dark to see where, but at least I knew who he was.

I swung the lamp again but missed. He lunged to his feet and grabbed for the cord. Hilda appeared behind him and grabbed him from the back but that lasted only a few seconds.

He bucked, turned around and hit her. I heard the whack.

I took advantage of the moment and hit him with the lamp again, this time a blow to his back, a square and solid hit.

He screamed. I went after him but fell over Hilda who was on the floor. I went face down onto the carpet, crawled a step, and lurched on my feet to see the door open. Light came in from the hallway. He was nowhere in sight, and I heard footsteps running away. The prick was gone.

I hit the lights and got to Hilda who was sitting on the floor.

"I'm okay. I'm okay," she said.

"You don't look okay," I said. Her nose looked swollen and her face was already bruising.

I was suddenly aware that my neck where he'd hit me hurt bad. I went down beside her, sitting on the floor. We clung together for a moment.

"Let me call the guard in the lobby," I said. I crawled to the end table and autodialed the phone.

"Stop that flower delivery bastard. He tried to kill me and my friend."

"He just went out, Miss Gabi. Let me call 911."

By the time I hung up, Hilda had come out of the bathroom with a couple of towels, wet and dry. She held a bloody washcloth to her nose. She handed me my kimono.

"Are you okay?" I asked, gingerly putting it on. It hurt to move my neck and shoulder.

"I will be. Who was that crazy son of a bitch?"

"A ghost from my past," I said.

"You need to call a medium and exorcise that bastard."

"Good idea," I said.

Macho wasn't a medium, but he was the one to call. I looked at the clock. It was late afternoon. Macho would be asleep, but he always answered the phone.

I dialed.

"Someone just tried killing me and my massage therapist. It was Alex Rose's brother. I didn't know he had a brother. He said I'd killed his brother and he was going to kill me." Somewhere in the garbled explanation, I started crying.

"Are you going to be okay?" Macho asked, sounding wide awake for once. His voice rang with urgency.

"I think I'm okay. I haven't looked in the mirror. I don't see blood. I mean, he bloodied Hilda, but not me."

"Did someone call the cops?"

"Not me. The guard in the lobby was calling 911."

"Shit, I wish there had not been any cops. I can't go over there until they are gone."

"I just wanted to let you know."

"I'll kill that guy. Are you sure you are okay?"

Hilda and me, we were bundled into the same ambulance. I had been on my feet to answer the door and let the paramedics in, but I had a blank space in my head between then and when I looked up in the ambulance with oxygen going into my nose. Hilda, who was lying next to me, was also getting the same.

"Are you okay?" I asked Hilda.

"I was so worried about you. Are you okay? You passed out."

"You look like hell," I said. Hilda's thick French braids were clotted with blood. Her nose was swollen, and I'm pretty sure she was headed for a pair of black eyes.

"You're beautiful as ever," Hilda said. "Your neck looks like you're turning into an eggplant map of Alaska."

I wasn't sure what that meant, but it didn't sound good. I couldn't turn my head because I was strapped down.

"What's the verdict?" I asked the paramedic. He had smooth skin, prematurely white hair and a handlebar mustache. He reminded me of Rich Uncle Penny-bags, the guy on the Monopoly game.

"Need to check your injuries. Both of you have some pretty bad bumps on the head." He turned to me and touched the frame around my neck. "And make sure you have no spinal damage."

I closed my eyes. I told myself this was not as bad as when Alex Rose sent me to the hospital.

Hilda and I were going to live. Fuck it.

"Can you turn the oxygen up a bit?" I asked. "And if you're doing requests, give me something for pain, but nothing that will put me to sleep."

"We're two minutes away from the hospital. They'll give you everything you need."

That's when I noticed the siren.

Hilda was released first. She came into the trauma room where they had me stashed in the ER.

"I'm taking a cab to your apartment to get my car. I'll call you later."

"Are you okay? Will the cops let you get your equipment?"

"I'm going to take a break, so they can keep it for a few days. Doc says I'm okay. I got three prescriptions I got to fill in the 24-hour pharmacy around the corner, then I'm going to try to stay in bed. But I hate to break my lifting schedule."

"I'm sorry," I said. "I'll pay you for all this shit. Don't worry."

"Girl, I'm not worried. This was not your fault."

They still had me lying down. I was waiting for the doctor to return. Hilda kissed me and left. I called Macho for the third time.

"I don't think they are going to admit you," he said. "Tension is waiting in the lobby."

As it turned out, he was right. I was not admitted either. The cat scan showed no sign of a concussion, and neither did the MRI.

"I don't see any need to keep you in the hospital. Go home. Stay in bed," the doctor said, "but be on the lookout for the symptoms listed on your discharge package. If you have symptoms, you follow the protocol, and come back to the hospital. I will see you in my clinic this time next week."

I was wheelchaired to Tension's car. He wouldn't let me stand up on my own but lifted me into the back seat like I was a baby.

In the car on the way home, Tension said, "I'm going to find this bastard. Don't worry."

"I'm not worried. I'm still flying high on whatever they had in that drip. The guy, he was a bully like his brother."

When we pulled up in front of my building, Tension got out

and opened the door for me. I stood with no problem.

"Take this. It's already registered in your name. If you want a carry license, you have to get it yourself," he said, showing me a small revolver and a package of bullets, and dropping them in my purse. "Next time, you'll be ready for him. Put it somewhere convenient, maybe in a drawer next to your bed. There's a schedule for a nearby shooting range. Get some practice. Get comfortable with it."

"Good idea. Thank you. I'll thank Macho."

I walked past the mess in the living room. Blood was all over my carpet, the lamp on the floor, and the bloody massage table was on its side. The cops had moved things around, too, and left behind fingerprint dust and tape. I had prescriptions to pick up, but I needed to sleep. I wanted to go to bed, but my phone rang.

It was Macho. "I'm in the lobby."

I told the guard to let him up.

I walked to the chair that sits by my apartment door and sat down, still feeling the medication in the hospital iv. I was drugged up enough to take a little nap between his call and the two-minute ride up the elevator. Thanks to that drip going for hours while in ER, I was feeling no pain.

I opened the door and fell back into the chair with a yawn. Macho lifted me off that chair, carried me pass the mess in my den, and off to bed like I weighed nothing. He tucked me in and then lay on the bed next to me, his clothes on, lights out except for a night light.

"I'm going to kill this bastard," he whispered.

I nodded to let him know I heard him. I didn't care if it was him or Tension who got Alex Rose's brother. I just wanted to sleep.

"Be careful. Love you, Macho." Then I remembered and tried to get up. "I have some scripts in my purse. I gotta go fill them."

Macho wouldn't let me get up. "Tension will do it right away.

Sleep now."

"Yes, love you, Macho."

"I've always loved you, Gabi."

Macho was an opportunist just as I was. We each served a need for the other. I was a good earner for him. Beyond that, I did believe he loved me, just as I loved him. No matter how we dressed it up, he was my pimp, but he was also my friend. God forbid I should call him my pimp.

The next morning, I felt like I'd gotten drunk and had a hangover. It was the drugs they had given me at the hospital. I walked through the mess. At the entrance was a paper slipped under the door.

I called reception. "I understand you have some meds for me. Please bring them up."

I spent the day in my room. I took the anti-inflammatory but not the pain pills. I was sore and I had bruising, but at least my brain was working fine.

I can't work with bruising anywhere on my body. I was fucked that I would be able to fuck for a while. I laughed but I wasn't happy.

At noon, a crew of six came in and stripped the carpet out of the living room, covered the furniture with plastic and painted the entire room. There was blood spatter in a few places on the wall, probably from Hilda bleeding and the bastard Rose. By midafternoon, the new carpet was in, same color as before.

When the sun set, I was in my living room that had no trace of the night before except for a slight smell of paint.

Macho called me when he woke up and after assuring him, I was fine except for being out of business for a little bit, I told him about the building management taking care of business in cleaning up my place.

"Kissing your ass so you don't sue them," he said.

"I'm the one who okayed the entry of the bastard thinking he was a flower delivery person. I should have known better."

"No way for you to know better," Macho said.

"Thanks for having Tension wait it out at the hospital and bring me home."

"No thanks needed. Did you get your meds okay?"

"I did. Thanks for that, too. I'm not taking the pain pills, can't handle the shit."

My next call was to Hilda who was a great sport about the banging she sustained.

"I'm going to be fine," she said. "I'm taking my pain meds and some other pills the doctor prescribed. Thanks for sending over my equipment."

The building management had arranged a messenger to deliver her suitcases, massage table, and everything else she carried to a session.

"No worries. And please track everything you are spending, including massages you can't do because of this shit, and I will pay you myself, or my renter insurance will pay you. I can send you some money now if you need it. I didn't even get to pay you for my massage."

"Gabi, be cool, I'm not worried. I'm good."

I had given a full report to the police that came to see me when I was at the ER. On the third day of being hunkered down at home, John, the lobby guard, called that two detectives wanted to see me.

"Miss Gabi, if you are not up to it, they can come back another time. They are standing right in front of me and told me to tell you this. Oh, and I have checked their identification."

"Send them up," I said, "Thank you, John. You are a sweetheart."

"Thank you, Miss Gabi. I hope you are feeling better."

I was in shorts and an oversize shirt that I wore untucked. I was barefoot and didn't plan on putting on shoes or slippers. I was comfortable as is. No makeup, but my mirror showed me a fading bruise on my chin. My other bruises were bad.

Peggy Rivera and Martin Mull showed me their identification at the door. I let them in. We sat in the living room.

"No relation," Martin Mull said. "I get asked that all the time."

Peggy said, "I saw the pictures of this room after the attack. You don't waste any time."

"I can't take credit for it. The building management got right to it."

Martin Mull said, "How do you feel?"

"Sore, but I'm lucky I only feel sore."

Peggy Rivera smiled. "I have good news."

Martin Mull said, "Rose is in custody."

"You just made my day," I said. "Can I get you coffee or coke?" I was on my feet. I wanted to dance right there in front of them.

"I'll take a coke," Peggy said. "No glass needed unless it's warm."

Easygoing cops.

"Not warm," I said.

Martin said he didn't want anything then he changed his mind and wanted a coke, same as Peggy.

When I sat back down, I was shown pictures of Rose, file pictures of him of when he was booked and sent to prison before, and still shots of video taken by the building security cameras in the lobby and the outside entrance.

"How did you catch him? I mean, where was he?"

"He was home. He's on parole," Peggy said. "A total fool, only out a week, and he comes over here, messes with you and your friend, and ruins his life for a very long time."

Detective Martin said, "Tell us about your encounter with his brother. I read what you said to the officers the night of the attack."

If he read it, why did he need me to tell him?

I was hesitant.

Peggy said, "It makes it easier for us to write the report that the district attorney will need to file charges. Let's give him a complete story."

"Can't they just send him away for the parole thing and not charge him for this? I don't want to go to court."

"It's up to the district attorney," Martin said. "This man could have killed you and your friend. He should be prosecuted for it."

"His brother was Alex Rose," I said. "It's amazing how much he looks like Alex Rose. I killed his bastard brother in self-defense when he broke into my bedroom. Why did he wait this long to come get me?"

"Only Rose knows that," Peggy said.

"The man is dead, and you refer to him as a bastard," Martin said.

"Detective, Alex Rose snuck into my bedroom and struck me with a baseball bat with the intent of killing me. He killed my baby. I had a miscarriage. What am I supposed to call him? What would you call the man who killed your baby?"

I could feel a shift in the detectives, even before they said anything. Peggy looked at me and nodded.

Peggy said, "I'd call him a fucking bastard."

Martin said, "Understandable. I didn't read that in the report."

I had no clue whose baby it had been. It hardly mattered now. I sometimes thought how my life might be different with a baby. I would never know the child. It could have been a client's offspring, or it could have been Alex Rose's. Better not to think of that dead-end road.

"What is this Rose's first name?" I asked.

"Phillip," said Peggy. "You hit him pretty good. Took twenty stiches on his back and I don't know how many on his shoulder."

I pointed out the brass lamp now back on the sofa side table as though it had caused no harm to Phillip Rose. "It sure came in handy. Saved my life."

"What do you do for work?" Mull gazed at me from the other side of his sideways nose.

"I just graduated from UCLA, but I'm a model," I said, "Beverly Hills Model Agency."

"Pay must be good. Great apartment," Peggy observed.

"Pay is good as long as the agent gets me the bookings," I said.

They both did a lot of writing. I had no question at all that they had taken down everything I told them, details about the house where I lived with my aunt, how Alex Rose may have gained entry to the house, and that it was his third time to do it.

When the detectives left, I had their cards and I was told they would be in touch after the district attorney decided on the filing of charges. I hoped the fucker would just go back to prison for a very long time, and we could forget this current event. Hilda might think differently, but it didn't matter. It was clear that the district attorney made the decision, not us.

My renter's insurance paid Hilda ten thousand dollars without much delay. She had a lawyer sue the building owner for security deficiencies. I could have done the same.

Macho said, "Hilda was your guest. If you sue the landlord, all kinds of things can come up during the litigation."

Macho didn't say not to do it, but it was pretty clear. Besides, it wasn't a lack of security that resulted in this attack. It was a flower delivery that I gave the okay for.

Where was the liability? Because of imaginary lawyers I saw on TV, because I toy around with the idea of becoming a lawyer, I like to mess around with legal stuff in my head. My knowledge only came from fake law, from watching television, when there was time to watch recorded shows that my VCR memorized for me: Perry Mason, Petrocelli, Paper Chase, Judd for the Defense, The Defenders, series like that. I thought I'd be ready to go back to work in a week, but no such thing. Bruises take a long time to go away.

I told Archie what had happened, and he passed the phone over to Homer. He insisted (his words) I drive my ass over to spend some quality time with him.

Homer claimed to have magic lips when he kissed me all over, including over my fading bruises.

"You make me feel like I belong here, like family," I said to Homer. I was comfortable at his house and around him.

"If it was up to me, you'd be here all the time," he said.

I was such an unbeliever. Words like that went in one ear and out the other.

Homer insisted I wasn't there for sex, but we had sex; Homer and me; Homer, Archie and me; and a lot of Archie and me with Homer watching. Bruising didn't stop my ability to fuck. I think so raw. It's like someone talking dirty to me. I seldom get the kind of client that I used to in Hollywood. Some guys get off talking dirty. I didn't mind.

I stayed three days at a time at Homer's resort home. I was finally getting to see more of the house. I never asked for a tour. It just happened that we'd end up in different part of the house for one reason or another. He had a gym with a boxing ring.

"The ring size is official," Homer told me. "My wife was into boxing. We had amateur boxers come over and box for the two of us, then we'd retire to the bedroom with the winner. Becky and I were very much into that."

I didn't show him my surprise. Not surprised that they had other sex partners. Surprised that they hired boxers to come in and box then lay the winner. How unique is that?

Every time I left, I went home with an envelope. I didn't feel as badly as before because I did give back. I fucked my brains out with Archie, not so much for my personal pleasure either. I gave the session my all to give Homer a great show. He loved to watch. He still hid somewhere but not always. It was more common to have him on the bed with us or on a chair or sofa a short distance from the bed in the master bedroom. When Homer was up to it, he took my encouragement and had sex with me. I wanted him to know I enjoyed having sex with him and that he was good and not as old as he thought he was.

"You're a tiger," I'd say, time and time again.

I assumed that Archie enjoyed the sex as much as I did. He was a hard person to read.

Even whores need sex. If Macho had been in my head, he'd correct me and say I was not a whore. An escort or a model, yes, but not a whore. Every time I got an envelope, I told Macho about it. He knew I was at Homer's.

"I got yours," I said, putting it in an envelope for him.

"You are as loyal as I am to you," Macho said.

Macho was no fool. He could have said he'd take a smaller cut since I was doing my own booking with Homer. Macho didn't say that, and it was okay with me. That was the deal. I know if I had needed help, he would have been there with a roll of bills for me, just as he had been when I first started with him. He might be seeing me as a friend, but also, he saw me as a good investment. There was no such thing as a free lunch.

I told Macho that they had jailed Rose.

"Good thing for him. Had I found him, he'd be dead."

I believed him. I think Tension was a guy you don't mess with. If you did, you wouldn't be around to be sorry.

Homer and I had lunch in a crazy den that had six slot machines. I had a club sandwich.

"I have an idea, Gabi."

"Afternoon sex?"

"That's a good idea, yes."

"Sure," I said, "After we eat or now?" I stood up and dropped my sandwich quarter to the plate.

Homer laughed.

"Sit down Miss Hot Knickers. Here's my idea: I sponsor you to law school. You live here and retire from your business."

I stopped eating and stared at him. Homer didn't stop eating.

"Why would you do that, Homer? Sooner or later you will have Archie show me to the door. It happens."

"No, I won't."

I know better.

I came around the table, hugged him from behind and kissed the top of his head as he continued to eat, then I went back to my chair to sit down.

"You are way too good to me," I said.

"Take the deal," Homer insisted. "Enroll in law school and make this your home away from home, if you don't want to give up your apartment."

I smiled. "You sound serious."

"I am serious."

"Why?"

He looked at me across the table. "Why not?"

"If I go to law school, I have to do it on my own," I said. "It will help if I can keep coming over for sessions." My smile was bigger. "I don't even know I can get in a school yet."

Homer finished eating. He wouldn't let up.

"You can get in. You graduated from UCLA with good grades."

"I am not ready. Besides, I make a lot of money."

"We can cut a deal."

"I have an apartment, a lease, a car payment. I—"

"You don't have to give any of that up," he interrupted. "Just move in here where it's safe. No one is going to bust in here."

We walked to the den and sat on a sofa.

"Tell me you'll think about it?"

"I'll think about it," I said.

That night I kissed every inch of his body. He moaned and sighed. He even purred a couple of times, then he went to sleep.

I found Archie in the theater room watching television.

"I'm out of here," I said.

"I didn't know you were leaving tonight. Let me get you an envelope."

I showed myself out, got in my car and headed home, a short drive away.

I was done with my bath and ready to hit the sack when I decided to call Macho. It had been a month and some days since I had worked, not counting Homer.

"Hey, you, how you?"

"How do you feel?"

"I'm ready for assignments starting tomorrow."

"I got one right now, easy six hundred, Sunset Hotel."

"That's close," I said. "I need thirty minutes before I can spring out of here. I have to start from scratch. Makeup, hair and I'm gone."

"Good girl. Tell me when you're ready for the details."

"Shoot," I said, picking up a pencil to write down the address. "I stay ready."

On my way to the client, I mulled over Homer's offer. He seemed serious. I would almost consider it, but Macho would have a heart attack.

I thought of the six hundred coming up. After I paid Macho his hundred and twenty, I would clear four eighty plus a possible tip that would be all mine. I was making money left and right from Homer.

After the date, I called Macho from the lobby of the hotel.

"Don't push it. Go home and rest. Tomorrow is another night."

At home, I showered, did my clean up routine, and went to bed. I could have asked for another client. Normally I would've. Taking it easy at Homer's had messed with the switch in my brain that keeps me in hustle mode.

Macho was right. Tomorrow was another day. I would do three clients if he wanted me to. My kind of business was the gutter, but I liked my independence. Living at Homer's full time would be unreal. I didn't belong there full-time. It would wear on me. Homer made me feel like a little girl in a huge candy store. I was dazzled by the house, the sex and the money I made without having to travel to a hotel. Homer was pure luxury. But nothing lasts forever.

The next afternoon before Macho reared his head, Peggy the detective called me with news on the case.

"The DA says you don't have to testify. Rose entered into a plea bargain. The main charge he is pleading to is assault with intent to commit great bodily harm."

"Peggy, he said he was going to kill me, not to mention what he did to Hilda. He face-punched her at the door and kicked her when she was down."

"Gabi, this is a serious charge. He's going to fry for what he did. The deal is five years with no time off for good behavior."

"He's out in five years then?"

"Nothing is a sure thing. Convicts like him pick up new charges for crimes committed in prison. He's a hothead. No telling."

I called Macho and told him what Peggy had said.

"I'm glad it's over, Gabi."

"That's it?"

"Yes, it's best this way."

"Fuck, it doesn't matter," I said. "I'm going to get ready for work."

"I'll call you soon as soon as something pops up."

What popped up was a basketball player with a jet, who paid three thousand on a credit card to have a model session on his plane. At ten-thirty that night, I was in an executive jet with a well-known basketball player headed to Dallas, Texas. He told me to call him Max. Max was married and had kids. I read that once in a magazine.

His big plane had an extra big bed.

"Looks like the mattress was custom made for you."

"I'm too tall for a regular size."

He was good humored, watching me as I undressed.

"Lady, you are the most beautiful white girl I have ever had on this plane."

"Liar," I said. I didn't follow basketball, but I knew who he was. The article I read about him once was interesting. More interesting was how much he got paid for a season.

"No doubt you have thousands of girl fans that would give you anything you want without paying for it, Max."

"That could lead to problems," he said. "I use Macho because I trust him. I know whatever I do with his ladies is not going anywhere, even if I do it at 35,000 feet."

We were in bed when his plane took off. When the pilot said we were descending and would be landing in twenty minutes, he rolled off the bed, took a shower, and got dressed.

"Magnificent is what you are," Max said. "I don't understand why Macho never showed me a picture of you before."

I looked up at him. He had an impossibly tall, lanky frame but he wore clothes well. He would be intimidating on any field, basketball court or office. His hair was trimmed close to his skull, and his skin was very dark, much darker than Archie's.

"I'm sure he's fixed you up with lovely women."

"He has, but you are off the charts."

He reached in his jacket pocket, dug out his wallet, and put a thousand dollars in my hand.

"I'd give you a bigger tip but that's all the cash I have," he said.

"Way too generous. Thanks."

"Soon as the plane is fueled, you'll be on your way back to Los Angeles." He sat down and patted the mattress next to him. "I want to do this with you again," he said.

I stood on the mattress, and he stood on the floor so that we were eye to eye.

"I want to do this again, too," I said. "You got the most delicious cock I've ever had."

I don't know if he believed me, but he smiled broadly and chuckled as if he did. Then, he was gone.

While the plane was being fueled, I showered. The rainforest showerhead was up high. I wondered how they got that much height in a plane. Everything in the bathroom had his name or his initials, including the robes.

We were airborne for about an hour when I sat down in the main cabin. The flight attendant asked me if I was hungry.

"How about a hot sandwich?" she asked.

"What you got?"

The sandwich was a pastrami, huge like Max would want it. I felt like a queen in my own plane, drinking diet coke and eating a hot meal that tasted just-made.

I told the flight attendant, Mona, "You're beautiful."

"It's you that's beautiful," she said.

"If you were a man, I'd let you fuck me."

"We have another hour and a half till we land. Let me know if you want to do it."

I figured she was putting me on, just as when I said what I said to be nasty. She had to know I was for hire and so did the flight crew, but they were all friendly and respectful. As we descended,

I asked Mona to sit across from me.

"Where do you live?"

"Dallas. All of us live there."

"Are you flying back when you drop me off?"

Mona showed her pretty teeth as she laughed a little, kind of a shy laugh. "Yes, but today the pilots have flown their limit. We're sleeping here. We go back in the morning."

It would have been easy—and cheaper—for Max to send me back commercial and save the expense of flying me back, not to mention lodging the crew and returning to Dallas. Max must be totally loaded.

"I'm going home," I said. "I don't live far. You can spend the night and taxi back in the morning if you want."

The executive terminal was right next to LAX where my car was in the small parking lot.

"Look at you. Nice wheels," she said when she scoped out my Corvette.

"Thanks."

I asked her to stay with me without any forethought. Maybe I was a little lonely. Until Macho launched my apartment, I'd always lived in close quarters with people. Independence was wonderful but coming home to an empty house was a whole other thing. I didn't let myself think about it, but I missed Serena more than I would have thought possible. I'm not saying Mona was a Serena substitute. She was just available. When I pulled in front of my apartment building, the attendant opened my door and greeted me, then greeted my guest. I led her inside. She was all wide-eyed at the posh building. It did have a classy ambiance.

"I'm in the wrong business," Mona said as we rose fast in the elevator. I was proud when I opened the apartment. It was, by my standards, a splendid home for me.

We drank a bottle of wine, music playing all the time. There was no sign that I had been attacked in that room. I made no mention of that experience, not even when Mona admired the lamp.

"What do you do when Max isn't flying?"

"I sit at home and get paid." She laughed. "He flies a lot though, and when he's not flying, his family and friends use the plane. I stay busy."

Mona was single. She'd broken up with a boyfriend six months before. "I go out partying and meet up with guys."

"Your boss is a real hunk," I said.

"I know, but that's hands off. His wife would have me shot."

I understood that Max was paying for privacy. He had to trust his crew. In my world, there was no such trust. I'm not saying I wouldn't be trusted to keep his secrets. I would. I just didn't believe I had anyone to keep mine other than Macho.

I opened the second bottle of wine.

"Hard to believe you never did it with him."

"I ain't never seen his dick either. You have. Tell me about it. Is he good?"

"What makes you think I've seen it?" I asked mysteriously.

Mona laughed. "You mean it's like a code or something?"

"I don't have a clue what you mean," I said.

In the wee hours of the morning, I showed Mona the bedroom that I used on a rare occasion with clients who wanted a private session. She preferred it to the one I think of as my bedroom.

"Can I call you every time I hit town for overnight?"

"I don't know why not," I said. "Nightgowns in that drawer. You don't even need to open your carryon," I said. "Make yourself at home."

I went to my room, brushed my teeth, removed my makeup and hit my comfy bed. Just as I was falling asleep, I heard Mona join me under the sheets.

"I hope you don't mind. I'm scared of the dark," Mona said.

With all the sex I'd had with Max, I wasn't after more. It's funny how curiosity drives me. I'd been with girls before but not at home, and not of my own choice. Mona was my guest. I didn't even know her last name. That made it more exciting. Mona turned out to be aggressive, and we got no sleep. At a little after eight in the morning, the doorman let me know the taxi was there.

"Till next time," Mona said.

"For sure."

I went to bed and slept like a baby.

June 1985

When I drove up to the house at two in the afternoon, Archie was outside waiting for me in his chef getup.

"Hey, you're supposed to be cooking?" I kidded as I got out of the car.

He kissed me and put his arm around my shoulder as we walked to the front door.

"Lunch is ready," he said.

"What're we having?"

"Exactly what you requested."

"You guys so good to me," I said.

Homer was waiting for me in the dining room. He was standing beside his chair.

"Wow, we're eating here?"

It was the first time I'd been in the formal grand dining room.

I hugged Homer and kissed him. He pulled out a chair for me to his right.

"You make me feel so comfortable," I said, as I took the seat he offered.

"I told you, move in."

"You're too sweet," I said, not wanting to go there.

"If you don't want to attend law school, fine. The offer stands."

"Tempting," I said.

The food smelled delicious. Fried potatoes and onions were in the air. I'm for simple food when it's my choice. I get enough fancy stuff when I work, and that includes going out to dinner.

The chicken tenders were crisp like I like them. I could tell they were fresh. My hamburger was well done, with no lettuce or tomato. I liked hot sauce and love the hell out of jalapeno chilis. The onion rings and French fries were perfect, still sizzling when they hit the plate. I hoped Homer didn't have a cholesterol problem. He ate like he had no problems, period.

"I hope you're ok with the menu," I said. "From now on, you or Archie choose."

Homer laughed. "This is what I have most of the time. Isn't that right, Archie?"

Archie said, "He loves this food."

I took a bite of my hamburger.

"I don't believe you."

Homer and me, we had a good relationship, but I could not forget he was a client. I was always thinking about what he would like, and what would put a smile on his face. I couldn't help changing how I am.

He was just a client. According to Tension, he was wealthier than I could imagine. I could imagine his rich daughter visiting daddy and her finding yours truly, the gold digger living here. Older guys and young women. We see that paparazzi snapshot, and isn't that what we all think, gold digger?

We were sitting in one of his dens, cozy on a narrow loveseat, drinking wine. Leonard Cohen was singing softly in the background.

"Don't nurse it. It's okay. Drink up. Be happy."

I sipped the fantastic wine, put the glass on the table in front of us, and leaned back into the deep, soft sofa. The fabric was plush, a vivid reddish maroon with gold stitching. More importantly, it was deep, and soft, and felt like a hug.

"I'd like to retain you for ten days. I have a couple of planes collecting dust out at the airport."

My whole body perked up. I scooted forward from the couch that was swallowing me and sat straight.

"You got planes? Wow." I played it like Tension never told us of the planes that had turned up in his investigation.

He shrugged. "My wife was a big spender. One of the planes is a long-range aircraft. I'd like to take you somewhere far away."

"Really?" He took me by surprise.

"Really," he replied.

"Why me, Homer?"

He looked at me thoughtfully for a moment and put his glass by mine before he took my hand. His palm was slightly calloused, less soft than I thought that a retired judge's hand might be but felt big and warm around mine. As I looked into his face, I saw past the creases in his face to the young man he had been. His eyes managed to be both impish and serious. He was still a very handsome man, and very charming. With the right shirt, he could look like a happy farmer. He gave me a serious look, a judge look.

"You give me a reason to wake up. I start looking forward to your next visit before you leave. I enjoy being with you."

"Homer, that's kind of you to say."

"Bull, it's not kind at all. It's true."

Still holding hands, I leaned toward him.

We kissed on the lips. The kiss gave me time to think of how to respond to his invitation. Why was I even thinking about it? If he had called Macho, Macho would have given him a price, and it would be done.

"I'll go wherever you want to go."

"Throw a country at me."

"Country?"

"Sure, country. How about ten days?"

"I'm in," I said. "The problem is that I like you. I have trouble charging you."

An overnight to New York got me five thousand on the high end, three on the low end. Ten days? I had no idea.

"Nonsense," he said.

"How about Venice?" I thought about my mom. My aunt said she had run off to Italy. I wondered what part of Italy. Why Italy? What made her choose Italy? She was brave to go on her own. Maybe I wasn't so brave going with Homer. I was mostly curious.

"I haven't been to Italy in a long time. Let's plan it. I need to get a crew rented, and the plane checked out."

Private planes were nothing new to me, but I'd never been a part of the planning.

"How much?" he asked.

I leaned forward and kissed him again.

"You tell me. I have a manager, but he knows I deal directly with you."

"Do you have to pay him much?"

"He handles me like a model. Twenty percent."

"Only you know if he's worth it," Homer said. "How about twenty-five thousand for ten days?"

My stomach jumped, but I didn't show it.

"Deal, Homer." I kissed him again, this time a peck.

He looked enormously happy. I was taking twenty-five thousand dollars from him, and he looked ecstatic.

"We will have a great time on this trip, I promise you," he said.

"I promise you a great time, too."

July 1st, 1985

Two weeks later, Archie drove us to the Santa Monica Airport.

"This is your plane? What is it?" I said. It wasn't as big as a commercial liner, but it was pretty big.

Homer chuckled. "It's a Dassault Falcon. Let me show you around."

I had flown in big planes with full-sized beds. His plane didn't have a bed like that, but Homer explained how the sofas folded out into beds, and there was a cabin with two sofas facing each other that unfolded into a queen-size bed.

"It's gorgeous," I said.

We had planned the trip together. "Best not to take chances," Homer said when we were planning the trip.

An overnight in New York for fuel, then we'd be off in the morning to cross the ocean, make another fuel stop, then on to Venice, Italy. The plane had a range of four thousand miles and didn't need many stops. Homer took no chances.

He hired three pilots and two female flight attendants. Julie was there to look after the pilots, and Betsy was there to look after us.

"We can have some fun with Julie and Betsy," Homer said, a mischievous smile on his face. "If you like them, they can stay the night with us in New York."

I thought of my night with Mona, flight attendant for my famous basketball star.

"I like surprises," Homer said. He leaned over to the side and we kissed. "Unless you mind, just tell me." We were buckled in, waiting to pull back.

I shook my head. "I don't mind, Homer. Anything goes."

I wondered if Archie was pissed that he was axed from this trip. I knew he was taking the ten days off. Sometimes when I was alone, I remembered the satisfying sex I'd had with Archie, but his absence would help me concentrate on Homer.

Julie and Betsy made the sofas into a queen bed complete with silk sheets, top and bottom. Halfway to New York, we were all in the bed. The top sheet drifted to somewhere on the floor. Julie and Betsy were pros. No telling where Homer hired them from, but they made sure he got all the attention he could want.

So, picture this: the cabin lights dimmed but not off. The portals open, showing the clouds, at least when it was daylight. The hum of the air conditioning. The steady roar of the engines. The creak of the bedsprings audible over the smooth mix tape the speakers were playing. We weren't talking but it was not completely silent. They worked him with four hand massage, kisses, and love bites while I rode him. Judge Homer thrived on the attention like the energizer rabbit. He kept going and going. I'd been with men much younger who didn't show half the energy.

Everything had been planned by Homer and me, then his travel agent did the bookings. Venice was to die for. Our hotel, Hotel Cipriani, was ten minutes from the Grand Canal by speed boat. Our suite was magnificent. It was elegant and almost as fancy as Homer's house, especially the bathroom. The staff at the hotel was constantly wanting to do for us. And shops were everywhere.

Designer clothes shops were practically in every block, on every corner. At first, I tried to pay for a dress I tried on. Homer didn't go for that and put up a fight. He was not happy until I gave up and let him buy, and even happier when I had a concierge find an Italian local to join us at the hotel.

Homer especially liked local talent. Gian turned out to be a pro who entertained couples, ladies, or gents who needed his company and services. He appeared in front of our door, well dressed and elegant after he made it through hotel security. He was as elegant out of his clothes as he was in them.

We were in Venice six nights. Gian was there for us on three occasions. He did me and Homer watched, seated on a chair next to the bed, getting up at times to get a closer look or to touch one of us. For me, it was an easy, sexually hot experience. Gian was a good-looking guy about ten years older than me. He knew how to please me, and more importantly, how to please Homer in voyeur mode. Homer and I had a blast. Every day, Homer suggested that I move in and start law school. I had already made up my mind to attend law school but not to live in at Homer's. The ten thousand a month allowance he offered me was tempting, but I could make that by working for Macho as usual plus Homer when he wanted me.

I could attend school, get ten grand a month and not have to leave the house to do the sex sessions. I felt like if I lived with Homer, I'd have to be a hooker twenty-four hours a day instead of following my regular routine living in my own place, not having to answer to anyone when I wasn't working.

"Homer, when you want me along on a trip, you don't have to pay me. This is heaven for me. My agent will just have to do without his cut."

"Don't worry about the money," he said.

"When you have other women come over for you, do you take them out like this?" I smiled. "I'm being nosey, sorry."

"I've taken some on trips but never out of the country."

Not that it mattered. I was in Venice like a princess.

We left one store, and an attendant carried our clothes to the hotel car.

"I feel like a princess. No, I feel like a princess who won the lottery," I admitted to Homer.

"I feel like I won the lottery having you around," he said.

He was sweet, though I knew he didn't mean everything one hundred percent. He was generous, and I treasured my time together with him. I wasn't buying into some fantasy that he was falling in love with me and we'd live happily ever after, flying around the world having fun.

August 1985
Not in Venice
Archie

I was pissed that I was cut out of the Venice trip. I wasn't told I was going then cut off. I was excluded. I heard them planning the trip when she was over, but neither one said a thing about me not going along. I stewed.

During one of his recent flings, Emma, the three of us took the smaller plane, the Learjet, and flew to Chicago. From there, we went to New York for two days. We had a ball. There have been a lot of trips since Becky died. I had never been excluded, until now.

I never get out of Homer's house. I don't have a regular day off although I'm reminded all the time to take off whenever I want as long as I tell him a day before. I get paid for every day I work, and I bank it all. I have nowhere to spend the money, for now. I'm a long way from my bartender job.

While Homer was in Venice, I bought everything I needed to go fishing. I spent hours on the Santa Monica pier where many fish against the backdrop of restaurants and wall-to-wall people. I put back the fish as I caught them. As a kid, I loved to fish back home. Now, fishing was killing time. A chance to fish and walk a few feet and feed off popcorn or some other favorite treats is one thing we don't have at Homer's.

I thought about going to Hollywood to pick up a lady, but that's hardly a treat. With all the pussy I got when the boss is home, I didn't need to go fishing for a woman to fuck. Before leaving, Homer encouraged me to call Virginia. Virginia is like the so-called Macho that Gabi has talked about as being her agent.

After three days of fishing, I stayed home and did some swimming, got in the sauna and later the wet steam. Homer's house is like a resort. I laughed at the thought that if he was gone long enough, I could get used to having the house and the household help to myself.

Eventually, I called Virginia.

"Hey V, I'm alone and need some you know what."

"You got it. What time?"

"V, all you ever send are white girls. I want a sister."

"I know exactly who to send."

I perked up. "Send her at nine."

I have a very cool bedroom in the main house and looked forward to showing it off. A taxi delivered her to the house and when she stepped inside and saw me, her jaw dropped.

"I gotta be dreaming. Is this your pad?"

I grinned.

"My name is Archie. You must be Eliana."

"I am pleased to meet you, Archie."

She walked up to me and we kissed.

1985
Los Angeles, California
Gabi

I went to see Macho at his apartment and found him up and on the phone. Tension was there, and another guy I didn't know. I did not have a session yet for the night.

When he got off, I said, "I need five minutes."

The phone got really busy once it was nighttime. Macho asked Tension to take calls.

He and I went into his kitchen and shut the door. I saw his set of black 'Fuck Crime' mugs, made fresh coffee for us both and gave us each a full mug. It was Macho's house, so I drank it his way, black.

"I'm all yours," he said, sitting down at a tall stool at his kitchen island.

I took a seat across from him.

"I have an application in at Southwestern, need to get accepted but I think it will happen. I am going to law school if they accept me. This is about Homer. I haven't made up my mind about his offer, but here goes. He knows I want to go to law school. Anyway, he wants me to move in. He wants to give me ten thousand a month to pay me for doing what I do for him, but he wants me to quit what I'm doing at the model agency with you. Okay, you got the whole story."

Macho was sitting motionless, his hand cupping the mug, and watching me without expression.

"I will miss you if you go," he said. "You say your mind isn't made up."

"That's another thing. We're going to Rome for a week. I'll decide then."

Macho laughed so he must not have been too upset with me. It was a real laugh.

"You just got back from Venice."

"I know, I'm sorry. You get the cut same as you did when I went to Venice."

He waved that off.

"You live up to our deal. I don't want to lose you, but I don't want to stop you from moving forward in school."

"Check this out, Macho. I'm going to law school whether I live with Homer or not. If I don't live with him, I'll keep working. That's where we are."

I got up and kissed him.

"I came to tell you and get your blessings in case I move in with him."

He kissed me back.

He swiveled his stool to face me. I walked around the island and sat on his lap.

"I love you, Macho. If you were the marrying type, and I was the marrying type, I'd ask you to marry me."

He quirked his eyebrow at me. I hugged him hard and he hugged me back.

Four days later, I was in Rome with Homer. Another memory.

Back in Time, Summer 1979
Los Angeles, California
Archie

Five and a half years ago, I was bartending at a Roger's Hotel in Chicago. I am a creature of routine. Every day, I got up at seven and hit the gym. I had a routine that included some weights, and a fifth-year kick boxing class. I'd clean up, have a late lunch, and work my bar shift from two till ten.

She sat down in my station at the bar in a white suit with a red summer scarf that only a person who didn't go outside in the heat would wear. She looked fit. She had class. She came across to me as more than designer clothes and expensive jewelry. She came across as being well-to-do, old money, gracious. She wore a wedding ring and a chain necklace with a big diamond.

She gave me the once over the way girls do when they're interested. She didn't strike me as a cougar, though she was more mature than the girls who hung out at the bar. I had no idea of her age. She could have been anywhere from forty to sixty. I figured her for a lawyer. She ordered a Margarita.

"Not too strong," she said and winked at me. She did nothing overt, but I felt a rush of heat from the eye contact.

"Not too strong coming up."

"You have a nice smile," she said as I worked on her drink.

I smiled at her.

I put in half the liquor and looked at her for confirmation.

"Perfect," she said. "How long you been working here?"

"Three years, ma'am."

"You can call me Becky."

I smiled at her. "My name is Archie."

"I know." She pointed at my badge.

At some point in every shift, a lady customer smiled with invitation or propositioned me outright. If I got caught taking up with a customer, I'd be fired. I'm not saying she wasn't sending her pheromones in my direction.It didn't feel like a proposition.

Becky ordered a second drink.

Our fingers touched. Sparks flew.

"Got anyone at home?" she asked.

"Not even a dog or cat."

"I like your smile, Archie."

When she was ready to leave, she signed the tab and wrote the room number of a penthouse suite. She took out a business card, wrote a number on the back, and tipped me a couple of twenties in cash. Women don't usually tip that well.

She put the card on the bar, face down, and slid it in my direction.

"My card," she said. "Call me tomorrow. Your choice. If you don't call, no harm done."

She didn't say why.

"Becky, thanks."

When she was out of sight, I turned the card over.

Becky Homer, CEO Roger Hotels.

She was my boss. The boss of my boss's boss. Hell, she was at the top of the food chain, the CEO. Roger Hotels was a global company that had seven different brand names that I knew of.

"This is Archie." I called the number exactly at noon.

"I'm glad you called," she said. "I'm flying home to Los Angeles in a couple of hours. Want to come along?"

She took me off guard, but I tried to control the surprise in my voice.

"My shift starts at two."

"You can come along for the ride. I'll take care of your work. You don't need to call in."

"Okay."

"Give me your address. I'll send a car. Pack light. You can shop in Los Angeles."

I was already dressed for work.

I took off the hotel bartender outfit, and put on jeans, a tee and a button-down white shirt. My shoes were white Vans. I dressed for a hot Chicago day.

A black-suited chauffeur showed up at my doorstep. It was a red-letter day. The whole neighborhood was checking out the black stretch limo that picked me up and delivered me to an executive airport that I didn't even know existed. It was a big adventure.

The security guard at the airport's car entrance put a sticker on the car's windshield and handed the driver a map. It's a good thing my window was up, because I might have hung my head out like a dog. I mean, I was cool about it, but this was all very strange.

"You are cleared to drive up to the tarmac. Just follow the road. I circled where Mrs. Homer's plane is," the security guy said.

The more nervous I am, the calmer I seem. I do things on impulse, but this was the most impulsive thing I've done so far. Everything seemed unbelievable to me. My nervousness doubled when I saw the big plane.

The driver whistled when he pulled up to the plane. "What a beauty."

The car came to a stop. I sat there, gazing at the plane. The chauffeur came around and opened the door for me. I hadn't needed for him to do that, but I was still taking it all in. I got out with my small duffle bag that held toiletries, an extra pair of jeans, shirt, underwear and socks. I started second-guessing my clothes. I wondered if I should have kept my work clothes on. I hoped she wouldn't be wearing a suit. If she was in a suit, I'd look like a tramp. I took a deep breath and went up the plane stairs. A flight attendant in a pink outfit greeted me.

Becky was barefoot, in shorts and a summery blouse. She looked ten years younger than I remembered.

"Archie, welcome. This is Liz, our flight attendant."

I shook hands with Liz and Becky.

Becky kissed both my cheeks. I've seen people do that. I mimicked her.

"Thanks for inviting me. This is my first time on a private plane."

Liz handed me a glass of white wine and showed me a wide leather seat across from Becky. We both had a window and there was a coffee table between us. My back was to the cockpit.

"After we lift off, I'll give you a tour," Becky said. "Thanks again for accepting my invitation. I know it was a bold move on my part, but that's how I am, like my husband."

"Oh, you're married?" I could hear the surprise in my voice. Stupid question.

She held up her left hand, the one with the wedding ring. Sure, I'd seen it last night. I don't know what I was thinking. I had not once asked why she wanted me to come along. For all I knew, she wanted me to bartend somewhere.

"I am," she replied. "My husband loves to watch."

"Watch?"

I sat back in the seat. Our eyes met. Her eyes flickered down my body and back up to my eyes. She licked her lips. She didn't have to say another word. I caught on.

And so, my life with the Homers began.

September 3, 1985

Last week she started law school and moved in at the judge's invitation. Homer had me set up breakfast in the big dining room. I brought them coffee.

"This is all I want Archie," she said. "I'm too anxious to eat."

"Why would you be anxious?" Homer asked.

"First day of classes," she said. She walked over to the heavy curtains and pulled them open. Light streamed into the room. The light shimmered on the draperies of heavy velvet. Somehow, the big, dark room sucked in and consumed the light. All was in heavy, dark colors, the furniture all ponderous and dull as Homer's law book collection.

It struck me that that is what Gabi has done for Homer—let some light in his life. The many women come through here don't seem to affect him as Gabi does. If only they didn't exclude me on their trips. It looks like she's here for a while. With her in school, I don't think they'll be going on many trips. Never know for certain.

When I left for the kitchen, she and the judge were standing up, talking about her classes. When I came back in with Homer's toast, the subject had changed, and they were both sitting at the sunny end of the table. I moved the place settings to where they had sat down and put a vase of fresh daisies beside the salt. I think Gabi once said something about liking daisies. She saw them and grinned at me.

"They're lovely, Archie."

When Archie left, I pulled the cheerful vase closer. The flowers certainly cheered up this mausoleum of a manor.

"I'm keeping my apartment, Homer. I'll live here, but I need a backup for the day you show me the door, and please don't say that will never happen."

"I'll never do that," he said anyway.

"I believe you believe that," I said and patted his hand. "Since there's no crystal ball that can predict unforeseen circumstances, I don't want to give up my apartment. I'm not always going to be the twenty-two year-old I am today, and I know it."

"You will always be beautiful," he said. "The apartment thing is your own decision to make, not mine."

"Thank you, sweets. You are not an allowance. It will be payment for all the sex you want me to have without limit. I just need a little time to study. I catch on fast. You won't even feel that I'm in school."

"You got a deal," he said.

"You will have the full package with me around," I told him. "Anything you want, when you want it. School will not interfere."

"I'm not pushy and you know it," he said.

I hugged him tighter and kissed all over his face. He laughed.

I know what he likes now. It isn't just sex. He likes attention, affection, touching, hugging, kissing, fondling. I knew how to give it all to him, and that's what I did.

The two-year accelerated JD at Southwestern University was going to be challenging, but I would have to find a way to keep my word. I had always been lucky at breezing through school with impressive finishes.

I drove myself to school in a new red Ferrari, a gift from Homer. I resisted but only a little bit. He gave me a bill of sale in my name and said I would be receiving a certificate of ownership from the Department of Motor Vehicles. I left my Corvette parked at my apartment's underground spot. I would have to sell it at some time in the future, but there was no reason to rush anything. I was thrilled with my new car. I spent two hours with the car salesman who delivered the car to learn how to use the five-speed manual transmission. I was given the choice to exchange for a 3-speed automatic transmission but was advised to stick to the manual transmission. I followed the advice.

Fall 1985

After I moved in, I found that Homer liked variety. Archie called a woman named Valerie to fill his requests for Barbies. After Archie would request a girl, then Homer might have sex with her or watch Archie have sex with her. Sometimes he wanted me sitting next to him while he watched, and sometimes, he didn't include me in the session. Sometimes I was in the action on the bed, but those times were with Archie or Archie and himself. I always thanked him for letting me play with them.

I was living like a princess without a penny out of pocket. As much as I was made to feel at home and at ease, I kept my mental state where I was okay if I was shown the door. I had my beautiful apartment waiting for me.

At times, I'd ask Homer to include me, and he'd say, "Are you sure? I don't want to take you away from your schoolwork."

"I stay caught up. Please don't worry about school."

I don't think he was already tired of me. My pussy had been around, but I wasn't worn out from the five plus years I'd been having sex for a living. One thing for sure, God kept my face beautiful. I didn't do much for my body, but I had a fine body. Maybe Homer really cared about my school. He was a judge, after all. It's a bitch being such a skeptic.

I never begged off. I always said yes when he asked. When I wasn't invited in, I'd spend the time on homework. One afternoon, Archie said that Homer was looking to party with two guys and me. Homer was finally going to let me engage with an outsider other than Archie. Cool.

"Did you already call to order the dude?" I asked.

He had not.

I asked Homer, "Is it okay if we give a little business to my ex-manager?"

"By all means," Homer said.

I called Macho.

"Long time," I said. "I miss you."

"Yeah, yeah, you miss me." Macho was a grump, but he was my friend.

"I wouldn't say it if it wasn't so," I said.

"Yeah, yeah, I know that."

"Listen, the judge said it was okay to send you business. We need a male tonight. It's for me, so send something good."

"You know all my talent is good, and fine."

"Yeah, yeah," I said, in a voice as like his as I could be.

That got a laugh out of Macho.

"I'll do a phone introduction so Archie can call you direct, instead of Virginia."

"I know her. She doesn't have what I have. I've talked to Archie. He once called, wanted to know how much I needed to terminate my agreement with you."

My heart dropped.

"He did what?"

"This was before you broke away from me. I told him your agreement with me was an agent agreement and all you needed to do was give notice if you wanted to leave. I think he was surprised."

"You got to be kidding," I said. I didn't know how to feel. Archie had invaded my privacy—What's the difference? He invades my privacy every time he spreads my legs. Furthermore, if Archie asked, he did so at Homer's command.

My mind was racing.

"Why are you spooked?" Macho asked. "He offered to pay to break any deal between us. I love money, but there was no deal to break."

"I'm not spooked. Surprised, yeah."

"Gabi, you should feel good about it. For all he knew, I had some hold over you. I could have been another Alex Rose. He was just looking out for your interest. I gotta go. What time you want the man there?"

Homer and I sat down to dinner. He asked about my classes.

"I had to do a paper on Roe v Wade. It seemed like a big assignment for someone just starting."

Homer laughed and kept eating. "Do you need help? I'm here for you."

"I got it. I did it already. I read the case."

He put down the fork and looked at me seriously.

"What do you think of Roe v Wade?"

"Imagine all the desperate women who died under the knife in dirty backrooms with people who didn't know what they were doing. Makes me sick. Let's change the subject. Sorry I brought it up, Homer."

"Your food will get cold," he said. "Have some more wine." He poured and resumed eating.

"Judge, I love you," I heard myself say.

"What happened to Homer?"

"Judge is more serious."

I reached across the table, and his hand met mine halfway.

"You so kind to me, Homer. I keep thinking I'm dreaming."

"You're good to me," he said. "Archie says you called your former agent, and he's sending us a guest at nine."

"Right, he is. I promise you will be so excited that you will squirm in delight."

"I can hardly wait," he said.

"Will you be on near the bed or in hiding?"

Homer downed his wine and poured another. The man can drink. "That remains to be seen," he said.

"I like it when you're with us."

"No room," he said, laughing. "Not tonight anyway. I wonder if I should have a bigger bed made."

"You got room for it," I said. "Or you could put together two kings."

"That's a thought," he said. "Remind me. I'll put Archie on it. Should have done that long ago. I can have a frame and headboard to go with it."

"Do it," I said. "That way there will be room to spare."

His look was like he was planning it already. I smiled at him. I don't think he noticed.

"I'm going to go take a hot bath and get ready for the big night. Is there anything special you want to see or do?" I got up, went around the table and kissed him.

He gave a sly smile and whispered in my ear. Even if he was a dirty old man, Homer oozed class. Even when he talked dirty, it didn't sound dirty.

"You're special, Homer," I said.

"That's what I tell you," he said. "The difference is that you are special."

I kissed him again and gave his crotch a little squeeze. Maybe a little more than one, just an appetizer for what's to come later.

Throughout the house, there were lots of pictures of Homer in his black robe. He was so distinguished. He looked like he couldn't possibly commit any kind of infraction, his face reflecting wisdom, discipline, and honor. Beneath that façade, Homer was human. I heard raunchy stories that happened during his judgeship. There were a lot of secrets in his chambers, hijinks performed by the man, not the judge.

"In those days it wasn't about watching. It was simply quick sex. What can I say? I'm a dirty old man. Even before I was old, I was a sex freak. My Becky did anything. She was into it. We would do whatever we did, the urges would cool for a day or so, and then I would be back on the hunt. Becky was away a lot, dealing with her hotels all over the world. I was practicing law, working my ass off. If Becky was home, I'd come home after work, and she let me watch men with her. When she was away, I found other erotic things to do. When I became a judge, I had to become more careful. I never got stung. I was lucky."

At first, Archie would tell me what Homer wanted. That changed during our trips to Venice and later to Rome. Archie wasn't on the trips. Homer was outspoken. Homer and I, we made everything work. He wasn't that kinky, or at least none of his kinks bothered me. We had a grand time in Venice and then again in Rome, but behind closed doors, even abroad it wasn't always just us. I didn't know a Macho in Venice or Rome, but I learned where to find men who could perform to his specifications, and not make waves. In Venice, the bellman made it happen. In Rome, I had to go out and find our playmates while he waited in the room watching television.

Looking at me dressed for school, no one would guess what I did for a living. No one could tell I'd had sex with so many men that I could not remember a fraction of them. Homer, with all of his kinks, was still an angel compared to me. I wonder if he thought about that. What was he thinking when he opened up his home to me? My history didn't seem to matter to him. The affection he showed for me was beyond anything I expected.

"You're still a baby. What are you, twenty-two?" he laughed. "Whatever you did so far doesn't count. You're too young for it to count. Just look at you. You could be in the movies or a model, for sure."

That's how Homer talked about me, to me.

November 1985

It took months for me to get used to sleeping at night, but eventually it happened. Then one evening, when I was sound asleep on my back, and I felt the bed shift. For an instant, I was back at Aunt Isabel's in the bedroom with my cousins, and Alex was breathing next to me in the dark. My heart raced with terror and confusion, then my brain shifted. I inhaled. I smelled and saw where I was, in the room that Homer provided for me. I know the face, the touch, the scent of his shampoo. It wasn't Alex. It wasn't Homer either. Archie.

"What's wrong?" I said, startled, but unafraid. "Is Homer okay?"

"I'm sorry if I scared you," Archie whispered as if someone else was in the room with us. "I want you. I want to be with you, alone with you for a change."

I sat up. I patted the edge of the bed.

"Sit," I said in a whisper to match his.

He was lying on his back on one of my pillows. He sat up and moved to the place beside me.

I put my arm around his shoulder.

"We can't do this," I said. "It has to be with Homer."

"He'll never know," Archie said. "I want you bad."

"He may not know, but I will know, and you will know," I said. "It's never going to happen. Especially in Homer's home."

The next morning at breakfast, I said nothing to Homer about the incident, and Archie never said a word about it. Knowing Homer, I wondered if Homer had sent Archie to see how I would respond. Archie never came back to my bedroom. For a handful of times after that night when we did it for Homer, the sex seemed more intense. My orgasms were explosive, and I guess, louder than usual. Homer was pleased. He said we were better than any X-rated movie he had ever seen.

May 1987

I had not seen my aunt in more than a year. We talked on the phone, not often but often enough. She called me. The conversation was always the same. Why didn't I live at my expensive apartment on Wilshire? Why was I living with a man old enough to be my father? I knew she was just looking out for me, but I didn't want her advice. I didn't need her concern.

In May, I received my JD (Juris Doctor) as planned. Homer did not attend my graduation, but my aunt, her husband, and children were there. It took a lot out of me to finish school that quickly. I started in September of 1985, a two-year program. I could have been held over, but I lucked out. After the ceremony, my aunt and her family took me for a late lunch. I'm glad family was there, or else she'd have given me the usual third degree. My cousin Serena was gorgeous. She was working at a car dealer in Los Angeles, selling cars.

"I would prefer doing what you did," she whispered.

I pinched her upper thigh.

"That hurt," she said.

"I gave her a love pinch," I said to my aunt and cousins. "She'll survive."

When I got home, there was a rainbow cake on the dining room table. *Congratulations Gabi* was written in chocolate. Homer handed me two gifts in Cartier boxes: a Cartier ball point pen, and a diamond bracelet, the diamonds just big enough to make it exquisitely beautiful.

"You are too generous," I told him.

"No such thing," he said. "You're a lawyer now. I am so very proud of you."

"It was hard, but it would have been impossible without your financial support and your mentorship," I said, kissing him.

I meant it. I did earn the ten thousand a month. It was not a freebie or an allowance like he had proposed at first.

Archie congratulated me with a hug and a gift. Inside the small box was a pair of diamond studs, beautiful stones.

"You shouldn't have spent this much money on me," I said.

"They were on sale," he said. I knew it was a joke because of the way he exchanged smiles with Homer when he said it.

"I love them," I said, putting them right on.

Homer put my bracelet on. I felt like a princess. We had cake and ice cream. Later Homer and I finished off two bottles of wine.

"Now it's the bar exam," I said. "I need to prepare for it. I need to pass."

"You'll pass," Homer said. "I have two tutors lined up for you, Niki and Don. Both are brilliant legal minds. Both of them clerked for me, and they are available for private tutoring. I hope you pick one of them to see you through the preparation process."

"Homer, thank you. I had planned to attend a prep class. I bet Niki and Don are expensive."

"You didn't let me pay for your school. Please let me pay this little bit."

I wasn't going to say no this time.

I picked Niki, but the choice was not easy. I liked them both. Niki was forty-five and packing about ten pounds of extra weight which she carried well. She was a pretty lady. A guy would say she had a fine ass, especially when she wore jeans. I wasn't hiring her for her ass, but her fine mind. The morning after I made my decision, I had breakfast with Homer and shared it with him.

"I thought you'd choose her," he laughed.

"Judge, don't get mad at me."

"Not a chance," he said, eating his usual hard dry toast and drinking his coffee. "Shoot."

"I will get more out of my study time if I move back to my apartment. Niki wants to work with me five days a week. At my apartment, I have nothing else demanding my attention."

I expected Homer to offer options, but he made it easy. Maybe he had been waiting for me to split.

"The bar exam is treacherous," he said. "If you think you need to be alone, do it. You got my full support. I think she's going overboard with a five-day schedule. It's your call."

"Judge." I touched his face. "Homer, stop the ten thousand a month. I'm totally solid, thanks to you."

"Let me give you the ten," he said.

I shook my head.

"When you want me to come over, don't try to pay me either. Please."

Homer smiled. He just stared at me. Our eyes were focused on each other.

"Oh, and my car. Have I told you how much I love that car?"

Homer laughed. "Every day since I got it for you two years ago."

I laughed, felt my eyes moisten.

That night we were alone in bed and I fucked him until he passed out. He had drunk too much but stayed hard enough for me to give him a long ride. I kissed him, tucked him in and went to my room to pack.

The next afternoon, I was in my apartment. My flawless, squeaky clean and lovely apartment. Archie brought me most of the boxes that wouldn't fit in my Ferrari.

Archie gave me a big hug and a number of kisses when he was about to leave.

"We're going to miss you," he said.

"My understanding is that you will call me when he wants me over."

Archie nodded.

"Why didn't you tell him you'd spend weekends at the house and not make it that you had to be requested?" Archie asked.

"I don't want him to think he's obligated to have me around. He put up with me for two years. It could be I overstayed my welcome."

Archie smiled, started to leave, and did a U-turn to hug and kiss me again. It was like he was saying goodbye or something. I mean, goodbye for real.

That night I had trouble sleeping. I kept telling myself that what I had done was the right thing. In the two years I was there, Homer had countless women and men in his bed. I was afraid I was abandoning him, and in constant fear that the new faces of people I didn't know someday would haunt me once I passed the bar and practicing law. I'd had sex with so many people who might remember me in the future. What if I got my license and got disbarred for moral turpitude because of my past?

Homer had graciously pulled me off Macho's list, but I was still whoring. Homer and Archie were confidential, but I was exposed every time a third party was called in for entertainment. Within three months of my moving in, I could predict when a barbie would show up for a session. I continued to be the loving romantic to Homer every chance I got. No wife or girlfriend would have given him the attention I did. I wasn't retired from the sex scenes. Homer and Archie got a lot of use out of me during the two years I was there.

I can't bitch about getting ten grand a month for two years. I had my fringe benefits too, including living in that great house, a horribly expensive car and jewels. Homer was too good to me. I hope he felt I gave him a good return on his investment in me.

I learned more in five days with Niki than I did in a month of school.

"Don't study," she told me. "Don't think law. Take the weekend off. Monday I'll be here, and we'll do it all over again for another five days."

I called Homer's cell number. He didn't answer. I called Archie.

"Hey, it's Friday night. Anything I should know about the weekend?"

"How did it go?" Archie asked.

"Intense like your sex," I said with a giggle.

"I'll tell him you called and get back to you."

"Cool, let it ring. I'm getting in the tub now. If you don't call until tomorrow, I may sleep in."

"Got it," Archie said.

I'm not a fool. Something was going on with Homer. He was either pissed that I left, or he was over me and moving forward without me on his menu.

How embarrassing.

I spent all that time there, and maybe he was burned out on me. Stress over fouling up my relationship with Homer made me toss and turn, but I finally went to sleep.

Archie didn't call on Saturday. In the early evening, I called my friend Hilda, but her phone was disconnected. I knew she had collected for the injuries she sustained when Rose's brother came after me, but I haven't heard from her in a long time.

I called Macho.

"What a surprise," he said. "Where are you?"

"I'm in my apartment," I said. I told him about graduation, moving into my apartment to study, and about Niki tutoring me. I told him how moving out of Homer's house seemed to change things, and now I don't know what is going on.

"I told you nothing lasts forever. If you're right that he's tired of you, don't lose any sleep over it. You're a lawyer now. I'm proud of you."

"I need a massage. Who do you use?" I asked. "Mine changed her number or something."

"You want a man or a woman?"

I realized I was horny. No sex for a week was a long time.

"Send me a dude who does it all," I said.

"It's on me," Macho said. "What time?"

"The sooner the better," I said, already excited.

"What color?"

"I don't care. Someone that doesn't talk much."

That made him laugh. Macho was in a good mood, maybe because I was back home. Maybe because Archie had given him a lot of business after I asked him to. I really didn't know if all the pawns who came over were from Virginia or Macho. I hope, Macho. I was so busy with school, I stopped being in contact with Macho for months and months. Horrible of me. If my aunt had not called me, I probably would have gone a very long time without talking to her, too.

I came close to calling Homer while I waited for my therapist to arrive; I managed not to. I opened a bottle of wine and put an ABBA cd on. Music filled every room, including the bathrooms.

Roger arrived with a massage table.

I gave him the once over. "You're really a masseur?"

He nodded and laughed. I liked him immediately.

"I told Macho to send me someone who does everything."

"I do everything," he said with a long, slow smile. "Want to start with a massage?"

"Massage after," I said. "Follow me." I tossed my robe on a chair and walked naked to my bedroom. By the time I was on the bed, Roger was a minute away from being naked.

"I assume you have condoms," I said.

Roger is bigger than Archie. That's big. He had his own condoms. I didn't have any that would have fit. All those years bareback, and all of a sudden, I ask for condoms. I got two hours of sex and a two-hour massage. I was a new me. The oil he used was not sticky at all, and the massage was delicious. The last few minutes of the massage, his fingers entered me. I exploded into an orgasm that left me breathless.

I tried to pay him.

"Macho got it covered," Roger said.

"Let me give you a tip," I said, reaching for my purse, and pulling out two hundred dollars.

"Can't take any money," he said.

"Can I book you on my own?"

"You have to call Macho."

I knew that.

Maybe Archie would call me Sunday.

I'd had nothing to eat since a tiny bit of cereal in the morning and two glasses of wine before Roger got there. I was hungry, but too wiped to get out of bed.

Sunday came and went. No call from Homer or Archie. Why did it bother me so? But bother me it did.

I guess that Macho is right. Nothing lasts forever.

It was late Friday afternoon when Niki said goodbye.

"Time flies. Enjoy the weekend. See you bright-eyed and bushy-tailed on Monday," she said.

"You're wonderful," I told her. I gave her a hug and kissed her right cheek then her left cheek.

Macho called me that night.

"Any calls from the judge?"

"Nope," I said. "I've been orphaned."

Mostly I was trying not to think about it. I was unsure if I was pissed more at Homer or myself.

"How you fixed for bread?" Macho asked.

"I'm good," I said. "I only have rent, and I owe nothing to anybody. Oh, and I still have the Corvette. I should sell it. Been sitting down there for two years."

"I'll ask around. Why did it take you so long? He gave you that car a long time ago."

"I didn't want to rush it. What if he had asked for the car back?"

Macho laughed. "Get serious, Gabi."

I joined in his laughter. "Anyway, get me a customer for the Corvette. Good thing my apartment comes with two parking spaces, or I'd be in trouble."

"Okay, I'll work on it."

"Thanks Macho. Now I have to work on passing the bar."

Macho said, "You always been smart. I know you'll pass the bar. You'll take it, and then after that, you got a couple months before you get results. I say this only looking out for you. If you want to make some fast cash on weekends, let me know. I'll get you top of the line work, top dollar like before or better."

"I could've had that ten thousand," I said.

"Why did you let that go? He can afford it."

"I don't want to be kept then chopped off without a word like I don't matter."

"Gabi, lighten up."

"You're right, my friend," I said. "I'll let you know."

"Yeah. Yeah. Do that. I want to hear from you, even if you don't want to work."

"I promise to be in touch," I said.

If I wasn't worried that someone one day would connect hooker Gabi with lawyer Gabi, I would have driven to a session, right then. I'm no angel. I can't take a chance. It's been a long road to get here. I'm a lawyer and only need to pass the bar to be an attorney at law. I don't want to fuck that up. I got to set Macho straight to stop tempting me. Damn him.

July 1987

Summer was in full swing, not that I'd know it firsthand. I spent all my time studying. Wednesday was always a tough day with Niki. It was like I wasn't studying for the bar exam. It was like Niki was putting me through law school again. I complained, but I loved it. She was a great teacher. I soaked it all in.

"They give the bar exam in July and February."

"You did the right thing not taking it this time around. You can plan on taking it in February, but I'd recommend next July. I will plan the study schedule accordingly. I'll give you tests along the way, to find your weak areas and work on them."

The idea of the pre-tests was chilling. I was good at taking tests; however, the bar exam was not the kind of test I was good at taking. In law school we were warned not to expect just a multiple question test or think that only one person graded your exam; multiple people checked your work. I was going over my notes when I got a call.

"Hey stranger, how are you?" Archie asked.

"Hey," I said, "What a surprise. I thought maybe you thought I had contracted a deadly disease. Six weeks and no calls."

"Judge has been busy. You know he likes variety. He wanted me to call you to see if you needed anything. Just tell me, and you got it."

Then he hadn't forgotten all about me. I pictured the scene in my head. They were doing their thing in Homer's bed, I'm guessing the three of them: Homer, Archie, and the Barbie flavor of the day. Maybe Barbie did something that reminded him of me, or, worse, did something better than me. Something made him think of me, though.

My throat locked up for a second. I felt like I was going to cry. I had a glass of iced tea and took a deep swallow so that I didn't give my messy emotion away over the phone. Stupid to be so choked up just because he called to see how I am. Hell, I was touched he thought of me at all. It would have been more touching if Homer himself had called.

"That's sweet," I said, keeping my voice even and cool. "I thought he was pissed at me or something, since I didn't hear from either one of you."

"Nothing like that. You're missed."

"Tell him I'm studying hard and thank him again for picking up Niki's tab. I'm set, I don't need anything. His friendship is all

I want. Yours too."

"You got that," he said. "I'll be in touch."

"Thanks for calling," I said. Ask him about the weekend. Ask.

"Listen here," he said. "Don't be a stranger. You call me if something comes up and you need anything at all, alright?"

"Loud and clear," I said. There was still time to ask about the weekend. "Thanks again." Then there wasn't. I was alone on the line. Why hadn't I invited myself over?

I stopped reading my notes. I walked over to my wet bar and got an open bottle of white from the refrigerator to pour myself a glass.

I sat in the living room, took two sips and set the glass down. The wine was terrible.

I may have felt better if Archie hadn't called. I was getting used the silence. It had been good to hear from him, but it raised my hopes and dashed them at the same time. Why should I feel upset? I had asked for the space so that I could study. Homer was just giving me what I wanted—though I'd thought the weekends would continue. I had made it clear, I would go there any day of the week, not just weekends. It's not like he's a dummy. He was a judge already. He had to understand what I said. I said I wouldn't charge him. I know he doesn't care about that, but I do. I wouldn't take any money from him. It's different now than before. He grew on me. Not like I'm in love with him. It's not like that. My feelings are hurt. That's what it is.

I looked at my diamond bracelet.

Even though I knew I would be with Niki and not leave the house, I put it on every morning after I showered. Same with my diamond studs.

I had elected to leave, and the door shut behind me. Just like that.

Macho called to chew the fat. I told him about the call. I knew better. Macho wanted me to go back to work, at least part-time.

"I shouldn't tell you this," Macho said.

"Tell me what?" Whatever he said would strengthen his position. He wanted me working for him. I was leaning away from being a lay for hire. Otherwise, what was the point of studying for the bar exam?

"Remember Bernice, dark short hair? I sent her twice in a row when you were there."

"I remember her. She's a doll."

"She's living there. She tells me it is temporary. She's getting paid each day. I'll get my end when I see her again. I'm telling you this, so you know how it works."

So. Bernice was the Barbie flavor of the day. I revised that to flavor of the month. I wondered if she had law school in her future. I doubted it. From what I remember, conversation is not her strong suit. I could not picture her addressing the argument structure of the reflective equilibrium. Besides, now that I think about it, she didn't aspire to anything close to law. I think she wanted to be a hairdresser, but she was unfortunately color blind.

"I know how it works, Macho. It's business. Good for Bernice. He's a generous man. She'll do well."

I went to bed picturing Archie and Bernice putting on a show for Homer. The two nights she was there with me, she and Archie and I played on the bed for a long time with the judge in hiding. Like all of Macho's girls, she had a special quality. If I were a man, I'd want to fuck her too. She's probably living in my bedroom there. My ex-bedroom. If Archie gets the hots and visits her room like he did me, would she turn him away? I doubt it. Homer had never asked me for that kind of loyalty. And if he hadn't specifically asked her for it, why should she provide it? Fuck it. Why should I?

It felt like the middle of the night when I woke up horny, clutching a pillow between my thighs and having a fruitless dream. I turned on the light, and saw it was just after midnight, the middle of the day for Macho. I told him I was having trouble sleeping. I didn't say I needed a man.

"My tutor leaves at four on Friday. I'm free after seven in case you need me to handle something like an out of towner that will never get a chance to see me in the future."

"I would never hook you up with a local. This is me."

He was happy to put me back in his rotation. I clicked the light off, and lay there in the dark, needing to get laid. It was almost funny. If I got lucky with the right dude, I'd get the sex I need and get paid for it. I stopped laughing and touched myself. It didn't take much to take the edge off. I finally got to sleep but dreamed of Bernice performing for Homer. What a miserable dream. Me watching Homer watching Bernice and Archie performing on his oversized bed that he had made after I gave him the idea.

No wonder I had trouble getting to sleep.

Thursday was a hard day, probably because I'd had so little sleep. Niki worked my ass off. She left early, and I relaxed by getting up to my neck in bubbles, thinking of what to order for dinner. When I was drying off, my phone rang. It was Macho.

"Remember the basketball player you flew to Dallas with?"

"Max. I remember," I said. I especially remembered his flight attendant Mona had spent the night at my place when we got back to LA.

"In two hours, he's flying to Texas. He said no one else will do but you. Two thousand to fly down with him. His crew will fly you back."

"It's four now. If he's leaving at six, I can't do it. Tomorrow is a study day."

"Two G's. Don't say no. He's counting on me. He's a good customer. You will be back in time to do what you do during the day with the tutor. The tutor works for you, not the other way around." Macho was being grumpy.

"I just got out of the tub."

"Perfect. And my take is thirty. I can't do twenty anymore."

"Macho, you know I love you, but I'm not going to pay thirty percent for this opportunity I don't even want, and I'm not game at all to change our deal we've had."

"Are you telling me you will do it?"

"Not for thirty."

"I let you go for years at lower rate than anyone else."

"Twenty-five percent for Max tonight."

"And on weekends. You said on weekends before."

"On Friday night through Sunday. I only want winners from out of town."

"Okay, twenty-five."

"You got a deal," I said.

"I tell you something. I would have let it be at twenty. I want you back."

"Never back like before. Back on weekends. Twenty-five is fine with me."

"Yeah. Yeah. I'll call you with details in twenty minutes."

"Okay," I said.

It was going to be close. If we left at six, it would be three hours to Dallas, and three hours back. We'd probably spend an hour or two on the ground at the Dallas airport. I'd be driving myself home at some time between two and six a.m. I wasn't looking forward to the drive.

I put on a killer outfit. I had many clothes I hadn't worn while I lived with the judge. By the time I was in the car, I felt good about it. I had to get back in time for my session with Niki, but I couldn't think of her. Macho was right. I could be late or tell her to take the day off. Fuck. All this stress over keeping me on track with my tutor.

It was Thursday night, but I was glad I took the gig.

Max's plane was at LAX like before. My name was at the private parking gate, but I had to show two forms of ID. I gave the guard my driver's license and passport and called the number Macho gave me to announce my arrival.

"I'm here," I said.

"Gabi, I'm glad it's you!" Mona answered. "I saw your name on the manifest."

At the foot of the airplane stairs, I ran into Mona, both of us hugging, laughing, chatting at the same time.

"Are we going to get together after?" I asked.

"If it goes like before, yes. We fly you back, and I hang at your house till my flight leaves in the a.m."

"That means you can sleep at my house?"

"I dig that," she said.

We walked inside the plane.

"Is he here yet?"

"In the bedroom." She pointed the way. "You got wine, champagne, strawberries, whipped cream and other goodies."

I kissed her cheek. She clung to my hand for a second.

"Wish I could watch," she said.

I walked in to meet Max. He was on the bed in his boxers. The television was on. He jumped out of bed when he saw me, picked me up, cradled and kissed me. He was so tall that his head brushed the ceiling.

I did what I was supposed to do. I flung my arms around his neck.

"I'm so happy to see you again," I said.

"Macho told me you were working part-time. I said I had to have you."

I kissed him.

"Max, you're so sweet. Look at what's growing through your boxers. You look delicious."

When he put me back on my feet, I grabbed his long stiff cock.

"I want to undress you," he said. "Is that okay?"

"Whatever you want, you got," I said.

"Anything?" He raised an eyebrow.

"Anything."

"The ride to Dallas is short. I want to do it all," he said.

Three hours is plenty of time. I had no problem sitting on his face like he wanted.

"Foreplay this time," he said.

"I love it," I said, feeling his monster tongue.

We never touched the wine or champagne, but he sprayed a whole can of whipped cream over my abdomen and pussy. He proceeded to eat it off me, and that led to sixty-nine, a delicious exchange. Sometimes I say no to that, but not to Max.

By the time he fucked me, I had come three times. Max had not come.

I tried explaining to him that it was my job to make him come, not the reverse, but it just made him laugh. He got on top. I wrapped my legs around his big body, and he slammed me until he exploded in me, overflowing onto my legs, my ass. It was stupid not to use a condom with everyone every time, but I had gone two years at Homer's doing it in the raw, and years before that without a condom. Max was not diseased. I hope.

I'd been in the big shower before but not with him and me in it at the same time. It was a squeeze to be in there with such a huge man. With shower gel, I gave him a body scrub that turned him on, but there was no time for a finale.

"Soon as we park, I need to be out of here fast," he said, while dressing in the bathroom. "Will I see you next time?"

I remembered he had a wife to go home to.

"I hope there's a next time," I said.

He kissed me with passion that had me bouncing with heat.

"Yes, next time." He handed me a stack of hundreds. "There's an extra thousand in there for you."

"The deal was two. The extra is not necessary," I said. He had given me a thousand-dollar tip last time, too.

"You're worth more."

I watched him cross the tarmac and disappear behind a gate, then I went back into the shower. It only took a moment to rinse off the gel that had rubbed off on me. After all, I'd been washing him, not me. When I stepped out, Mona was there to hand me a towel. She used another to help me dry off.

"How was it?"

"Fucking delicious," I said, licking my lips.

"You got anything left?" Mona asked.

"I got a lot left," I said. "Can you handle it?"

"Yep," she replied, "I sure can."

"You'll stay at my house tonight?"

"Can't do it tonight, but we've got this bedroom for ourselves as soon as we are wheels up. I made a deal with the pilots. It was a trade. I spend a night with them."

I smiled. "A threesome. Nice."

"We are a tight team. It's not the first time. The deal is that I—we—will not be disturbed during our flight back to LAX. I have an IOU date with them, whenever we arrange it."

"Nice. Let's grab a sandwich before we take off. I'm starved," I said.

"I already ate but I have a nice selection for you like before. The pilots will be busy getting ready for the trip back. We'll be back in the air by midnight. I'll fix you up."

Once in a while, Macho had a client who wanted two women. Once or twice the client was a woman wanting another woman or two. With the judge, anything could happen. A few times, he'd wanted another woman and me. I don't look for encounters with women, but when it happens, it is at someone else's request—except for Mona. Mona was like pay dirt for me.

I didn't even remember her last name. All I knew is that she worked for Max as a flight attendant and had a dirty, suggestive mouth that turned me on.

The two plus hours on Max's bed with Mona were as gratifying as the time with Max earlier that night. Mona was spectacular. In our intercourse, she was dominant and knew exactly what to do to me to shoot me into space.

"What if Max were to walk in?"

"What a turn on that would be," Mona said, taking my fingers and pressing them inside her. "Like that," she moaned.

We were wrapped in each other until the wheels touched down. We rushed to get dressed and to say our goodbyes.

I palmed five hundred dollars to Mona.

"No, you're nuts. I can't take pay for that." She tried to refuse, but not too hard.

"Please take it. It's just a little bit. It's a gift, not pay."

Max was a fantastic fuck. So was Mona. What a score. Two grand, an extra five hundred, and countless orgasms for me. Three with Max, then with Mona, I quit counting.

I looked at my watch as I climbed in the car.

Three a.m.

I was feeling the lack of sleep. I'm pretty sure I nodded off to sleep while driving home, but made it home intact, miraculously. At home, I showered and fell into bed, and set the alarm to go off later than usual, not long before Niki would arrive at nine.

With great effort, I made it through six hours with Niki. After she left, I fell into bed.

My phone rang. I looked at my watch. I'd been asleep for three hours. It was Friday night, and it had to be Macho on the line.

I picked up and didn't even try to sound like I was awake.

"Mmm," I said, and yawned into the phone.

"You forgot to call me last night after you got back," Macho said.

"I'm sorry. Out of practice staying up nights. I was tired like you wouldn't believe."

"I have something for you in two hours."

"What is it?"

"It's easy money. That's what it is."

Easy for him. All he had to do is sit on his ass. I did a Macho, "Yeah. Yeah. I bet."

I drove to the Bonaventure in downtown Los Angeles. I went through hell getting through law school. I'm beating my ass studying for the bar. What am I doing hooking at a hotel blocks from the courthouses where I will be practicing law?

What the fuck is wrong with me?

I got on one of the glass elevators with the spectacular view of Los Angeles lit up at night. I went to room 1212 and rang the doorbell.

A young man answered the door.

"Carlos?"

"Peggy?"

"Yeah, I'm Peggy," I said in Spanish. "Macho said no English."

"I speak little bit. You speak wonderful Spanish. Come in."

Carlos was not bad looking. I doubted he was even thirty.

"How do you know Macho?" I asked, taking a seat in the plush living room.

This was a big suite. I wish I had not asked such an intrusive question. I was rusty at the skill of casual conversation.

"He's a friend of my father. I'm from Mexico City."

"Here I am." I gestured with my hands.

He watched me expectantly. His dark eyes followed me. I was wearing a little summer halter dress, not much to it. I untied it, and it fell to the ground. I turned my back to him to pick it up and toss it over the back of the chair tucked into the hotel's desk. I could feel his eyes on me and turned around wearing nothing but a thong that wasn't much more than string. I sat on his lap, put my arms around him. I could feel how happy he was to see me. I straddled him, facing him, did a couple of shimmies with my hips.

He liked it.

I slipped off his lap and sat beside him but left my hand on his crotch. I could feel the hard ridge of his excitement through his jeans.

"You're beautiful, Peggy."

I kissed him lightly. "You are too," I said.

I climbed into his bed and beckoned him to hurry.

He undressed as he walked into the bedroom, tripping in his excitement.

That's when I noticed his unusually long thing. Pretty soon, it stretched out like a bat. Carlos was thick enough, and longer than ordinary.

"Te gusta?"

"Me encanta," I replied

If he wanted me to go down on him, he had to be wearing a condom.

"My condoms are not big enough for you," I said. I thought of the masseuse Macho had sent me when I told him the same.

"I don't like condoms. I pay extra for no condom," he said.

"Me neither," I said. "But I got to use them."

He got out of bed and rummaged through a suitcase open on a bench, tossed a handful of condoms to the nightstand and lay down. I snatched one to put on him, and his dick went limp.

"Relax," I said. "Lie down and let me work on it."

It came to life.I opened a new condom and put it in my mouth, positioning it to roll down. He was too long for me to pull it all the way down with my mouth, but he was excited that my lips were on his cock. I gave him a blow job through the condom, then I got on top. After a while, I got on my side. He came into me from behind, and that worked great. Too great. I didn't feel when the condom slipped off. I don't know if he let it come off or if he helped it along, or if it was an accident. I was too excited to notice anything but how the friction increased. Years of fucking with no condoms, why the drama about the condom falling off? I went to the bathroom and used the bidet to wash the mess away, then showered. I came out of the bathroom naked, the same as I had walked in.

"Can we do that again?" he asked.

"If the condom falls off, I stop," I said.

He was very good looking.

"Okay."

He handed me a new condom.

He put the condom on himself without a problem.

"Going to cost you extra for taking the condom off last time," I said.

He smiled mischievously. That's when I knew for sure.

"I pay," he said in English. "No problem."

I rolled on my side. He fucked me for what must have been an hour. Fucks like this and Max the night before are not usual, but were home runs, like prizes for coming back to the biz. Was I back? With Homer, it was the same business.

When I came out of my second shower and got dressed, Carlos pulled out a wad of hundreds from a drawer. He gave me the thousand Macho had worked out with him then he counted out two thousand more.

"A tip," he said in English.

I kissed him on the lips, not passionate, but not the kind I give clients.

"Mission accomplished with Carlos," I told Macho on the phone.

"Want another one in Beverly Hills?"

"I'm out of shape," I lied. "Tomorrow, I'm in."

"Yeah. Yeah. Go home and rest. Good girl."

When I got home, I douched with vinegar then with my regular douche, twice. I took another shower then hit my comfy bed and knocked out right after.

Sunday, I did two clients. I told Macho, "Don't call me until Friday night, no matter how good the deal is."

"Yeah. Yeah."

July 29, 1987

The last Wednesday of July, while in session with Niki, I got a call just before we broke for lunch. I didn't answer the first time, then it rang again.

"Let's break a little early," I told Niki.

She left as she usually did, to lunch at one of the eateries in the village.

I answered the phone on the fourth ring, but no one was there.

I headed to the bathroom. The phone rang again. I got it this time.

It was Mona, crying.

"What's wrong?"

She wailed.

"I'm fired! His wife had a video camera hidden in the bedroom. She has a tape of you and Max and of you and me."

Mona was crying so that I could barely understand her.

"Take a deep breath, maybe four, then talk."

"She came to my apartment and slapped me four times. Called me a dyke and a slime ball."

"What a bitch," I said. "If she's got video, fuck, she'll be coming after me next."

"I don't think she knows who you are."

Mona was crying again.

"Have you got anything holding you in Dallas besides the job?"

"Besides the job I got fired from? Nothing," Mona said.

I wasn't worried that Max's wife would come find me, but that any minor arrest might affect my state bar application. Max had as much to lose as me. His wife could cause a scandal that would hit the media. I don't need anything that I have to explain to the State Bar. When I killed Rose, that was self-defense. My law school counselor told me that self-defense was not going to affect my admission to the bar once I passed my bar exam.

I told Mona she could stay with me for a while until she found another job or figured out what she wanted to do. I told her how busy I am during the week, but I didn't tell her what I was doing on weekends.

She had to know I was hooking. I needed to let Macho know. This was a crisis. I didn't call him because even if he answered the phone, he'd be too asleep to comprehend. I'd call him later.

Niki returned from lunch. I could barely concentrate during the afternoon session.

That night, the lobby guard called to tell me Mona had arrived via taxi from the airport.

She came in my apartment carrying two suitcases. We hugged. There were no tears.

"That's an impressive bruise on your cheek. How do you feel? Do you want an ice pack?" I asked. I'd had one in my freezer ever since Alex's brother had 'dropped in.'

She sat on the couch and accepted the pack that I'd wrapped in a towel.

"Sorry to be a bother."

"Hey, we're kind of in this together," I said. "I can't imagine she showed you the video."

"No, she didn't."

"It's not so bad, but I'm surprised you didn't put concealer on it."

"I didn't see it till I went to the restroom on the plane."

"What a bitch," I said.

"I'm pissed at Max," Mona said. "He's a pussy to allow his wife to do this."

I sighed. I disagreed but wasn't going to argue about it. He was a pussy, all right, not for failing to control his wife, but for promising fidelity, and then fucking up. Not that I think that men are capable of fidelity. Okay, so I'm a hypocrite. I wasn't about to start quizzing the dates Macho got me to see if they were screwing around on a wife. I wouldn't have cared anyway, like I didn't care Max has a wife. I knew it. Mona had told me the first time I met her.

"What's the wife's name?"

"Lily."

It seemed like a good time to change the subject. I hadn't had breakfast or lunch.

"Are you hungry?" I asked.

"I am. What you got to eat?"

"Not much."

She stood, followed me to the kitchen, and watched as I opened the refrigerator door. Not much in there except for con-diments on the doors, a pint of milk that had gone bad, coffee cream, and a six pack of cokes. I tossed the milk in the trash and shut the door.

"I love cooking, and I'm good at it." Mona giggled. "But I need something to cook."

"For now, I can have food delivered fast."

I opened a drawer beside the refrigerator and pulled out a handful of take-out menus. I tossed them on my dinette.

"What do you feel like eating?"

"My treat," Mona said.

"Don't sweat the small stuff."

I called Macho to tell him about Max's wife, the videos, and my new roommate Mona.

"The wife called her a dyke."

Macho didn't comment about my after-Max party.

"Have they tightened security at your place?" Macho asked.

"They have two rent-a-cops now instead of one. I'm not worried. Besides, she doesn't know me. Max doesn't have my phone number or my address. Can't see how his wife could get to me."

"Jealous women with money hire private investigators. But any questions would lead to me, not you," Macho said. "I'll send Ben over there. Call security and let them know he's a PI working for you and to let him in and out of the property."

"What's his full name?"

"Ben Sanders."

"Got it."

"Tell the guard to log his name and after twelve hours another PI will replace him. I don't have the name yet. Sanders will let them know."

"I hate to put you through this expense," I said.

"Yeah, Yeah. Don't worry about it."

We put Mona's suitcases in the extra bedroom, but she got in bed with me.

"Hook me up with your pimp. I'm willing."

"No chance I'm going to get you in to this filthy business I'm trying to pull myself out of."

Mona laughed.

"I fuck. I just never get paid. The pilots the other night, I gave them head, I let them fuck me, one at a time, then both of them filling me from both ends. It's not like I'm innocent."

"No," I said.

Lights went out. Mona began to massage me. I lay back and enjoyed it, then I wondered how she got so good at it.

"Where did you learn to massage like this?"

"Massage school before I started working with Max. I didn't finish school. I figured I didn't need to. I loved my job with Max."

"Has he called you?"

"He's not going to call me. For all I know, she shot him. She was pissed."

"You've got options," I said. "The pilots might be good recommendations if you want to get another flight job."

"Lily will fire the pilots. She had to figure out they knew what Max did on the plane. When she came to my house, she kept asking me how many women had been there, for how long, and why didn't I tell her. She's so full of shit."

"You could go back to massage school if you still think that fits with what you like to do. If you stay in LA, there is a demand for massage. I know I love it."

"I can do that, but I think the bread is in what you do when you aren't studying. I totally would dig it."

"You aren't listening. I'm not going to help you get in that business. Besides, the guy that I work with is fussy, and I don't think he's taking on anyone new."

"Maybe he will if he sees me," she insisted. "Or do you think I'm not hot enough?"

"You're hot enough. Trust me. You don't want to do this kind of work."

I hardly knew Mona. I didn't know how persistent she could be.

"Trust me, I do want to do that kind of work. I've been giving it away way too long."

Mona massaged me until I went to sleep. In the morning, I woke alone.

I'm not a breakfast person, but Mona woke up hungry. We got up early, walked two blocks to a popular all-day breakfast restaurant on Wilshire Boulevard. We got a table by the window, and while we ate, I told Mona about my schedule with Niki.

"I'll be really quiet in my bedroom watching TV or something. Or I'll come out and walk around and get to know this great area."

"At least you're safe from Lily here," I said.

"Lily." Mona shuddered. "She's going to get over it. Besides, how would she find you? She's not going track you down to LA."

I poured syrup over my pancakes and took a bite.

"Did I ever tell you about this bastard pimp I had when I was just a kid? I once saw him almost beat a guy to death with a baseball bat. He loved that bat. He came over to my house and went after me with it, once."

Mona raised her eyebrows.

"What a motherfucker. Did he hurt you?"

"He put me in the hospital, but I killed him."

"For real?"

I heard her gasp aloud, then she choked over a bite and spent a good minute getting her breath back.

"For real. I took the bat away from him and slammed him so hard that it killed him."

"Motherfucker deserved it," Mona said.

"He did."

"You're not thinking of killing Lily if she comes over here?"

"The building has security. I doubt she could get upstairs." I took a swig of orange juice, and one of coffee. "If she fucks with me, you never know."

When we got back to the apartment, Niki called to say she had the flu.

"Stay home until you're well," I said. Soon we were going to cut back to three hours, three times a week. Niki had a list of books for me to study, and a plan for me to work. A month before the bar exam, she'd be back every day.

We wandered into the kitchen. Mona opened my refrigerator and looked it over again. She looked in my little pantry. It was nearly empty.

"I should study," I told Mona. "Fuck it. I'd rather hang with you. My tutor is sick."

"Let's hit the market. I'll go shopping and fix you lunch and dinner. You don't have to blow money ordering out."

"You don't have to cook," I said.

"I want to. I promise. Of course, we could always go roll around in bed before we go to the grocery. I'm all worked up after this story of how you put this guy under."

"Hey, I'm not proud of it."

"You should be."

"How about you spoil me with a heavenly massage?" I asked. "I have oils. Follow me."

I led her to the bathroom and showed her the box of essential oils. I picked out lavender.

"You will love the massage," Mona said. "I promise."

On a napkin, I drew out the route to the store. Mona left and I sat down with pile of books. In the afternoon, Macho called.

"Are you up early?" I asked. It was two in the afternoon, which for Macho was very late or very early.

"I haven't gone to bed yet. You'll never guess who called."

"The president," I said.

Macho ignored me. "Max called. His wife asked him to leave. He's staying at the Ritz Carlton in Dallas. He plans to get the video and says for you not to worry. He plans to give Mona a good severance package as long as she keeps everything quiet."

"I am sure she will agree to that. Are you pulling Ben and the other guy?"

"Not yet. I am keeping in touch with Max until this blows over. I promised him there will be hell to pay if his wife shows up here, or if she sends some tool."

"I'll shoot her," I said. "You know I have a gun, and it's legal."

Macho laughed. "Sleep with it handy, sweetheart."

"Get Max to ante up Mona's package. You can be our liaison."

Mona got back from the store and put her purchases away. I told her about my conversation.

"You know, I have eleven thousand in the bank. I can use the compensation, for sure."

"You'll get it," I said. "Max is generous."

"Max is a chump, letting his wife throw him out of his mansion. Lame is what he is."

"I have an extra car you can use," I said. "It's been sitting for a very long time, but the other day I had the auto club come over to give me a jump, and it started right up. I took it to the car wash, and it works fine."

"You don't mean the Ferrari?"

"No, it's a Corvette. Cherry, baby. I love the car. I should have sold it two years ago."

"That's way too expensive for me unless you hook me up with your guy."

"I'm not hooking you up with my agent. You can borrow the car. I'm not asking you to buy it. Not even sure what it's worth now."

"I'll go study while you cook," I said.

"You like walnuts in your salad?"

"Love Waldorf salad."

Niki confirmed that she had the flu. It would be a week before she could get back.

"No sweat," I said.

Friday night, Mona sat in my bedroom and watched me get ready to meet up. She had already gone into raptures over the contents of my closet and was rambling on about how great my clothes were.

She counted my shoes.

"You have forty-four pairs of shoes," she said. "I never stay in one place long enough to get that many."

"Another reason not to get in this business. Macho requires designer stuff."

"Sweet. I'm jealous," Mona said. "At least get me an audition with Macho."

"No."

Los Angeles, California
Mona

When I enrolled in massage school, Gabi agreed to let me move in permanently. She put off requiring me to pay my fair share until I became an earner not dependent on my savings. She let me use her Corvette and soon it was true love. Eventually, I would have to buy the car from her. It was precious. She kept it like it was brand new.

After I'd been there for about a month, Macho told Gabi that a local lawyer contacted him and wanted to see Gabi and me. We went to an address in downtown Los Angeles and met with the attorney who was representing Max.

We took an elevator up to the fifth floor. It wasn't the fanciest office building I'd ever been in, but it wasn't run down, or anything. The elevator was directly across from the double doors to the firm. The lawyer we were there to see was one Tomas Lopez. The firm name was Lopez, Song & Myers. The receptionist was chewing gum and typing when we came in. She notified him that we were here, and he came out to lead us to his office. Black hair thinning around the edges, a nice shade of tan, penetrating eyes, starting to get some silver in his temples. He wasn't six feet or an athlete, but he was buff like a lot of California guys. I'd do him— not that he was looking at me that way. I did wonder if he'd seen the tape. We followed him to his office. He held the door open for us and was completely respectful, so maybe he hadn't.

He introduced himself, and we sat down. His office wasn't huge, and it had the same industrial carpet as the reception area and hall. On the wall opposite the desk was an ornate gas fireplace. His desk was painfully neat, and he sat with his back to a wall-to-wall bookcase full of important-looking books. The chairs Gabi and I sat in put our backs to the fireplace. The chairs we were in matched, but they weren't particularly comfortable. I sat forward, with my feet flat on the floor. Gabi's taller, and sat more comfortably, with her legs crossed. She's got great legs. Tomas Lopez had to notice.

"Max wants to pay you twenty-five thousand each in exchange for a release and a non-disclosure agreement. You will never disclose anything you know about Max, events on his plane, or anywhere else you may be aware of."

"I don't know what Mona wants to do but I'm not taking twenty-five thousand. The invasion of privacy is horrendous and mind boggling. Any deal I agree to will include my getting the original video tape along with a sworn affidavit from Max that there are no copies."

"What she said," I said, raising my hand. "I agree. And what she says, goes."

The lawyer was not happy.

"I happen to know you graduated from Southwestern. Are

you planning to litigate this?" He scoffed at her degree like it was a joke. "You were hooking."

Gabi kept her cool. Her face was expressionless.

She shrugged. "Mr. Lopez, is Max going to testify that I was hooking?"

He blushed.

"I'd be careful accusing me of hooking, unless you have proof."

I was watching Gabi. She was cool and calm, but her mouth wouldn't stop.

"You called us. I wasn't the one who started this. I have nothing to lose. Max, on the other hand, is a famous athlete. If this scandal goes public, what will happen to all those endorsement deals of his? Even without the tape, I can make a lot of noise."

Gabi stood up to go, and I was right behind her.

The lawyer cooled his jets and asked us to please sit.

"What do you want, exactly?"

Gabi sat down. So did I. She leaned forward in her chair.

"I never planned to do anything about it," Gabi said. "You asked us here to offer us a pittance in exchange for silence. I'm throwing it back at you. A hidden camera without my permission, without Mona's permission. That is serious shit."

"I'm waiting to hear what you want."

Gabi nodded. "I want fifty thousand for each of us. It's chump change for a guy like Max, and it is better than your starting offer. Furthermore, I want the video tape. I want a notarized affidavit under penalty of perjury, signed by Max that there are no copies. If there are copies, there will be hell to pay."

"If I get this, you can bet your life there are no copies," Tomas Lopez said. "I concur that Max has more to lose than you do."

"Get the tape and the money. Mona and I will watch the video to confirm it was taken that night. I will agree to burn the tape right here in your fireplace."

Tomas Lopez smiled.

Two weeks later we were back.

This time, he greeted us with a smile.

"Call me Tomas," he said.

Gabi and I watched the video in a private meeting room sitting side-by-side on a leather sofa at his office. We kept advancing the tape so that we saw short bursts of it. The gum-chewing secretary had given us a pitcher of ice water, two glasses, two cokes, and shut the door, leaving us alone in the room. Some very hot moments in the Max and Gabi video made us exchange looks and sheepish grins. Same was true in the video of us together. I had never seen myself in a sex video.

"Have you ever seen yourself doing this in a video?"

Gabi shook her head and said, "Never, ever. It's hot. I'm going to be soaked if we don't skip through some of this."

We signed, got a check for fifty grand each and watched the attorney burn the video.

"When you pass the bar, come see me," Tomas told Gabi. "I like your style."

Then Gabi said to Tomas, "Did you watch the video?"

The blush shot across Tomas's face.

"I did not watch the video."

"Tomas, I bet this fifty thousand of mine you watched it," I said.

"He's a lawyer," Gabi said. "He'll never cop to it. Hope you enjoyed it."

"Gabi, come back when you get your license. We're a boutique, a small firm, but we are blessed to have a whole lot of interesting cases."

"I'll call you," Gabi said without turning around. She headed for the door, me behind her.

Gabi gave Macho a quarter of the fifty grand. She said he had it coming. She told me she felt like she'd practically blackmailed Macho's client, and it was only right that he got his cut.

I sang all the way to the bank. I felt like the luckiest rich girl in Westwood, California.

"I can pay you rent now."

We agreed that I would pay five hundred a month, no utilities. I would have taken anything Max offered, but Gabi made it possible to get the fifty and the video.

It was a good deal, thanks to Gabi.

The next bar exam was scheduled for February 1988. January and February, Niki came over daily. Gabi cut out her Macho work. When she accepted a session, it had to be special. The money had to be over norm and the client had to be older and from out of town. Mostly she studied. She took the test. It was months before they published the grades. Gabi ran out to find a newspaper in the middle of the night to catch the morning edition of the LA Times.

She did not pass.

I found her the next morning curled up on the couch, crying her eyes out, the newspaper with her name not in it folded to the list. I made her coffee and an omelet, but food didn't help. She was devastated. Before it was even seven in the morning, a dude named Archie called. He was the spokesman of her friend the judge. The judge had not seen her name on the list of passing lawyers. All I knew about him is that he'd paid the bill for Niki and was offering to keep paying her fees.

"Thanks for the offer," she told Archie in a voice that sounded perfectly normal. "Tell the judge I am grateful for everything, but I'm going to study on my own. I know what to expect, now."

She hung up, crying. She took the phone off the hook.

"I can't remember ever flunking a test," she said, crying.

We got drunk that night and stayed in bed the next day with a hangover. I missed massage school. Gabi refused to answer her phone, in case it was Macho who didn't know yet she flunked.

I graduated from massage school. I was already a good therapist and I got it totally together when I finished the Los Angeles
school. I took the test for my license and passed it. I got licensed
and found a job at High-End spa just five blocks from the apartment. I was the youngest, least experienced therapist but I had
one thing going for me. I was hot. Even with the uniform I had
to wear, I looked damn good.

I was heavily in demand, mostly by men. I did not break the
rules. I was careful to never touch the genitals, and I didn't accept
offers to do anything erotic. I had a couple of regulars who had
this thing about rubbing my ass or my leg, but nothing too drastic.
I let it happen, but I never made a deal to do anything in exchange
for extra money.

After four months, I got fired. They said business was slow but
that was bullshit. The old-timers got rid of the competition,
namely me.

I got even by going into business myself. I did outcall. I bought
the best wood massage table made, a heavy mother. You have to
have a strong table, especially if the client happens to be on the
big side. I had to buy a bigger car. The Corvette was too small for
my table and my supplies. I got a Toyota 4runner, brand new. It
was a sad day when I gave up the Corvette.

The regulars called me to come over to their office or their
home, and freed up from High-End, I got little more flexible on
the touching. Touching was no big deal to me, even the ones that
found their way to my bare skin while I was busy massaging them.

Gabi advised me not to fuck them. "Even a hand job can bite
you in the ass. It's not worth the bigger tip, the risk of losing your
license."

I followed her advice.

In July of 1988, Gabi took the three-day exam again. The night before the exams began, we smoked a joint and got buzzed. It was months before the results came out. Gabi didn't run to find a newspaper in the middle of the night to catch the morning edition of the LA Times.

She passed. Gabi was twenty-five when she became an attorney at law.

Los Angeles, California
Gabi

I made up my mind long ago that I would apply for a job with the Los Angeles County Public Defender's Office. I had enough money put away to supplement my income, so it didn't matter that the pay sucked. The pay with the District Attorney's Office was not any better.

The day my name appeared that I had passed the bar, I got a call from Homer. Not Archie. Homer.

"Congratulations, Gabi," Homer said. "I'm very proud of you."

"Judge, thank you. What a surprise to hear from you. It will make my day."

"I haven't called because I wanted you to have the space to prepare for the exam. Here we are. You are now an attorney at law."

I chuckled. "You are a day early, judge. I'm not being sworn in until tomorrow. It means so much that you called."

"I miss you," Homer said. "When you get settled and sworn in, come over. I'd love to see you."

"I'll call for sure," I said.

"By the way, the senior partners in many law firms owe me. Let me know if I can put in a word for you and give you a running start."

"You are so sweet, Judge. My plan is to apply with the Public Defender's Office. I want to get a feel for doing criminal work. I figure it's a good place to start."

"Good move. If you take to criminal, do two years with the PD then jump over to the DA and do two years. You'll come out of there with a ton of experience and ready to hit the criminal practice of law."

It wasn't the first time he'd given me this advice, and it was good advice. He knew from experience what he was talking about because he'd been a criminal lawyer and then a judge.

I want to make big money. I want to be happy. I hung up the phone with a sense of disbelief. He didn't call for two whole years to give me space. I didn't believe that was the reason. He was busy with his hobby. Sex. I figured if Judge Homer called me, I'd get a call from Archie. Archie didn't call.

A lawyer doesn't have to attend a ceremony to be sworn in. Some have a friend of the family who is a judge who will do it. A week after notification that I passed the bar, I joined two hundred and forty men and women at the Hilton Hotel for the lawyer swearing-in ceremony by a California court judge followed by a Federal court judge. I only invited Mona. As far as Aunt Isabel was concerned, I was already a lawyer. I didn't feel like making a big deal over it. Everyone who mattered to me, like Homer or Macho, already knew.

How could I not think of all the times Macho had sent me to this great hotel in downtown Los Angeles on 7th & Figueroa? I repeated the words of the oath, and I didn't tear up at all. I was all grown up now. Mona and I left the ceremony in my Ferrari. It was night already, and traffic was a bitch.

"Are you done with Macho?" Mona asked.

"I should have been done with him months ago. Three days ago, I was turning tricks. I'm a risk-taking fool."

"I'll buy you dinner," Mona said. "We can celebrate."

"Deal, I'm starving. Where do you want to go?"

"My treat, your pick. We are celebrating you."

"In that case, I want Tommy's," I said, laughing.

Tommy's is a short distance from the Hilton. I had a hamburger and a hotdog, both with the famous chili. Mona ordered the same.

"I hope you didn't pick Tommy's to save my wallet," Mona said.

"Not a chance. I love this stuff, and you know it."

By the time we got home, we had to run for the antacid.

"It never fails," I said. "Great stuff but the heartburn is horrible."

"What now?" Mona asked.

"Let's watch some TV and I'll give you a massage later," I said.

"Hey, I'm the therapist. I'll give you a massage."

"I was hoping you'd say that."

I love Mona. The day will come when she would move out, and when that happens, I will miss her big time. Living alone had never bothered me before. Now, I'm used to her being there in the morning, after work and all nights.

When I was working for him, I saw Macho only once or twice

a month when I gave him his percentage from my cash customers and collected what he owed me for tricks who paid him with a credit card. It's a piece of cake when you are working with a person you trust. This time when I went to see him, Mona weaseled herself along for the ride, and finally met him.

"Nice digs," she said in the elevator. Macho did live in a nice building, and his apartment was, as always, as sharp as a magazine cover. I could tell Mona was impressed by the apartment, and by the man.

Macho and I conducted our business quickly and efficiently. I took a thirty-second bathroom break and came out ready to hustle myself home. It had taken half of a minute for Mona to make herself available to him.

"I'm doing good with my massage business," Mona told Macho. "But I wanted to meet you. Maybe you and me can make a deal."

"I already told her no," I said.

"You're doing good with massage," Macho said. "Let it be."

Mona didn't push it. Neither did Macho.

But when I got home, the phone rang, Macho on the line.

"She's very nice. How old is she?"

"Don't encourage her, Macho," I said. "Please."

"Okay."

"Besides I thought you had all you wanted with what you have."

"I do. This Mona is nice. I like her. I'd like to see her without clothes."

"Her body is better than mine."

Macho laughed. "I don't believe that. If you change your mind, send her over."

I didn't change my mind. A month later, she went to see him on her own.

I filled out an application with the public defender's office and a week later, I was interviewed. Two days later, I was interviewed again, this time by the boss, Joseph Michaels, head public defender for LA County.

"Why do you want to work here?"

"I want to help the men and women who don't have funds to hire a lawyer," I said.

"The money is nothing to brag about."

"I don't think it's so bad," I said. "There are fringe benefits like medical insurance, dental and IRA. I read that on the application."

"That does not start until you pass the probation period."

"I have savings to supplement what I'll make here. If you hire me, of course."

"Are you looking to make a career with us?"

"I don't think so. You never know though. If I like it and everyone likes me, anything is possible." I didn't mention wanting the experience.

I was hired as a deputy public defender. I even got a badge that looked like a cop badge. My immediate supervisor was Jerry Jacobs, ten years with the PD office and at least that many years older than me.

"Why the badge?"

He shrugged. "It's a thing. Been going on for decades. You don't like it?"

"I love it."

I was given an office the size of a closet. No fancy expensive desks, no decorating. Everything was utilitarian. I had a bookcase full of files, and a battered metal cabinet with hanging folders and more files. Jerry's office was no fancier, and maybe three times larger. It wasn't luxurious either. I didn't care. He had a picture of his wife and three kids on his desk.

"Lovely family," I said, looking at his family photo.

"Thanks," he said. "I noticed on your application that you are single."

"Yeah, no one will have me," I said.

"Initially, you will be going to court with me, to watch, and only to watch."

"Got it," I said. "Observation only."

By the way he stared, I knew he liked my looks. I pretended not to notice.

Very little of my expensive, extensive wardrobe crossed over to the courthouse. As soon as I was hired, I bought five masculine-tailored but well-fitted two-piece suits and shirts. I wore no jewelry. I did wear my Rolex, a gift from a prince when I was hooking. I would keep that secret. I also used my designer purses and shoes, but I used them with an eye for utility, not fashion. I had enough to swap shoes and purses for weeks.

When anyone saw me parking, my red Ferrari made a splash. At work, my car was legend. Whenever anyone asked about it, I told the truth, that it was a gift from a friend when I started law school. I never said who the friend was, and eventually people stopped asking.

Jerry had fourteen arraignments, all scheduled before one Hon. Lyon Trippe.

Jerry met with the clients in the holding area where the prisoners are locked up, and I tagged along. In thirty minutes, Jerry talked to each of the fourteen clients. He'd introduced me quickly, and then moved on to the pitch. The clients each got about two minutes of his time. I paid attention to everything Jerry did, but I especially paid attention to what the clients said. Their situations were identical but unique at the same time. I was fascinated.

"The judge will ask you how you plead after the prosecutor

reads the charge. You will say not guilty. At that point, I will ask the judge to review your bail."

There was no time to take many questions.

Jerry was used to this job. Because I was so interested, I could tell that he was burned out. To him, these were just people who had been caught committing a crime and claimed they had no funds to hire private counsel. He did not seem to take them as his clients. I could be totally wrong, but I don't think so. With volume like this, how can you properly represent a client? I stayed positive. It was way too early to get negative.

I especially noticed one of the clients whose name was Luke. He was the squeaky wheel. He complained that the bail they set when he was booked was $25,000 on a petty theft charge.

"I have a job," Luke said. "If I'm not at work tomorrow, I will be fired. I can't post that much bail."

Jerry listened to Luke as he had listened to everyone, but I guess he'd gotten calloused. He must have heard the same story a hundred times. Who to believe? I figured you have to believe your client if you had to convince the judge your client was truthful about everything and that their words have merit.

I was watching the door and saw the crowd inside.

"The courtroom is packed," I said, just before we went in.

"Arraignment court always is," Jerry said.

Jerry introduced me to the judge in open court. I felt a little flattered when the Honorable Lyon Trippe welcomed me to his courtroom as a new member of the bar. I should have been nervous, but I wasn't. I guess I've been performing for so long that there was no shy left in me. The courtroom was full of a random collection of people. I got the feeling they were all nervous, intense and respectful. In the back of my brain, I hoped I'd never meet up with a judge who had seen my pussy.

I had been silent this whole time, as Jerry had told me to be. Jerry was on his feet, with me sitting next to him, minding my manners, and paying attention with every fiber of my being. When they called Luke's case, I listened carefully to the fast dialogue among the DA and the judge and Jerry. I could see Luke was sweating bullets and watching the legal professionals back and forth like a tennis match.

"Do you waive the reading of the charges of petty theft?" the DA asked.

"Luke Washington waives the reading of the entire document," Jerry said.

"Is that correct, Mr. Washington?" asked the judge.

"Yes, your honor."

"How do you plead to the charge of petty theft, shoplifting at Robinson's Department Store?"

"Not guilty," Luke said.

"I'll set the preliminary hearing for three weeks from today. Does that work?" Judge Trippe asked Jerry and the DA.

Both agreed the date was good.

"Your honor, on bail, my client respectfully requests that you reduce the amount to a more affordable amount," Jerry said.

"Any objections?" Judge Trippe asked the DA.

"We recommend twenty thousand," the DA said.

Jerry didn't argue.

"Bail is set for fifteen thousand," the judge said.

"Judge, I can make five thousand," Luke said. "I talked to a bail bondsman."

"Bail is set to fifteen thousand," the judge said.

I got up, side-by-side with Jerry.

"Your honor, may I be heard on the matter of bail?"

I felt Jerry turn to look at me. My eyes were on the judge. The judge had already ruled, and I figured Jerry couldn't be any angrier than the judge. I didn't know much court protocol, but for sure, you don't argue with the judge. You wait until the next hearing and bring it up.

"Counsel, go ahead on bail," Judge Trippe said.

Counsel. That was me. For a second, my confidence drained, at least until I started talking. I knew he was giving me a break because I was wet behind the ears. A virgin lawyer, at least until I left the courtroom today.

"Your honor, our client has a job he will lose if he doesn't show up for work tomorrow. This is his first offense. He's never been in trouble before. He has a wife who is pregnant. I respectfully request that you release him on his own recognizance."

The judge was smirking. Okay, well maybe the smirk was a smile. He asked the DA if he had any objection. I felt like a toddler taking my first few steps, but the end of the road looked miles away, a swimmer, too many strokes to the edge of the pool.

Jerry was silent, his expression anything but encouraging. I think he wanted to choke me.

The DA said, "Your honor, I haven't verified that this is his first offense."

"A few minutes ago, you recommended bail at twenty thousand," Judge Trippe said. "How can you make an informed recommendation if you don't have the defendant's rap sheet?"

"Sorry your honor. The case was just handed to me this morning."

"Mr. Washington have you ever been arrested before for any reason?" Judge Trippe asked.

"No, your honor, I have not."

"If I release you on your own recognizance, do you promise to return three weeks from today? Will you return on all dates set by the court until this matter is resolved?"

Luke Washington swallowed. It looked like he was having trouble with his emotions. I felt deeply empathetic, teared up myself, but I think I managed to hide it.

"Yes, your honor. I promise."

"Defendant will be released on his own recognizance," the judge ordered.

"Thank you, your Honor," I said. I sat down, feeling humble and grateful.

Jerry said, "Thank you, your Honor."

I could not read his expression.

"Call the next case," the judge said.

Not all of our cases were called in order. It took three hours with one ten-minute recess in which I went to the ladies' room to defer Jerry's chewing me out. We were done at noon.

At noon, we walked upstairs to the office.

"You got lucky with the judge. If he had cut you off, it would have been very embarrassing for you, for me and for our office. You can't grandstand."

"Last thing I want is to make waves," I said. "I'm sorry if I embarrassed you. That was not my intention. When you didn't bring up it being the client's first arrest, I figured you missed it. I felt like I needed to say something."

"I'm not embarrassed, and I'm not pissed," Jerry said. "Tomorrow, try and sit still and watch. As soon as I think you are ready, I will set you free to take the load off."

"Thanks, Jerry. I'll spring for lunch if you'd like."

"We have a lot of paperwork on the cases we just arraigned. We may have a peek at what is scheduled so far for tomorrow."

"Are you saying we're not having lunch?" I wasn't complaining but it must have sounded that way. Jerry laughed. It was the first time I heard him laugh.

"Let's hit the cafeteria," he said, "Sometimes their soup is good."

We sat next to a window overlooking the run-down neighborhood, parking lots everywhere. The state of California building had been demolished, and the lot had been vacant for long time. The Hall of Records needed a facelift, and some tagger had obliged.

"Do they let them paint the walls or they do it at night?"

Jerry said, "Both. If the work is nice, they don't paint over it. That one has been there a while."

I smiled. "It caught my eye."

The good thing about my massage business is that my office is my phone. I spent fifteen hundred dollars for a Panasonic cell phone. I've been wanting a cell phone. The one I got is big but fits in my purse. The service is expensive, you pay per call and even pay for calls coming in. I don't get that many calls, but I love how available it makes me to my clients. Gabi refuses to get one. She says she won't carry around a brick.

I have no advertising. It is all word of mouth. The three clients from the spa I worked in started recommending me. I give out business cards with my name, license number and phone every chance I get. I use public bulletin boards. At the market where I shop, three of my cards are on the bulletin board, and also at two gyms near the apartment. I got a client call right after I first posted my card, and now, he's a regular. I don't make advance appointments. I ask them to call me on the day they want a massage or sometimes I can book for the next day to keep me free if I need to do something else and to avoid the client calling to cancel or reschedule. I probably lose some business because of this, but the freedom is worth it to me. Gabi says it makes no sense to her. For me, being spontaneous is best.

Macho told me to keep my figure as it is, not to gain or lose weight.

"You are perfect as you are."

I didn't think I was perfect. I thought I had too much ass, but if Macho said I was perfect, I wasn't about to argue with him.

"You'll make a lot of money with me. Next year, I may send you to the Cannes Film Festival. A girl like you, you'll come back with a ton of money."

After we shook hands on the deal, Macho gave me a whole night of coaching. His phone rang non-stop, but he made time for me, and offered to advance me money to buy clothes. I told him I was set. He said he'd ask me for permission to fuck me, but he doesn't do it with anyone associated with him. Just his telling me that got me wet. Forbidden fruit, I guess.

"It's too bad. I bet you are hot stuff."

I was in the center of his designer living room when he said to take off my clothes. I didn't just shuck them. I got a tall stool from under his kitchen counter and used it as a prop, tossing my clothes on it as I undressed. And I didn't just undress. I did a careful striptease, while maintaining hot eye contact, peeling down stockings, turning my back and sliding down my blouse while looking over my shoulder, propping one leg up to unbuckle my heels, the works. The shoes were last. When I was done, I was naked except for a garter belt, thong, and a plain black choker that had my house key on it. I froze, one leg propped up on the chair, the other bare, tiptoe on the floor. I was leaning forward, and my hands on my right ankle, still with the hot eye contact, about three feet from his face.

He said nothing for about thirty seconds. I held the pose as he walked around me, looking me over. He gave me a sharp slap on my ass, and then came up against me, pressed his body against my ass.

He pushed my head forward until my back was parallel to the floor. I had to grab the stool, but I didn't lose my balance. His hands moved to my hips. I could feel the hard ridge demonstrating that his interest was real, but he didn't have sex with me. He put his hands on my shoulders and pulled me upright, using his body to keep my balance. One foot was still pointed on the chair, and my hands were gripping the top of the stool.

He went back to his couch, sat down, and leaned forward, one hand to his chin in the 'thinking' position.

"Turn," he said.

I stepped to one side instead of backing away from him and turned.

"Slower."

I did as he said.

The third time, I turned very slowly.

"Stop shaving your legs and underarms. Get waxed."

He explained how much pubic hair to leave. "Never shave it all off."

I had thought it a waste of money and I had heard it hurt like hell, but at least I knew now why Gabi went to a salon.

"Macho will have you spending half of your income on clothes," Gabi said.

She wasn't far off. I bought three complete outfits to work Macho's clients, from shoes to purses, and they cost a pretty penny. "I don't know about half, but if I make enough, I'll buy what I need. I wish we wore the same size. I'd buy some of your stuff."

"My clothes aren't for sale."

"I didn't mean anything by it. Just that with your lawyer job now, you're not wearing most of the good stuff."

"Not to the office. I got a life. I need my clothes."

Gabi can be grouchy. I do love her though.

While Gabi was at work, Macho's photographer arrived. He took pictures for more than two hours. I kept changing clothes, Macho wasn't after nude pictures. He was after pictures of a model in expensive clothes. There were several nude shots. The plan was that once the photos were with Macho, I would start working. I signed a model agency contract. Gabi had told me Macho put it in writing. He must have a good reason to want contracts with the women he represents.

Macho sent me off on my first modeling session. That's what he called it. I was told to call him my agent. The client was forty or so. When he opened the door, he gave me a friendly hug.

"I am Buddy," he said. He was wearing a hotel robe.

"My name is Ann," I said.

I took off my full length Dior coat that had set me back two thousand dollars. It was a perfect coat for Los Angeles. It would never work back home in Dallas where it gets really cold in winter and way too hot in summer. Underneath, I was wearing a fitted peach-colored cashmere sweater, matching skirt, and a colorful leather cummerbund, with undertones of peach. Purse and shoes matched the belt. You can picture how soft and fitted it was. Cashmere is like a furry second skin. I bent down to adjust my stiletto, and as I stood, let my hands slide up my legs, so that the already short skirt hitched up a little.

He gave a whistle and ran a hand over my hip where the fabric had just gathered.

"You are gorgeous, Ann."

"You too, Buddy."

"Want payment now?"

"No need."

"Good girl," he said. "I have beer and wine if you are interested."

"Do you have a Coke?"

"I don't," he said.

"No problem, Buddy. I'm cool."

"Are you nervous?" he asked.

"Not at all."

"Good. I'm one of the good guys. You don't have to worry."

"That's good to hear," I said with a little laugh. "What's the plan?" I said, reaching for the clasp of the cummerbund to take it off.

He stopped me.

"Ann, wait. I want to do something I been thinking about. Humor me."

"Sure, Buddy. What's your pleasure?"

"Lift your skirt and let me see your ass. I'm an ass man."

I've always been a little worried about my ass. There's more of it than I like, but I didn't hesitate. I turned around and pulled the cashmere up. I felt a tug, and my thong dropped to my ankles. I started to kick off my shoes. He put his hand on my forearm to stop me.

"Ann, leave those pretty shoes on."

"Sure," I said.

I felt a kiss right at the crack of my ass, a fast, little kiss. I got a chill.

"Here's what I'd like. Leave your skirt up and lean over the bed, lie down and raise your ass. I will stand behind you at the edge of the bed."

Buddy took his robe off. He was big, and he was hard.

I stepped out of my thong and left it on the floor. I could feel him watching my ass as I walked over to the bed, turned so we were face to face, and touched him. As I watched him put on a condom, I could tell he was impatient for me to bend over. The soft cashmere was still clinging to my hips as I turned my back to him, slid up my sleeves, and went face down on the bed. I felt him grip my hips, pull my ass upward and toward him. He touched between my legs with his hand, pressed one finger deep, then two.

"No need for lubricant." He sounded pleased.

He was right. I was soaking wet.

He entered me. I thought he was all the way in, but he pushed in another several inches. He began moving in and out of me. I came noisily several times.

Each time I did, he said, "You're a hot one."

He did me for over thirty minutes. My clothes were damp from perspiration, but my body was feeling really good, if you know what I mean.

"May I shower really quick? It's okay if you say no," I said.

Buddy laughed.

"Ann, be my guest. Take your time. There's a real nice bathtub if you want to use it."

I kissed his cheek. He redirected my mouth to his lips.

"You have a fine ass, Ann. I need to request you again when I'm back in town."

"Love to," I said. "Work it out with Macho."

When I left, he gave me five hundred dollars plus a hundred tip.

I would have had to do a lot of massages to match this. I wouldn't always luck out with a good fuck like Buddy, but it was a fast way to earn money. I wasn't giving it away anymore.

I called Macho to tell him I was done and ask what was next.

"Go home and relax. Tomorrow is another night."

"Are you sure?"

"I'm sure."

I didn't get a goodbye in. He hung up.

I got home early enough to catch Gabi awake. I told her about my call and how he hung up.

She laughed.

"That's how he is. He's not angry if that's what you are worried about. I bet he called Buddy to find out if everything went okay."

"He does that?"

"Customer service is what keeps him on top. He does that."

"It went okay. Want to hear about it?"

"Sweets, you can tell it to me when you go to bed later. I'm hitting it now."

"I'm tired, too." I was still pumped full of adrenaline. I wasn't really tired. "I wanted Macho to send me on another modeling thing."

"I wish you weren't doing this," Gabi said.

I bet she'd said it so many times to me, she was tired of hearing herself.

"I righteously don't have a problem with it," I said.

"In that case, I righteously don't have a problem with it either," she said with a huge yawn.

I showered again and went to Gabi's bed.

Her bedroom was pitch black and totally silent. She insists on a totally dark bedroom. If there was an earthquake and the power went out, we would have a problem finding the door to get the hell out of there. In my bedroom that is right next to hers, I have two nightlights going at night.

I always worry about earthquakes, especially at night. Maybe it's because I'm not from California.

"Are you asleep? Do you want me to go to my own bed?" I whispered.

I heard sheets rustle. It sounded like she was patting the bed.

"Come keep me warm, sweets."

I cuddled up to her. She smelled like the fragrance she always wore, Ralph Lauren. The sheets smelled fresh out of the dryer. With both of us working, splitting the household chores and a maid coming in weekly, the apartment was probably the nicest place I've ever lived in. It's sure better than the crowded, chaotic hen house I'd lived in when I was stewardessing.

"You got to promise that when you want me to get my own apartment, you will tell me. I still have money in the bank. Even without Macho, you know I do okay with my massage business."

"Why do you bring that up now?" Gabi asked, rolling over to face me.

"It's the Macho business. I'm not familiar with it. What if it brings heat to where the hooker lives? I'm the hooker, and I'm in your home, and you got a job with a badge. I don't want to get you in any trouble."

Gabi sat up. I followed. We faced each other in darkness.

"As long as you don't bring jobs here, I'll be fine. From now on, I will give you a receipt for your monthly rent and you write me a check. No more cash. If anything ever comes up, you're my roommate, you're a therapist who models part-time, and that's all."

I hugged my friend.

"Thank you, Gabi. I've been worried about that."

"It's good to worry. It keeps you on your toes. If Macho sends you, there won't be a cop where you are going. No entrapment waiting to happen."

"I understand."

We lay back down.

"Want to hear what this stud I saw tonight wanted?"

"Stud?"

"Well, you know, dude, guy. His name is Buddy."

"Yeah, like my name is Oprah," Gabi said with a laugh. "Tell me but don't get mad if I fall asleep before you finish."

"I never get mad at you," I said.

I touched her and she was wet.

"Gab, when do you plan to get laid?"

I didn't get an answer and realized that she was asleep already. I got out of bed as quietly as I could and managed to find the door. The little night light in the hallway led me to my room.

I went to bed and organized my thoughts. Gabi had told me the stories about her work hours with Macho. I knew if I kept working with Macho, I would have to learn how to sleep days because business was nights. If I got comfortable and secure with Macho, I had to give up my massage business. I don't see how I could do both, unless I split the job like Gabi used to, and only did massages during the week. All I knew is that some of my massage clients were two-hour massages. That's work. I'd be exhausted if I went from doing a two-hour massage to a client like Buddy who pounded me for thirty minutes. No matter how good it was, I would have to bluff. I gave myself a month to see how it went.

December 1988
Los Angeles, California
Gabi

Jerry and I were having lunch on Olvera Street, a long walk from the criminal courthouse but it took more time to drive. We had taquitos, four each. I ate chicken taquitos. His were beef, loaded with guacamole. Both of us had *Aguas Frescas*. I had tamarindo and he had watermelon.

We walked outside to sit on a wooden bench that has been there longer than the years Jerry and I have both been alive, added together. The place was famous for their taquitos. It had been chilly at first but after the brisk walk, I was feeling pretty good. I had walking shoes on, and my court shoes were stowed in a drawer in my desk. Lucky for me, my sleek leather trench coat was warmer than it looked. Jerry was wearing a coat that looked more substantial, but the tip of his nose was turning a little pink.

I carried a small journal where I kept important notes, thoughts, and reminders. In addition to all these other things, I kept track of how many arraignments we did every day. I opened it and put it on the table to thumb through as I was eating. I'd been working with Jerry for five weeks. Thirty-five days.

I put away my journal. Jerry had bought a copy of the LA Times and was going through it fast.

"We've done four hundred and one arraignments," I told Jerry.

Jerry laughed. "What are you doing? Keeping score?"

"Keeping track. Imagine a criminal lawyer in private practice getting paid to do four hundred and one arraignments in five weeks."

Jerry said, "We're getting paid."

I'd gotten to know him pretty well.

"I mean, really paid."

He looked at me.

"I know what you mean. These are just arraignments, a tiny piece of most cases. The cases still have a lot of work ahead."

"I know," I said.

"I'm not making a pass," Jerry said. "You are way too pretty to be a public defender."

I knew how to do a sexy laugh, and that's what I gave him.

"We have a bunch of pretty ladies at the PD office, but I'm more interested in knowing how I am doing as a deputy PD."

Jerry made his big announcement like it was nothing.

"We'll know next week. I plan to let you handle some of the arraignments while I sit by and do what you been doing."

I whooped aloud. Some of the people around us looked my way and smiled.

I stretched both hands across the table and grabbed both of his while they were holding open the sports section.

"Jerry, that means so much to me."

I was smiling all the way back to the courthouse.

December 1988

The courtroom was as crowded as ever. Jerry was beside me, silent. Across the aisle was the DDA,[2] Johnson.

"Your honor, our client waives reading of the entire complaint and is ready to enter a plea."

"Mr. Gardener, how do you plead to one count of grand theft?"

"Not guilty."

"Let's check the calendar, Counsel. Three weeks is rough for preliminary. Does Mr. Gardener waive his rights to speedy trial?"

"Your Honor, he's in custody, bail is fifty thousand. We can't waive at this time."

"Okay. Three weeks from today in Division four. Any objections?"

"Not for us," I answered for the PD Office.

DDA Johnson had no objection.

"On the matter of bail, what do we have?" the judge asked.

"Your Honor, we request bail to be set at one hundred thousand. Mr. Gardener has three prior arrests for grand theft auto and a long list of other arrests. We consider him a flight risk if he is released on bail."

The judge looked at me.

"Your Honor, Mr. Gardener has a number of arrests, it's true. However, he has no convictions except for a DUI five years ago to which he pled guilty. He was never found guilty on the grand theft charges. I respectfully request that your Honor consider reducing the bail amount to a more reasonable amount that our client may be able to post."

The judge's decision was rapid. I had learned that's how Judge

---

[2] Deputy District Attorney

Bailey ruled. "Bail is set at twenty-five thousand dollars. Everyone is ordered back in three weeks for the preliminary hearing."

"Thank you, your honor," I said.

This was my fifth case that morning. Jerry had not gotten up from his chair to bail me out or help in any way. On the surface, everything was wonderful, but every man I saw in the courthouse sent my mind reeling. I tried to remember if I had ever seen him before. They all looked familiar, from the shiftiest con to the judges that sat in arraignment court. I wonder how much longer I'm going to be haunted by fear of recognition. I'm not stupid. There is no proof that I had sex with anyone and got paid for it. My word against the accuser.

Why do I worry?

November 1989
Los Angeles, California
Mona

I didn't make a big deal out of killing my massage business. When I got a massage call, I told the client I was going away for a short time and that I would be in touch when I returned. I wasn't sure yet if it would be six months, a year or ever. Eventually I stopped getting calls. I didn't bother going around to remove my business cards. I figured that they got thrown out anyway, before long.

Macho gave me one project a night, and I was okay with that. I got home early most of the time. I went to sleep only a little later than usual. I tried to be very quiet when I came in so that I wouldn't bother Gabi, and often I tiptoed into my bedroom without turning on any lights to keep from disturbing her. I set my alarm early so I could fix breakfast for her in the morning, though most mornings, breakfast was just black coffee and toast. Her days started early. After she left, I'd go back to bed and sleep until I thought I had enough.

After a year, I was still living with Gabi. I purchased very expensive clothes and that put me into the model escort category with Macho. A client called wanting a hot looker to attend a party with him and after, anything goes. Attending a party with a client paying two thousand for the night meant a big affair of some kind. My clothes and makeup and how I carried myself was of great importance to Macho.

I did well. He kept giving me that kind of work when it came up. I accumulated a substantial amount of cash during the year, and I occasionally deposited the cash in the bank knowing that I would have to file a tax return just as I did when I was on payroll with Max. Filing a tax return helped me maintain the credit I had, namely credit cards. My credit history from Texas followed me to California. If I needed to buy a car again, I didn't plan on paying cash like I did my first car after I got the fifty thousand from Max. I would buy it on credit. If I moved to my own apartment, my credit check would be better than average because earnings play a big part in how the credit companies evaluate a person.

"I can't remember the last time I paid any serious taxes," Gabi told me. "I only bank what is absolutely necessary to pay my rent and car. The rest I always kept in cash. I didn't file taxes for the two years I was with judge. I never asked if he was writing it off as some kind of service or as a gift or what. Not like me to be so stupid."

I said, "I filed late before when I worked for Max. You pay a penalty and that's it."

"For now, I'm going to defer filing tax returns. The taxes on ten grand a month for two years could wipe me out. I pay tax on the money I put in the bank. I use the cash I keep stashed for shopping and to sit there as security. My stash."

I've done well in the fourteen months I've been at the PD office. Because I am doing more important work like filing motions on behalf of our clients, I've been bumped up to a larger office with more access to an assistant and investigators who worked for the deputies. I've handled three trials without a jury, two of them with Jerry sitting second chair and one with only me and a newbie. The PD office is so busy, you can advance quickly. Jerry's recommendations and laudatory reports have been a tremendous help in my advancement.

I had a twenty-eight-year-old client, Tim, who was busted with a gallon bag of marijuana in the trunk of his car. He was charged with possession with intent to sell and distribute, a serious felony. He had one prior conviction for joyriding, a charge reduced from grand theft auto. He served two months in the county jail and one-year probation. He fulfilled his probation. Two years later, a cop stopped him because his right taillight was out. After he was pulled over, officers searched the vehicle and found the stash. I filed an illegal search motion asking that the case be thrown out based on the unlawful search without probable cause or having a search warrant.

"Show me your colors," Jerry said. "I think he's lying so best you handle it."

"If you weren't married, I'd give you the best blow job you've ever gotten," I told Jerry the day he gave me the case. We flirted hard-core, but it was just talk. He reminded me of the fast food manager I'd had as a kid, where I kept my promise of giving him a hand job, a quid quo pro, for sure. I have not fucked him and had no plans to do so, but we had a dirty, flirty mode of conversation.

My client, Tim, had a dirty mouth but was soft-spoken. He flirted. I didn't flirt back. He and I were in court, and Jerry was not in court with us. The first officer on the stand stated that he pulled Tim over for the brake light being out. During the stop, Tim seemed nervous, and that resulted in the search.

"You know that Tim's nervousness is not probable cause for a search. How long have you been with the LAPD?"

"Eight years."

"Officer Hanley, you know better."

The second officer was anxious. He reminded me of a sex client trying not to blush or show his uneasiness once I was naked and ready to attend to his needs.

"Officer Blake, you were in the passenger seat. Did you observe the right brake light off on my client's car? And before you answer this, please keep in mind you are under oath."

Officer Blake was quiet.

"Mr. Blake, did you understand the question from counsel?"

"Yes," he replied.

"Please answer the question," the judge said.

"I don't think the light was out," he spoke in a low voice into the microphone.

"Please repeat that a little louder," I said.

The judge interrupted. "I heard him, counsel."

"Officer Blake, why then did you stop my client's car?"

He hesitated again.

"I believe we made a mistake," Blake replied.

"Who decided to stop the car, you or your partner?"

"Both of us," he said. I knew he was lying, and so did the judge.

"That will be all, Mr. Blake. Thank you."

"Your honor, I move that the entire case against my client be dismissed. The only evidence in this case is the bag of marijuana that was found as a result of an illegal search."

The judge addressed the Deputy DA. "Mr. Blossom, do you have anything to add?"

Blossom looked embarrassed, but this was not the first time an officer had lied.

"Nothing to add, your Honor."

"Motion to dismiss is granted," the judge said and banged his gavel.

"Thank you, your Honor," I said. "Can my client have a court release and not have to return to County?"

"Sheriff will release the defendant forthwith."

"Your Honor, thank you," I said.

When I walked back to the office, my panties were wet with excitement. (If you are wondering about my panties being wet with excitement, they were. A woman can get off without touching. I can.) I love this work. I love to win on behalf of my clients. I walked upstairs to Jerry's office. The clerk must have called to tell him the results because he was standing up and clapping. My assistant Betty had come in, and she too was clapping. Betty returned to her duties. I sat down across from Jerry.

"Do we go after a cop when he lies?" I asked.

"The DA won't do it. It's a nothing case. If this case got publicity, a DA might make noise and get the officer suspended for a while without pay."

"Seems like an officer who takes the oath should honor the oath. If he lies, damn, it can't be right. If I was a Deputy DA, I wouldn't let him off that easy."

Jerry laughed. "Yeah you would. Deputy DA is too busy to jail a cop who was doing his job getting bad guys off the street."

"You're thinking like a PD."

"Of course," Jerry said. "Are you ready for another good case?"

"I am," I said.

It was Friday afternoon. Everything but me was winding down. I was turned on. I didn't tell Jerry. I couldn't remember the last time I had sex. If it wasn't for Mona, I'd be a train wreck. Too bad sex isn't stored like a battery. If that were true, I've had enough sex for a lifetime. But I like sex. I missed it so much, I went home and called Macho. Normally Macho sent hugs and hellos with Mona when she went over to settle her business, and I sent my hugs and hellos back with her. I hadn't talked to him for a while.

"Last year, you sent me a masseuse, Roger. Remember?"

"I remember. It was my treat."

"Is he still connected with you?"

"What time you want him?"

"Eight," I said.

I let security downstairs know he was coming, not that my life is anybody's business. I figured the massage table Roger would be packing would be self-explanatory. When I had sessions in Mona's room, I would meet the client at the parking gate, punch in the code, direct him to park in my second parking spot, and we'd come up the elevator together without stopping at the lobby level.

Mona was getting ready to work that night when I told her I had ordered a therapist.

"I don't know him," she said. "But I can make time to do that for you."

She was sitting in front of a makeup mirror and putting on her work face. I kissed the top of her head, her face and gave her a nibble on her left ear.

"You do everything for me. I love you," I said. "But I want to feel a big dick inside me. This dude Roger is a hammer."

"Okay, have fun. I have a session at eight."

"That's early," I said.

"You know how it goes."

"I do," I said, remembering my past, not so long ago at all. I kept working practically until I was sworn in. I'm a nut case.

Roger arrived with his massage table and a friendly smile. I did not remember him being as fit as he was. Maybe he'd been working out for a year, or maybe it was the job that made him fit.

"I'm all yours for the next four hours. Want to begin with a massage or the other?" he asked, just as before.

"Other," I replied, walking toward my bedroom. "Leave the table."

He followed me into my room.

I never got a massage. For three hours, we had sex every imaginable way possible. The down comforter was on the floor, the sheets were mostly off the bed, and both of us were lying there, exhausted, wearing nothing but the smiles on our faces.

"You got an hour left," Roger said. "Let me give you a massage."

"Not a chance. I don't think I can walk. Hand me my purse. It's right over there."

Roger got to his feet. I watched him. He was a good-looking

guy with the kind of body that looked better without clothes. I remember when I'd first asked for Macho to send someone. I'd wanted someone who didn't talk much. He certainly lived up to that. "Over there," I pointed again to my purse.

"It's on Macho. Sorry." He picked his clothes up off the floor, and, still naked, gave a sharp bow, like a dancer, and a curl of floppy dark hair fell over his eye. He shook his head and brushed it back.

"Roger, not fair."

"He's paying me. I'm good."

"Are you sure I can't give you a tip?"

"I'm sure."

He carried his clothes with him into the bathroom and took a shower while I fell asleep. I felt a wash of air float over me as he wafted the top sheet over me, and then the comforter. I heard the door close. I don't know how much time passed before I forced myself out of bed and went to the bathroom to clean up. I lay in a tub full of hot bubbles, thinking how I should have let him give me that massage. Even without it, I felt better. Three hours in bed used to be nothing for me. I'd be asking Macho for my next gig, but now, my life was different. I worked hard in other ways. Defending a client as I did today is very stressful. I found warm flannel pajamas in my dresser, a Christmas gift from Aunt Isabel, and pulled them on.

When Mona closed the front door, my clock was flashing 3:15. Mona opened my door to check in on me. The door creaked softly, and I could hear her breathing.

"Are you done for the night?" I asked.

"Yes. I'm sorry if I woke you," she said.

"I'm a little restless."

Mona sat on the edge of my bed. The only light was from my clock, not enough for me to see anything.

"Was it good?"

"Roger is a specialist," I said with a sleepy laugh. "How was your night?"

"I had two dates, all good."

"Mona, come sleep with me when you turn in, please."

"Give me fifteen. I'll be back."

"I'm lonely."

Mona leaned in and kissed my cheek.

"Not for long."

I wished she had not taken up with Macho. She claimed she didn't mind the work. I had felt that way when I was working. Every session, I hoped I'd get a special person, and most times I didn't.

Mona got in bed, spooning me. She kissed the back of my neck, sending chills through my body. She was kissing my ear when I went out.

Saturday morning, Mona was still beside me. It was close to nine. On a weekday, I would be in the office.

"Want to go for breakfast or sleep in?"

Mona opened her eyes. Smiled. "Let's eat at Sandcastle."

Twenty minutes later, we were in my car headed down Wilshire Boulevard to Santa Monica then Pacific Coast Highway to Malibu. The restaurant was on the sand, and open for breakfast, lunch and dinner. I ordered a Denver omelet and a side of crispy bacon. Mona had steak and eggs. There was more food than we could eat, and we stowed the extra breakfast bread in a bag in the car.

Truth be told, it was a good thing we'd dressed warmly. We walked along the beach for a while. It was brisk, but the ocean is always invigorating.

"I'm sorry I didn't let you sleep," I said.

"I'm good," Mona said. "I didn't go to bed that late."

I laughed. "It was four."

"I'll take a nap this afternoon."

I told her about my motion win the day before.

"Lucky for me, Roger is still with Macho. It's been a year since the last time."

"Nobody leaves Macho," Mona said. "Like, he doesn't kill you, he just stays on you until you come back just like he did you after you left your judge."

"You're right. I did leave Macho and came back. When he knew I wanted to leave, he said to go. I love that grump."

"Me too," Mona said. "You're special. You're the queen. Macho loves you big time."

"He says that?"

"All the time," she said.

"We did it once before I worked for him, then never again. He never touched me after that first time."

"He told me the same thing. Doesn't stop him from rubbing up against me. Doesn't get past that. Does he have a big one? When he presses against me, I feel it. I wonder."

"Been long time, but he knows how to please a woman. That, I remember."

"You blushed," Mona said.

I smiled at her. "You know I do that."

"Macho said I have a jeans ass, whatever that means," Mona said.

I took a step back and watched Mona take a few steps. She has a fine ass, a jeans ass for sure. We were walking where the sand was hard and wet. She didn't slow down, and I had to run a few steps to catch up. We headed back and spent a couple of extra minutes getting the sand off so that we didn't track it into the car. My Ferrari was not the only one in the parking lot. Malibu equals money.

We got back in the car and headed toward home.

"You dig the work, huh?" I asked Mona.

"Yeah, I dig it. I like to fuck, and to get paid for it. I'm kind of an exhibitionist. When I undress in front of a dude, I get a thrill. Has nothing to do with the looks of the dude."

We giggled together, then Mona yawned.

"Looks aren't everything," I said, remembering Alex.

I went silent, remembering Alex Rose, his hole in the wall apartment, the people he would drag in off the street. Everything about that time was horrible, but if I hadn't been through it, would I be a lawyer now? I started to say something, but she let out a soft snore. My passenger was asleep.

March 1990

Motorola came out with a flip phone half the size of Mona's cell phone. The MicroTac was still a brick, but I was lured by the convenience. It was cool to stay in touch without having to find a phone to call someone. Reception wasn't always good, but I tested different areas at the courthouse and in my office. There were good spots and not-so-good spots. Most the time, reception in my car wasn't bad. Using it was a learning experience. I learned where not to initiate a call from.

My client, Manolo Sanchez, was fifty-five years old, a widower. He was in court for a violation of probation. His probation officer recommended to the judge that probation be revoked, and Manolo be sent to spend a year in the county jail, the original sentence that had been suspended. The original charge had been drunk driving. Manolo had failed his probation officer's drug test.

"One of the conditions of probation," the DA said, "was that Manolo Sanchez could not drink any alcohol or take any drugs not prescribed by his physician. We concur with the probation officer's recommendation that bail be revoked and Mr. Sanchez be remanded into custody to serve the original sentence of one year in the county jail."

"Your Honor," I said. "As far as the barbiturates are concerned, we have a letter from his doctor stating he prescribed pain medication to Mr. Sanchez because he's worn away the cartilage of his knees, and he has succumbed to arthritis. This morning I gave the letter to the probation officer, the district attorney, and your clerk. Mr. Sanchez admits he has a drinking problem and will return to AA immediately if your honor will reinstate his probation."

"Your Honor, if he knew he has a problem, why didn't he start AA before he violated his probation?" the DA asked. "He can attend AA while serving his time at the county jail."

"Your Honor, my client has a good job which he will lose. He's a good man with an admitted problem of alcoholism. Your consideration to reinstate will be greatly appreciated by my client."

With his sternest expression, the judge stared at my client.

"Mr. Sanchez, you have a problem. You know it. Why did you not seek help? I should have ordered you to attend AA as a condition of probation, but I didn't know you had a problem. I was under the impression the drunk driving resulted from bad judgment when you were out with friends."

"Your Honor, if I can speak?" Mr. Sanchez spoke up. He was dressed in a cheap suit, and smelled of inexpensive aftershave, but he was clean, and clean-shaven. He stood with his hands clutching each other nervously, but with a contrite expression on his face.

"Go ahead."

"I promise Your Honor I will attend AA no matter what you do today. If it is available in jail, I will join the group there. If you release me, I will join AA immediately. I promise never to be back here on a violation again."

The judge looked at the Deputy DA.

"Anything further?"

"We rest on the matter as previously stated, your honor."

It was my turn.

"Your Honor, I respectfully request that you extend my client mercy one more time. He's sick and admits it. I believe that is the first step."

The judge looked down at some papers that were in front of him. It was probably only an instant, but it felt like a long wait. I could hear people behind me in the crowd getting restless.

"I am modifying the probation order," the judge said, "to include that the defendant will join AA within forty-eight hours from today and provide proof to the probation officer of doing so. Furthermore, he must provide proof to the probation officer each month that he's attended no less than two meetings per week. Probation is reinstated and defendant shall be released from custody forthwith."

"Thank you, your Honor," I said.

I shook hands with the Deputy DA. "He'll be back," he said to me in a low voice.

"No, he won't," I said. Of course, neither of us knew for sure.

I had two other hearings that day. The public defender's office is crazy busy.

I sent my accountant the W2 of my first year's income with the public defender's office. The taxes deducted from my paycheck were insane.

"You don't have dependents. If you did, you'd be paying less."

"Am I going to get a refund like everyone else does?"

"Not everyone else get a refund. I'll call you when I have a tax return draft. Consider buying a house or condo. You can write off the interest, taxes and maybe you can have a home office that you need for work. We can work that in and save something there."

I loved my apartment. If it was a condo, I'd try to swing a purchase. I received the forms from the accountant in the mail and mailed them in with checks. I was in pain for two days. I got over it. The taxes withheld did not cover what I owed the internal revenue and franchise tax board.

"If I knew I could get away with it, I'd moonlight with Macho on the weekends for the extra money."

"I have money," Mona said. "Will that help?"

"I barely broke even with what I pay out and what I bring home from work."

"Gabi, raise my rent. I'm cool with that."

I hugged her.

"No way," I said. "Your being here is a big fringe benefit."

Mona was getting ready for work. She was already dressed in some short oriental-looking red dress. She sat down in front of the makeup mirror. Our eyes met in the glass.

"Cheer up. Go to a movie. A nightclub. Maybe you'll see a guy you want to bring home."

"Imagine if my past gets out. How the dude will feel knowing that Gabi has been laid by thousands of men?" I asked.

"Don't exaggerate," Mona laughed. "Go to a movie. Some good ones are playing down at the village."

I ignored her. I said, "I've been thinking of going in for a consult about this vaginal rejuvenation that doctors are doing now. It tightens your pussy."

Mona stopped what she was doing and looked at me over her makeup mirror.

"Are you saying the vinegar Macho swears about doesn't work?"

"You tell me. You use it too."

Mona got up, laughing.

"Gabi, you are hilarious. Your peers at the office should hear you when you talk like this. What a blast that would be."

When Mona left, I went to my bedroom and put on **In the Line of Fire**, a movie I just bought a few days before. I felt sorry for myself. Maybe a dose of Clint Eastwood would cure me. What a fool. I felt a wave of gloom wash over me.

I remembered Max. I remembered the luxury of a plane ride to Dallas on his bed, two thousand and a grand tip. I wondered what ever happened to him and his marriage. Mona says she's not in touch with anyone in Dallas who knows Max. All we know is what is on the sports page when he's playing. I shouldn't have held him up for the fifty I got. I should have just negotiated with the lawyer for Mona but not for me. Macho got his cut but said it was no big deal.

"Eventually, Max will call me for a hookup," Macho had said. "A guy like him never leaves for good. He likes pussy and he knows I have the best in the business."

I watched Clint, but my head was everywhere except on the screen. At midnight I was tossing and turning. I took a sleeping pill and went out.

My client, Tess, was twenty-one and attending LA City College. She was a pretty girl, slim, and nervous. Her eyes were dark brown, her hair was straight and black, and she wore it in a pony-tail. Her parents lived in Wisconsin and sent her five hundred dollars a month to help out. She worked part-time at Dupars Restaurant as a waitress for minimum wage, but she said her tips were okay. The TV she'd bought for fifty dollars at a pawn shop finally showed its last picture. She wrote a check in the amount of two hundred forty-five dollars to Fry's Electronics for a small television. She sent out five checks on the same day to pay monthly bills that totaled just under five hundred dollars, the amount her parents sent her on the first of the month like religion. Her checks bounced. She was arrested for writing checks with non-sufficient funds. The charge was for the Fry's check, not the others.

"This all started four months ago when my dad had a heart attack. He survived, but he was in the hospital for a week and laid up for a while after that."

"You didn't get your five hundred, so all your checks bounced." I said.

"Exactly. That wasn't all. The bank closed my account, just like that," she snapped her fingers. "And when I went in to find out why, the operations officer said my account was barely six months old, and they do not tolerate accounts that bounce checks for insufficient funds."

"You have nothing saved?"

"The money I make at the restaurant pays for my books and rent and the money my parents send me I use on the other bare essentials. I have nothing left every month."

"How is your dad now? It's been four months."

"He's okay now. It was rough for my parents for a while. They work for a living, you know."

"That sucks, I mean, your arrest over a two hundred forty-five-dollar check."

"I paid off all my bounced checks with cash I made at work. I tried to pay Fry's, but no one could find the bad check or a record of it."

"You shouldn't write checks unless the money is in the bank," I said.

"I know but I told the salesclerk that my check would not verify that day I issued it, that I expected money in the mail in two days. The clerk laughed and said it takes a long time for a check to get to the bank, and I had nothing to worry about."

"Are you sure you had that conversation with the clerk?"

"I am positive. He was young and friendly, probably a student himself."

My client was out on a one-thousand-dollar bail that her parents arranged to post with a local bondsman. She spent a little over twenty-four hours in county jail until bail was posted. Neither she nor her parents had the funds to pay for a private attorney, and that's how I fit in the picture.

I told Jerry about my client interview.

"There is no intent."

"You need the salesclerk to remember that conversation. I don't remember ever putting up a defense like this on an NSF case."

"Jerry, if the DA doesn't dismiss after I explain, let me do a jury trial."

"Gabi, no."

"Jerry, the DA is not going to dismiss. I know, and you know."

"Bench trial. No jury, not over a check for two hundred forty-five dollars. Besides, you haven't done a jury before on your own."

"Maybe it's time."

"Try the case if you have to. No jury," Jerry said with finality.

The DA offered a plea bargain. It was a misdemeanor, ten days in county jail with credit of one day for time served while waiting for bail, and a one-year summary probation. I took the offer of the plea bargain to my hesitant client.

"If we take this to trial and lose, the judge could give you more time, fine and probation."

"What should I do?"

"As much as I want to try this case because of what you told the clerk, I don't want to take a chance on losing."

"Try the case," Tess said. "I want to win and get my arrest expunged."

"Are you sure?"

"I'm sure."

"Your Honor, the Deputy DA offered my client a plea deal," I said. "But she never intended to defraud Fry's, and I believe we can prove that."

The DA said, "Your Honor, I have the check in evidence with

two stamps on it. Not Sufficient Funds and Account Closed. Fry's redeposited the check after it was returned. The account had been closed. I see intent."

The judge said no more. He read off some dates. We picked a date for trial without a jury.

"Tess, you can still change your mind," I told her as we walked out of the courtroom.

"I need to get out of this without any time in jail, fine or probation."

A week later, we were in court. The DA had an accountant from Fry's who took care of depositing checks and handling checks that did not clear the bank, and the clerk to testify about waiting on Tess, selling her the television and accepting the check for payment.

I had Tess.

Frail and anxious, shaking like a vibrating bed, she faced the judge. Her voice was meek, and trembled when she talked. Her hair was in a ponytail again. Her gray dress probably came from Sears three or four years ago, nothing fancy. That she looked very young was in her favor.

The DA was brief with the accountant, Mrs. Geiger. She stated her name, how long she'd been on the job and identified the check as the one turned over to the police.

It was my turn at Mrs. Geiger.

"Wouldn't it have been easier for your company to sue my client in small claims court instead of going through all this?"

"Objection, your Honor," the DA said. "The defendant tendered a check in violation of Penal Code 476(a). Fry's has every right to do what they did."

I said, "Of course, I didn't mean Fry's had no right to file a criminal complaint. I only asked if small claims court would be a wise choice, as Fry's is paying for the time Mrs. Geiger and the salesclerk are here in court. This expense is incurred over a two hundred forty-five dollar check."

"Fry's files on all checks over two hundred dollars in hopes of sending a message that we will not tolerate NSF checks. We have so many you would not believe," Mrs. Geiger said.

I ended it there.

"Thank you, Mrs. Geiger."

The salesclerk was a young kiddo. I'd be surprised if he was twenty-one. He'd come to court in blue jeans, a windbreaker and worn tennis shoes crumbling around the edges. A shock of curly hair on top of his head was cut to stand straight up like a badly pruned hedge. High curving eyebrows gave his face a perpetual look of surprise. The DA asked his name, how long he'd been working for Fry's. Did he remember the accused? Did he remember selling her the television and accepting the check in payment?

The clerk remembered Tess, and yes, he remembered accepting a check in payment.

It was my turn again.

"Do you remember any conversation you had with the accused about the check she gave you?"

"I don't understand."

"Did the accused tell you whether she had funds in the bank that day to cover the check?"

"Your Honor, objection. Leading the witness."

The judge said, "Overruled."

"Your Honor, may the stenographer read my last question?"

The judge nodded.

"Did the accused tell you whether she had funds in the bank that day to cover the check?" the stenographer said.

"I do remember her saying that the check would not verify. Something about she had money coming in two days and as soon as it arrived, she would run and make a deposit to cover the check. Is that what you mean?"

I smiled at him to make him feel more comfortable. "Yes. Why do you remember her saying that?"

He blushed, hesitated, then said, "She is a very pretty girl. I wouldn't forget her. And what she said about the check, that was unusual. It stuck in my head."

"Did you let her have the television after she told you that only because she was pretty?"

His cheeks turned bright purple, like a pair of beets. Blushing furiously, he said, "No, no. I figured it would take a few days for the check to get to the bank. She didn't look like a person trying to steal a television with a bum check."

"Objection your Honor to this line of questioning."

"Granted," judge said.

The DA closed with short monologue. "The accused wrote a check knowing she did not have the money in the bank, took the television home, and never paid for it."

"Your Honor, my client tried to pay Fry's for the check on three occasions by going to the store, but no one could find the check. My client never received a letter or any notice from Fry's that the check bounced, but she knew it bounced because the bank sent her a notice. That's why she was trying to pay for it in cash. As for intent to defraud, there is no intent. 476(a) states in part that when check was issued the accused had to know there were insufficient funds; she admits to that. However, when she told the salesclerk that the check would not verify and she planned to make a deposit in a couple of days, that destroys the intent to defraud. The salesclerk could have refused to accept the check at that point. He didn't do that. Knowing what he did about the check, in my opinion, he removed the criminality of the transaction. I respectfully request that your honor find my client not guilty of the charge she is being held to answer. Thank you."

The judge removed his glasses, set them down, then picked

them up and put them back on again. He spent about a minute in silence digesting what had just been presented to him.

"Interesting presentation. I can't remember anyone arguing about intent to defraud on a single check. I don't believe the accused intended to defraud Fry's, and I make this determination based on the testimony of the salesclerk, and the argument by counsel. It's almost as if Fry's' salesclerk extended credit to the accused, and the check was merely the evidence of the debt. Case is dismissed. Bail is exonerated."

"Thank you, your Honor," I said.

Tess stood there in shock, trembling. She had tears leaking out of her eyes.

"Thank you, your Honor," she said.

The judge removed his glasses and said to Tess, "Young lady, be safe. Do not write a check unless the money is in your account at the time you tender it to someone."

"Yes, your Honor. I am very sorry."

When I turned around, I saw Jerry sitting behind us.

"You did good," Jerry said.

"How long have you been here?"

"Long time," he said.

"You are lying," I said, forgetting Tess was next to me, and giving him a little shove.

Outside the courtroom, we hugged. "Easy does it with a checkbook," I said.

"I haven't opened a new account," she said. "I may just leave it like that."

"Good. Be sure you pay Fry's today. If they give you the same as before, ask for Mrs. Geiger directly."

"I'll do it for sure."

Jerry waited for me to finish, and we walked upstairs to the office.

"You may not have been as lucky with a jury, having to explain the intent defense."

"I agree," I said. "Thanks for that."

We walked through his office door. I looked around. The room was empty, and no one was in the hall or paying attention to us.

I whispered, "I owe you a BJ."

Jerry laughed.

I knew he liked me.

I knew he wanted me.

He was married with kids.

Saturday morning, we had breakfast at home. Mona made pancakes. She had on a pink nightie, fluffy scuffs, and an apron that had a pattern of cherries all over it. I sat at the kitchen table while she flipped pancakes at my stove, then she sat down, and we dug in.

"I'm working every day of the week and weekends."

"You mean, every night of the week and weekends."

"Exactly."

"Macho doesn't expect you to work every night. Let him know when you want time off."

"I'm not complaining," Mona said. "The money is good. Macho said I can go to Cannes in May for the festival. He said to ask if you want to go."

"I've been before," I said. "It's twelve days of big money. You'll make a killing there. Gotta dress smart. Macho's connection there is Guillermo, the Macho of Nice and Cannes. He'll keep you busy. The sessions are with persons from across the globe."

"Did you make lots of money?"

"I did good. I stayed in an expensive hotel, against Guillermo's recommendation. I loved it there and I loved the hotel. I would have brought more home if I hadn't done the hotel thing and if I hadn't shopped as much as I did."

"Sounds hot."

"It's a lot of work."

"Would you risk going?"

"I can't do it," I said.

Mona was laughing.

"What?"

"I think you want to go."

I laughed, too.

"I can use the money, for sure."

"You can get laid and paid. Who is going to know you getting paid? It's just you going out on a date while vacationing there. You're a lawyer. You tell me, am I wrong?"

"I'll think about it," I said. "I have vacation time coming. Haven't taken one yet."

"We can have fun," Mona said, excited.

"It's fun but everything is non-stop."

"I hope you go, but only if you will be comfortable and not looking behind your back."

I laughed. "Honey, at work, I have that problem ongoing. Maybe being in the South of France, I'll not have to worry like I do here."

The IRS sent me a letter advising me that I was selected for a tax audit for two years prior to my working at the Public Defender Office. I faxed the letter to my recently hired accountant Herman Smith, a CPA who Macho referred to me.

I asked Herman, "How do they pick who gets audited?"

"Everyone you ask that question has a different answer."

"I just filed my tax return, why me?" I sound like one of my clients.

"I need the returns you filed," Herman said. "Did you file before the return I did for you?"

"I filed. The income was only enough to cover my rent, car

payment, insurance and few other things. I paid my creditors by check."

"You should be okay then."

"I hope so. Why me?" I said again.

"I will handle it. Don't worry about it."

"No way I'm not going to worry about it," I said, sounding bouncier than I really felt. Herman charged me eight hundred dollars to prepare my tax returns, four times as much as I paid at H&R Block when I was hooking and reporting the bare ass minimum. Now that I was a lawyer, even though I wasn't making much money with the PD, I knew I'd need the professional preparer. Eventually I'd make more, and taxes would only be getting more complicated from here on out. Herman only needed my tax returns for those two years, and the paper trail backup. H&R Block would have told me to go fly a kite.

Herman let me know his opinion after he met with the auditor. "She's a snob, but I've dealt with snobs before. She said the modeling income from your tax returns is interesting, now that you're a lawyer. I told her you were pretty and smart. Pretty enough to model. Smart enough to pass the bar. I asked if she had kids. She has a nineteen-year-old daughter who graduated from high school but doesn't want to go further."

"She sounds like a disappointed mom."

"She wants four more years of tax returns. Did you file going back four from the two we have?"

I know there were three years I didn't file.

"Send me the years you filed. I will handle."

"Herman, thanks. That's a big load off."

"We may have to file late returns. Let's see what she'll go for."

"How do I know how much I made?"

"We estimate. You aren't alone, Gabi. Many have this problem."

"I'll put it in the mail in the morning."

My overseer for trial work was Carlos Montanez, a lifer like Jerry. Carlos was a big guy. He dressed well, but I'd seen him put on at least fifty pounds while I've been with the PD. The button-holes on his shirts were strained. He'd been with the PD for fifteen years, sedentary the whole time, but he was a workaholic who rarely took lunch if it didn't include a meeting. Instead, most of the time, he ate at his desk. Other deputies told me I was lucky to have him. He handled big cases, including homicides. I wasn't ready for that type of case. I'd have my own vote but no one else.

My first case as Carlos's second chair was before a jury. It was a nighttime burglary, the worst kind for both the victim and for the accused if found guilty. Penalties for daytime burglary were bad, but not nearly as harsh as for the night burglary of an occupied residence.

Our client was Miguel Lopez. He was tan, black-haired, and a little on the shaggy side, forty-one years old, unemployed and a guest of the county jail. I interviewed him alone in the attorney room at county jail, a week before the trial. He wore the county uniform. I took notes on everything he said and answered his questions as best I could. He was most emphatic about wanting to get out from behind bars.

"So, tell me exactly what happened."

"What happened is I didn't do it."

The homeowners had picked his face from a book of mugshots at the police station. The camera was found at the apartment Miguel shared with several others. His name wasn't on the lease.

Carlos and I interviewed him together two days before the trial.

"We can continue the trial," Carlos said.

Miguel did not want to put it off. "No continuance. I want to get this over with."

In his opening, the deputy DA said the case was very simple. The defendant had entered the house without forced entry, saw the camera in the living room, picked it up and went looking for small items he could carry. He opened the door to the bedroom. Mr. and Mrs. Munoz woke up, turned the light on and screamed. They got a good look at the defendant. They have identified him and will do so again today during the trial."

Mr. Munoz was a medium kind of guy. Medium tall, medium weight, medium short hair. His hair was a middling brown, not light enough to be golden, not dark enough to be brunette, not bright enough to be red. He was a faded man, in faded beige, and his wife looked like his twin in drag. I guess that can happen when people are together a long time. Truth is, you could look at both Mr. and Mrs. Munoz for an hour straight, turn away, and not be able to list a single physical characteristic that stood out.

The deputy PD was first chair. In his opening, Carlos said he didn't dispute what the deputy DA had presented except that the defendant sitting at the counsel's table was not the person who entered the house to steal anything. He simply was not the one who committed the crime.

"We have the landlord of the apartment where the defendant was living and where the camera was found. The apartment is rented to a man we have been unable to contact. Finding the camera in the apartment is not proof that the defendant committed the crime of burglary."

The trial went for two days. Carlos gave me a number of opportunities to question the DA's witnesses and ours. I questioned the cop who dusted for prints when he was on the stand.

"You collected samples from the door and from the apartment. Did you match any of the prints collected to the defendant?"

"No," he said.

We went into the science of fingerprints and the protocol for the collection of the prints for this particular burglary.

We already knew he had from earlier testimony when the DA questioned him.

"Did you find fingerprints on the camera?"

"Yes, we found the defendant's fingerprints on the camera."

"Any other prints?"

"Yes."

"More than one?"

"Yes."

Carlos cross-examined the husband and wife about their identification of defendant.

"Yes, that is him right over there," Mr. Munoz said.

"Do you sleep with your glasses, Mr. Munoz?" I asked.

"Of course not."

"Did you have your glasses on when you saw the defendant?"

"I don't think so. I can't recall, exactly."

"Mr. Munoz, it's okay not to remember. You testified this happened fast. You said one minute you were asleep. The next minute you heard a noise, woke up, turned on the lamp by your bed. You saw a man. Glasses or no glasses?"

"I don't remember."

Carlos questioned the wife.

"Are you sure this is the man?"

She hesitated a long time. "I was. Not so sure anymore. I'm sorry."

Mrs. Munoz started crying.

At four-thirty that afternoon, the jury went out.

They announced they had a verdict in under an hour.

"Not Guilty."

We headed upstairs.

"Do you think he did it?" Carlos asked.

"I believe our client," I said.

He winked.

"Good job, Deputy Gabi."

"Back at you," I said, matching his smile.

"We're hitting the tavern," he said, putting on his coat. "You coming with?" Jerry asked.

For the first time, I accepted the invitation.

The tavern was a block from the courthouse. PDs, DAs, and cops congregated there after work. It was badly lit, crowded and loud. Carlos, Jerry and I were at a corner table. I drank a draft beer, and joked around with the guys, but all the while, my dirty mind filmed a mental movie of a threesome with my two bosses. Carlos was as married as Jerry. Long before it was closing time, I went home alone. It was a joke that a girl like me was practically doing without. At least there was Mona.

My CPA called often about the progress of my audit. He filed late tax returns with estimated earnings of modeling jobs that I hadn't reported. He told me getting the auditor to accept the estimated amounts as enough was like pulling teeth. The IRS didn't care what modeling entailed. It didn't help that on my list of assets, I showed a Ferrari and Corvette, unencumbered. All the lady auditor wanted was that the IRS get their cut. Months after the audit started, I signed off on the auditor's findings that I owed forty-five thousand dollars. Herman thought I should not ask for installments because the auditor could file a tax lien and keep it as public record until the amount was paid in full. I sold the Corvette to a car dealer. I could have gotten more if I had time to advertise, but I had been putting off selling the car for far too long.

When I needed cash, I pulled out no more than five thousand at a time and deposited the money. Couldn't do it with forty thousand. With forty thousand in green cash that I had left in my safety deposit box from my street work, I went to Macho.

I arrived when it was after dark so I would find Macho awake.

Macho wrote me a check for the cash without charging me any fees.

"This breaks me," I said to him.

"Get vacation time and go to Cannes. You know how it works. Mona can learn from you. At least this time, you'll have her for company."

"I've been thinking about it since Mona told me," I said. "There's still a little time before the festival."

"Nothing to think about. Just do it. You can make this forty in ten days there."

"I'll do it."

"Good move."

"The hooking doesn't bother me. It's the fear of getting found out that spooks the fuck out of me."

Macho nodded. "You're not going to be found out."

"Tell Guillermo I need the heavy money dudes but to leave some for Mona."

Macho chuckled. "That Mona is fabulous."

"I hear you are getting some."

"I never mess with my models, but Mona draws me in. I only touch, nothing else."

"I can't believe you just said that."

"She's sweet."

I was going to ask if I wasn't sweet anymore but held my tongue

"She likes you."

Mona is like the sister I didn't have.

The next day, I visited Herman in his one-man office in downtown LA. I thought he'd had a home office, but obviously he had enough business that he could afford the office and a receptionist. She was on the phone the whole time I was there. The reception area had six chairs, and no windows.

"Miss Guerrero? Herman is waiting for you."

The receptionist waved me in, though another woman was waiting when I arrived. She was beautifully dressed. Fantastic legs. Probably one of Macho's girls. I didn't know her.

It was a good thing I had been paying him while the audit was ongoing, or I would have owed him a ton when the audit was complete. As it was, I had to ante up the full balance, just under three thousand. I signed off on the IRS agreement and handed him the check for him and for the IRS.

"Thanks. It would have been a train wreck if I'd had to work with this lady," I said.

"That's what I do for a living," he said. "I doubt you'll get another audit for a long time."

Macho had recommended Herman. He had to know that I hooked for Macho under the guise of modeling, but he never mentioned that and neither did I.

When I got home, Mona wasn't dressed for work yet. It was only six, because I'd taken off early to meet with Herman.

I was wearing what looked like a man's pinstriped suit. I dumped the jacket over the back of the couch and pulled my pockets inside out to show how empty they were.

"Well, I paid off the IRS and my CPA, and now I'm broke. I can't remember how many years it's been since I actually ran out of cash."

"I got plenty," Mona said, hugging me tighter.

I stuffed the pockets back in properly and pulled my sweats off of the stack of clean clothes folded on the dryer. I didn't bother going to my room to change, just dressed in the little room off the kitchen where the washer and dryer was. It only took a second to rejoin her in the kitchen.

"You're so sweet to offer," I said. "I'm cool. I told Macho I'm on for Cannes. I'm going with you."

Mona squealed and started jumping up and down, then grabbed me by the shoulders. We were both jumping up and down, bananas with excitement.

Wednesday afternoon I was late and rushing from one court to another. I saw the smile on his face before I digested who it was. I knew I had met him before. He had a head of black hair, fuller than I remembered it, and the silver around the edges looked very distinguished. He stopped directly in front of me with his hand out, and I had no chance to avoid him. I accepted his hand and shook it, a smile on my face. The corridor was like all busy court houses. It was jammed and noisy in a respectful library kind of way. You could practically smell the anxiousness in the air.

"Gabi, I recognized you immediately."

I smiled. "Max's lawyer Tomas Lopez," I said. "Good to see you," I lied.

"I've seen you couple times before in court when you were busy. No time to say hello."

"I wish I had more time," I said. "I'm late in Division J."

"Molinero. She doesn't like late," he said. "You're with the Public Defender's office?"

"I am," I said.

"I told you to come see me when you passed the bar."

I remembered he did.

"Hey, you never know," I said. "I'm getting my polish. Might come see you." Another lie.

"Do that. In case you forgot, here's my card. Give me yours."

I had no choice. I reached in my purse and gave him a business card.

A handshake later, I was off to Division J. Who knows where he was heading.

I seldom feel so anxious. I say seldom because I can't remember the last time that I was so shaken up. I walked into that courtroom with visions of Max and me cavorting in his plane. My past had just caught up with me. I hoped there were no copies of the video we burned in Tomas Lopez's fireplace.

My case was called a minute after I arrived.

"In the case of State of California v Juan Perez, I see counsel for both sides are present. Are you ready for trial?"

The DA answered he was.

"We're ready, your Honor," I said.

"Okay, we're going to be trailing this case. It might be a couple days before we get to it. Everyone will be on call. Mr. Perez, work out something with your attorney. Two hours before I expect you back here, she will reach out to you."

"Yes, ma'am," my client replied.

I walked back to my office, shut the door, and pretended to be busy by opening up one of the case files stacked on my desk. I'd known this was going to happen.

"Please don't let this be the beginning of the end," I prayed. Maybe I was a horrible person sin-wise, but I'd be lying if I said I didn't believe in God.

When I got home, my hands were full with my briefcase and a bag of groceries. I plopped everything down at the door, and a honeydew melon rolled on the carpet as I got my keys out. By the time I'd done that, Mona swung the door open, holding a huge Reuben with one bite gone.

I picked everything up, shunted the melon back in the bag, and walked in.

I told Mona about my internal crisis when I'd run into Tomas Lopez in the courthouse.

"Chill," she said, waving around her sandwich. "He said he'd seen you before. What's he going to do? If he says anything, he's implicating Max. Not going to happen."

Mona was right. I was too close to this. I wasn't thinking.

I took a bite of her sandwich.

"Yuck. Mustard," I said, fake-wiping my mouth and giving her a kiss.

She held her sandwich out of my reach. "Yours is on the table. Mustard free, even if it is a Reuben."

"I feel better already," I said.

"When you get back, I'll give you a great fuck," she said, blinding me with her smile.

That smile. No wonder Macho was drawn to her.

I clapped, blew her a kiss and started into the kitchen. "In that case, hurry back. I can use it."

I love my job at the PD office. I was moving up. Though I was still limited on what kind of cases I was given, when I went to trial, I had a second chair of my own. I was not trying to move too fast. It was too dangerous for a client if their attorney fucked up, especially in a trial. I took the responsibility seriously. The cowboy that was in me when I got hired had tempered. I felt good about myself.

I always wondered if my academic ability was an inherited asset from my mom or Armand Rana or whoever my real dad had been. Wherever it came from, I had a knack for researching the law. I researched at work. I seldom took work home to my apartment. If I needed to work late on a case, I did it at the office where I had a library filled with law books.

I was dead asleep when Mona came home but she never failed to make breakfast for us. I slept later than usual for a work day, but the fragrance of bacon and coffee that Chef Mona was putting together roused me from a sound sleep. I walked in the kitchen while she was at the stove. I planted a kiss on the back of her neck. She wore a long white button-down shirt. She liked men's shirts. A medium fit her long, and the shoulders were crazy-wide. Her ass was just barely covered. A cigarette pack was in her shirt pocket, and I knew from experience that there was no tobacco in there, only a couple of joints. The sleeves were carefully rolled above her elbows, so they didn't interfere with cooking.

"Good morning. Did you sleep?"

"Morning, Gab. I slept a few hours. I had a five-hour job. Came home late."

"Let's see, five hours. Seven hundred?"

"I got a thou, including tip."

"I'm sure you deserved it."

"I did. He got it all."

I turned around.

"He got it all, like all?"

"Yep, like all."

"I'm afraid to ask."

We sat for breakfast.

"I don't understand how I don't get fat," I said.

"Because you work your ass off," Mona said. "Like I do."

"I work it off, but not like you," I laughed. I'm sure she worked it off in her way, but I did a lot of running up and down in the courthouse, and we frequently walked to eat lunch in the neighborhood, often coming back at a run or close to it. I had good reason for keeping a pair of walking shoes, and a pair of neutral heels in one of my desk drawers.

"Do you miss it?"

I laughed, almost choked on a mouthful of bacon.

"Miss what? Getting laid? Pampering strangers with complete access to my body? Douching four times a night? Showering and bathing at least that many times? Changing clothes three times a night? Do I miss it? Maybe I miss the occasional righteous sex, the rare patient man not in a rush to come, the occasional man who got me to orgasm."

I laughed. Mona laughed with me.

"Tomorrow I'm going to do you," Mona said. "I'm buying a new penis. What color do you want?"

It was early still, and I hadn't seen any clients yet. I had a cup of vending machine coffee on my desk, and a stack of cases to look over before I got started on my day. The phone rang, and I picked it up.

"Gabi, this is Tomas. Tomas Lopez."

"I recognize your voice. Good morning," I said. "What's up?"

"I want to invite you to lunch. Doesn't have to be today. Any day you are free."

I hesitated. After running into him yesterday, I was not surprised he called. At least I did not panic. Mona was right. If he made a big noise about me, he would be sinking the Max ship. Or at least he'd be putting a hole in the hull. Slow leaks can take you to the bottom. They just take longer, that's all.

"Tomas, we were adversaries when we did business. Why would we have lunch?"

"I told you back then I like your style. Look at you now, a member of the state bar, a deputy PD. Who knows where you'll move up to next? I want you on my side."

"You have a sense of humor," I said.

"Believe it. Don't say yes to lunch because you think you have to. I'll go away quietly."

I took a sip from my mud-flavored waxed-cardboard cup and set it far from my pile of folders in case the phone cord accidentally knocked it over. It had been known to happen.

"Call me next week and I'll know better how my calendar looks. I hardly know from one day to the next what is being changed."

"Gotcha. Have a great weekend."

"You too, Tomas."

I couldn't stop thinking about the call. I was not anxious or fearful anymore, only curious about what he wanted. Did he want to fuck? Did he think I was still for sale? I would not fuck him, not even under duress. Not a chance. Maybe he just wanted sex. He's a man after all. Blackmail? I would never cave to blackmail. If he made a move like that against me, it would be war. I would have him beaten to a pulp. I wondered if he still represented Max.

Would I do it with Max?

Damn right, I would. I'd pay him. That's how good he is.

I was still thinking about the call when I was in the courtroom. I laughed to myself and patiently waited with my client for the judge to call his case. The client was being held on a domestic abuse charge, with fifty thousand dollars bail.

This case was not the norm. Like her husband, the wife had also been arrested for domestic abuse. Her bail was the same as his. A neighbor had called in the cops, and they found them duking it out. My client had two black eyes. I hadn't seen the wife, but the report said she was bruised. Their six-month-old twins, a boy and girl, were taken in by child services after the arrest.

"Your Honor, I haven't discussed this with Mr. Dyles because there's been little time to talk. This case came at us fast. I'm wondering if you would entertain a motion to combine my client's case with that of his wife, who is also in custody. She is being arraigned in another division as we speak. There is so much to get done in this case. There are twins involved, currently in the custody of child services."

The matter of his bail would also be heard on Monday when his wife was present in this division. The judge asked the Deputy DA what his position was.

"Your Honor, I have no objection to combining both cases."

"I'll find out what court has the matter and I'll speak with the judge," our judge said. "I don't think you need to file a motion unless there is an objection on the other side."

"Thank you, Your Honor," I said.

"If you are ready, let's do the arraignment and continue this matter until Monday at ten a.m."

The judge never asked if that was a good date and time. He wanted this case expedited, and so did I. I felt bad for the twins, babies too young to know where they were, or comprehend the nightmare their lives were descending into. Sometimes it is better not to make babies.

Still March 1990

Friday night, I was dressed in jeans and Mona was dressed like an expensive doll, ready to work for Macho. We went to Macho's in our own cars. She was planning to go straight to a gig after our talk.

Macho's apartment was a lot like mine, except he had three bedrooms; I had two; he had three and a half bathrooms; I had two and a half; he had a balcony overlooking Wilshire Boulevard; I had no balcony overlooking anything; he owned his; and I rented.

Currently his den was his office, but he liked to change it around alot. Mona and I were on wing chairs across from a big desk. Shelves along one wall held stacks of scrapbooks. A couple of filing cabinets held more photos. One wall was floor to ceiling framed black and whites of models who called Macho agent. I don't think they were all currently working for him, but the last time I'd walked away, Macho had given me my picture off the wall.

"The best money while you are in Cannes will be from clients who see your pictures," Macho said. "Gabi, you know this."

"I can't do pictures anymore," I said. "Not even in Cannes. Not a chance."

"The pictures don't have to be nudes."

"I can't, Macho."

"You already have my pictures," Mona said, looking at her eight by ten on the wall.

"I need new ones to send ahead to my man there."

Mona said, "Sure, tell me where and when."

He looked at me. "Gabi?"

"Nope, can't do it. Tell Guillermo I haven't changed." I smiled at Macho.

"I know better than to argue with you."

"Macho, what if I install myself like before at the Carlton, and I do my own hustle? You know I will still cut you in."

"Bad idea. You stayed at the hotel, but you didn't do your own hustle. You will not get the high-dollar people like our man there does. You should know this."

"Okay, but no pictures."

"Headshots, that's all. How about it?" Macho would not give up.

"Give Guillermo one headshot and if he has any pictures from my last trip, order him to burn them. If you love me like you say, you'll make sure of it."

Macho came around his desk, I stood up and he hugged me. I hugged him back.

Mona said, "I should carry a camera."

Saturday morning, Mona woke me when she slipped in bed. It was six ten in the morning. She smelled just-out-of-the-shower-fresh and her breath was Crest. She loved that toothpaste.

I opened my arms, and she moved into them. Her skin felt like warm, soft silk. I took a deep breath, inhaling the sexy smell of her shampoo.

"Are you just getting home?"

"Yeah. I slept though. Client wanted me to sleep over, after. I got five hours and split when I woke up. I'll make you breakfast when you're ready to get up."

"Keep hugging me," I said. "I got no love going, no one to hold me. Hug me. I feel like I'm wasting away." I laughed to temper the insecurity I was revealing. I hated to be feeling sorry for myself. I was still young. Damn me.

"Poor baby," she said.

She touched me through my boy underwear, kissed me lust-fully, coaxing me to a quick but explosive orgasm.

"You need a boyfriend," Mona said.

I laughed.

"That way you wouldn't have to work me, huh?"

"I love working you," she said.

"I told you before why I can't hook up with anyone serious."

I thought of Max's lawyer wanting to take me for lunch. There was a catch there somewhere. I was sure of that. Men are strange. Someday, when she was no longer a hooker, I bet Mona would be reluctant to hook up with a man permanently. The secret does not stay secret forever.

We split to the village down the street and had breakfast at Mama Wilshire, a twenty-four hour coffee shop on very expensive turf. The restaurant had a fancy ambiance, and dramatic architecture, soaring ceilings and a massive crystal chandelier like something out of Les Misérables. A host led us to our table and presented huge menus that only had a couple of things on each page. It looked more like an invitation than a menu, and each dish had a loving portrait, with a paragraph below, describing it.

Mona had cheese stuffed French toast made of brioche. I had braised hash with a long list of herbs and topped with a poached egg. We each got coffee, breakfast potatoes, and shared a basket of yeast-raised rolls. Butter came to the table molded in delicate half-moons and served on ice. There was a good crowd, but it was a subdued bunch. Maybe everyone was in shock over the prices. I just wanted to splurge.

"Why did you decide to do Cannes?" Mona asked.

Our little blond waitress delivered our coffee, so I waited till she left to answer.

"It's about the money. For years, I've had a stash, and now it's gone. I can't make it back into the green with my paycheck from work. Maybe one day, when I'm in private practice, I'll look back on these days with some romanticized glow. Now I gotta do what I gotta do. I need my stash back."

"I'm glad we're going together, but if you are uncomfortable, let me give you twenty thousand. I got it. I won't even miss it."

"You're going to make me cry," I said, putting my coffee down.

"I mean it," Mona said.

I took her hand and squeezed it.

"I know you mean it, but that's not the kind of money I need. Homer was giving me ten thousand a month for living there with him while I went to school and for attending to his needs and desires. This audit went through what I had left after paying tuition plus my Corvette, plus my nest egg. Fuck. I need some fuck money."

"You need the sex, too."

"Well, we'll see about that. You know that in this business it's rare that we're going to get a good lay."

"You got that right." Mona lifted her mug of coffee, and we clicked.

While Mona was working, I arranged for Roger to do me for two hours. No massage, just sex. I told Macho that I was paying, and I did.

"You said you were out of money," Macho said.

"I am, but I can pay Roger. I feel bad you are picking up the tab for me to get fucked."

"As you wish," Macho said.

Roger ended up giving me three hours for the price of two.

"A token of my appreciation," he said. "Sex with you is magnifico."

Sunday morning my room still smelled of sex. I should have changed the sheets.

I told Mona, "Problem with these high-rises, we can't open a window."

"You can if you have a balcony apartment."

"Smart-ass, five hundred more a month. Not a chance. I wasn't complaining. The smell is a turn on. Roger is a stud and then some."

"I should try him out," Mona said. "You wouldn't get jealous, would you?"

"Get serious." I laughed.

Mona laughed too. She was a tease.

"I guess you don't need the new strap on I bought."

"You so dirty," I said.

"That's so true."

"You didn't really go out and get one, did you?"

I get turned on so easily.

"I did. it's chocolate colored, and an interesting size. Want to see it?"

I said, "Yes, show me." We were open with each other, so without bullshit.

"I'll go get it. Want me to put it on?"

April 1990

Jerry's boss, Harry, was my boss too. He was not as nice as Jerry, but we were close enough to joke around. Harry was outspoken about cases I was handling, he was handling, cases he wished he could handle personally, and cases he wished his boss would let him give to another deputy.

In his office, I sat across from Harry. It was not even nine in the morning.

He said the jefe—the head honcho of the Public Defenders' Office—had received a letter from a prisoner named Rose.

"You know him?"

I felt the punch in my stomach.

"There are two Roses in this world I will never forget. The first one is Alex Rose. I killed him in self-defense when I was a kid. I wrote it up in my application when I got this job, and the State Bar is aware of it. I didn't put in the whole story. He killed the baby I was carrying, and almost killed me."

Harry nodded. He had to know.

"The second Rose is his brother. Phillip Rose broke into my apartment. He faked being a flower delivery person. He meant to kill me. He attacked me and a massage therapist who was there with me, sending us both to the hospital. Why do you ask, Harry?"

Harry took his glasses off and looked at me.

"Rose wrote that when you killed his brother, you were a prostitute and his brother was your pimp. He writes that you should be neither a lawyer nor a public defender. I read the letter. It is a total hate-fest."

"He's full of shit. He said the same thing to the cops that arrested him. I wasn't a lawyer then, but he told them I was a prostitute in Hollywood. He had no proof because it's a lie."

"It is only a letter from a nut case. I'll write a report for the boss that we had this conversation. If he has any questions, I'll let you know."

"Can I get a copy of the letter?"

"Gabi, you don't want a copy of the letter. Let it go. I didn't sleep all night sweating how I would tell you about this. Thanks for making it easy."

"You didn't believe it, did you?"

Harry got up. He smiled.

"Of course not."

"I'm curious Gabi, how old are you?"

"Twenty-seven."

He shook his head and smiled. "I can't even remember when I was twenty-seven."

I gave him a smile that I know he liked.

I hoped he didn't believe it, but even if he believed, there was no evidence. The PD was not going to send an investigator to prison to interview Rose simply because he wrote a hate letter about me to the boss here. No proof, period.

I thought about the upcoming days in Cannes next month. Even if someone took pictures of me with a man and then another man the next night, that doesn't make me a hooker. I know what evidence is, and there is no evidence of what I did before or what I plan to do in Cannes. Fuck it.

I walked out of Harry's office, fuming over that bastard Phillip Rose discovering that I am a lawyer now, and where I work. Rumors spread in prison. Maybe he met someone I represented who was sent away. I haven't won all my cases. Shit happens.

On my way home, my brain wouldn't stop.

No one can prove what I did. Even a client who paid me is not evidence. I was never arrested for anything. I'm clean. I've always worried, and I still worry, but there is no hard evidence. I do sweat over maybe running into someone I had sex with but I'm a lawyer. I know about evidence. Real evidence, not just hearsay.

Fuck Rose.

When Rose gets released and comes looking for me again, he's dead. Let's see who listens to him when he's lying in a pine box, six feet under. Motherfucker.

I told Mona and she told Macho. He called me.

"Next, he'll write the state bar."

"Probably already did," I said. "I haven't heard anything. The bar is not going to take any action unless they have a complaint and evidence."

"That's my girl," Macho said. "Don't let anyone bully you."

"My boss is being a champ about it," I said. "No one is bullying me. As for Rose, he's a snake. It's a wonder he's just now surfacing."

"I'll find out what his status is," Macho said.

Macho had connections. For all I know, I may have fucked a warden, or a dozen of them who owed him favors. Ex-cops have connections. Especially feds like he was. Besides, what did he need connections for? It's not like he would have him snuffed. Would he? No way.

Mona had a week off, that time of the month. The first night she was off, we went to the show, then to dinner. The next night we went to another movie and then to dinner.

"This is a welcome break in my routine," I told her.

"A break in my routine, too."

I went to work during the day, and we found something to do when I got home. I got her to go with me to the shooting range. We went to Sears where she bought a Colt 38. We planned that she would go shoot with me every two weeks. While at Sears, I seriously considered buying a shotgun, but I had second thoughts. Shooting practice only took an hour, and I was damn good.

Sometimes we just lay like broccoli and watched TV. On Saturday we went to Santa Monica Pier. The weather was chilly, but we are crazy. We had lunch there, like we were dating. We knew we looked hot no matter what we were wearing. We were attention getters, everywhere we went.

If you are in the business I was in before lawyering, you lose the desire to have a boyfriend. Don't let anyone tell you different. Sure, I need to get laid, and I love getting held while lying in bed, and I love someone touching me. What I don't want is a full-time man. Besides, what man would want a wife or permanent live-in that had that many men? First thing a guy asks is how many men you had. Eventually, the truth makes the relationship go up in smoke. I traded in the mom-housewife fairytale to Rose first, then to Macho. Between running into Tomas Lopez at the courthouse, and the rat fink writing the public defender chief that I was a hooker pimped by his brother, I'm being paranoid but with just cause. If Tomas has a copy of the video of me having wild sex with Max on his plane from LAX to Dallas—but I don't think he does—that doesn't prove me a hooker. That only proves I had sex with the famous NBA star named Max. And unless Max testified that he paid me for that sex, there is no evidence.

I never was into another woman. I did it when a client wanted it, but I was never into it. It's different now, with Mona. We haven't given up men, but I love the relationship. I know it's a relationship. We're not just room partners or occasional lovers. In public we behave. No sense offending anyone with behavior they feel is questionable, offensive or taboo. No nasty talk outside the apartment. I don't know who has a dirtier mouth, me or Mona. We are not children anymore but our enthusiasm about going to Cannes is like kids about to take a ten-day trip to Disneyland.

May 10-21, 1990
Cannes
Mona

I flew with Max to every state in the US, but I never traveled outside the country. I am excited like never before. I didn't have a passport until Macho put it on a checklist for the trip to Cannes. We flew in coach from Los Angeles to Nice with two fast stops. I pretty much chattered my way across the Atlantic. Gabi hasn't talked much, shushed me when the stewardesses cut the lights in the plane, but kept smiling.

When we landed, Gabi called Guillermo to let him know we had arrived and when she was done, gave me the phone to say hello to him.

"Are you ready to make money?" he said. His English is better than mine.

"More than ready," I said.

An hour in a taxi took us to Cannes. The taxi driver Jean-Michel wasn't beautiful. In fact, he was kind of chubby and hairy, and reminded me of that comedian, Dom somebody or other, but his accent was killer. I could have come a hundred times just listening to him. I asked so many questions about where we were that he talked to us like a tour guide. I watched Nice through the car window all the way to the Carlton InterContinental where Gabi stayed before. You can tell it's a foreign country, but it looks good and interesting. Pointe Croisette looks like Miami if it was built on a hill with hotels across the street from the beach instead of on the water. There were a ton of bike riders along the riviera. There was some crazy driving through complicated tunnels, and when we surfaced, there were buildings piled up on buildings on mountains, so it reminded me of Disneyland, except so old! The cars here are tiny, but Gabi warned me ahead of time, so I packed everything tight and didn't have a ton of bags. We packed casual day stuff, two day-dressy outfits, and seven different outfits for work at night, everything designer.

Gabi showed me how to roll the clothes so that nothing got squashed or wrinkled. Nine pairs of shoes. Mink coat. Gabi already owned one. I had to buy one, and it set me back five thousand dollars. Cannes would be comfortable but cool, especially in the evenings. We each had two bags, and the taxi driver managed to squeeze everything in his mini car.

Everything in the hotel is white. When we walked in, I swear I was almost blinded. Gabi, she was cool as a cucumber, but she's been here before.

"Are you excited?" I asked her.

Gabi nodded, grinning. "Of course. My first time, I was as bubbly as you. Difference is I was alone with no one to share the bubbles."

We laughed entering the hotel, and a bellman followed us with our luggage. Macho wasn't going to spring with the bucks to pay for our room in this palace, and neither was Guillermo. Macho pushed Guillermo to find a way to book the room, and it was done. My understanding is that it was not easy. Gabi said that on her visit before, she paid for her own room, and Guillermo worked that booking. There are many hotels in Cannes, but this one is special, a favorite of many important people who attend the festival, actors, producers, directors and studio big shots, just a few of the guests who stay there.

Our room was not a suite or anything fancy, but it was beautiful, had plenty of closet space for both of us, two queen sized beds and one big bathroom with a tub and separate shower. The ocean view was crowded with so many yachts like pictures I've seen in travel magazines.

I opened the suitcase to put things away and pulled out the small steamer I'd brought.

"No," Gabi said. "Put that away."

She put in a call to housekeeping to send a room maid.

"Put everything you want pressed on the bed," she said, and started going through her own clothes. Gabi gave the maid a ten spot, US.

The maid smiled broadly, chattered a mouthful of French and took the clothes with her. It was late afternoon.

The glass doors opened to a fake balcony, fancy cast iron railing with no actual space, but when it was open a nice breeze of French beach air was blowing in. I swear it smells different. We were lying around in our underwear. The temperature was in the mid-sixties, not exactly summer. It was wonderful. I loved it. Gabi agreed every time I asked.

"Jet lagged? Need to sleep?"

"I'm too excited to sleep," I said.

Gabi sat up on her elbows. "Are we were going right to work?" she asked.

I don't remember answering her. We fell asleep.

It was dark, a little after eight, when Gabi's phone rang. I sat up.

"Hey, Guillermo," Gabi said into her phone. "I think the customer will get more for the money if we wait until tomorrow."

We ate nothing and conked out. Four hours later, we were wide awake.

"I got it solved. I brought sleeping pills," I said. Then we were both out to the world.

Guillermo said he lived in Cannes, but I'm told his main house is in Nice, a short, hectic, crazy drive away. The last time I was here, I saw him three times. Like Macho, he lives on the phone. Last time, he had a portfolio of pictures of me, some dressed up, some with not much on, some he'd taken himself, and some from Macho. This time he only had a face picture. I don't know if he had the old pictures. My outcome from this venture depends on how he pitches me. He has a lot of beautiful pictures of Mona.

We were up early, both too excited to eat, and went out by the pool, an irregular shape, very mod. The hotel was between us and the beach, but we had a view of a sliver of ocean, and of course, May sea breezes. The breezes are what stung us with a chill. The pool was heated, probably why there were people in it. We had no plans to actually get wet, but the cold wind chased us in. Before getting out of the pool, I waved over an attendant, and he brought us two hotel robes. The sun kept peeking out and disappearing behind clouds. When it shined, it warmed us up.

My cell rang. It was Guillermo.

"I have something for you. Dinner and after. He's been a client for the past two years, a good one."

"I'm in," I said.

Mona was lying on her stomach. Her cobalt bikini matched the pool water. She turned her head in my direction, listening.

"How about Mona?" I asked.

"It's early. I'll call her as soon as I have one. Be in the lobby at eight tonight. The client's driver will pick you up and deliver you to the restaurant."

"How much?" I asked.

"Five hundred an hour," Guillermo said.

"What if overnight?"

"Five hundred an hour."

I wish the PD would pay me five hundred an hour for the work I do. If Guillermo had been there in person, he would have seen my smile.

"Hey, what's up?" Mona asked, rolling over, sitting up and taking a sip of a tall glass of icy mineral water.

"He's going to call you soon as he lands one. He got one for me, maybe someone I did before. I don't know."

I didn't know why I went first.

"Cool," she said. "Should we eat? Or are we going to not eat on this trip?"

I could hear her stomach growl from where I was sitting and waved the waiter over. We ordered hamburgers and ate them poolside, a pitcher of lemonade parked on table between our recliners, a patio heater keeping us comfortable. We no longer needed our robes.

I have such a suspicious mind. Nobody would come here from LA to watch me work. Who from home would be watching me all the way in the South of France? Even if they were and I'm seen with a guy here and there, I'm just dating. No one would see money exchanging hands. I'm covered. Why do I keep thinking crazy? We were being watched. Of course, we were being watched. We were looking our best, and there were plenty of other guests, many of them male, most of them classy-looking older men, probably loaded with money.

I was excited about the prospect of raking in some serious money to take back home. I felt insecure without my nest egg. In twelve days, I could rake in thirty-five thousand or thereabouts.

Cannes population goes from seventy-five thousand to over two hundred fifty thousand during the festival. Everything is packed. The clients I serviced in the past were not involved in movies. They were here for the ambiance, to be a part of the excitement that vibrates here day and night. They could have fucked wherever they came from, but maybe that wouldn't have been as much fun as doing it in Cannes. One thing is for sure. If they called Guillermo, it was going to cost them a lot more than they would have paid back home. I'm just saying. Everything is expensive. Mona and I wanted a slice of it, and we had what it takes to get it.

It was the first night of the festival, and my first night on a date.

May 1990
Cannes
Mona

Guillermo set me up with a couple from New York.

"Call him Mike. He has connected with me for the past four years. He's a good guy. I think the girl with him is a girlfriend from the US."

I'd done a few couples back in LA but not many. I'd manage.

The driver dropped me off at the hotel that was very nice, but probably not quite as top drawer as the Carlton. He gave me the room number. Top floor.

I knocked at the door.

He opened it in his robe. He was probably in his sixties and seemed nice.

"You must be Mike," I said.

He did not confirm or deny the name, but he kissed me on the lips. We said our hellos, and then I followed him through the big living room equipped with a piano, bar, and lots of seating. He led me into the bedroom where he introduced his companion as Penny. A cutie. I'd guess she was in her thirties.

Penny was in a white dress, her bare legs crossed as she sat at a glass-top table near the bed. A bottle of Dom Pérignon was in a cooler. Without asking if I wanted any, she poured me a glass. She was made up like she had either been out or planning on going out then changed her mind. Probably the latter.

"Thanks," I said. "My name is Trish."

"The booking agent told Mike your name," Penny said.

"Penny, you are gorgeous," I said.

She blushed.

Mike took a seat beside Penny. I sat across from them, lifted my glass and they did the same. We drank simultaneously. Mike finished his whole glass in a long gulp. Penny finished hers too. When in Rome...I emptied the glass and put it on the table.

"What are we doing tonight?" I asked.

Mike said, "I want to watch."

Penny blushed.

"Should I take my clothes off?" I asked.

Mike chuckled and said, "Wonderful. Yes."

I got up. I was in a simple sundress (except that it was Dior, and not simple.) The midnight blue and cream striped-silk gown skimmed my body. The waist was cinched with a satin bow belt. My seamstress had cut the floor-length dress so that it was quite short and put in a Velcro closure to replace the halter's three hooks that would have made it a nightmare to take off by myself.

I didn't make a show of it. One snap, and the belt was on the chair. I stepped out of my heels. One pull at my seamstress's quick Velcro release, and the dress slipped down my body, leaving me in a pair of boxer-style fitted panties in black lace. I draped the dress over the chair's back, walked over to Mike's chair and leaned over him to kiss Penny's lips.

Penny stood up. She was about my height. She kissed me back. I focused on her as her robe came off, leaving her as naked as the day she was born.

"You are breathtaking," I said.

Penny went for another kiss.

"I like you, Trish."

Penny and I moved to the bed. She was not shy, and this was not her first time. She pulled off my undies. Before I could start on her, she was kissing me over my entire body. Mike scooted his chair next to the bed, smiling, and drinking champagne. I could see she was already excited and made it a goal for Penny to come for the first time with my mouth. She wrapped her legs around me and detonated like she'd been storing gunpowder in there.

I took my time getting her back to speed, turned Penny on her stomach and matched what she had done to me. I took my time with the foreplay, and explored her body with my mouth, leaving no place unvisited. I moved her on her right side and worked her as she moaned, groaned, and thrashed around, making a wreck of the bed. Mike was laughing and clapping at one point, but I wasn't paying attention to him. I was following Penny's responses and could tell what she liked. I rolled her over on her back, my mouth found her breasts, my hand found her wetness, my fingers found her spot.

Penny exploded for the second time.

She was a noisy New Yorker.

While Penny cooled, I tried to get Mike on the bed with us. He was the shy one. He stayed in the chair. Kneeling under the table, I worked his thing with my mouth. Penny watched and yelled directions from the bed.

I was with Mike and Penny for three hours, then showered and dried my hair. When I came out of their bathroom, Mike handed me twenty-five hundred dollars.

"Please come back and see us."

"You got it," I said. "Let Guillermo know when."

Bare ass naked, Penny walked me to the door. She kissed me the way Gabi and I kiss each other. "Thank you, Trish," she said. "Is your name really Trish?"

I smiled. "No," I said, door open, ready for me to walk into the hallway. "Is your name really Penny?"

"It is," she said. "Penny Lewis. Mike is my husband."

I called Guillermo from the lobby.

"All good. I'm done with Mike and his wife."

"I thought it was his girlfriend."

"Only they know for sure," I said. "Headed to my hotel."

"Are you tired? Can you do another one at the same hotel?"

"You bet. I'm in the lobby."

"Perfect. Let me call him and tell him who to expect. Trish, correct?"

"Yup, for the next twelve days."

May 1990
Cannes
Guillermo

I'm busy most of the year, but nothing compares with how busy the Cannes Festival is. After the festival, I go from seventeen dolls to five. Word of mouth gets me the business. If a client hates the visit, I send someone else, free.

I manage everything from my cell phone, and before that, my house phone. Now I can be anywhere and take a call. If a client wants to see a picture, I send my runner, Joe with an album of who is available. It's not true that everyone hates a messenger. Everyone loves Joe.

Joe runs in the morning to visit the ladies and collect my commission from the night before. If a client calls for a male model, I send Joe. There's nothing Joe can't do. He plays both sides of the fence and has an unforgettable face and body. New business comes from bellmen, bell captains, front desk clerks and concierges from hotels in Nice and Cannes. Joe handles anyone who calls me with a lead that pans out. He doesn't get much sleep this time of year. He gets around the heavy traffic in his Harley. The locals know the bike. Where-ever the bike is, Joe is close by.

One of the hottest dolls I have during the festival is from California. She's been here before. She looks like a movie star. My friend Macho in Los Angeles sent her with another doll whose photos are seductive, even to me. I must see her before she goes home.

May 1990
Cannes
Gabi

I was in the lobby of my hotel about to sit down when he walked right up to me like he knew who I was. He was not dressed like a driver would be back home, and I was not surprised since I'd been here before. The weather has a lot to do with what we all wear. He had on white linen slacks and a matching linen shirt with three quarter length sleeves. It was chilly for shorts, but locals are used to the weather. His shoes were off white, and he wore no socks. He looked like a tourist with money to spend. I liked the look.

"Miss Kylie?"

I smiled and nodded.

"Ma'am, my name is Felix. I am here on behalf of Mr. Jones."

"Yes, I was expecting you." I wanted to laugh at the name, Mr. Jones.

We crossed the lobby and went out the front doors of the hotel where it was extremely busy. Cars lined up with no occupants either ready to be parked by valet or picked up by their owners.

It was temperate for May, and the breeze off the Bay of Cannes was intoxicating. I love the smell of the ocean.

Felix led me toward the massive overhang of the hotel entry with its hundreds of lights shining down on the cars and people entering and exiting. Beyond the lights, the night seemed exotic and a little mysterious. Each night here was always an adventure. Felix opened the door of a white Mercedes limousine that was double-parked, ready to drive out.

"Ma'am, the drive to the heliport is about twenty minutes. Please help yourself to whatever you wish." He pointed out the bar.

"Heliport?"

"Yes, Ma'am. Mr. Jones is meeting you in Monaco. It's a short flight."

Guillermo had not said anything about flying to Monaco. I would call him.

"Felix, all good. Let's go. Thank you."

On my last trip here, I came to Monaco to see its castle perched high overlooking everything. As a day tourist, I walked around the city. I looked forward to this unexpected flight. I had known that every day here was going to be an adventure.

Felix closed my door, got behind the wheel and masterfully got us into the flow of traffic. From the back seat of the car taking me to the heliport, I called Guillermo. "I didn't know I was going to Monaco," I said in a low voice.

"I didn't know either. Mr. Jones is solid. Don't worry. He's loaded. I'm not surprised."

"I'm good," I said. I thought about the five hundred an hour. When was I on the clock? I'd have to play it by ear. Good thing I was wearing my full-length mink. It was in the late fifties and Monaco would probably be cooler. Of course, I wasn't expecting to be outdoor camping, but you never know.

I called Mona, but there was no answer. She was probably with the couple. I wondered how she felt about handling a couple. She always said she could handle anything. When she'd been getting ready tonight, she'd been so excited. The memory made me laugh.

"Everything okay, ma'am?"

"Felix, all good. I was thinking of something funny."

"Yes, ma'am."

I was as excited as Mona had been. This Mr. Jones was a mystery, and I was full of anticipation. As we drove up, I saw a blue helicopter with two pilots was already waiting for me. I said goodbye to Felix and hello to the pilots. I kept my cool, but the flight was a thrill; and though we flew through darkness, bits of the landscape and some of the yachts we flew over were brilliantly lit and spectacular. We landed at the Hotel de Paris. On the approach, I saw at least fifty people outside the casino across the street from the hotel. One of the pilots gave me a hand stepping down from the helicopter.

I saw a smiling man walking toward the aircraft. He wore a white blazer with dark slacks. He looked Hispanic to me, probably in his sixties, dark hair, silvering around the edges. He wasn't tanned but had a creamy olive tone to his skin. He had a very agreeable face, dark eyes, substantial eyebrows, and was impeccably groomed.

He kissed both of my cheeks, European style. We walked to the elevator hand-in-hand like we knew each other. I assumed he was not American, and as soon as he started talking, he proved I was right.

"It's difficult to get seated at a good restaurant when the festival is going on," he said in accented English. "I hope you don't mind the helicopter ride."

I squeezed his hand. I laughed. "Don't mind at all. The night view was fantastic."

"Day is better view," he said.

I nodded in agreement.

At Le Louis XV Restaurant overlooking the casino, a pristine window table was waiting for us. White linen cloth and napkins. Gold and white frescoed art lined the inset of the tray ceiling like it was an Italian church I'd studied in my undergraduate art history class, instead of in a French restaurant where I was actually about to eat. We sat across from each other.

"Beautiful," I said.

"It is you who are beautiful," he said. "Have you been to Monaco before?"

"A day trip several years ago. I feel like a princess," I said. "Thank you."

"You look like a princess."

I don't blush as a rule, but I felt my cheeks get hot. There was something about him that humbled me, and that was not me at all.

"Thanks," I said. "Kind of you to say."

The wine steward poured wine in Mr. Jones's glass. I figured he knew what he drank.

"Champagne or wine, Madam?"

"Please, I am Kylie," I said to the steward. "I'll have the same."

My dining companion smiled and said, "Pleased to meet you Kylie."

"Felix, the driver, told me he was picking me up on behalf of Mr. Jones," I said.

"I'm a fool. Forgive me for not introducing myself. So sorry. My name is Bilal Dashti." He raised his glass. My glass met his with a click mid-way across the table.

"May I call you Bilal?"

"You must," he said. "Guillermo told me your name is Kylie."

I smiled. "Pleased to meet you," I said again.

We toasted again in silence. I was aware of the servers moving around the room bringing food to a large table of well-dressed Asians. Actually, everyone here was well-dressed. The server's uniforms looked like formal office wear, black pants and coats, red ties, white collars. A serving station in the middle of the dining room had four tiers of wine glasses that sparkled like jewels.

"Kylie, you are beautiful, exactly like your picture. When Joe showed it to me, I was not interested in looking any further."

"I'm glad you picked me," I said, laughing.

"It seems unfair that we pick, and the lady doesn't get the same opportunity."

I could always walk away, walk out. He's right though.

"You are a handsome man," I said.

"My turn to say thank you," he said.

"Do you live in the South of France?" I asked.

"I live in London, originally from Kuwait."

"Nice," I said.

"You prefer Kuwait or London?"

"London," I said with a smile.

"Have you been to London?"

"Actually no. I've been to Paris and only dreamed of going to London."

"It's good to know that you dream of going to London," he said, leaning forward, and looking intensely into my eyes. He had nice teeth. Maybe he wasn't sixty yet. He wasn't weathered.

I never took to French food, but I didn't say anything. I ordered a Salad Niçoise to start and was delighted to see that lobster thermidor was a choice.

Our conversation was about business. I would not in a million years tell him I am a lawyer. Like many men I was paid to dine with, Bilal liked to talk about himself. I listened to him talk about being an investor in the volatile commodities market. He was successful because he could not be outsmarted, and he had limits.

I said 'amazing' way too many times. Dinner was delicious. I ate just enough to be comfortable, but I couldn't say no to the waiter's suggestion of chocolate souffle and espresso. Bilal ordered Louis XIII brandy. I would have passed, but there was no way to decline graciously, so I accepted, and then got treated to the ceremonious way they served it tableside. I had never had it back home where a pour of it cost over five hundred dollars. I could feel the brandy all the way to my toes. I wasn't used to hard liquor. I must admit it was not bad.

In the restaurant, only Bilal and the waiter had a clue what it cost.

I stopped myself from asking too many questions. I thought we might be staying at the Hotel de Paris where we just eaten, but instead of going upstairs to a room, we took a walk to a noisy helicopter. We boarded at the heliport.

"Where are we headed to?"

"Cannes," he said.

"Lovely."

We were seated thigh to thigh, his hand on my knee as we lifted up and into the vast, dark, night sky. We kissed. Just a kiss.

Felix and the beautiful white car were waiting for us when we landed. When we pulled into my hotel, I figured he was dropping me off, but Bilal got out too.

"Are you staying here?" I asked, when he emerged from the car and took my hand.

"I am," he said. "This is where Felix picked you up?"

"Yes. I'm staying here."

"I love this place," he said.

"Me too," I agreed.

We walked through the busy lobby to the elevators holding hands. Bilal liked to hold hands.

His suite was magnificent. I think seven or eight of my hotel room would have fit inside. He had more rooms, a full dining room and living room, and the living room had a full bar. My room had carpeting and a fake balcony. His room had a rooftop patio, and marble floors under Persian rugs. Even though I have been with so-called royalty, men that have the title of Prince and entertained them in private homes in Cannes and in huge suites like this one, I was impressed. Who wouldn't be? I know a man like Bilal who spoke of his business the way he did would want me to rave about the luxurious palace we were in that had to be costing him at least ten thousand dollars a day. I raved over it.

The dinner and drinks had been wonderful, but I suddenly felt either the effects of the wine, or what could be jetlag. I did not want to show any sign of being tired. Still holding my hand, he went to the bedroom without stopping at the living room bar, which pleased me greatly.

"Bilal, do you mind if I freshen up? A shower would be great."

"Good idea," he said, pointing out which bathroom was his and which was mine.

"If you'd like, I can soap you down in the shower," I said. "Or we can use the two bathrooms."

At his request, I filled his huge jacuzzi bathtub.

"Will we fit?" he asked, feeling my ass as I leaned over to test the temperature of the pouring water. "We will fit nicely," I said.

I turned around and hugged him. His penis was hard, not straight, over to one side but he was big.

"Very nice, Bilal," I said, going on my knees on the marble floor. "I'll work this while we wait for the tub to fill. Is that okay?"

"Over here," he said, moving back to a settee.

"Perfect," I said, positioning him so he was sitting on the cushion, and my knees were on a towel doubled over.

I turned off the water, positioned myself between his thighs, and listened to him moan in pleasure.

"I knew you would be like this," he said, leaning back against a wall.

Bilal got it working for the third time and took me doggy style. You don't have to be middle eastern to like this position, but I knew from experience that at some point, they want it like that. Older men tend to go flaccid faster in this position. When he did, I attended to his penis until it got hard again, and then we'd start over where we left off. Bilal blamed the food, then the liquor. A big shot like him, making excuses to a call girl. I tried to make him feel better about it.

"We've been at it for two hours. Nothing's wrong with your big dick. It probably needs to rest a bit." When it was ready again, I said, "You see, you're back."

Bilal smiled.

At four in the morning, he walked me to the door of his suite. He was in a hotel robe and slippers. I was in my outfit of the night, and in my purse was ten thousand dollars in hundred-dollar bills. We knew each other quite well at this point. He held the door open for me and we kissed. A passionate kiss. I did not pull away. I let it continue until he stopped.

As I took the elevator to my level, I couldn't believe the energy I had. I don't know where the second wind had come from. I let myself in our room. Mona was passed out. I hoped she'd had a good night.

I had bathed before leaving Bilal's suite and used the bidet to douche. Our bathroom had a bidet. Maybe all the rooms did. We had disposable travel douches just in case. Protocol was to call Guillermo when done for the night, just as with Macho back home. I called Guillermo. Like Macho, he doesn't sleep nights. I told him how much I made.

"Good girl," he said. "I'll send Joe about noon."

"Did Mona do good?" I asked.

"She did okay, took care of two modeling sessions."

"We came long way. Be sure you keep taking care of us," I said.

"Don't worry. I got you covered. Mona, too."

The window was open. I could smell the sea air, but there was no draft. It was a cool night, a nice night to be under the covers. I slipped into my bed, naked as I had been earlier, and went to sleep listening to Mona's breathing.

The routine is simple. Before Guillermo hits the sack in the a.m., he calls me. I take down how much each girl said the client paid. Guillermo sets the price unless she gets an hourly as Gabi did, a hit of ten grand.

Guillermo gets mad at me if I call his dolls putes.

"They are ladies. Models, not putes. You get it?"

I came to work for him two years ago. Best way for me not to stumble and call them putes or catins is not to think of them that way. I know his five local regulars personally. The ones that travel to Cannes, I don't know.

I'm the one who takes pictures to a customer who wants to see a picture. I call them models when I'm doing this. God forbid Guillermo finds out I called them catins or putes.

I have the album, so I know what this Gabi and Mona look

like. They are at the Carlton. I never came to dolls at the Carlton before. It's too expensive. It's stupid to pay what they charge here. They don't host in their room. Why fork out the dough? I've been here before to do a trick, but I know no one at this hotel. I'm the only guy that Guillermo has so I handle the guy bookings.

I went through the door. It was bright, but it still took a second for my eyes to get accustomed to the inside. The place was too posh. Tall imposing columns, gold and white. High ceilings. Why pay such fancy hotel fees? What's the benefit of high ceilings and the whole staff looking like they're set to go to a formal ball? I gave a fiver to the spiffy guard stationed at the lobby elevators. I wanted to blow my nose on the perfect triangular tip of the white handkerchief sticking perfectly out of his vest pocket.

"I'm here to see the ladies in room 215."

He looked at the five. "You don't look like a terrorist," he said.

"Pas aujourd'hui," I said. "Not today."

I left him laughing and got in the elevator.

I knocked on the door at 215. I wasn't expecting it to be opened so promptly by the Americans. One of them, anyway.

She was fetching in her picture, even more so in person. She smelled warm and coconutty like sun-warmed skin balm and was walking around barefoot in a string bikini that had less material in it than my left sock. She'd clearly just come from laying out at the beach, and her hair was streaked every possible shade of blonde, honey, gold, and brown, and her eyes matched the hair. She smiled at me, and I felt weak at the knees. I wanted to pour a jar of warm honey all over her and lick it off. But I can't react like that to the models.

"You must be Mona," I said, being cool.

"You must be Joe," Mona said.

"You got that right," I said.

"Love your accent. Oh, you're a jolly one," Mona said with a beautiful smile.

"Come in," the other one said from inside. Had to be Gabi.

"I'm Joe," I said loudly in her direction, though I hadn't seen her yet. I stepped inside. From where I was standing, I could tell Gabi was still in bed, under blankets.

"Glad to meet you," I yelled.

"Here's seven hundred fifty," Mona said as she handed me cash.

"You're short five hundred," I said.

Gabi stood up naked and stretched. God help me, she was standing in a ray of sunlight that made me wish I was a painter or the guy she'd been with last night. Her body was so fine, I swallowed hard, and it became an effort to not make a fool of myself. She shrugged into a robe, grabbed a pile of money on the bed-stand, and walked towards me holding her cash. She was a looker, and she had more of a presence than Mona. Of course, that vision of her stretching in the sun was going to stick in my brain for a good long time.

"Ten percent we take home for Macho. You should know that," Gabi said.

"Who is Macho? A partner I don't know about?"

"You're not jolly. You're a smart-ass," Gabi said.

Her hair was just chin length, wildly rumpled, but perfect curls, mostly gold. I knew girls who sat at a salon for hours to get that look, but she had just gotten out of bed. She was beautiful, savagely sexy, better than the picture I had in the album. Beautiful but not so friendly. I took the cash. Tomorrow was another day.

I called Guillermo when I hit the lobby.

"Both the Americans shorted me," I said.

"You woke me for this? Didn't I tell you that they pay fifteen percent?" Guillermo said.

"Sorry to wake you. No, you didn't tell me."

"I just told you."

Every girl he has was busy last night. He has a gold mine. I rode my motorcycle to the Park Hotel where six of the models are staying. At the Park, everyone knows me. Same at the Hideaway where the other ladies are staying. The models have separate rooms. The only ladies that know each other are the locals, and they live in their own places. Not every girl pays Guillermo the same. One lady, Luiza from Romania pays forty percent, but I keep these details in my notebook. She was one of the out-of-towners I didn't know. In her picture, she had dark eyes, and lots of dark hair. For all I know, that's a Romanian trait.

"You must be Luiza," I said.

She opened the door in a nightie. Luiza is fine-looking, hot as fire. Dark bedroom eyes. Dark hair.

"You must be Joe," she said with a smile. Teeth not as straight as the American girls, but white. She handed over her cash while I was still standing in the hall.

"Want to come in for coffee?"

I smiled. "I want you. If I come in, I have you," I said, leaning in.

"You got any money?" she asked.

"I do, but I don't pay."

She laughed. "In that case, Joe, have a nice day. See you tomorrow."

She shut the door. If I had been a millimeter closer, it would have banged my face.

Two hours after I started, I was done collecting. I still had to pay two contacts who had sent leads to Guillermo. A bartender and a waiter each got a fifty from me from Guillermo. I'm free until Guillermo wakes up, then I will deliver the money to him. I stopped at the Playa Restaurant on the beach, had a late lunch, and went to my apartment to catch up on sleep.

May 1990
Cannes
Mona

After Joe left, we hit the buffet in the lobby. It serves from seven in the morning until three in the afternoon, and there's quite a spread. Various brightly lit tables were set up, some of them with four or five tiers. The portions were tiny, but there were a gazillion separate brunch-style dishes. I snagged a half grapefruit with a cherry in the middle, and a flower made with petals that were slices of a bunch of different kinds of melon wrapped together in a slice of Canadian bacon that the waiter called prosciutto. I found a shot glass of some kind of fantastic soup he said was bouillabaisse, and the waiter brought me a half-full bowl of it. Of course, the bowl was the size of the bathroom sink back home. The dessert table was like a rainbow, tons of shot glasses with everything from whipped cream to chocolate mousse, and every possible color in between.

We were both starved.

"I haven't had anything to eat since the hamburger we had by the pool."

"You should eat," Gabi said, devouring a plate of breads and cheeses, and going back for a bunch of tiny bite-sized quiches of different kinds, rumaki, stuffed mushrooms, and something that had crab in it.

"I am eating, if you haven't noticed."

"I had a great dinner with a Kuwaiti. Salad Niçoise, lobster Thermidor, chocolate soufflé."

She told me about the helicopter trip to Monaco.

I told her about the couple, and my second session, which was with a Middle Eastern man at the same hotel where I did the couple.

"I got $2,500 and check this out. The Arab after, he gives me twenty-five hundred. Apparently, that's what Guillermo charged him for two hours. I fucked him once, and it wasted him. He wasn't more than forty, good looking too. Small dick, but it worked, not enough to satisfy me but what else is new. Anyway, I showered then sat around with him watching television until the two hours were up."

Gabi laughed. "You scored."

"I did. I felt bad. It's a lot of money for what I did."

"Oh please, Mona. Lighten up. If they couldn't pay, they wouldn't play. If we wanted to stay in the hotel and do our own scouting, all we'd have to do is hang around the lobby downstairs. Security can't say shit because we're checked in here. We could score. I offered to do that when I spoke to Macho. I even offered to give him his cut, but he shined it on and said it wasn't a good idea."

"Gabi let's stick with G, whoever he is. You got ten grand. I got half that and it's only the first night."

"I'm kidding. I talk it, but I don't want to pimp myself."

Gabi finished everything she'd from her second round and came back with a plate full of shot glasses of fruit concoctions. If I ate like her, I'd be fat. I was slowly eating bouillabaisse, a bowl of clams, lobster, crab, shellfish, shrimp. Every drop was a mouthful of heaven, and I was savoring it for all I am worth.

"This G is a mystery," I said.

"You'll meet him," Gabi said. "He doesn't show often but he'll be around."

"Great. I want to meet him," I said.

Gabi rolled her eyes. "You get excited about the littlest things," she said. "He's just a high-end pimp. Nice guy though."

"I'm not excited. If you called Macho a pimp, he'd shoot you."

Gabi laughed.

"Yeah, Macho is an agent, a manager, not a pimp. And you are weirdly excited, like that bowl of soup is going to make you come." She picked up her spoon and aimed it at a juicy chunk of lobster in my bowl. I crouched over the bowl, moved it closer, and put my arm out to intercept her spoon fake-guarding it. I grabbed a shrimp fork, stabbed the lobster chunk and shoved it in her mouth. That shut her up for a good ten seconds. Her eyes rolled back in her head a little bit, and she moaned. I should have kept my mouth shut.

"I don't like working for a pimp," I said. "I prefer manager."

"Okay then, Guillermo is not a pimp. He's our manager."

"That's more like it. Have you fucked him?"

"No, I met him maybe three times on my last trip. No pass from him. No fuck."

"Is he fuckable?"

"I imagine he's very fuckable." She shrugged. "He's black. He's a good-looking dude."

"What are you thinking about?" Gabi asked.

"Max."

Gabi smiled. "He was a hunk."

"Why past tense?"

"Because he's gone from our lives."

"I read in the paper that he's retiring," I said, getting up for dessert. One of those pistachio mousse desserts had my name on it.

"Yeah, this year," Gabi says. "I read it too."

"I wonder if he's still married."

We walked together back to the buffet.

"I wonder," Gabi said picking up an apple tart with one hand, and a tiramisu with the other.

May 1990
Cannes
Guillermo

Joe's chopper was parked in my parking garage. We met at my kitchen table, me with my phone in hand, trailing the long cord. The house phone has been ringing since I got up, old customers who don't have my cell number. I haven't had time to count the money he collected today, but I would do that soon. He put my first espresso of the day on the dinette in front of me. I lit a cigarette, sucked a lungful of smoke, and put it down on an ashtray. A client was talking in my ear as I motioned for Joe to get some coffee for himself. During the Cannes Festival, I'm up and on the phone by five in the afternoon with two hours less sleep than I like to get. The city was bustling, busier than ever, and my phone reflected that.

I took swig of the coffee and listened to the client who was about to tell me what he wanted.

"Joe showed me a picture yesterday of the girl named Trisha. Is she available?" Bilal Dashti asked.

"I can make her available. Did you enjoy Kylie?"

"She's a winner."

He laughed. I laughed. I laugh a lot with customers.

"Trisha and she are bunking together at your hotel. Both from Los Angeles."

"I didn't know."

"I don't want to sell you more than you came for. You could do a three-some if you wish."

Dashti was silent for a moment. "Are they both available?"

"At this minute they are. When I take the next call, that might change."

He laughed. "How much for both? Doesn't matter."

"It matters," I said. "Two thousand per hour, five hours minimum."

"We went from five hundred an hour to two thousand. What happened?"

"You got two of the best, and they make ten each or more in a night. Two thousand with a five hour minimum for both is half of what they normally make."

"My room at ten," Dashti said. "Call me back to confirm."

"Yes sir, will do that."

Joe saw my cup was empty and served me a second espresso.

"Merci, Joe."

I dialed Gabi's phone. "Is Mona with you?"

"You mean Trisha."

"Sorry, I know the names. Is she there?"

"Sitting right next to me."

"I got a request for the two of you."

I explained.

"That means the most we can make tonight is five each," Gabi said. She didn't sound convinced.

"That's not a bad night," I said. "I have calls to make. Yes, or yes?"

I heard Mona say that she was okay with it. I remember from before that Gabi can be difficult. She was always on top of how much she was going to make per night. After the ten she made last night, she's going to want that much every night, but she agreed to the date.

"One more thing," she said. "Give me one of your winner Arabs that pays upwards of twenty thousand. You know who they are. We got the clothes and the class to handle anything."

"I got you covered," I told her.

After I confirmed with Dashti, I hung up. Right away it rang again. Another client. It was going to be a good night.

May 1990
Cannes
Gabi

It will be righteous to make five thousand a night, after commissions. I would go home with the money I'd like to have back in my stash. I did not tell Guillermo that, but I did tell Mona.

"You such a good negotiator," Mona said. "Thanks to your skills, Max's lawyer paid me some real money."

"Paid us," I reminded her.

We arrived in front of the double entry doors to Bilal's suite at ten on the dot. He glowed with delight when he saw us. Men in his position are not always so gracious. Bilal was openhearted and nice. The intimate hours we'd spent together the night before gave me a pretty good picture of his character.

He was dressed in a white linen suit, blue shirt and shoes.

"You're all dressed up," Mona said.

"Yeah," I said, "You look great. What's going on?"

"We're going out on a yacht with friends if that's okay with you."

His smile was like a dare to say it wasn't okay.

"Yachting, here we come," I said.

"Should we go down and change?" Mona asked.

"You look pretty, but don't worry. Our host has clothes if you want to change what you're wearing."

Our host? It took longer to drive than it would have taken to walk, not that we had on shoes for walking. Driving had been a good idea. We used the time well, and fell all over him, like we were famished to have him. We smothered him with kisses and teasing. He loved it. The bath I'd given him yesterday erased all traces of 'first date jitters' and gave today a head start.

It was a big, big boat. I mean, yacht. It was parked by a slip barely long enough to accommodate it. I hadn't counted how many decks, maybe five. I have no clue what boats cost or what kind of wealth it takes to own a yacht like this. The upkeep must be astronomical. I wondered what the gas mileage was.

"This is amazing," I said.

"Crazy amazing," Mona said.

I looked for an indication that it was not a private yacht but found nothing. Five minutes after we were aboard, Bilal introduced us to the owner, Rob Sphere, a Londoner and friend of Bilal's. Rob wore a black shirt, white slacks and shoes. They hugged each other, kissed each other, and then we were finally properly introduced.

"Both of you look la-di-da," Rob said, "But would you like to get comfortable?"

It did not sound like an order. It was more like a gracious invitation.

"What do you suggest?" Mona asked.

"We will have fun," Rob said.

Bilal said nothing, just nodded in agreement. A waiter was handing Rob and Bilal drinks when we followed Ingo up a deck to Ginger, a red-haired beauty younger than we were. The dressing room we undressed in was made of polished inlaid teak, and Ginger hung our clothes in a walk-in closet. We sat on benches and were provided identical drawstring linen pants, matching plunging neckline blouses, Gucci sneakers, and a Gucci hoodie with a zipper. Apparently, we were all supposed to dress alike. There was an unlimited supply of the outfit.

"Nice," I said, holding up a pair of the brand-new sneakers. "Can we keep these?"

"All of it is yours," Ginger said. She was in the same outfit, down to the shoes. She offered socks. We passed.

"I suggest you put them on. It will get chilly when you are on the deck outdoors," Ginger advised.

We followed her advice. The hoodie was light but very warm, maybe because we were still indoors.

Ingo walked us to the top deck where Bilal, Rob, and at least ten people were sitting around eating hors d'oeuvres and drinking drinks. The music was blaring. Below us, onlookers were gazing at the yacht and snapping pictures. It was late in Cannes, but late is when Cannes comes to life.

"We thank you for the comfy clothes, Rob," I said.

He waved off the thanks. A waiter came to get our orders.

I counted five women dressed as we were, and four men we had not met yet dressed in suits. I guess the clothes were just for the women.

A bell rang.

"We are heading out," a voice said over the loudspeaker. He introduced himself as the captain, welcomed us all aboard, made some jokes, and explained that we would be heading to Nice and back.

"Is this exciting or what?" Mona asked.

"For sure. I never made it to a yacht before," I said.

Mona took my hand and squeezed it, then let go and touched Bilal. Bilal took her hand. Rob got close to me.

"Let's sit over here while we pull out," he said, motioning to a sitting area away from the other passengers. I wondered if we were going to meet them. We should have done so when we came on board.

I wondered if the plan was to hook me up with Rob. I had no idea what lay ahead. Mona and I were going to have to play it by ear. I moved closer to Rob on the cushioned seat we were on. The sky was cloudy. I wondered if some stars would show through. Bilal and Mona were in the next seat. We put out to sea. Ginger came around with a bag of knit hats.

"In another three weeks, the weather will be beautiful. To-night, the wind has a bite to it. It's cold. Put it on," Rob said.

I loved his British accent. So much for my hair. I put it on and over my ears. He smiled.

"You're as beautiful as Bilal said."

"You are nice to say that, and so is Bilal," I said.

We were moving slowly along the coastline. Rob took my hand and walked me down to a cabin on the level below. The ceiling was beautiful, some kind of exotic wood I had never seen before, and big rustic beams that supported the upper deck where we had been sitting.

This level also had a bar, a bartender, and a nice-looking young man doing the serving. I could see the lights of the coastline twinkle through the windows. Bilal and Mona joined us, and the four of us sat at a table about ten feet from where the other guests were. Rob asked what I thought about the communist party in Russia giving up control months back.

"Unbelievable that Gorbachev stood by and watched the USSR dissolve," I said, "But not so unbelievable after Beijing brutally crushed the demonstrators in Tiananmen Square, and crushed democracy there with their military. The world's opinion of how Tiananmen Square was handled will haunt China, maybe forever. So, I'm not surprised he did not turn on his fellow countrymen."

"He is a gutsy person," Rob said.

"I think the next big thing is that East and West Germany will be reunited."

"What do you think of Mandela getting released?"

"South Africa should have done that long ago," I said.

"I agree," he said. "Mandela will become a legend."

"Yes, no doubt."

"Do you believe the cold war will really end this year as they say?"

"If the cold war ends, my money is on Gorbachev getting the Nobel Prize this year."

"I hadn't thought of that. Did you read that somewhere?"

"I didn't read that. I'm just thinking this is Gorbachev's year. If he keeps going along with the way the world is changing, how else can he be publicly rewarded? I say he's a winner."

Rob laughed. We clicked glasses and drank. I waited for more poli-quiz questions, but that was the end of it.

Blal and Mona had their own thing going and were paying us no attention.

I stood to watch the lights outside, and when I looked back, all the other guests were naked and doing each other as though we did not exist.

I clapped my hands. Rob looked at me and did the same.

"What a surprise. I wondered who the guests were."

"He is filled with surprises," Bilal said.

"He sure is," Mona said, raising her glass of wine. "So cool, Rob. Thank you."

Our host never offered a reason for having these people put on erotic performances, and I didn't ask. Each couple was doing something different. The lights were low, and the music was quiet enough that we could converse without yelling.

"Do you like?" Rob asked.

"I like," I said, returning his kiss.

Bilal and Mona were whispering to each other across the table from us. Rob led Bilal, Mona and me to a level below the orgy where we split up. Rob and I went to one bedroom, and Bilal and Mona to a compartment on the opposite side. It was not a threesome at all. I could see how comfortable Mona was, how well she got along with Bilal. She was loose and happy. It was a great evening.

Rob liked to tear into things.

He pulled off my Gucci hoodie, blouse and pants, leaving me topless with my panties on. He stripped me naked, but it didn't hurt. It wasn't alarming. I squealed like he expected me to, and then I matched him, and tore off his clothes. Because his clothes were more substantial, it wasn't easy, and I told him it wasn't fair. He never stopped laughing or grinning, and neither did I.

Rob had a good size bat between his legs, and he got right to business with no foreplay, unless you count how hot it was watching the erotic sideshow. He was on top, then he wanted me on top. What we were doing turned me on enough that we didn't need lubricant. I didn't have an orgasm, but he fucked for a long time. He sweated a lot, but he smelled good.

Around one in the morning, a waiter came. Rob ordered clam chowder served in a sourdough bowl and I followed suit. Our food arrived loaded with crackers already in the bread bowl, easy to eat and delicious. He poured the white wine the waiter had opened for us, and we drank it in the glasses he delivered.

"You don't look like a call girl," Rob said, sipping wine. "And your conversation is impressive."

"I try to stay current," I said, then whispered, "I even graduated from college." I regretted it as soon as the words were out of my mouth, but then said quickly, "How does a call girl look?"

He was sitting up on the great big bed against pillows, and I was sitting with my legs crossed in the center of the bed facing him. The blue and white sheets had a nautical theme.

He avoided my question, not revealing what he thought a call girl looks like.

"You're a smart woman. You speak eloquently."

"Thanks, Rob, but you're the genius. Just look at this yacht."

I laughed and he grinned broadly.

"Do you come to Cannes often?" I asked.

"I'm here for every festival and again in August. I keep my boat in Marseilles."

"I would have trouble leaving this palace."

"I always have trouble, yes. My home and my business are in London."

Maybe he thought I would ask what he did for a living. I didn't.

We talked for more than an hour with him in a short robe with no underwear. It was funny, and I had to keep the laughter inside. The clothes he'd given me were in shreds on the floor, but he gave me a shirt of his to wear. We moved to a round table near the bed.

"I know nothing about boats. Where did you find this remarkable yacht?"

"Actually, I had it built. It took almost a year and a half. Want to hear the story?"

"I do," I said, pouring him more wine.

He had a wife and she loved boating. They had a number of

boats, mostly small ones. The largest was forty-four feet. He liked the sea, liked piloting the small boats they had, but it was his wife who loved the sea. When he started making more money, they bought a bigger house, bought more cars than they needed, bought an airplane they used maybe once a month, and then they started looking for a yacht. They couldn't find one like his wife wanted. She wanted the master cabin to have two full bathrooms, not boat bathrooms, but huge bathrooms with a tub.

"We talked to a boat architect who met with us more times than I can remember and when the plans were finished, he found us a boat builder. We named the boat Cilla, short for my wife's name, Priscilla."

"And when the boat was finished, did she love it?"

His expression darkened. He suddenly looked somber and troubled.

"I'm sorry. Did I say something wrong?"

He bowed his head for a moment, then raised it to look me in the eye.

"I'm sorry. My wife was diagnosed with cancer while the boat was in construction. She never saw it completed."

There was such sadness in the way he spoke. I was crying sympathetically without even realizing. He reached across the table and wiped away my tear with his finger.

"It's okay," he said. "The boat is three years old."

The mood lightened after he talked of other things. He spoke a little of London.

Rob finished off a glass of wine with another toast and went to bed. I went down on him while his big hands fondled me. He fingered me into unexpected ecstasy. My orgasm was an explosion. My excitement and my mouth on him brought on his explosion. He actually howled, and it took about a minute. His response was so extreme that we both laughed until we were in tears.

It was six in the morning when I kissed Rob good-bye. He opened my purse and put cash in it.

"This is for you," he said. "Bilal will take care of your friend."

"Thank you," I said.

I walked out of the bedroom, and found Felix waiting in a chair. Mona came out of Bilal's room.

"Ladies, I drive you to hotel," Felix said.

Bilal stayed on the boat.

"B is wiped out," Mona said. "He says that he's going to sleep for a few hours before going back to his hotel." She took my hand as we walked.

"B like Bilal?" I asked.

"Yeah, he said to call him B."

"Cool," I said.

I was half asleep on the ride back. Somehow Mona and I made it into the elevator and back to our room. We showered, and met in the bedroom, both of us in hotel robes.

I didn't open my purse until Mona plopped down next to me.

"How much did he pay you?" I asked Mona.

"Ten," she said. "He told me Rob was going to pay you."

"He did. Let me see what he put in here."

It was quite a bunch of bills. I counted aloud by the thousands. "One, two, three..."

Mona's eyes got big when I passed ten thousand. "...fourteen, fifteen. Fifteen thousand,"

"Fuck, we made twenty-five thousand between us," Mona whispered. She looked shocked but also happy.

"Not quite. Pull out the money for Joe and I'll do the same. I need sleep. When he shows, I want him gone without delay."

"Let's see, Guillermo got us five thousand each. His commission and Macho's cut is based on the five each. The extra is a tip and we don't pay on tips."

Mona got excited.

"I didn't think of that! That's right!"

"If this had been an hourly like I had last night, Guillermo and Macho would be paid based on the number of hours the client paid for. On the tip, the same applies. We keep our tips."

"I understand," Mona said, "You think I'm a dummy?"

"Based on five thousand, we each give G seven-fifty and Macho five hundred."

"Got it," Mona said. "The tips are fantastic."

"I love Cannes," I said.

Mona said, "I cleared eighty-seven hundred and fifty. I'm so excited I won't be able to sleep."

Mona closed the blackout curtains and set the thermostat to seventy-two degrees.

We were both on my bed. I got under the covers, and put my head on the pillow, turning to face Mona.

"Did you cum?" Mona asked.

"I did. I came with his fingers. It was delicious."

"Bilal goes soft a lot. He's so nice though. I think he enjoyed himself."

"If he gave you ten big ones, he enjoyed himself."

Mona yawned hugely.

I laughed at her and patted the extra pillow on my bed.

She lay down on top of the covers, groaning a little.

"I'm too tired to move."

"Stay if you want," I said, turning off the last light remaining.

She managed to get under the covers.

"Hold me."

I don't know where the robes ended up, but our bodies were entwined.

May 1990
Cannes
Mona

Guillermo can't get enough. He sent me to a third gig at sunrise after two sessions that between them went seven hours. It was an easy one just like he predicted. Guillermo is keeping us super busy, doing Gabi and me righteous.

Gabi got us upgraded to a better room with a safe. It's a bigger regular room with two bathrooms. We have to pay more but we want the extra bathroom and the little bit larger room. With our earnings, we needed the in-room safe. Gabi says when we go through customs in Los Angeles, they will want us to declare all cash over ten-grand.

"Are you really going to do that?"

"Fuck no," Gabi said.

We laughed.

We haven't been paired since Bilal and Rob, so we have plenty of stories to talk about when we have our late lunch.

Guillermo laughs a lot. I never know if he's laughing at something I say or if it's just a nervous thing. At home, when a dude is anxious, he laughs like Guillermo. Who knows? Guillermo says that I better let Macho know how well he's taking care of us. I tell him that Macho will know when he sees his cut. We've been here six working nights, and we're doing well.

Gabi and I hugged, then I left the room a few minutes before ten. Gabi's session was at eleven. Normally I take a car to a hotel or wait in the lobby. Tonight, I was supposed to meet the driver in front, a driver named Jimmy in a four-door black Lincoln sedan that would probably be double-parked. I went alone in the elevator to the lobby. The door opened, as usual for that time of night, to a crowd. The entry was packed with people dressed to the nines and outside was a raging herd of cars. Traffic during film festival week in Cannes is like grocery lines at Ralph's after an earthquake, so many people arriving and leaving, a typical madhouse.

Cannes really wakes up after seven.

One foot out the door, and I regretted leaving my mink upstairs. The cold hit my skimpy dress with a vengeance. It was too late to go back for it. I stood there getting my bearings, looking over the crowd before I spotted a black sedan at a distance pulling parallel to cars along the curb. I walked between two parked cars and along the busy driveway. Making my way through all the people getting in and out of their cars was a mess, and Jimmy was just a short distance away. To my left, cars were driving along the double lane driveway in the opposite direction as the arrivals. The crowd was practically shoulder-to-shoulder. I squealed as an arm snaked around my waist, lifting me off the ground. I heard a car door open, and I was shoved in the back seat of the car—wrong car!—and dumped face down on the floorboard. I got slammed so hard I lost my breath, but still made a noise when my face slammed into the carpet. A big hand pressed the back of my head to smash me face down. I was hemmed in. No space, no room down here.

"What do you want?"

"You want to live, woman? Shut up."

The accent was foreign, Russian maybe, but the English was clear.

"I have no money," I said.

"Shut up."

I didn't say another word.

The hand crushing my nose and mouth against the carpet had me struggling to breathe. I could feel the car moving slowly in the bumper-to-bumper traffic.

I don't know when I've ever felt so terrified. In my ears, I could hear my heartbeat racing.

Tears leaked out of the corners of my eyes. The pressure of the hand at the back of my head was unrelenting, and I struggled for air.

I'd only had a flash of a glimpse of the outside of a car that wasn't a black limo and had seen no faces yet. A new voice spoke from the front seat.

"He's going to release his grip on you. Stay down until we get where we are going." A woman's voice. French accent. Good English.

The hand disappeared from my head.

I turned my face to breathe, gulped some air, and saw only dark carpeting, and some black shoes inches from my face. Men's shoes. Not a hell of a lot of room back here. I could feel a chill emanating from the floorboards and shivered inadvertently.

"Okay," I said. "What do you want?"

"Shut up!" The man. Stern, angry voice.

What did he have to be angry over? I was the one being kidnapped. I was terrified and pissed off but managed for once to keep my mouth shut.

The car moved faster. When it got darker, I presumed we had moved from beneath the overhang of the hotel. We made some turns off of the beach road, terrifying really, because that is the only street in Cannes that I am slightly familiar with. The car was moving at a steady pace on what felt like a winding road. The windows were closed, and the car stank of the perfume the kidnapper bitch was wearing.

"I been watching you," the man said. "You dress expensive. Making good money for your pimp, yes?"

I didn't answer. Not even sure it was a question. I did not believe he'd been watching me. I work every night in hotel rooms and sleep most of the day. He's full of shit. I felt a pull on the hem of my dress, a hand on my panties, a hand touching me, yanking at the lace.

"This ass can make someone a lot of dollars," the man said. I matched the voice to the hand. I get paid when I'm touched. I gritted my teeth but said nothing.

"I agree," the woman said.

The car stopped. I heard metal, not a garage door, maybe a pull chain on a pull up door. I couldn't tell. The car moved again and stopped. I heard the metal again.

A car door opened. I could feel the car vibrate, probably the driver door. The woman spoke from outside.

"Get out of the car. Keep quiet and speak only when you are spoken to. Our intention is not to hurt you or harm your pretty face."

To get out from the position I was in, I had to crawl in the dark. My neck ached. I got to my feet, and brushed carpet debris off of my dress, and found myself in a residential driveway. The front door had an amber light above it.

I tried to make sense of what was happening, but it was unreal.

This could not be happening to me. In my head, my brain re-played the guy saying my ass could make someone money. That sounded less like kidnapping and more like slavery. My right leg cramped, and I stumbled. The man grabbed the top of my right arm and yanked me upright. I did not look in his direction but shook off his hand. I focused on the woman in front of me. Shorts and high heels. She moved like a young woman, but I had not yet seen her face. I hoped she would get stuck on the uneven stone and fall on her ass.

The door was opened by a young woman about my age. She kissed the bitch I was following and smiled at me.

"Don't be afraid," she said.

As the door closed behind us, I finally saw the face of the bitch from the car. She was a little older than I'd expected, and so heavily made up that she could have looked like anything under all the paint. The bastard who had tossed me in the car and pawed me had a big shapeless nose, overgrown eyebrows, a cleft chin, and needed a shave. The driver must have stayed in the car.

The man grabbed my arm again so that I would move forward. The bitch noticed.

"She can walk on her own," she said.

I wanted to kick him in the balls. I wanted to bitch slap the bitch. It sounded like she called the shots. Apparently, she was behind this. The girl who answered the door moved into the front room of this house. I wondered how she fit in. Hell, I wondered how I fit in. I wondered what the fuck is going on.

I stood in the lobby of my hotel for five minutes and then I saw him, my target for tonight, Misha. So many people were milling around that if I had wanted to sit, it would have to be on the floor. All the furniture was occupied. I used to worry that I looked like a hooker, but I was dressed as well as or better than the women sitting around the lobby of one of the top hotels in Cannes.

Guillermo said he'd known Misha as a client for several years and not only during Cannes. He was about forty and change, crew cut dark hair and a raw moustache, strong nose, visible cheekbones, very masculine. He smiled as he approached. He was tall and lean, but not thin, and the cloth of his suit was superfine, a better quality than I was used to seeing on the lawyers back home.

"Kylie, you are more beautiful than your picture."

He kissed my lips lightly. I caught a whiff of some expensive smelling cologne. His face was more rugged than pretty.

"And you are very handsome," I said.

Misha raised his arm a little. I placed my hand on his elbow, and we walked through the entrance.

"My car is right near the doors," he said.

A valet opened the door for me as we got in a red Ferrari with the top down. Misha got behind the wheel. I had not expected this. It was great. I would never bring up that back home I own a Ferrari.

"Guillermo told me we were going to a show first," I said.

The car was in bumper-to-bumper traffic moving away from his parking spot.

"We are. I hope it's okay."

"Of course, it's okay," I said with a giggle. "You speak great English. Where are you from?"

"Moscow. My business is with many English-speaking people and I've caught on."

He took his eyes from the traffic for a moment and stared at me. We weren't moving.

"Kylie, you are beautiful."

By the time I looked at him, he was watching the traffic again. We moved forward an inch or two.

"You're kind of beautiful yourself, Misha."

May 1990
Cannes
Guillermo

I was at a restaurant where I eat all the time, where I know everyone. Getting a table is not a problem, even when the place is booked. All my dolls are booked again, but my phone never stops ringing. If I had three times the girls, I'd have them booked. Beside the napkin, my cell phone is on the table, its light going on and off. The nights are long and full of spontaneous requests. My dolls finish a session and are willing to keep going as long as there is demand. It's non-stop.

The restaurant was packed. When I stood, a waiter rushed over to see if there was a problem. I motioned to the phone so that he knew I was not leaving.

"Hold on," I said, headed to the parking lot door in the rear. "It's too noisy. Sorry."

The door slammed behind me, shutting the noise inside.

"Okay, you got me. Who is this?"

"Guillermo, this is Marty. Your girl Trisha is a no show."

"Impossible."

"My driver waited thirty minutes out front, and she never got there."

"Marty, give me your number. I will call you right back. Don't worry, I'll make it up to you."

"I counted on you. I'm at the party without anyone like I planned, but after I need it. I am not sleeping alone tonight."

"I promise you will not sleep alone, and you will not have to pay a dime."

I took out my little phone book and punched in Mona's number.

No answer.

I redialed.

No answer.

I wanted to call Gabi, but she's in a session.

I called Joe.

"Get over to her room. Call me back on my house phone. I'm on the way."

"Be there in fifteen," Joe said.

Everyone was booked. I looked through my list for dolls who wanted in, who would have made the cut if I kept six girls instead of five.

"Gianna, you know who this is?"

"Honey, I know your voice. Guillermo, why are you calling me?"

"Are you working?"

"Yeah, slave pay."

"Are you working this very minute?"

"No, right this minute I am naked, alone at home in a bubble bath. What's up?"

I heard the splash of water.

"You dress up. I'm going to send you out with someone. I'll pay you. Do this right and I may let you in. Got it?"

"Honey, I got it. How much?"

"A thousand US."

"For how long?"

"Never mind. I'll call the next in line."

"Wait, don't do that honey."

"I'll call you back with the address. You got to dress up. Understand?"

"Honey, you've seen me. I dress well."

"You're right Gianna."

I called Marty.

"This doll Gianna is a cutie, twenty-five, local girl. Where and when do you want her to meet you? It's on me."

"Where's Trisha?"

"She may have gotten sick. You'll love Gianna, I promise."

Marty had not seen a picture of Mona. He took my word for it, just as he was going to take my word for it about Gianna. Gianna does not have polish, but she has everything else.

I went back in the restaurant to have the waiter pack up my dinner, drove home and unpacked my meal on my desk where I can talk comfortably on a phone without a hundred people talking, chewing, and clanging their silverware in my ear.

My desk phone rang. I picked it up expecting it to be Joe, and I was right.

"What's the scoop? Is she in her room?"

"I knocked on the door. No one answers. At this hotel I can't push in. They have card keys."

"This is not like her at all. Ask around for her. You got a picture."

"She might be tricking on her own," Joe said.

"Say that again and I'll kick your ass."

"Sorry, G. I'll get back to you. I don't know anyone here."

"Money talks," I reminded him.

I took a bite, but dinner was cold, and my appetite gone. I tossed the food in the trash. Against my better judgment I called Gabi. No answer. I looked at my watch. She was probably at the show. Damn. I hate waiting.

Something was wrong.

May 1990
Cannes
Gianna

I work it on my own. When I'm on the street with competition, guys on the prowl will motion for me to come to their car so they can talk through the passenger window. I know I look good. I can't pay for designer, but I don't use my knockoffs unless I'm on to something bigger than usual. I've been trying to get on with Guillermo. His reputation is over the top. He can pimp me anytime. I'd make money for him and me.

I know and get along with Guillermo's five locals, but they got no influence with Guillermo, even if they want to help me, which, no telling if they do or don't. I tried to get in with him for the festival.

"I got plenty," he said. "Maybe next year," he said.

He called out of the clear blue sky. It must be that he is in a pinch. Something's up.

When Guillermo hung up, I got off the phone and looked around my place. My apartment's small, but all mine as long as I pay the rent on time each month. No children, no fool man, no roommates. It was warm inside, and I stood naked in my bathroom to run the hair dryer. When I was done, it hung board straight no matter what. No point using sprays or gel. I brushed and flossed my pearly whites. Thank you, Lord, for giving me these beautiful teeth.

In my bathroom mirror, floor to ceiling on one wall, I look good. I'm slim, fit, shapely, no wrinkles. I look young for my age. I smiled at myself, high-fived my reflection like an American movie star. A thousand will go a long way.

I picked up my bottle of Dior. The guy who sells me knockoffs swore it's the real deal. He bought it from someone who stole it from a perfume shop. I never put too much on, a dab behind my ears, between my breasts, a touch on each cheek of my ass, and right on my clit. It stung.

I went through my outfits and picked a faux Chanel black dress. If you untie the barely-there straps, it falls to the ground. Not even the designer would guess it's not the real thing. Faux Chanel patent leather shoes to match and a matching purse. What I didn't have is jewelry. Chanel should be worn with jewels, but I'm a rule-breaker. I could pull it off.

I wanted to take a bus, but dressed like I am, I took a taxi to the JW Marriott. Never been before. I didn't want to act awkward, so I didn't react, but the ceiling went up three stories. I wanted to look at the bar and the restaurant, but it was a blur as I went past, straight to the elevator. The client is the important thing.

The elevator guard greeted me like I was a guest. I got off on the sixth floor. The room was way down the hall. I knocked first, then saw the button for a doorbell. I pressed it. He opened the door, looked me up and down. He looked like money. He was healthy, well-fed, maybe in his forties. He had an accent, but his French was good. He was in slacks, no shirt, looked like he was just undressing. He seemed comfortable in his own skin. He smelled tasty.

"Marty is my name."

He wanted to shake hands. I moved up close and kissed his lips.

"You are a knockout," he said "Wish you had gone to the party with me."

He shut the door behind me. Party? I didn't ask. Nice big corner room, windows on two sides, luxurious drapes open revealing the lights of Cannes glistening. Plush carpet.

"I'm Gianna."

"How about a drink, Gianna?"

"Soft drink, if that's okay with you."

"I have a refrigerator full of choices. Come choose."

I followed him, a little dazzled by the high-quality hotel room, but his bare back made me feel an instant connection with him. I mean, he's comfortable with me. It's like the room was putting on airs, but he wasn't.

I picked a Coca-Cola. He opened the bottle for me at the bar, and I stopped him from giving me a glass.

"I'll drink it from the bottle. Thanks, Marty. Can I call you Marty?"

"It's my name. Is Gianna your real name?"

I nodded and took a sip. "It's my name."

I sat on the living room sofa as he got a Coke for himself and poured it from the bottle into a glass with ice. He sat next to me. The suite's living room was twice as big as my apartment. I saw the bed in a whole other room.

"Did Guillermo tell you what happened?"

"I don't understand?"

Marty said he arranged for a date with Trish, one of Guillermo's girls. I didn't recognize the name. He sent a car and driver to pick her up, but she never showed. He called Guillermo to complain, and here you are. I'm the here you are.

"Here I am," I said, and put down the drink. I turned to meet his eyes squarely and put my arm over his shoulder.

"I promise you won't be sorry."

His glass went on the table by mine, and we slipped into a hug. It's a lot of contact because my designer knockoff is for summer, and there was not that much to it. His skin was warm, and a little damp like he was fresh from the shower, but his hair was dry. A touch of hair across his chest. His party shirt was draped on a chair. Definitely designer. No robe on. Just slacks, so he was just getting comfortable after the party.

"I love your scent," he said.

"In that case, you love Dior. What's your pleasure, Marty?"

"What's yours?"

"I'm yours, and you don't have to pay."

"Guillermo is a man of his word," Marty said. "A stand-up guy."

He stood. I stood with him, clinging to his delicious skin. He released me from the hug, looked toward the bedroom, then at me. He was much taller than I am. He'd been to the beach and had a nice tan. I smelled a hint of aftershave, who knows what. I didn't recognize his cologne, but I could tell that it was expensive. I don't know about colognes anyway.

"I'll show you the bedroom."

He held my hand and led me. I saw his shirt tossed across a chair, and a white suit draped over a hanger, definitely designer. Gold cuff links on a dish. Solid gold cologne bottle. Marty smelled and looked like money. A tip would be wonderful.

I thought I'd make it so good he wouldn't have a choice.

I took the lead. He was standing by the bed. I slipped off his slacks as he watched me. I brushed lightly against him as I followed them down, dropping to my knees. He pulled me close, dragged me back on my feet, full body contact all the way. He was already hard, upright.

He was naked on the edge of the bed, his bare feet on the carpet.

He slipped his hand down my back, sliding against my skin, sliding his hand across my back, unclasped my bra one handed. A big hand, and warm. I found myself swaying in his direction. The bra didn't fall off, still under the dress. He tugged the narrow strap of my dress over my shoulder, and then nothing, just looked at me. He stopped. He was waiting. I read his eyes and took a few steps away from him to undress. The dress slipped down my body, and I made love with him with my eyes while he was watching the clothes come off. His eyes were hot on my body. The thong I wore dropped to the floor. I turned my back to him, and bent to pick up the lacy little bra, thong, dress, and lay it all on the back of a leather armchair as if my knockoff was the real deal. He liked my ass. I heard the intake of his breath and turned to face him.

I licked my lips.

He licked his. They were slightly open. He was almost panting, and his eyes were consuming my body.

I walked up to him in my heels, nothing else on my body except Dior. He was still sitting, but reached out, planted both his hands on my ass, one on each cheek. He grabbed a handful, and pulled me toward him, ducking so he could kiss my belly button. First my belly then my face. I sank down on the bed with him. The liquor on his breath was an aphrodisiac. He was a prize. I wouldn't forget this night.

May 1990
Cannes
Mona

I was ordered into a brightly lit bedroom with no furniture, a boarded-up window, and four recessed lights glaring down on six young women in various states of undress, all of them sitting on the carpeting. I heard the click of a lock when the door shut behind me, and I walked straight to the other door in the room. I opened it, but it was just a bathroom, not the exit I hoped for.

I turned around and put my back to the bathroom door, trying to assess the situation, and looked over the faces of the women trapped in here with me, all of them young and beautiful, not a one of them approaching thirty. I slipped off my heels, took a position in the center away from the wall, and facing them all. I missed furniture, but at least guns weren't in the room with us, and I was a hell of a lot warmer than I was on the floor of that car coming over here.

"Anyone speak English?"

They spoke up one by one.

"I speak English," one said.

Another said, "I understand."

They all either spoke or understood it. I guess you have to in Cannes, assuming that's where they are from. I was upset, angry, outraged, but they were all cool, as unconcerned as a room full of stray cats. I couldn't be sure how they felt about me, or how they felt about anything at all.

"None of you look worried about this. Am I missing something?"

No one answered directly. One laughed, a couple of them shrugged.

"Where are your clothes?" I asked. I felt naked without my purse, but I was the most dressed of any of them.

One said she was taken from a hotel where she was taking care of a client who set her up. She was in stiletto heels not meant for walking, bra and underwear. She ducked her head, and a thick mane of frosted Italian-dark hair curled over her shoulder and over her barely covered breasts.

"Who are these people?"

White short shorts, white top, no underwear answered. "The one who had the key to open the door is Rachel. I heard someone call her that. The other woman is Liz."

Rachel was the bitch who answered the door. Liz must be the one who rode in the car.

"Who is the man?"

"Idiot," the first girl said, in a Spanish accent.

All of them laughed.

"What are we doing here?"

"We are being sold to men from Romania or Budapest," a girl said.

"I think a gang in Marseilles," said another.

"Rachel say I maybe get lucky and get a Prince in the Middle East, live like queen." She giggled.

I was stunned by their lack of concern. "You think this is all good then?"

"Be happy, Miss American," the giggler said in her broken English. "Being sell is better than beaten, throw in dirty cell, no loo, no carpet."

"There are six of you and me. There are more of us than there are of them. Why are we letting this happen?"

"There are more. We not see them all. We have no weapons, nothing."

That bastard idiot had taken my cell phone. Probably took all of theirs, too, if they had them. It was a fucking nightmare. It could not be happening.

The talk went on into the night, a welcome distraction from the pain in my neck. We exchanged names. I had asked them if they were all hookers like me. They were. One by one, they said how'd they'd been swept up. To me, it was like a nightmare, even more so because I had learned how the others had been kidnapped too.

"How can you afford that?" the Spaniard asked, pointing at my Chanel dress, a strappy black number that came with a big round chunk of costume jewelry in the cleavage. The dress itself barely reached past my underpants but had a couple of sheer veil layers that stopped four inches above my knees. As long as I wasn't facing a mirror, it felt longer. More distinctive were the sheer gloves that came up over my elbows, and the fake sheer sleeves that fastened to my upper arm, hung almost to the ground and wafted when I walked. It was a very flashy dress, and I doubted anybody but Chanel could pull it off.

"I put a lot of what I make on clothes," I said.

"You must have a good pimp."

"What good is that now?" I asked.

After a while, I went to the bathroom, surprised how nice it was. I checked my face in the mirror, relieved my lip was not cut, and that my nose looked fine. There was a shelf of makeup products, various shampoo bottles in the tub. Our kidnappers were concerned about our appearances, and keeping us undamaged, no doubt to keep our appeal for the buyers.

They were hypocrites. It made me mad. The whole situation got me boiling, and I shot out of the bathroom and knocked on the locked door. No one came, so I pounded on it. Didn't take long for the turnkey bitch, Rachel, to unlock the door. The idiot walked in and poked me hard in the chest.

"Do that again, and I will beat you until you pass out."

"Yeah, do that and you won't be able to sell me, you motherfucker."

"What is that word, motherfucker," he asked Rachel.

Rachel ignored him and pointed her finger at me. "I got six girls to sell. I don't need you. Give me any trouble, and he won't have to beat you up. I'll kill you."

She started closing the door. I caught the doorknob.

"Give us water and food, bitch."

"All in good time. Now back off. Get with the others. Get away from the door."

"You will not get away with this," I yelled in her face.

The door slammed.

I sat up, my back against the wall. No one commented on my outburst. The one who might be Italian patted my hand. The one who might have been a Spaniard gave me a pitying half smile. I was getting more upset, but everyone else was settling down.

Two of them were now lying on the floor, maybe asleep. None of them looked as panicked or anxious as I felt. I was too pissed to cry, but some rage tears might have come out of the corners of my eyes.

I wondered how long it would take Gabi to figure out I'm missing. It felt like forever, but it was early. The evening had barely begun. She was going to a show, dinner before the sex.

I had been stupid to agree to getting picked up outside the hotel.

May 1990
Cannes
Guillermo

I finally stopped calling Mona's cell phone. The phone was either shut off, she was in a bad spot of town with no reception, or someone else had the phone. I didn't want to do it, but I called Macho in Los Angeles. It was afternoon there. I got his machine. Probably like me, he sleeps during the day.

"Macho, this is me, Guillermo. Have to talk to you."

I waited a few. The machine beeped, and I heard his voice.

"What's up?"

"I don't know what happened to Mona."

"What you mean?"

I explained.

"That girl is never late."

"I will call you when I find her."

"You better the fuck do that at lightning speed."

"I sure she's okay. Don't worry, Macho."

"I am worried. Call me back."

I knew I shouldn't have called him.

Again, I called Gabi. If she answered, she would tell me the same thing. Mona is never late; she is never a no show.

No answer.

Joe called me on the house phone.

"G, I got this valet who says he thought he saw a girl being forced in a car, but he didn't see the girl's face. He was thinking at the time that it was a pissed off husband and his wife."

"What kind of car?"

"It might have been a black GMC."

I had a pretty good idea who it was.

"Did you get the time this happened?"

"He can't be sure. Maybe about ten."

That's the time. Ten sharp was her meet.

"Joe, get your ass to my place right away. We got to move fast."

Mona had been kidnapped.

I looked in my phone book for her number and called Rachel.

"Guillermo, what do I owe the pleasure of hearing your voice?"

She answered the phone in French, and that's how I responded.

"Rachel, you got one of my girls. Don't make the mistake of denying it."

I'd had a problem with her twice before. Two of her people ended up dead, and she came close to dying too.

"We don't work the hotels where your girls stay during the festival."

"Rachel, you got one of my girls."

"Impossible."

"She's staying at the Carlton."

Silence.

"Rachel, you better the fuck answer me. If I come over there, I promise I will make everyone there dead, including you. You know I don't bluff."

More seconds passed in silence.

"Are you there?"

I heard her asking someone where they got the last girl. She was pretending for my benefit. Bitch knew damn well where they picked her up.

"Rachel, fucking answer me now."

"How do I know this is your girl we got at the Carlton? You told me where to stay away from and we do. I want no problems with you."

"You got big problems. Get her on the phone. Get her right the fuck now."

"Wait. What is her name?"

"I'm coming over. You hurt that girl, and you are dead. No one will miss you anyhow."

I disconnected.

Joe arrived. I had my gun over my shoulder, and one for him too.

"What's up? Why you got that machine gun?"

"Rachel has Mona."

I handed him an assault rifle and lead the way to my car. We got in and headed for Rachel's.

"She doesn't learn, does she? That fucking bitch. Fucking with your dolls again."

"I'm going to kill that bitch once and for all. Think of the favor I will be doing the world. Rachel has two fears when it comes to me. One that I will kill her or someone in her little gang. Two, that I call my cop friends to mow her down."

"Why not let them?"

I shrugged. "Right now, I need to get Mona out of there."

"Rachel is only thirty," Joe asked. "How did she get so strong?"

"She's not strong. She hires guns and has a market for women. I should have killed her last year when she took one of mine for the second time. I'll be dead meat if Macho's girl gets sold as a slave."

"I keep hearing Macho. Who's that, G?"

"Mona and Gabi are his. He was a drug enforcement officer too good at his job. He was accused of stealing millions of dollars during a bust. They couldn't prove it, but he was forced to resign. Now he runs girls in Los Angeles. I don't know how he got mixed up in this racket, but I do know he's the kind that shoots first and asks questions later."

"Like you," Joe said.

"Crazy like me, exactly."

Joe laughed.

"You got a bonus if we free Mona."

He quit laughing.

"Let's do this," he said.

May 1990
Cannes
Rachel

"Dago, come. I need to get that whore you brought here from the Carlton."

"What you mean get?"

"I don't have time to explain. Come."

I walked to the bedroom door, unlocked it, and Dago stood right behind me just in case.

"Hey, you, American. Come over here."

I looked at the whore. Pretty eyes, slim, creamy skin, dressed like a runway model. Why did G take it so personal when one of his whores falls in my net? I stay off his turf. Mostly.

"Where's the water and food, bitch?"

Dago reached past me and grabbed her hair; I slapped his hand away. He gave me a confused look. I ignored him and talked to her.

"If you want out of here, don't give me any shit," I told her in a low voice. "Step out."

Dago shut the door, locked the deadbolt with my key and handed it back.

"What's going on?" the American asked.

"You didn't tell me you worked for Guillermo."

"You never asked, bitch."

"Call her that one more time, and I will slap your teeth out," Dago said.

"She works for G. Put her ass outside the gate. He's coming over right now, and I don't want any problems."

We walked through the front room toward the door. The American was balky. Dago grabbed her arm and tugged her along with us. She was dragging her feet and complaining.

"Who is G?"

"He's the guy that killed the dude you replaced."

"So? I know he's coming. I'll shoot him when he gets here."

"You'll never see him coming. He was a cop. His squad executed criminals instead of taking them to jail. He's a dangerous bastard."

"I left my shoes," the American kept saying. "I want my shoes."

I stopped at the door.

"Dago, for fuck's sake. Go get her fucking shoes before I shoot her to shut her up. Here's the key." She didn't react, so I suppose she doesn't speak French.

Dago released his death grip on her arm, and I stared at her until he came back. She stared back like she was a prize fighter, chin up, arms crossed, big chip on her shoulder. Too bad I called quits on her. Sell her, she'd lose the chip in minutes.

Dago is big, strong, all brawn, no brains. All he knows is fighting and shooting. I can't afford a shooting in my own house. I have brought girls here three, maybe four times during festival week. My contacts come, inspect, pay me, and it is over. When the festival is finished, we move on to another location.

Cannes is my home, and this is my house.

My life would be so much easier without G. Last year Guillermo came in shooting like a fool. I had to pay three of my neighbors to keep their mouths shut so they wouldn't report the shooting. The year before, another man of mine was planning to take one of Guillermo's girls but G shot him before he could do it. I'm going to get him once and for all, but not here, and not now.

Dago handed the American her shoes. I grabbed her by the shoulders.

"You tell G I don't want trouble. If he comes storming in here, I'll kill the girls in that room. Tell him."

She looked at me like I'm crazy. I was so furious that I couldn't keep my lip from snarling. She must have seen I mean business. For the first time since she's been here, she finally shut up.

She nodded, somehow managing to look compliant, and still looking like she had that chip on her shoulder.

"Guillermo is coming here?"

"He'll be here any minute," I said in English. "Dago is going to open the gates. You wait out there, understand?"

"I get it." She looked around. "Where's the bitch that brought me here? I'd like to punch her in the face."

"Get out of here before I change my mind."

She followed Dago out.

When Dago came back, he slammed the door. I was in the living room watching the monitor displaying the entry to the property. The American was standing in the dark, but I could make out her shape, illuminated slightly by the property light above the gates.

Liz came out of the bedroom where she had been napping.

"What is all the commotion? It woke me up."

"That was the whore American asking where you were," I said. "She asked for the bitch that brought her here."

"Which one was she?" Liz asked.

"The last one. The one from the Carlton," I said.

"American piece of shit," Liz said.

"She works for Guillermo. Remember him?"

I waited a few seconds for the light to dawn. She looked at me in horror.

"Remember what he did to Tario and Antonio?"

"He's fucking crazy. His girls don't stay at the Carlton. How were we to know?"

I didn't answer. A car was at the gate. Must be him.

"That looks like a machine gun out of a movie," Liz said. "Crazy man, *fou*."

"Check that runner of his. Look at the rifle he's got."

"We have guns. Why don't we take him on?" Liz asked.

"I'd love to do that," Dago said.

"Shut up, both of you. He's connected with police brass here and in Nice and who knows where else. I am thinking of getting rid of the snake. When the time is right."

In the monitor, Guillermo hugged the girl and walked her to the car. His runner looked straight at the camera, smiled, and pointed his weapon. We all jumped when we heard the shot that killed the camera. The monitor went direct to snow and static. We listened to find out if the car drove away, or if G was coming through the gates.

Five minutes passed. The house sits back far from the street. We didn't hear the car.

"They're gone," I said. "When these girls are sold, we go after that bastard."

"Good idea," Dago said.

"Let's feed the whores. The buyers will be here in an hour."

"You could have gotten a lot of money for that American,"

Liz said.

"She was killer-hot," Dago said, rubbing his hand over his abdomen. "I wanted her."

I punched his stomach. He bent over as if I hurt him, but he was laughing.

"You got the hots for all the whores that come through here."

"That one is special," he said. "Smell my hand. It smells like her. It smells good."

I shoved his hand away from my face.

"Go wash your hands."

He didn't obey right away, but stood there inhaling his hand, like the fool he was.

"It's just perfume," he said, laughing.

"Let me smell," Liz said.

May 1990
Cannes
Gabi

The crowds were not as bad as they had been in the beginning of the week. Misha confided he knew the main producer of the film we saw. It was his second time to see it. His first time was the second day of the festival. Because he was considering investing with the producer, he came to see it again. After the show, he drove us in his hot Ferrari convertible through the chilly night to the JW Marriott. I would have frozen without my mink. The plan was to order room service in his suite.

The suite was as grand as I anticipated. Lots of white. Orange acrylic top on the bedroom dresser, more mod than luxurious. White modular sofa. White gauze drapery around a four-poster bed. I checked out the bathroom when he called room service and ordered for both of us: oysters, lobster, bread and cheese, plus champagne and strawberries. I found a spa tub, separate shower, but didn't check it out. The food was delivered quickly, and Misha slurped the oysters as I nibbled on the lobster and him. It was not long before we had shucked off our clothes and got to business.

Naked on the bed, we fondled each other. Nibbled strawberries and fondled again. Between bouts of steaming each other up, Misha talked. A lot.

He lived in Paris, but it wasn't a French accent I heard. He was definitely international.

"I drove over. I visit Cannes often, not just for the festival."

"Fun," I said, my hand on his jack hammer.

His fingers were snuggled in my wetness.

He was paying a lot of money to talk. What could I do but respond to his conversation? I felt I needed to be interactive. He told me he's in construction. He builds high-rises in London and homes in Paris. He employs over a thousand men and women.

"Women in construction?"

He laughed.

"Some of my best steel workers, carpenters and electricians are women."

"Fuck." I said.

He laughed at my reaction and got on me. He'd been going on for so long that he'd talked himself out of his erection. I gave him a little encouragement, and he was soon up for the challenge.

The surprise of the evening was when he went down on me. I tried to get in a position to do him at the same time. He resisted sixty-nine and stayed down there until I finally had an orgasm that was extraordinary. It took so much out of me, I lay there collapsed on the bed with a huge smile on my face, feeling ripples and aftershocks for minutes afterward. It was hard to believe how lucky I'd been on this trip.

I knew he was not middle eastern. I couldn't remember a middle eastern who ever went down on me. In this business, I'm not surprised that men don't do it. I can't blame them. Misha didn't know my pussy is the most sterilized pussy in Cannes.

"Misha, I should pay you for that," I said after. It was a while after. I had to recover.

He laughed, a real belly laugh. He apparently got off on getting me off. Nice.

"Can I ask your nationality? You said you were born in Russia?"

"My father was Italian, my mother Russian."

"They made a beautiful Misha," I said, caressing his face. I kissed him.

"Kylie, I like you. You must come see me in Paris, I will give you my card."

I smiled. I'd heard the line so many times.

"Lovely," I said. "I will be sure to do that."

At three in the morning I was fresh out of Misha's wonderful spa tub and waiting for the elevator to take me to the lobby, then I was going to hail a taxi to the hotel. I'd scrubbed off my makeup of the night, and hadn't bothered to reapply it, but that didn't matter. The hall was deserted. I was not expecting to see the beautiful girl who was in the elevator when the doors opened.

"Hard night?" she asked as the doors closed. The elevator started moving downward.

"Nah. It was a great night," I said.

"I was lucky, too. My name is Gianna. What's yours?"

"Kylie."

"Pleased to meet you, Kylie," Gianna said.

We shook hands. I looked her over.

"Likewise," I said. "I like your outfit, Gianna. Chanel?" I sniffed. "And Dior. Nice."

"Your sable coat has me in awe." She flashed me a big smile, beautiful teeth.

"This old thing," I said, joking. "More precious than gold, especially in a car with the top down."

We stepped out side-by-side and walked together in the lobby. Both of us headed to the entrance.

"You got a car or taking a taxi?" she asked.

"Taxi."

I was wrong about three in the morning being quiet. The area in front of the hotel was buzzing with activity.

"So many people outside, you'd think it was the middle of the afternoon in Los Angeles. Busy. Does anyone in this town ever sleep?"

I told the doorman I wanted a taxi. He looked from me to Gianna.

"One or two?"

I looked at her. "One, we'll split it. I'm going to the Carlton. I'll enjoy the company."

"I'd love to, but no." Gianna looked disappointed. "I'm going in another direction. Thanks for offering."

As the doorman was out hunting taxis, Gianna and I talked.

"You can have the first one," I said.

She shook her head. "You go first."

I smiled at Gianna or whatever her real name might be. I put my hands on her shoulders and kissed one cheek then the other. She kissed me back.

"I think we could be friends. Come see me at the Carlton. I'll be here for a few more days. Let's do lunch or something."

"Really?"

The taxi had pulled up, and the doorman was holding the door open. I kissed Gianna again. I could tell the taxi driver was getting impatient.

I gave her my room number. "My roommate and I don't get

up until about two," I said.

I waved at her as the taxi pulled away in the night. She was getting into a taxi of her own.

I was cozy in my coat and savored the salty ocean air as we sped down the Boulevard de la Croisette with my window open. Finally, I rolled it up. The cab was nice, probably new. I remembered the cabs back home in LA reeking of tobacco and sweat, likely to have inches of crud on the floor. This one was pristine. I sat back in the leather seat, closed my eyes and thought of my date of the night. How unexpected it was that rich Misha devoured me like he did. Just the thought gave me chills, and a hot flash of sensation. Did he have a wife? All that consideration for me, and I walked out with five thousand plus a two thousand tip.

How many cases will I have to handle as a lawyer in private practice to make that much? I don't know the answer. I've never been in private practice. I thought of Homer, my former benefactor. He had practiced criminal law, and he said he made lots of money. Of course, his wife had also had the hotels and billions. I didn't want to think of Homer. He'd let me down. He pooped out on me, never reached out for me again. What had I expected? I was lucky he let me stay at with him all that time, and not to mention his paying me ten thousand a month. I believe I earned that money; it was not a gift. I fucked him and anyone else he wanted me to have sex with, while he watched.

The taxi pulled up to the entrance of my hotel. I let him keep the change, and once I reached the lobby, I turned on my phone, and dialed Guillermo to let him know how much I made.

Before I said a word, he snapped at me.

"I called you six times," he growled like a mean dog.

"I can't answer my cell during a session. What's the matter?"

"Mona's home now," he said. "But she was kidnapped last night."

I couldn't get to our room fast enough.

He kept talking, explaining what had been going on while I'd been with Misha. I ran to the elevator.

"She's okay. The girl is a roughneck. She made me proud tonight. She really handled herself."

"Guillermo, I'm almost to my room."

"Tell her I love her and I'm proud—"

I cut him off. "I'm here. I'll call you. I'll call you back." I dropped my phone in my purse, and fumbled with the key card. It took three attempts to open the fucking door. I talked to Mona through the closed door. Not that she could hear me. Finally, I got the door open.

"Mona, are you alright? I just heard."

My bedside lamp was on. Hers was off, but she sat up when I landed next to her and bounced her awake.

I hugged her.

"Did you get hurt? Tell me the truth. Tell me everything. I didn't know anything happened to you till ninety seconds ago. My phone was off. You've got to tell me everything. You've got to tell me you're okay."

I pulled back from the hug to look at her. Her eyes were moist, and her lower lip was trembling.

"To make a long story short, I was almost sold to a Romanian gang. Or a Hungarian gang. Or something. There was this woman named Rachel. She's a monster."

I hugged her. I started crying. She started crying. We were a mess.

"You'd never know I went through this with no tears," she said between sobs.

After a while, Mona lay down. I turned the light off and went to the bathroom to undress.

I noticed a dress in the trash. I pulled it up. I remembered the dress—Mona's pride and joy. It had fake sleeves, and gloves made of net, and it had cost her a fortune. The gauze that hung around the hem was partially ripped off. It had a bad tear along the bottom seam, the zipper was messed up, the gloves were ripped, and the fake sleeves that made the dress so unique were nowhere to be found.

What a waste.

Damn that Rachel. I should find a bat like Alex Rose had, and club her to death for scaring Mona like she did.

Thinking Mona was asleep, I was extra careful when I got in my bed.

"I want to sleep with you." Her voice was so meek that I barely recognized it.

"Sure baby, or I'll come to you. Whatever you want."

She didn't bother to answer, just got in my bed. We hugged.

"I don't want to hurt you. Did you get injured anywhere?"

"My neck hurt like hell earlier. It's okay now. I'm okay. They were rough but didn't hurt me or the others." She talked for a few minutes, telling me about being grabbed off the street, shoved into the back seat of a car. I squeezed my hands into fists as I listened to her story.

"...Then out of the blue, she and the idiot took me out of the room and set me outside the gates. When I was outside waiting for Guillermo to pick me up, I wondered how I would know it was him. I had never met him before."

"Like I said, he doesn't show up much. I wonder how he found you."

"Guillermo and Joe told me something about it on the drive here. Joe found a Carlton valet that saw me being pushed in a car. Guillermo had history with Rachel. He had run-ins with her in the past. She's kidnapped hookers to sell as slaves before. He guessed she was the one who nabbed me."

Apparently, all Guillermo had to do is make a phone call.

"She released me, just like that. I feel bad for the six others left behind. I told Guillermo about them, but he ignored my pleas to rescue them. But he meant business. He and Joe, they showed up with a machine gun and a rifle."

I wondered what he would do with them.

"I am never again going to meet anyone outside a hotel," she said. "That was stupid to go find a black sedan in the front of a pack of cars and find a driver named Jimmy. What the fuck was Guillermo thinking? I should have said no. I know how crazy crowded it gets out in front of this hotel. It was totally stupid for me to agree."

"Me neither," I said, nodding in agreement. I hugged her, then it was lights out, and dream time.

My cell rang. I was feeling dopy and disoriented. I disengaged from Mona and reached for it, couldn't get it. I sat on the edge of the bed and fumbled in the dark. I pulled the phone from the charger.

"Who is this?" I said somewhere in my sleep.

"I talked to Guillermo. He says Mona is okay. Is it true?"

My head cleared a little at the sound of his voice. "Macho, it's you. I should have called you. I'm sorry. She's okay, sleeping right here next to me, sleeping like a baby."

"Come home if you want to," Macho said. "You can cut it short."

"We don't have that long to go, and Mona is not going to want to quit now. Me neither. It was a fluke."

I didn't hang up. I dozed off, and I woke up with the phone in my hand. Still dark. Still not home. I tried to put it on the bedside table but the nightstand at the hotel isn't where mine is. The phone dropped to the floor, and I dropped back to sleep.

I was out.

Joe arrived the next afternoon. Same old scrawny Joe, but he was looking good to both of us now. He wasn't armed. He was just his usual self, with his ever-present messenger bag.

"About time," Mona said. "We're starved and waiting on you."

I handed Joe Guillermo's share for the Misha session.

Joe waved it off.

"G said you don't pay today," he told me, then turned to Mona. "He sends this."

He handed her a fat envelope. It was stuffed with bills.

"G says there is four G American to cover what you were going to make with the session you missed."

Mona and I exchanged glances.

"How about lunch, Joe?" I asked. "Mona says you're her hero."

"I would love to, but I have to run. I'm late getting the others. Next time."

And he was gone.

"What a guy," Mona said, getting tearful over the envelope she was examining. "G is something else."

"So is Macho. He was worried. He called while you were asleep and said we could shut it down and come home."

"Come home early?" Mona perked up. "No and hell no. We're not done here."

"That's exactly what I told him you'd say," I laughed. "Let's eat," I said. "Enough with the tears." My eyes were burning, ready to flow.

We were in the hall when the room phone rang.

"Don't answer it," Mona said.

"Okay, I won't."

We walked out of the elevator at the lobby level and headed for the buffet. Halfway there, through the usual crowd, I spotted her at one of the lobby phones. It took a moment to dredge up her name.

"Gianna," I said loud enough for her to turn to face us.

She saw me, glanced down at the house phone in her hand

and hung it up.

"I just called your room."

"Well, here I am," I said, giving her a hug like we knew each other a long time. We caught up with Mona, I introduced them, and we walked in the restaurant.

Mona and I ordered orange juice and coffee as though it was breakfast, and Gianna followed suit.

I pointed at the buffet, which was lunch extraordinaire. "This goes on till three," I said.

"It was nice of you to invite me. Thanks again," Gianna said.

"I dug you soon as I saw you in the elevator. We met last night at the Marriott," I explained to Mona.

"We almost took a taxi together until we figured out that we were going in different directions."

We split to pillage the buffet. Mona and I each brought back a plate for ourselves plus a plate of bread for the table. Mona got muffins, I brought fruit scones, and when Gianna saw what we'd done, she went back and got croissants and a cold plate of butter.

"Are we in the same business?" I asked.

"You are much too classy to be in my business," Gianna said,

"You think?" Mona gave her an arch look, nodded, and said with a straight face, "We're in the same business."

Looking stunned, Gianna glanced from Mona to me.

"At the JW, was that a score?" I asked.

"It was a score for me. Absolutely."

"You have the hottest accent and yet speak perfect English."

"Thanks. Plenty of practice here, especially on movie week."

"I did okay myself," I said, "but Mona here was kidnapped last night and almost sold as a slave."

"No!" Gianna said.

"Yup," Mona said, eating her way through a pile of mini quiches. "A fucking nightmare could not have been worse. I didn't get beaten or anything, but I was furious and helpless, especially when the cavalry showed up, rescued me, and left six people behind. I don't wish my worst enemy to go through what I did."

Mona gave Gianna a quick recap.

"I've heard of those animals. Word is one of them is a woman." Gianna put down her fork and clutched her coffee.

"Two women that I know of," Mona said.

"You have a good manager?" I asked Gianna.

She laughed. "Manager? *Un proxénète*. You must mean pimp. That is the American word, right?"

I looked around. No one seemed to be listening. I wondered if anyone was paying attention to our conversation. Lots of people were sitting around us, but they all seemed to be wrapped up in their own conversations and eating.

"I like manager better," I said.

"I don't have a manager. The one I want won't let me in."

"You must have a way. You two met at the JW. I've been there. It's primo real estate, like this hotel."

"Last night was a lucky break. The guy's date didn't show up, and the pim – I mean, the manager sent me on the house as a consolation prize."

It was too much of a coincidence. Mona stopped eating to look at me, then we both looked at Gianna.

"What's the manager's name, if you don't mind sharing?" Mona asked.

"I call him G."

"G short for Guillermo?" I said.

Gianna looked up from her coffee, comprehension dawning even before the words came.

"You know him." It was more of a statement than a question.

"Yup. He showed up at the kidnappers' place with Joe and a machine gun to rescue me."

"Damn, what a coincidence is that? I must have had your date last night," Gianna said. "Mona, he was a prize package. I'm sorry, but I'm not sorry."

May 1990
Cannes
Guillermo

At this end of the parking lot there are only parked cars. No one is close by. Fifty feet or more from here, people are getting out of their cars and valet attendants giving or collecting claim tickets. They're in brighter light, Hollywood bright like a glamorous movie set, but here the streetlamps only illuminate a weak arc. I come to a stop when I see three figures appear between cars. One is Rachel pointing a silencer at me. Her bitch, Liz, pulls a gun out of her purse. A dude I've never seen before is with them. Big, stocky, needs grooming, stupid grin. He's got a gun out, too. He must be her new muscle.

"I don't hear any brave talk. No demands, G? What's wrong? Lost your tongue?"

They laugh; the muscle laughs loud, a braying mule. Rachel and Liz hiss like the snakes they are.

My gun is tucked in a holster behind my white blazer.

"I should have killed you last night," I say.

"You should have killed me," Rachel agrees. "Let me hear you beg. Maybe I'll kill you fast."

"Let me do him," the man says.

"Don't you dare," Rachel says, training her weapon on me. She aims at my midsection. My head. My midsection again. She's enjoying this.

"If you shoot, that gun's going to throw you, Rach," the guy says. "You got no practice with it."

The bastard's jabber gives me a window of opportunity. I pull my gun, but the bastard shoots. The impact knocks me back but not down.

Rachel shoots. He's right. She falls on her ass, gun pointing skyward.

I am hit. Still standing. Wish I was next to the snake to grind her under my heel like an ant.

Muscle takes another shot at me. Damn. I stagger. Stumble. Keep my footing.

Rachel is up. She shoots. Misses. Don't see Liz. There she is. She runs. Everything in slow motion. Muscle fires again. I go down, knees slam into the parking lot, knees excruciating. I drop face first to pavement. Three dents in me, hot blisters of pain, feels like being struck by a baseball bat.

"He's dead," muscle says. "Let's go."

"I want to shoot the bastard," Rachel's voice. She's close.

"He's dead I'm telling you. They're coming this way. Let's move."

I'm not dead. Too much pain to be dead. They, however, are good as dead. If help is coming, whoever they are, better hurry.

May 1990
Cannes
Joe

Before G goes to bed every day, he calls to let me know how much each girl owes on my pick-up run. My phone rings at three in the morning. It may be another problem like the kidnapping yesterday, so I am leery when I answer.

"Come get me at Hospital. Pierre Nouveau. Hurry up."

I'm clubbing on my motorcycle. I can't use that. What's he thinking? Hospital might mean he needs transportation. I take my bike to the JW and hire a Mercedes. I know the valet, and he promises to keep my bike in front. Damn place is packed, so the driver moves at a crawl.

"Allez, allez," I say. "Press the pedal and let's get there fast," I tell the driver. We go back and forth in French.

"You want me to fly? You got wings in your pocket? You see

the traffic?"

The driver moves out of traffic and at a good clip, moving when he can, and winding around clots of traffic on the Boulevard de la Croisette when he can. I pull out my cell and call.

"I'm in a car headed your way. Traffic is a mess. I'm worried. Why are you there?"

"I was shot. I want out of here. Hurry up."

"Shot and you want to leave the hospital? I presume it's just a graze?"

"Joe, don't give me any lip. I have things to do."

G didn't look well. His slacks had been scissored-off mid-thigh, his knees bandaged. His white blazer had three holes in the chest, and it was draped over the foot of the emergency room cot. When I got there, he was wrestling with a nurse, trying to put on his holster, while a nurse was trying equally hard to prevent him.

The nurse lost.

"Get my coat," he said, pushing away from the bed.

He was on his feet but looking ashen. His holstered gun was not concealed as it normally was when he was out in public. The emergency nurse followed us down the hall, telling him he needed to get a room. G ignored her.

He asked where I'd parked.

"My bike is at the Marriot. We've got a car waiting at the front entrance."

He just grunted at me. I tried to help him in, and he growled at me.

"Take me home," he snarled to the driver, "and then you can go away."

"Drop me off at the JW," I told the driver. "I'll pick up my bike and meet you at your house, G."

Before the sun came up, we were at Rachel's gates. I saw the security camera had not been replaced. G, carrying a camo back-pack, reached in, and pulled out a green ball. It wasn't a toy.

It was a grenade.

"Where'd you get a grenade?"

"Connections," he said. "Don't ask."

G pulled the pin and tossed the grenade. He counted off the seconds, then there was a thundering blast. A garden wall collapsed, and foliage around it caught on fire. He pulled out a second grenade, and tossed it too, toward another garden wall that was still looking salvageable. I covered my ears and the earth shook again. Then it wasn't looking so salvageable anymore. Through a haze of smoke and fire in the garden, I could see the house was untouched. The house lights flashed on. G started moving toward the street. I was right behind him.

"In the car," he said.

He got in the passenger side. I got behind the wheel. His head was turned to face Rachel's property. If anyone had left the house to investigate, they were hidden by the night. Portions of the yard were in flames.

"Where to?"

"Home to wait. Get the fuck out of here. Allez."

I headed to his house where my bike was stowed in his garage.

When we pulled up to his house, I was prepared to spend the night on the couch. I'm no Florence Nightingale, but he didn't need to be alone.

"Drop me off, take the car, and go home," G said.

"That woman and her people are coming after you," I said. "I'm not going anywhere."

"You do as I fucking say. I know what I'm doing."

G is the kind of person you don't contradict. I quit arguing.

I could tell he was hurting by the way he walked towards his house. Each foot hit the ground softly, toe heel, toe heel, and he moved like he was barefoot on broken glass.

"G, I should stay here," I yelled at his back.

He ignored me, just kept on walking. I stayed there watching until he was inside. The porch lights that were on went off.

I thought of sticking around close, but I drove the car home.

I wanted a drink or a joint.

I couldn't take a chance. I need to stay totally alert.

I waited, the television on mute, cell phone in hand.

May 1990
Cannes
Guillermo

I closed the door behind me and hit the lights in and out. The grenades will let her know that I am alive. I'm alive thanks to my vest. I got used to the vest in my former life as a cop. I was lucky the bastard shot at my chest. That's how they train you, go for the bigger target. He figured he'd kill me for sure, a bigger target than my head. I knew that without a grenade launcher, I couldn't lob grenades all the way to the house. Last year, it had been a challenge to get the gate open and then walk the distance to the front door my boys and I shot through. I only used two of the four grenades my friend provided. I didn't want to risk killing any innocent women who might be inside the house.

I watched the sunrise through the window. Rachel is a night-dwelling creature. She wasn't coming during the day, so I felt like I'd bought some time.

I called Joe. "Everything is good for now. You do the rounds, whatever they say they owe, collect it, make a note. I'm going to bed. I need to be rested up for tonight."

"Count on it, G. I got your car."

"Keep that for today. I got the other car. And thanks, Joe."

From the time I got dressed to leave, I've been antsy. It wasn't about me. It was about Mona getting kidnapped again. Guillermo told her the client's driver was picking her up in our hotel lobby. He booked her with a festival regular, and she'll be getting five hundred an hour, five hours minimum. The client is staying in a mansion walking distance from city center.

I mentioned we'd met Gianna, and Guillermo said he was booking her for festival week. He said his problem was not with Gianna, but that he had enough girls without her. Truth is, I bitched and moaned until Joe came out to our hotel to take pictures of her. Mona and I had fun dressing her up. Joe did a double-take, and when G saw the pictures, he was pleased. The pictures were in G's words, magnifique. She was beautiful.

We agreed to meet the next day for brunch, then Gianna split to get ready for her gig.

Guillermo hooked me up with a late festival arrival.

"I got you five thousand for five hours. Good news is that he's at your hotel. Penthouse suite. I'm going back to my favorite restaurant for the dinner I didn't have when I got the call about Mona."

"Don't remind me about Mona's horrible experience," I said.

After he hung up, I remembered flying by private jet to New York, doing a session in a hotel, and taking a commercial flight back to Los Angeles in the morning, all for five thousand. Five hours for five thousand is a win. You get spoiled when a client hands you ten-thou for the night. I'm human enough to want to make ten every night. It doesn't work that way. I thanked Guillermo heavily for the fix.

"I dig Gianna," Mona said, fastening her strappy sandals and standing up.

"Me too. We'll see her tomorrow."

"Totally cool," Mona said as she looked at herself in the mirror. "I know we're hooking. Still, I dress up like this, it feels like a date. How dumb, huh?"

I stopped, turned and walked up behind her, our images in the mirror.

"It is a date," I said.

Before I left, Mona and I hugged.

"Be safe," I said. It was just words, but my hands kind of refused to un-hug her. She was ready to go, and I was still hanging on for dear life.

"Gabi come on. You can let go. I'm good. The kidnapping was

a freak thing."

"Not so freaky. You said he told you he'd been watching you."

"That was bull. He said it, but he was just trying to get me spooked."

I gave her a peck on the lips, and we went our separate ways for the night.

I took the elevator to the top floor. I guessed we were not going out for dinner, but you never know. I had been in this playhouse of a suite before.

I rang the bell to Keith's room at exactly ten pm.

I love this suite.

When my date for the night opened the door, I saw snow on the rooftop, and guessed he was in his sixties. He could have been older but not younger. His hair was not doctor-grown, or a rug, or bleached. It was just white. His skin was taut, his features strong and regular. He had a nice smile, good teeth. He was a class act, like the suite we were in. He looks so good now that I bet when he was thirty, he must have had a barnful of women chasing after him, and not because of his money. Gray eyes with a sparkle. White slacks, white shirt unbuttoned and untucked. Bare feet. His hands and feet showed his age more than his face.

His eyes were focused on my face. He met my eyes. I saw mischief in his expression.

"You are much more beautiful than your picture," he said.

"You are too kind," I said, stepping inside the room. "My name is Kylie. Pleased to meet you."

We shook hands.

"I'm sure Guillermo told you that my name is Keith. The pleasure is mine. Please come in and make yourself at home."

I walked in the familiar living room where another man in whites greeted me. A bottle waited in a silver bucket near the sofa. If sofas could talk, or I were the blushing type, I'd be covering my ears and eyes, and be the color of a beet right now. Thankfully the sofa was keeping my secrets.

"Hello, ma'am. My name is Roger. What can I get you to drink?"

"Wine is fine. Thank you."

"You are very welcome," Roger said.

He sat me on the sofa.

Roger reminded me of Archie, and not because they were both black. It was the combination of the smile and charm. Roger was a new face, and not dressed like hotel staff. I figured that Roger didn't come with the room but belonged to Keith.

Keith took a seat in a wing chair to my left, and we clicked glasses. Though I don't claim to be an expert, I had learned a lot about wine when I was living with the judge. I did know good from very good and excellent.

The wine was exquisite.

"I understand you arrived later to the film festival than you'd planned," I said.

"I did. Couldn't help it. Unavoidable business in Nevada. Almost didn't make it at all. I'm sure glad I did so I can have the pleasure of your company tonight."

"Pleasure is mine," I said.

"I thought we'd have finger foods unless you want something heavier."

"I'm good. Whatever you wish. Can I call you Keith?"

"Please do."

He put his glass down and moved next to me.

"You're killer handsome, Keith."

Room service delivered several trays of food. Keith's partner, Rossi, joined us. She had a perfect beach tan, and was dressed in a cropped, manly plaid shirt, and short shorts that barely covered her ass. She offered us a plate of the largest prawns I'd ever seen. Prawns are just big shrimp, but I'd never seen them so big. They were pan fried in butter, and as big as my hand, too big to be called finger food, but still delicious.

"Roger and Rossi travel with me when I'm on business or pleasure."

"Sounds great," I said.

Roger smiled and poured a round of wine.

Room service came up again and brought their dishes straight to the suite's kitchen. Rossi served us each a banana split covered with a mountain of whipped cream and cherries.

Keith's exuberance over the dessert was like a kid's, excited and bubbling over. I played along, and he loved my reaction. Rossi pulled out bibs like the ones you get in an Italian restaurant when you order spaghetti and meatballs and made a big deal about putting them on us. I don't know why the bibs were so liberating, but we made a mess devouring the banana split, with Roger and Rossi adding to the fun with their own bibs, splits and gobs of ice cream all over their faces. I could see the joy was real and spontaneous. This was just how they were. I wondered if Keith was married, if he had someone at home, or was it just Roger and Rossi. I didn't even know where he was from, not yet anyway.

After I visited the bathroom to clean up the remains of dessert and wash away all the stickiness. Roger and Rossi went off to the kitchen, I asked Keith what his pleasure was.

"Let's hit the bathroom. One of them has a fantastic spa tub, very big," he said in his cheerful way.

I didn't mention I had been in that jacuzzi before.

"And then...?"

"I'd like you to bathe, and let me be there."

"And then...?"

"One step at a time," he said with a mischievous grin.

I was glad I only ate one shrimp.

"I'm in. Lead the way, Keith. Can I have a bunch of bubbles?"

"Rossi will fix it up. She brings all that."

Prepping the tub took almost thirty minutes. While we were waiting, I drank the rest of my wine.

"It is a big tub," she said.

"Lots of bubbles?"

"Lots of bubbles," Rossi said.

I could tell Keith loved his wine and enjoyed watching me interacting with Rossi. We were on the second bottle. We got up, and he grabbed the next open bottle, and gestured for me to follow Rossi to the bathroom. Her shorts were short and tight. I could tell Keith noticed. I was mesmerized, maybe a little drunk, or was maybe getting horny already. I was getting excited, maybe because what came next was unknown. I didn't know if Roger and Rossi were a part of Keith's thing, but I was moved. For sure, I was moved. I was excited. Rossi was adorable.

The electric light was off, but it wasn't dark. Candles were lit. The entire bathroom gleamed in candlelight. Mirrors, walls, light marble was so reflective. It was like walking inside a mirror made of candlelight.

The jacuzzi was filled with bubbles. It was a thing of beauty. Half a foot of bubbles rose over the top of the tub, like the head of a beer. Like the whipped cream mountain on top of the banana split.

"Do you approve? Or should we put more soap?" He laughed. A cute laugh.

"I don't think we could get more in there," I said, laughing. "I love it, Keith. Thank you, Rossi. I don't know how you got it so high! Can't wait to get in it. It is for me. Is it for me?" I turned to look at Keith. The wine bottle was on the marble counter, and he was holding his glass of wine.

"It's all for you," he said. "Rossi will hang your nice clothes. Will you humor me?"

"Anything you want," I said.

I didn't know he was around until Keith said, "Roger open a

bottle of champagne and bring it here."

"Champagne. Nice," I said. I never mix wine and champagne, but it didn't seem right to tell him that.

I faced Keith. Rossi came up behind me and unzipped my dress. I stepped out of it, and she slipped it on a hanger. The front was form-fitting, short and short sleeved, and entirely covered with iridescent white sequins. The back plunged to my hips. My shoes were iridescent white also, but they were in the den by the sofa.

"This is a beautiful dress."

"Thanks, Rossi."

There was no bra to take off. It's not like I could wear one with the backless dress. I was left naked except for a red bikini while Rossi went somewhere with my dress.

"Position yourself on the widest edge of the spa. Yes, like this, humor me," Keith said.

Again, I was strongly reminded of Archie when I was with the judge. Archie was like a choreographer positioning me so the judge could see more. I wasn't sure if Keith was going to push me in the bubble bath, but instead of being worried, I was giggling. Rossi returned in her birthday suit.

"This is going to be chilly," Rossi said.

I saw in the mirror that she took the champagne bottle from Roger.

Roger and Keith were both fully dressed, except for their bare feet. Keith was clearly enjoying himself. Roger was there, standing at attention. I could see how excited he was, and both of them being there was making me steam. I'm a whore. I should be immune. I should be over all this. I shouldn't steam so easy. It was work. It was a job. It was a session. But I was steaming. I worried it would show through my panties, but then why should I care? Why should they care? Besides, they couldn't see that part of me. I was kneeling where they positioned me on the edge of the spa.

Like me, Rossi was bare except for underwear.

Rossi poured the Dom Perignon on me.
"Slow. Pour it slow," Keith said.
"Yes, slow," Rossi said. "She is lovely."
The cold champagne was a shock to my skin, but I laughed and laughed. It was shocking, bracing, stinging, sharp, brisk, chilly. I gasped and laughed again.

I wished Mona was here. I watched Keith standing there, just a foot away from me.

"Pour it, Rossi. Slowly."

I was pretty caught up in sensation, but I saw in the mirror that Roger disappeared, maybe not out of the bathroom but I couldn't see him anymore. Too bad. It was a rush to see him with his big smile, and pretty teeth, and the big attentive ridge in his pants. I turned my attention to Rossi. She was probably Keith's age, but she had a beautiful body, a young body like Mona's. Not that I'm old, but I'm turning twenty-seven next year. I'm older than Mona, not getting any younger. Still young enough to earn big dollars in this crazy business.

Keith moved closer. He slowly removed my panties. Rossie drizzled champagne on my ass, only now without my panties, it was running down between my cheeks, shocking my tender bits. Keith used both of his hands to gently part my ass to the stream.

This was a first for me. The sensation was indescribable, bubbly fizz running down my skin and over the most sensitive parts of my body. I felt like an ice cube, or a sugar cube, or maybe a mound of ice cream, melting, and being melted and effervescing into a froth.

The pouring stopped. By then my eyes were shut, but I opened them to see that the champagne bottle was empty. Keith told me to relax, to get in the tub.

He left Rossi with me.

"Get in," I said.

"When he comes back, I will."

I smiled at Rossi. I closed my eyes and felt a buzz from the wine. Keith returned in a hotel robe. I heard him pull the vanity seat up next to the spa, and I opened my eyes. Rossi stepped into the tub with a large sponge. She turned me and sponged my neck, my shoulders. She lifted my arm and worked it with the sponge. A wealth of bubbles slopped around the surface of the water, floating mountains of bubbles, and I was still beneath them.

"Get up sweetie," Rossi said.

I stood there in water almost to my knees, my body coated by foam. Rossi handed the sponge to Keith.

"Move close, sweetie."

Rossi urged me to the edge of the spa within Keith's reach. He poured body wash on the wet sponge and squeezed it foamy. He sponged my neck, my shoulders, my rib cage, my breasts, slowly, thoroughly, deliberately. His eyes were twinkling. I didn't have to do anything. Rossi moved my body parts so he could reach. Arms, hands, underarms. She lifted a leg, moved my foot to where I had been when I had been reclining. More champagne appeared, and she poured from the fresh bottle, rinsing down my body, my leg, and my other leg. Keith moved up my leg, he was on my perfectly manicured pussy, Rossi moved one hand between my legs and held me there. She knew exactly where to place her hand and fingers, where to hold me. Then they turned me around. He sponged my back. He did not miss a single spot on my body.

It was erotic.

I never saw Roger.

After all the soapy foreplay, I ended up on a bed. I had been on that bed before, but not wound up with so much foreplay. The silk bedding was turned down. Not the hotel sheets at all. Keith packed his own bedding. It was monogrammed. The initials on the pillowcases were KJM.

The lights were very dim. He was there, but I was facing wrong to see his body. Rossi was there too, on the bed, not helping him precisely, but part of the action. I heard a faint pumping sound, and she put my hand on his penis. It was not what I expected. It was hard as hammer handle, and it was long and thick. A penile implant. He lay down. I could see the gleam of his teeth, his smile.

"Sweetie, you are on top," Rossi said.

I mounted the erect stiffness and rode him in slow motion.

"He can handle whatever you got, Sweetie. He's not fragile. Don't worry."

"In that case, I'm going to fuck you silly."

"Yes, silly," he said, with a laugh.

I leaned down to kiss him and then straightened to a sitting position, gyrating on the unrelenting stiffness that was not going to get placid. A dildo is rubberish. In comparison, a penile implant is a real cock with real skin. I fucked him with gusto that was genuine.

Inches from me, Rossi sat on her knees. She was there for Keith who didn't seem to need any help or assistance. Rossi was not there to add to the sexual scene. Nevertheless, I looked at her every chance I had, stealthily. I was attracted to her. She knew it. She kissed Keith who was out of breath. She kissed me.

"Yeah, I like that," he said.

Was it my motion, or Rossi's kissing me that he liked? He didn't say. I kept doing him, and she kept her lips on mine.

I left Keith asleep.

In the master bath, I used the bidet and showered, making liberal use of the bath products they had so many of, and ignoring two unopened bottles of Dom Perignon. Two empties were in the otherwise empty bin, and I hate to admit that I picked them up just to gawk at them, as if to confirm the improbable bath had played out the way I remembered. I found a larger-than-hotel-sized bath towel to wrap myself in, and when I came out, Rossi dried me off, brought my clothes, and helped me dress and handed me my underwear, still wet from the champagne, and in a plastic bag.

"I'm going to frame these panties," I said.

Rossi laughed.

"You are a very special woman, Kylie."

I kissed her softly. She kissed me back. What was it with me lately? Was I leaning toward women?

"You are the special lady," I said. "You are gentle and kind to him."

"I love him very much. Roger and I both do."

When we came out of the bathroom, we tiptoed through the master bedroom to the parlor where Roger handed me an envelope.

"Hey, where you been?" I asked.

He didn't answer the question.

"He told me to give you a good tip. It's in here. It has been a pleasure meeting you, Miss Kylie."

I kissed him.

"Thank you both. Everything was delicious."

I walked to the door with them on either side, arm-in-arm. Roger held it open. I turned around, kissed my open hand, tapped Roger's lips, then Rossi's.

I took the elevator to my floor and found that Mona was not back yet. I sat on my bed and counted the money. Ten thousand dollars. Fuck. Amazing.

What beautiful people.

I called Guillermo to tell him how much I'd made, but he didn't answer.

I called Joe.

"Where's Guillermo? I got five thousand. The tip doesn't count."

"He's a little busy now. I'll tell him."

"Are you with him?"

"No, he's home, but he had a little accident."

"Is he okay?"

"He's going to be fine. Good night Kylie. See you tomorrow."

I decided I was going to call Mona to make sure she wasn't kidnapped, but first I set out the money for Joe and put the rest in the safe. I picked up the phone to dial Mona, and in she walked. I tossed my phone aside, then picked it up and plugged it into the charger.

"Gabs, how's it going?"

"Just got in. Call Joe. Guillermo isn't answering. How'd you do?"

"I did good. I love it here."

I love Cannes too. Everything would have been perfect if Mona had not been the victim of what she went through.

The lights were out, and the curtains drawn so we would not wake at the crack of dawn. The only light in the room was from the red lights on our phone chargers, which I had covered with a towel.

"I should wait until tomorrow to tell you about my night, but I can't wait. I have to tell you. You won't believe it."

"I hope it makes me cum," Mona said, "I didn't even come close."

She rolled to face me. The percale rustled, and the blanket over me moved slightly, and I could smell the perfume of her clean skin.

Our return to LA was coming up. The last thing I wanted to

think of was my return to the Public Defender's Office. Cannes felt different than my first time. I made a lot of money then. It wasn't just the money. It was having Mona with me. Us, together. I liked Gianna. A fun trio, hustling the best we could.

"C'mon sister. Shoot." Mona's voice was disembodied, soft, close in the dark.

I shook LA off and told Mona everything.

May 1990
Cannes
Joe

I got my bike and got an early start to do the money pickups, an easy thing since I hadn't shut my eyes all night for worrying about G. I started with the local dolls who work year-round with G, and then I visited the two hotels the others were staying in. Around one in the afternoon, I rang Kylie and Trisha's room. I know their real names, but to keep it straight in my head so I don't fuck up when I show their pictures, I think of them by their stage names. That's true for all the dolls. Not all of them use a stage name. The newcomer, Gianna, it's her real name.

Trisha answered the door yawning. I noticed the yawn. She was in a see-everything nightie and yawned with her whole body. A man can't help but respond to that.

"Hi Joe, we overslept." She yawned again.

My heart nearly stopped. In a good way, I might add.

She did a yawning stretch that did my heart good, and stepped away from the door till the back of her legs hit the bed Kylie was in. Her eyes were shut, and she flopped backward on to the mattress and scrambled under the covers. Head on pillow.

"Come in. Money's on the table."

Normally she isn't this friendly. Then again, it looked like she was already asleep.

I looked over at the beds, Kylie was stretching like a cat under the covers.

Kylie sat up and patted a spot on the bed next to her.

I walked over but didn't sit.

"Hey Joe, come in here and tell me about the accident Guillermo had. Is he okay?"

Trisha sat up. "Accident. Accident?"

She knuckled her eyes, reached for the table, and handed me two envelopes, as usual, one envelope from each of them, with their names written on the front.

"He's okay. Have a nice day," I said, starting for the door.

"Hey, hold your horses," Gabi aka Kylie said, catching hold of my belt from the back, and hanging on.

Trisha was still sitting up, still yawning from time to time.

"I can't talk about it. Let him tell you."

"Is it that bad or what?" Trisha asked.

I made the mistake of saying, "It could have been worse."

"Sit down," Kylie ordered. She'd let go of my belt, and clambered on top of the bedding, sitting on her knees. I got a quick look before she put her legs together. I know I got an instant hardon. These Americans are fine.

"Sit down," Trisha said.

I didn't sit down.

Kylie had let go of my belt, but then pulled on my shoulder bag where I keep all the cash.

I sat.

I wrapped my left hand around the shoulder strap as though they were going to take it. How stupid of me. In a split second, they double-teamed me. Their faces were inches from me. The fragrance of them. Gabi put her face an inch from mine, her eyes penetrating.

"We need to know."

"Here, let me get him on the phone for you." I pulled out my cell.

Trisha slapped my shoulder, not hard. "Spill the beans, Jacko."

"He will hang me if I put his business out in the street."

"Not in the street. Right here. The three of us. What the fuck is it already?" Kylie asked.

Trisha grabbed my growing hard on.

Smiled at me. She's got the devil in her, that femme.

"We got him turned on," Trisha told Kylie.

I called myself getting up. Trisha pulled me on the bed by my dick.

"Tell us." Kylie said.

"...and you get a hand job," Trisha said, emphasizing her words with a knowledgeable tug.

I didn't make the decision. My thing did.

Like an idiot, I told them. By the time the cat was out of the bag, Trisha's hand was not on my dick. Her fingers were splayed over her mouth in disbelief.

"He told you it was that bitch Rachel, the kidnapper?"

"Not alone. The three of them assaulted him."

"And the vest saved his life," Gabi said.

"He wears it when he's out. Who knows who's gunning from the next corner? He was a cop once. A well-known cop."

"I had a feeling this was bad."

"Don't worry about G. They will not get away with it. They thought they left him dead, and now they know better after the grenades."

Trisha grabbed my dick again.

"G is not your easy-going person. If he learns I told you this, he will be on my ass."

"We will never say a thing to anyone," Kylie said.

"I hope Rachel doesn't come after me," Trisha said. Her grip tightened just enough to keep me interested.

"Rachel's beef is with G. Besides, by tomorrow, she and her team could be history. I'm not in on G's plans, but he's not going to be forgiving."

I just know he's not going to forgive and forget. He's not the type.

"Don't tell us that part," Trisha said.

"I don't know that part, anyway."

They were silent. I knew just how to break the silence.

"Okay, I already told you, I want to fuck one or both of you."

"Hand job," Kylie said, placing her hand over Trisha's hand that was on my cock.

There was something about the way they both squeezed it, or maybe how they kissed each other while they were doing it. I came on myself. Both their hands released me. Kylie tossed me the cover off her pillow. I used it to clean up. They were laughing.

Mona/Trisha jumped off the bed, leaving the nightie behind, and sashayed the long way around the bed with what might be the sexiest walk I have ever seen. Naked, she stood in front of me.

"If you can get it up, you can fuck me," Mona said.

That girl has a mean streak a mile wide. I could get to like her. I got off the bed wishing I didn't have places to go and things to do. I kissed Mona. I kissed Gabi.

"Next time," I said.

"You know, Joe, you are one good-looking dude," Gabi said, giving me the once over. "I hadn't noticed before."

"Thanks?" I said.

I took two steps to the edge of the mattress, bent down and she didn't try to avoid my kiss on the lips. I kissed them both again.

"You are beautiful," I told them. "Both of you."

The sun was shining. The afternoon was warm for late May, but chilly on a motorcycle, even with the leather jacket. I headed to G's. He would be asleep at this time of day. I normally wait until early evening to roust him, but today was not a day of routine anything. Something was cooking. He would just have to wake up when I ring the bell.

May 1990
Cannes
Guillermo

I would have punched Joe for waking me when he came over, but I had planned on getting up early. I hardly slept anyway. I knew Rachel would not dare come during daylight hours. I wasn't answering my cell phone in case it was her checking to see if I wasn't dead, as she tried to figure out if I was the one who threw the grenades.

Joe handed me the day's cash and two envelopes. I put the cash in the safe, didn't count it. Only Gabi and Mona put their cash in an envelope with their name on it. I was fond of the two Americans. It didn't matter that I put my life in danger rescuing Mona. It was almost like being back on the job.

"Joe, I trust you. Don't ever disappoint me."

Joe started to say something, but I put my hand up.

"You take all the calls today. You answer my phone, you say,

"You got Joe. G is busy right now.' You know the dolls. If someone wants to see a picture, tell the caller you work alone, and they have to take your word that the lady you are sending is the cream of the crop. In other words, you work out of your apartment. You got that?"

"I got it," Joe said.

"I'll be using my back-up cell," I said.

I handed him the cell phone I use as the date line. He took it with an awed expression. I watched until he pocketed it. He always has this look like he's afraid of me. He must not know I love him like the son I never had. Well, maybe not that much.

"Rachel or one of her people might call to see if I'm dead. I ain't answered the phone at all since we came back last night. You got that?"

"I got it."

"You know the prices. You sat here long enough to hear me talk to clients. Damn, boy. You know the business. You got that?"

"I got it. Yeah, I know the business. Never like you, G."

"No time for you to kiss my ass. I want you gone. If I need you, I will call you. I'm depending on you to attend to business. I want my dolls to work tonight. All of them. You got it?"

"I got it."

"You got the photo album with pictures, but you ain't going out to show anyone pictures tonight, you got it?"

"If someone wants to see a photo, I tell them to take my word for it that the doll I am sending is cream of the crop."

I smiled at Joe. He ain't used to seeing me smile.

He looked at me with a damn serious face.

"Good boy, Joe. Don't disappoint me."

I reached for my phone book, my bible. Every doll who has ever worked for me is in there, every client name. All my business is in that journal.

"Where are you going to be?"

"Ain't going nowhere," I said. "Why are you still here?"

He stared silently. His forehead was creased in worry. He looked like he was going to say something, but he was thinking before he asked what he wanted to ask.

"You planning on Rachel coming for you?"

I matched his serious look and pointed to the door.

"Take care of business."

"Got it, G."

It was still daylight. I had time. I showered, dressed, made food. An appetizer, really. Two great chunks of cheese, stuffed olives, spicy hot orange jelly. An assortment of crackers. I love crackers. I carved the cheese, stood and ate in my kitchen. Poured a glass of Sauvignon Blanc and savored the meal. If all went as planned, I would be heading for a late dinner.

When it was dark, it was lights off inside and out. I heard traffic through a cracked window. Nothing out of the ordinary. My neighbors garden like fiends. I breathed deeply to calm myself, smelled cut grass and flowers. Poppies. Lily of the valley are blooming, iris, valerian and genet. Spring in Provence-Alpes-Côte d'Azur.

My backup cell phone was on my desk. No one had the number. I almost called Joe, but it was too early for him to be very busy.

Hurry Rachel. Where are you? I know you're coming.

I waited in the dark.

May 1990
Cannes
Mona

In all the days that we'd been in Cannes, we'd never hung around in bed this late.

"G could have been killed and it would have been my fault," I said.

"You weren't the cause, just the catalyst. Joe said they have a history. Two dead on Rachel's side in two years. You were just the most recent spark."

The room phone rang.

"This is Mona, I mean, morning, this is Trisha."

Gabi gave me one of those how-dumb-can-you-be looks.

"Morning?" Gianna chortled. "Are we doing dinner? It's too late for lunch."

"It's Gianna," I told Gabi.

"Invite her in."

"Come on up. We're just getting out of bed."

Gabi was emerging from the bathroom when Gianna rang the bell. I let her in. Gabi and I were in hotel robes. Gianna was in the threadbare blue jean short shorts that were all the rage back home.

We had ten seconds of a group hug and kiss.

"Gianna, if the shorts were any shorter, your pubic hair would show," Gabi said.

Gianna looked down at herself, laughing.

"What pubic hair? No, I promise, no."

She has the cutest accent.

It was late in the day but early for us.

Gabi and I put on bikinis and loaned one to Gianna.

"Gianna, if I were a man, I'd fuck you," I said, patting her perfect ass.

"She uses that line all the time."

"Trisha, you can fuck me any time you want, free."

The pool attendant fixed us up with a cabana by the pool where we ordered off the menu. It didn't matter at all that we missed the buffet. Gabi and I don't usually drink in the afternoon, so we can head out on our dates with clear heads.

"Wine is good for you," Gianna said.

She's so French. I drank to make her feel comfortable, just enough to feel bubbly. Gabi says I don't need to be bubblier than I already am. The sun set at eight fifty. We got back to the room at nine.

"I split now," Gianna said. "I need time to get pretty."

"No need, Gianna. You can use one of my outfits tonight."

I showed her the closet I was using. I could tell she loved everything in there.

"Mine have the labels," she said. "Yours are real. I don't want to be responsible if something happens. If I get a run, or snag something."

"At home, you want the big bucks, you got to look like big bucks from head to toe," I said. "I'm not sure that's true here. But you can wear anything I've got." With the festival almost over, there was no reason to change the routine, but I often wondered if Gabi and I shouldn't just dress in Cannes wear. Or maybe that's just an excuse to go hit the shops.

"Bullshit," Gabi said, reading my mind. "You just want to shop." And to Gianna, she said, "Come on. Think of the travel time you'll save. Stick around. We should hear from Guillermo soon."

I could tell Gianna was happy to comply.

"I will miss you when you go back to America," Gianna said.

"We're here now, so let's be together." Gabi opened her closet, too. "Pick out something."

"I'm not sure Guillermo will give me a job tonight."

"We will make him," I said.

Gabi's phone rang. She picked it up and listened for a minute before she responded.

"How come you're doing G's job tonight?"

Gabi covered the phone with her palm.

"Joe is booking tonight," Gabi said. She took her hand off the mic and spoke to Joe again.

"Is he okay?"

Gabi turned the phone in my direction. We heard a pause at Joe's end of the conversation. No answer spoken, but it was louder than words. Gabi put the phone back to her ear.

"Gianna is with us. If you ever want another hand job from us again, you best book her."

I laughed. Gianna looked inquisitive, like a little bird.

"Tell me. I won't forget," Gabi said, scribbling something down on a pad. "How much?" Her eyebrows raised. "Good work,

Joe. Thank you. Do you want to speak with Mona and Gianna
now, or call them on their cells?"

Fifteen minutes later, Joe set me up, then in another ten, Gianna. I felt good for Gianna. She's transparent about how little
she makes on the regular without G, and how badly she wanted
Guillermo to represent her. Joe fixed it for the three of us to meet
at ten. We were dressed and had time. The hotel room rang.

"Gabi, it's Rossi?"

I didn't know who Rossi was. I felt curious as I handed the
phone to Gabi.

May 1990
Cannes
Gabi

Why would Rossi be calling me? Maybe Keith wanted a session tonight. I can't do it unless it's after the one I have.

"Rossi, hi. This is Kylie."

"I had to pull a lot of strings to get your room number." Rossi laughed. "But not under Kylie. Just Mona."

I laughed a little. "Yeah, my stage name in Cannes. Sorry."

"No worry. When do you go back to Los Angeles?"

"We have four more nights," I said. I figured she wanted to book me.

"Keith told me to find you and offer you the suite. We're leaving tomorrow morning, and we're committed for three more nights after tonight."

"Rossi, geez, I can't afford ten grand for one night, much less thirty grand for three."

"Try fifteen thousand a night," Rossi said. "He likes you. If you don't take it, it will go to waste."

"Oh my. I don't know what to say."

"Say yes. That's it."

"Can I do something for him?"

"He's got it handled for tonight. No sweat, Mona. It's a pleasure for him to do it. He told me to tell you that."

As I hung up, my eyes were tearing. Gianna and Mona had their hands on me when I screamed. They were so jolted, they screamed in sympathy. We messed up our perfect makeup.

"What happened?" Mona asked.

I told them why Rossi called.

"That's forty-five thousand dollars. Three nights, my God," Gianna said.

"Gianna, you are moving in with us. The place is huge. I mean huge," I said.

The three of us took the elevator then split to different places in the enormous lobby.

A woman in sneakers, shorts, and white blazer carried a sign with my Cannes name: Kylie Jones.

"You are dressed to the nines. Lovely," the woman said in English with a lilting Spanish accent.

"Thanks for the compliment."

"My name is Nina. Car is right by the entrance."

"Good to meet you, Nina."

Although this was the safe way to be met, I have to admit I thought of the kidnappers. If I had to, I felt certain I could kick this girl's ass if she tried anything.

Nina was headed for the car that the doorman was standing by. A white Rolls Royce.

"You have to be kidding me. I've never been in one of these

beauties."

Nina smiled proudly, holding the back door open.

"What year?"

"It's a 1962 Silver Cloud, an amazing machine."

I slid across the slick leather upholstery and felt like a queen.

It was no limousine and there was no partition, but it was a big car with an expensive vibe. I've seen them from a distance, but never up close or inside. I wasn't being kidnapped in this car. Of that, I was sure.

There are a whole mess of hotels in Cannes and Nice, but great hotels like the Carlton and the JW were few and far between. It was not at all unusual to end up in the same hotel on successive nights. The men who could afford Guillermo's rates were monied people and almost always staying at the JW, the Carlton, or in their own yacht. Nina delivered me to the JW. All the way there, heads turned, and people stopped and gawked.

Like at the Carlton, the drop-off area in front of the JW was always a madhouse but spotting the dollar sign on wheels that the Silver Cloud is, a valet raced through the obstacle course to where we were double-parked and opened my door before Nina had even gotten out of the car. I felt like a princess getting out.

"I got the car," the valet told Nina.

"Thanks. Fix you up later."

Nina and I walked through the crowd and in the hotel, I know better than to ask a lot of questions. I knew from Joe only that Marco was his name, he was from Spain, and his moniker was as likely to be his as Kylie Jones is mine.

Nina walked ahead just a little bit leading the way on and off the elevator to the rooftop penthouse, a suite I had been to before. There are only two of these big suites in the hotel, and they are both on the fourth-floor penthouse. Nina had a card key for the door. She was no driver for hire. She belonged to someone in this room, that is, worked for someone.

Nina opened the door, and for a moment, my view was blocked. Then I saw him, young, solid, lean, the youngest session I'd had in Cannes. He couldn't be more than thirty. I got a pretty good glimpse of his physical condition immediately. He was wearing only a towel, so I guessed he was going to or from the bath.

"Kylie, this is Marco Pliego," Nina said.

He wasn't tall, maybe five foot eleven. He wasn't buff either, but he looked solid. His stomach was flat.

"Kylie, pleasure." He had the same accent as Nina, delicious to my ear.

He kissed my lips first, then took my hand.

"I was going to get in the jacuzzi. Join me, please." He stopped.

He looked at me like he had just noticed a spider crawling on my face.

"What is it?" My smile was automatic.

"Kylie, you are so dressed up. Maybe you aren't up to a hot jacuzzi."

I could understand his response. I was extremely dressed, covered from head to toe in Chanel. Clinging white woven jacket, long tight sleeves down to thirty gold bangles on each wrist. Massive gold bangle earrings, gold choker but it couldn't be seen. I had on a hat, big white-brimmed back-tilted thing with a white rose with black leaves on the underside of the brim. Black hose, ordinary black patent leather heels. At my throat was a sleek gold choker, but it couldn't be seen under the black woven dickie at my throat. A fringe of black peeked out from under the skirt, giving the impression of a wool dress extending from throat to hem under the jacket. Only there wasn't a dress underneath. Just the hose.

I raised my hand and pawed in the air in his direction, laughing.

"I'd love a hot jacuzzi. Where can I take all this off? How do you want me, bare or…?"

"Bare," he said. "Pretty please. Nina will show you to the dressing room."

"Great. Is there somewhere I can place my jacket?"

He nodded toward a closet. I turned to look toward the patio, so I was at an angle away from them, and unbuttoned the buttons. It took some maneuvering because of the bangles, but I'd practiced this, had sewed the dickie to the jacket so I didn't have to fool with it. I swept off the coat, and stood before them in my hose, shoes, bangles, hat and choker. I loved the look of shock on both their faces, followed by suppressed laughter as we all behaved as if we were in a formal situation. Nina stowed the jacket in the closet.

Chuckling quietly, Marco passed through the sliding glass door to the patio. I saw candles burning in the night, and smelled incense. From this angle, I could not see the view, but it had to be spectacular. Cannes was always lit spectacularly.

Nina put her arm on my bare shoulder. Her nails were long, pointed, and painted white. "This way, Kylie."

Mostly naked, I walked behind her. The dressing room adjoined a big bathroom. It was big, but not as big as the suite I'm going to be in tomorrow. I felt a frisson of excitement for the night tonight, and equally for the suite we were moving into tomorrow.

I saw Nina taking off a shoe.

"Oh good, you're joining us," I said.

I dropped my ridiculous hat on the commode, followed by shoes, stockings, earrings, and bangles. Except for the gold choker, I was as naked as the day I was born. Nina was still undressing.

"No, you're joining us."

I thought that girl is a bitch, but I said, "I should have guessed. You're way too pretty to just be his driver."

It took Nina a while to take off the chauffeur get-up. I waited till she was done.

"Keep saying nice things like that, and I'm going to like you," Nina said. "I'll see you out there."

I waited a few seconds after she was gone before I followed. The big entrance, you know?

I walked outside.

They had already gotten into the jacuzzi and were sitting side-by-side with big smiles. Marco whistled. Nina's smile was so big, I figured she was putting on. I did a three-sixty slowly so he could see, Nina put her fingers up to her mouth and whistled loud.

I laughed.

They laughed.

Normally you don't want the water very hot in Cannes, but that May night, it was nippy. The very hot water was great. A tangy salt breeze was coming off the ocean, and music from the lobby-level restaurant was a lovely backdrop.

Marco was between us. He put his arms over our shoulders so that we were very cozy. The remote was inches from Nina's shoulder, and he switched on the jets. Bubbles, eddies, thrusting streams, and whitewater burst all around and under us, like we were a batch of happily boiling lobsters. If I could have moved six inches, the jet below would have hit me exactly where I'd like it.

"This is wonderful. Thank you," I said.

"No, thank you for coming over," Marco said. "Nina and I like company."

I smiled as if I understood what he meant. I still didn't know what I would be doing, or who with.

A man in a white summer tux came around bearing three glasses of wine on a tray. He was older than the three of us, but not ancient by any means. He was clearly a butler, and also un-fazed by our nakedness. I wondered if his service was provided by the hotel or if he was one of Marco's entourage. With only two of these giant suites on this floor, it was probably up to him to attend them both.

"Is wine okay?" Nina asked.

"Perfect," I said. "Thank you."

We toasted Cannes. We toasted the lovely night. It was when we toasted each other that questions came up. We set the glasses by the remote.

"You are American?" Marco asked.

"Yes. My dad was Italian and my mother, Mexican."

Those were the last words spoken in English.

"Do you speak Spanish?" Nina asked in Spanish.

"I do," I said in Spanish. "You speak perfect," I told Nina.

"It's my first language," Nina laughed. "I'm happy you speak our language."

"We speak in Spanish all night now," Marco said.

"De Seguro,"[3] I said, cheerful as all heck.

Their Spanish and my Spanish differed a little. We shared a language but have different accents. They spoke like they were from Spain, with an accent Mexicans don't have. Maybe Castilian.

Nina lifted Marco's arm and gently rested it on the back of the jacuzzi and moved beside me. As I was now in the middle, I put both of my arms over the shoulders of my new friends.

"When I heard your name is Kylie Jones, I figured you were a gabacha."

"Jones is my stage name."

I bet Kylie is stage, too," Marco said.

Nina said, "Don't be mean to my new friend, Marco."

Nina kissed me. I liked it. Maybe she wasn't such a bitch.

"I'm not mean. She's my new friend, too," Marco said.

Laughs all around. We drank, and the butler refilled our glasses. I pretended to sip to keep from getting too drunk.

---

[3] For Sure

"Eres preciosa, Kylie, mira como me tienes mi verga parada,"[4] Marco said.

We changed positions in the water. Marco's arm snaked around me, and Nina's did too. I faced Marco and kissed him on the lips, then Nina. Nina caught my lower lip between her teeth, teasing. It didn't hurt; it was playful, and I found it moving. I found our wine breath aromatic, like an aphrodisiac.

The butler returned with more wine, then set the glass table that was also on the balcony. I didn't exactly watch him, because I was too busy playing with Marco and Nina. He rolled in a cart loaded with finger foods.

One by one, we stood, and climbed out of the water. The water hit me around the midriff. For a Jacuzzi, it was pretty deep. The butler held out robes for us to put on. He was very cool about his job, and we were pretty cool about standing around naked. Maybe it's a French thing, or a butler thing, or maybe the guy just loves working around naked bodies.

"You have an efficient butler," I said.

"All of them on this floor are fantastic," Nina said.

That answered my question.

"You come to Cannes often?" I asked.

"Lately we have. We're opening a store here and in Nice."

"Oh, cool," I said.

"Nina, tell her what kind of store," Marco said, picking up a plate and handing it to me. "Help yourself, Kylie."

"Thanks," I said.

Lobster tails were out of their shells and cut in big chunks, righteous finger food to dip in a selection of sauces. We stood there picking and eating, because there were no chairs.

"Marco and I are partners in a clothing line for men and women."

"All brands or your own?"

---

4 You're beautiful, Kylie, look how you got my dick standing

"Have you heard of Nina's?" Marco asked.

I connected the dots. Nina has a bunch of stores in Los Angeles. They are everywhere, I think.

I looked at Nina, feeling, well, something. Maybe it was awe. "You're that Nina," I said.

She nodded.

I kissed Nina's cheek as she chewed.

"In other words, Nina is not a stage name. It's your real name," I said.

"Yes," Nina said, laughing. "Now tell us your real name."

I thought I was smarter than this, but I must not have been, because I heard myself answer—as if I wanted this second life to take on a life of its own and show up five years from now to shake hands with LA Gabi, atty at law. It was as if I had no control, which is bullshit.

But they asked, and I answered.

"Gabi is my real name."

"I like that name better than Kylie," Marco said. "Fits you."

Nina picked a cloth napkin off the table, dipped it in a glass of white wine, and wiped a dab of a spicy avocado sauce from the corner of Marco's lip.

The eating continued.

"Me encanta tu nombre, Gabi."[5] Nina said.

"I've been in your stores in Los Angeles," I said.

"The important thing is do you buy in our stores?" Marco was laughing, happy.

"She didn't get the Chanel number she's wearing tonight at our stores."

"I shop at your stores," I said.

Nina nudged me with her elbow.

"We have nice clothes at a fraction of what you paid for the

---

5 I love your name Gabi

outfit you arrived in before we had you strip to the way you came in this world."

"I came prepared," I said.

"You were dressed like an onion, many layers," Marco laughed. "I did not think the layers would come off so easy."

"Tell me more about your stores," I said.

"We have 456 stores," Marco said. "Everything is made in Spain except for some items we manufacture in different countries where labor is cheaper. When we do that, we normally supply the raw material or finished fabric from Spain."

"That's a lot of stores."

We took seats at another table next to the one that was serving as a buffet.

"How do you manage something so big?" I asked.

"We have a great team," Marco said.

"I am totally impressed. You are so young, both of you."

We chatted for a long time. The talk stopped, and our food settled. I drank no more wine and switched to Coca-Cola. Marco and Nina did the after-dinner drinks. I passed on the lava cake except for a few bites Nina fed me with her fork. We ended up in the bedroom. Nina went down on me while I went down on her, sixty-nine-style. It was one of the few times that it was a true sixty-nine, because we were almost the same height, and our bodies lined up right. Marco played with the two of us, his dick hard all the time. His manhood was of average size, like the rest of him. He and Nina were as clean as could be, and totally eatable, but when it was Marco's turn, he passed.

Nina said, "He's expecting someone."

We were on the bed. Nina and I had reached orgasms and now required a pause.

Unlike some of my other sessions, this couple liked a room filled with lights. That was okay with me. I had nothing to hide except my public defender credentials.

The company Marco was expecting turned out to be a young man who showed up dressed for clubbing in a hot town. Sleeveless orange silk top with a zipper down the front and a Chinese collar, skin-tight black pants. I didn't ask if Joe sent him. Joe was handling the business tonight. The butler didn't step in the bedroom, but I got a glimpse of him when he admitted Marco's companion. Normally, I get a sense of preferences, but I had figured Marco wrong. After all, he was aroused being with Nina and me. He was hard the whole time we were rolling around together, though I may have missed something. Marco got off the bed. The young man couldn't have been more than twenty-two years old. They greeted each other—handshakes, then hugs—and excused themselves. I didn't see Marco again. I looked at Nina.

"Okay, I get it. Now what?"

"Yo puedo seguir toda la noche,"[6] Nina said.

She threw herself at me and we wrestled and laughed a whole lot. Nina was beautiful. I wondered if she designed the clothes. I was so curious. Rob Sphere was a multi-millionaire too. It wasn't the money that impressed me about Marco and Nina. It was the smarts of them putting such a successful business together. So many stores.

The best way to describe it is that we had sex in bouts. We'd go and go and go, then we'd come apart and lie there, breathing hard, out of breath. When the breathing slowed, the words came.

"What made you come over to pick me up? Why not a driver? And who owns that gorgeous car?"

Nina's laugh was a funny giggle. I couldn't believe I had not liked her at first. What a difference a language made.

"The date was for me. I wanted to be sure I liked what the guy on the phone said was the crème de la crème. If I had disliked you,

---

[6] I can go all night

I would have given you money and split."

It was my turn to laugh.

"Oh, you are so mean."

"That name was a turn-off until I saw you all dressed up. I realized why this guy on the phone charges so much."

Nina kissed me after she said this, and I kissed her back.

"I have nothing against gabachos. We make a lot of money in America. I like to make a connection with my bed partners. I changed my mind about you when I learned you were of Latin descent. The Latin in you helped to do it."

"And what do you think of Kylie Jones now?"

"Te amo, Kylie Jones."[7]

She laughed.

"And the car?"

"It's a company car. It's a twelve-hour drive from Madrid to Cannes, but we plan on being here several weeks. I had one of our runners drive it up here. It's a fun car."

"I love that car," I said, "And you are the cutest, most beautiful, sexy, erotic driver I have ever met."

Nina blushed.

"I'm going to turn off the lights then I want you to repeat that again."

I hugged her like I sometimes hug Mona, a face-to-face hug while we were lying on our sides, rubbing our noses together, giggling or laughing, making each other feel divine with hands and mouths.

The sun was coming up when I put my clothes back on. I rolled up the hat, and dumped it in my purse with the bangles so that I didn't look quite as overdressed leaving as I had arriving.

I kissed Nina goodbye. She opened the safe as I was pulling my stockings on. Naked, she walked past the robe puddled on the

---

[7] I love you, Kylie Jones

floor, to escort me to the door. She handed me an envelope with the money in it.

"This is not payment for sex or the good time we had together. It is a gift," she said.

I was moved by what she said and still moved the more that I thought about it. We hugged halfway in the hall, halfway in her room. It was a long hug. Nina had not been eager to let me go.

When I got in the elevator, I thought about what she said. Nina was lonely. I don't think she wanted me to leave.

In the lobby, I called Mona to tell her I was on my way.

"I was worried," she said.

I laughed. "I'm intact. Don't worry. On my way. Is Gianna there?"

"She went home to pack some stuff and will be back in the afternoon after we move to the suite."

"We're going to have fun," I said.

Once back in the hotel room, I sat down on the bed and took the cash from the envelope to count it. I counted, and kept counting. I was shocked by how much was there. Nina had given me twenty thousand dollars.

Mona's eyes goggled.

"Fuck, what did you do for that?"

I told Mona about Marco and Nina.

I got in bed and called Joe to check in.

"Are you still in charge?"

"I think so. Did you get the five?"

"Five? Is that what you charged them? You didn't tell me."

"Gabi, you didn't ask. Yeah. Five."

"Yeah, I got it. I got more but the rest is a tip."

"I know the rules," Joe said. "See you this afternoon."

I went to bed with Mona, hugging her the same way I had hugged Nina.

"You know, Mona, I like men more than women in bed. I haven't jumped the fence. Still, I feel so close to you. Tonight, I felt close to Nina. A few nights ago, with Rossi, I didn't feel as close. I felt okay about being with another woman."

Mona kissed me.

"I get it, Gabi. I'm the same way. I never messed around with another woman before you came along, and now it's a part of what we do. Am I saying it right?"

Half asleep, I said, "I'll tell you after we get at least seven hours of sleep."

"Deal," Mona said.

May 1990
Cannes
Guillermo

I thought of leaving the front door unlocked, but I didn't do that because it smelled like a trap. Too easy. There's not much traffic, and my house sits back fifty feet from the street, one of the few properties that has grass in front. I have no gates. If Rachel had a grenade like the ones I tossed on her grounds, she could do some damage if she had the arm to toss that mother fifty feet.

I listened for noise. I didn't think Rachel or that young girl that was with her in the parking lot were professional enough to get close without making a mistake, a noise, dropping something or talking to each other. As for the fuckface that shot me, I don't know.

I didn't leave law enforcement with medals, but I had good friends I send dolls to when they need a girl, no charge. The chief is a client. I operate a business without police problems and didn't have to pay anyone cash to keep it that way. All I needed was for Rachel and her twisted people to be in my house with guns. I will wipe them out, and it will be totally legal.

I wondered how Joe was doing.

Did he book all the dolls?

I forgot to tell him to include Gianna, damn. Maybe I would give him a call to let him know when I got back to my office. I was not hanging in one spot. I was quietly making my way around the house, checking the rooms one by one. Moving kept me alert, but between rounds I retreated to my office for ten minutes or so.

I heard an explosive bang. I got up out of my chair and stood there in the dark, pointing at the open doorway from the hall. My office is down the hall from the living room where they had to come through once in the house. I scooted quietly toward the door to the hall and saw a fragment of splintered oak in a stripe of light where none should be. My front door was gone, blown open with one shot of a powerful rifle.

"Are you here motherfucker?" It was Rachel. Her voice was distant.

I thought of shooting her, not killing her, then fucking her right here bent over my desk. A mean bitch like her, I would fuck her to death. I wondered if she knew how many women she had sold as slaves. Rachel could win a beauty contest, a beautiful woman. I always wondered how she got in the business of capturing women and sending them off as chattel in foreign countries, no doubt, never to return.

"Don't be chicken, motherfucker. Where are you? Come to mama," she spoke in French.

The man's voice said, "He's not here, I told you. The house is dark. Been dark for hours."

The bastard was watching the house.

I heard the girl's voice. Must be the girl who ran off when the shooting began at the parking lot. Why would Rachel bring her?

"Check every room. I want that motherfucker dead."

I saw the light of a flashlight shining down the hall. These fuckers were amateurs at this.

"I'm in here, Rachel. Come get it, bitch."

I could see the reflection of the flashlight move. It pointed down the hallway, then in my direction toward my voice. Briefly I made out three figures backlit by the streetlight. It was the youngster who had the light. Rachel was leading them. Without a word or warning, she shot in my direction, not the rifle from the parking lot. The bullet hit my chest. It knocked me back but only a little. The flashlight turned to the group. I saw the face of confusion. Rachel had not figured on my vest. I pulled the trigger on the machine gun, fifty bullets in ten seconds. They went down wordlessly. No threats, no cussing, nothing. Sadly for them. Way too easy for me.

I made it to the switch and my office was flooded with light. It was a jolt for me after waiting in the dark for hours. I used the house phone on my desk to call the police.

In my office, after the coroner had collected the bodies, Lieutenant Caron took my statement.

"Why the machine gun?"

"It happens to be on top of my credenza behind my desk. I had cleaned it a couple of days ago and didn't put it away. It was a gift from Captain Brodeur many years ago, way before your time."

Lt. Caron said, "I didn't ever meet him, but I sure have heard of him. Very nice gift. It saved your life."

"It sure did," I said.

"Are you sure you don't want to go to the hospital?"

"The EMT bandaged it up. It didn't break the skin, but there will be a hell of a bruise."

I didn't tell him it hurt like hell and added to the discomfort from the three shots from the night before.

The coroner sent over an independent service to clean up the bloody, ugly mess. I made a deal with the cleaners to sanitize the affected rooms, but I would have to get a contractor to replace the door, and deal with the bullet-holes. The blood on the walls was a mess that would take a lot of work, and what the machine gun did to my office was a crime.

The sun was rising over Cannes when the cleaning crews left. There were bullet holes everywhere. My office and hall stank of hospital, but everything was clean. My front door wasn't pretty.

I surveyed my office, which was a disaster area. I lived alone and had three bedrooms to pick from, not counting the master bedroom. I unplugged my office phone and carried it into a spare bedroom to plug it into the dedicated office line and dropped the phone book on the card table in that room. It would do as an office for the time being. I walked back into my office, dumped the tiffany lamp, electric typewriter, ream of paper, and cup of pencils into the seat of my desk chair, rolled it into the new office, and arranged everything on the card table. Done.

I sat in the chair, adjusted the angle and dialed Joe.

"Joe, long night. I'm going to bed. Don't wake me. I'm hurting but fine. Handle the calls the same way tonight. I'll start back tomorrow night. Got it?"

"I got it. Want to know how we did last night?"

"No. I trust you. Don't fuck up. Forgot to tell you, find a session for Gianna."

"I did last night. She did good. Gabi and Mona pushed it. Was that okay?"

"Good boy, thanks."

I disconnected.

I called a detective with the homicide division. He was asleep, but I gave my whole spiel to his answering machine. "Josue, G here. I'm sure you heard about those people who broke in my house last night. The woman, Rachel, got hauled off to the morgue, but she was in the kind of business where there is bound to be a lot of loot in her house."

I disconnected.

Josue would be up and running in no time at all.

I was pleased that my bedroom was spared from the mass of bullets. I undressed, took two sleeping pills and went to bed. I'm a side sleeper, but my chest burned with pain. I lay on my back and waited for the sleepers to kick in. I was extremely hungry. All I'd had to eat yesterday was the cheese when I got up. Tomorrow was another day. At least I survived the battle. Next to me where a woman should be was a shotgun. The cops took the machine gun as evidence. Eventually, I would get it back.

Seven hours later, I woke up. It was daylight still. I got up, barely made it to the bathroom. My chest was black and blue but looked mild compared to how I felt. Adrenaline kept me going. I was feeling like a cripple. I got in the shower, but the impact of the water was more than I could handle. Rachel's shot from yesterday was the only one that had left a scab. The EMC had bandaged it. Now that bandage was the center of a fifteen-centimeter bruise. The cuts happen when the Kevlar is dented. How bad the bruise is is based on a combination of the force of the bullet, and how the Kevlar distributes the force.

I went back to bed and called Joe.

"Bring me the money and handle it again tonight. I hurt bad."

When Joe came a short time later, I had to push myself to let him in. The break-in had not damaged my door chain or two sliding bar locks. I hurt too much to fasten the bar lock at the foot of the door.

"Put the cash on the table here," I pointed at a coffee table. "I need to lock the door and don't want to walk back here to do it."

"Got it, G."

"Thanks, Joe. I need you right now."

He gave me a thumbs up and headed out the door. He kept walking toward his motorcycle parked curbside.

I didn't bother with the money. I headed for the master bedroom.

It must have been thirty-six hours since I had the cheese and crackers. I was hungry but I needed to rest. Food could wait.

It was crazy that on this trip, we've upgraded three times in this hotel, from one of the most basic rooms to the best in the place. The new suite had three bedrooms, a media room, even a small kitchen, but we weren't doing any cooking. Who is rich enough to spend fifteen thousand a night on accommodations then give it up to a woman you've only known for a handful of hours?

The suite was so fantastic, I was reluctant to leave for work.

Mona and I had already made enough money that we could have taken the next three nights off, relaxed and savored our accommodations. We talked about it, but in the goldmine that Cannes was to us, we were too greedy to do that. Gianna wanted every bit of work she could get from Guillermo's boy, Joe. She needed the money. She said she had never made this kind of money on her own. Each payment she received was life-changing.

Anyway, we got our gigs and left the suite at different times to get together with our dates.

May 1990
Cannes
Mona

The first night in the new suite, we each started off in our own bedroom, but we woke up together in Gabi's room, the master bedroom. Gianna blended perfectly with us. She wanted to take us around Cannes to show us the sights, but we resisted because we couldn't bear to give any suite time away. We ordered in and didn't find out until the end of the first day that Rossi had arranged for room charges be added to the bill. Keith was paying.

We partied.

We finally arrived at the date printed on our tickets home. I felt lucky we'd added two days after the festival was over, but even so, like everything else in life, we ran out of nights. Business slowed down the last night, not as much money, not as many hours, and though I thought it was crazy that checkout time was twelve PM, it had given us a whole last day. You have to figure that the three of us always got in about sunrise and then we needed to sleep at least until one. That's what we had done since we got to Cannes with exception of oversleeping once or twice. While staying in the big suite, we did not oversleep. We wanted to use up every waking minute to enjoy the lavishness of it all, especially the jacuzzi in the private gym located in the suite.

We packed our bags and put them by the door. Gabi and Gianna and I sat on the balcony with an almost midnight snack: bowls of lobster stew, our last meal. We split a couple of pastries in thirds so we could try them all.

"I promise I'll let you know when I get my visa to visit the US as a tourist," Gianna said.

"Do that, and we promise you can come stay with us for a while."

Gianna said she wanted to visit Los Angeles, Hollywood, Universal Studios, and take a tour to check out the movie stars' homes. I told her a dozen times we didn't live in Hollywood, but she understood we were just a short ride away.

"I hate for this to end," I said.

"You and me both, sister," Gabi said.

"Moi aussi," Gianna said, almost in tears. "I suppose life will go back to normal now."

Gabi reached across the table and held Gianna's hands. "Maybe. Maybe not. Excuse me a sec. Gotta powder my nose."

She went inside. I heard her dialing. Gianna and I finished our little bites, sipped lemonade over crushed ice, and followed her in. We caught the tail end of the conversation. Really, it was just the goodbye.

Gabi hung up the phone and grinned like she'd won the lottery. No, like she was so full of some happy secret that a bright glow was coming out of her whole being.

She looked at Gianna. I had a pretty good idea who had been on the phone.

Gianna was standing there in my pink shirtdress that looked like something Audrey Hepburn would have worn, with a wide belt and a long pink bead necklace. I said it was not my color. Her fingers were laced and at her mouth like she was praying, and she was staring at Gabi.

"What's up, doc?" I asked.

"Not a thing," Gabi said to Gianna. "Except a little birdie told me that you're officially on G's dance card now."

I squealed, and jumped up and down, just like Gabi did. Gianna burst out crying. We had just enough time to fix her makeup.

We said goodbye to Gianna in front of the hotel with our taxis waiting. She took her taxi home, and we took ours to the airport. Gabi and I looked back at the Carlton glowing like a queen of the night as we drove away. The trip had been unforgettable.

"Liar," Gabi said, snorting. "Too tight on you? That was your favorite dress."

"You're the liar," I said. "Give me a break. Powder your nose? Best phone call, ever."

Guillermo took over for the last two nights we were there. We never told him that Joe told us what had happened. He never told us why he took off those nights. He only told us to be sure and come back. We had to double-team Joe again to get the truth about what was up with G. It was a blast except we were not happy G caught people breaking in his place.

Gabi and me, we took to Gianna. We even took to Joe. We made some serious bread on this trip. I was worried about the ten thousand cash limit you are allowed to enter the US with. Gabi wasn't worried, and she had more money than me. We had it in our carry-on purses, bags, and moneybelts. I didn't trust putting cash in our checked baggage, and neither did Gabi.

At the airport, we were offered an upgrade to business class with seats next to each other for five hundred each. We took them up on it. It was heavenly. All that room to stretch like loaded cats. I love my life. Just think that without Gabi, I'd still be a stewardess for Max with a nothing paycheck. I owe so much to Gabi. Except for the sex, she's like the sister and brother I never had rolled up into one. I'm such a pussy ass bitch. Sex on my brain. Don't I get enough at work?

We boarded the plane. I was blown away by business class and couldn't wait to get a better look at all the perks. I picked up the brochure in our welcome packet. Our seats were straight up, seat belts on, the plane was moving back, and flight attendants were demonstrating emergency procedures. I had so many hours of air-time with Max, I didn't have a single worry about flying. Finally, the stewardesses were done. I flicked on the reading light, relaxed against the headrest and opened the brochure. For just a second, I turned to look at Gabi. She sensed my eyes on her. We held hands as the plane blasted us into the sky.

May 1990
Los Angeles, California
Gabi

When we got home, the never-get-tired girl, Mona, went to the grocery store and came back with bags of food. Her plan was to cook up a storm twice a day for the four days until I went back to work. That didn't happen. What did happen is that we got out of bed to order in, we'd eat, then go back to bed. The nine-hour time difference was a killer. I couldn't remember how I handled the jetlag before. Certainly, I would not forget how it got me this time.

We stashed our cash earnings in my home safe. I planned to take most of it to my safety deposit box. Five thousand, maybe ten in the house safe was more than enough in case of an emergency earthquake or even an epidemic. I felt secure again. I counted out Macho's cut and gave it to Mona who was going to see him before returning to work tomorrow.

I've had it with taxis and drivers. Driving my Ferrari with the top down felt sweet. Every time I get behind the wheel, I think of Homer who gave it to me. I thought of him all the way down Wilshire Boulevard to the courthouse at the public defender office. The freeway was faster, but I didn't mind the drive. I totally dig my wheels.

I had a good rapport with the attorneys at my office. At the PD office, we joked that we had a revolving door because of the fast personnel turnaround. Rarely did a lawyer stick around more than a year. I wasn't a lifer by any means and didn't plan on staying forever, but it felt good to come back to a bunch of friendly hellos, good mornings and welcome backs. People missed me.

On my desk was a luscious four-inch orange-frosted cake and a note written in long hand that started with 'Welcome back,' and ended with 'Jerry.' I took my camera from my desk and snapped a picture of the cake. Jerry was no longer my direct boss, but he was my best friend here. He joked that he wanted to have sex with me, but he was married with kids. I think if he really wanted it, it would have happened, although the adventure with Max's wife Lily and the hidden video camera had taught me to stay away from married men.

I called Jerry on his cell to thank him for the cake. He was running to court, as usual.

"Hey, we need to do lunch. Let me know. Tomorrow works for me."

If we went to lunch, it was to Olvera Street, a good jaunty walk. The taquitos there were to die for, well worth the walk.

"I'm in," I said.

As I had planned before I left, my calendar had no appearances until tomorrow. I needed today to go over case files. I felt like I had a full case load, but Marshall, my supervisor who assigned cases, might think differently and hand me more. I feel bad for clients in custody waiting for trial or a deal who have to wait longer to get through the process. Many clients on bail want to delay. Being in custody makes a big difference.

I am thankful my short-term memory can store and organize important facts about each case. It's not unlike freshman midterms when you're cramming before exams. From the facts, I build a defense. By the time I went through my case load, it was after five in the afternoon. On my drive home, I went over the high priority cases, those who were in custody, and those who were out on bail. I had a variety of petty crimes, misdemeanors, and nine serious felonies, including a manslaughter case and an armed robbery. The manslaughter was out on bail. The armed robber had no bail. I tried to get him bail. That was my job as his lawyer. Society might be safer if he wasn't out right away. He was a client who kept saying if he was out on bail, he could borrow and earn enough to hire a private lawyer instead of a loser PD.

Public defender lawyers are not seen as warrior lawyers by those who need us. We're a last resort. It's either us, or they ask the judge if they can defend themselves. Most times, that's not going to happen. I would want a private lawyer too. All the years I broke the law by selling my body and never got caught make me a better lawyer. I was lucky. Who better a defender of alleged criminals than someone like me? I give one hundred percent for my clients. I do it because it's the right thing to do, and it's my duty, no matter how many other cases I have to work on. And I have more empathy with them than they will ever know.

Marshall Biker left me a message to call him when I was back from court. We were in the same building. Marshall was in his sixties but that doesn't matter anymore. What matters is that he's married with adult kids, two of them lawyers in the district attorney's office.

"Welcome back young lady. I missed you. If I was younger, I would ask you to marry me," he said.

"Not sure how much your wife would like me sharing her sock drawer. Just because you missed me, the answer is yes. I'm flattered, Marshall. Tell me about the case you are assigning me."

"It's a night burglary and attempted murder of the homeowner. The judge was going to assign private counsel until we learned that the victim is going to recover."

If there is a death in a case, the judge often assigns the case to private counsel and the county pays the lawyer.

"Has he been arraigned?"

"He has. Johnson handled that, and then the judge was back and forth on whether to assign the case out to counsel or let it stay with us. Trial in six weeks. Check it out. See if you need to file motions."

"Got it. Send me the file, or I'll have Sandra go get it."

"It's already on its way."

I reviewed the file. Robert Lopez. Not much there. I had the arraignment notes, conversations with the defendant and the public defender who handled the arraignment, and the police report, which was incomplete. The defendant claimed he was in San Diego when the burglary occurred. The DA filed the case because the badly injured victim identified my client. My client was thirty-five years old, unemployed, no felonies on his record, but he did have a history of three arrests. Bail was set at $100,000. Lopez was in custody at county jail, unable to make bail. Mugshots are never good, but the face on Lopez's mug shot was good-looking enough to be on the cover of one of those romance novels that Mona was always reading.

When I got home, Mona was heading out.

"You're out early," I said.

"Yeah, it's a dinner, and after, a party dinner or something. How do I look?"

"Scrumptious," I said.

"I thought so," she said with a laugh. "I ordered you a pastrami with killer onion rings and fries. Got here an hour ago. You need to microwave."

"I thought I had an appointment with a can of soup. Pastrami and goodies will make my night."

I turned on the small TV in the kitchen and it droned on while I, in pjs and socks, made a cup of instant coffee, warmed up the food, and sat down to eat. After one sip of the instant, I tossed it and brewed a half pot of real coffee. Then the pastrami was cold. I put it back in the microwave, and finally I sat down to eat. Halfway through the sandwich, I poured a cup of the brew, black. Not as good as the hotel coffee, but not bad.

The evening news was on, but my head was in Cannes. Behind my eyes, I replayed my memory of the nights we were there. I worked every night and so did Mona, except for when Rachel had her. I was lucky that I had no bad experiences. The clients were great. Mona wasn't as lucky, but she shook off the kidnapping and worked the next night. She's strong. Love that girl.

A call girl only has so many years, and then the gravy train's over. Even if your body looks good and you get plastic surgery, you're never twenty again. And what happens after that? You either find some other way to earn bread or you work for peanuts. Good thing I have a license to practice law. I wish I could figure out something for Mona. What will she have to fall back on? I'm pretty sure being an underpaid stewardess or massage therapist won't cut it any longer. Will she get married and divorced when the dude finds out what she did? For that very reason, I will never get married and live a lie. That's what it would be unless I told him. Yeah right.

It wasn't even eight, and I was not sleepy, but I went to bed. The TV was on, keeping me company. I knew if I waited it out, after a few days, my body would turn night back into night. In Cannes, I'd be figuring out what I was going to wear for the evening. I don't miss the strangeness of the business, but I do miss dressing up and going out on a blind date. The only thing I knew when I headed out was how much Guillermo had charged for my services. I should be grateful of where I am today. I am grateful.

I can't say I miss the sex. Usually clients don't care if a hired hand gets her jollies or not. That was not true with several of my clients in Cannes.

I hope I don't live to regret giving my cell number to Marco and Nina. Both know my name and that I live in Los Angeles, but neither has a clue that I'm a lawyer. I'm sure they dumped the number. Why would they keep it?

I put the TV on mute. Why is it that a TV screen, even a silent one, is like having someone else in the house? But it wasn't enough. I was wide awake. I went to the den to get a book but couldn't find anything I wanted to read on our small bookcase. I thumbed through Mona's dog-eared collection of paperbacks. I pulled out one of the novels, purple cover, naked-chested man with impressive biceps. It was set in medieval times, but his clothes could have come from Calvin Klein, and he rocked that scruffy forty-eight-hour barber-be-damned need-a-shave-look. That was Lopez, all over. This afternoon when looking at his mug shot, I pictured him on the romance novel cover. I laughed at myself and put down the romance.

No book. I'm bored sick, and it's not even nine. This is what I face until my body figures out that night is for sleeping. Life at night at home. What a bummer.

I turned everything off. Lamp. TV. I had a wrestling match with my pillow getting it just right.

Fuck it's early.

I pictured Lopez. My client, the burglar. I actually remembered his face except it was plastered on that lurid purple cover of Mona's Love's Sweaty Armpits.

I fantasized. I rolled over on my back and pictured the stranger on top of me.

Fuck.

No one was giving me brownie points for facing the long night cold turkey. I finally took a sleeping pill and launched into dreams of Lopez naked except for a medieval doublet floating in a pastrami boat on the pier outside the Carlton.

My date picked me up at the apartment building where Gabi and I live. When Macho arranges that kind of a hookup, I'm outside the door with the doorman, waiting for the ride. Tim was driving a Porsche 911, a black beauty that looked marvelous under the lights of the Century Plaza Hotel where we attended the party. Macho said my date was Tim Wells. At the party fundraiser for a state senator, a whole lot of people called him by that name, so it probably wasn't an alias. I actually met the senator. Boy, would he pee in his pants if he knew what I do for a living. I glanced at the papers by our plates. We were sitting at a top tier table, and the paperwork said each plate cost ten thousand. Ten thousand. Tim had paid twenty thousand big ones for two seats at a dollhouse banquet. It wasn't rubber chicken. I say dollhouse because the dinner was a bunch of courses of tiny dishes with one bite of food that was so fancied up, it was completely unrecognizable, like one sliver of unnaturally colored radish with a bunch of spices on it, or one cube of meat stabbed with a stick of rosemary. Male waiters in formal wear were running back and forth bringing one bite at a time. One of the salad courses was a frozen peeled grape. I kid you not. Somebody would bring out a massive tray of, say, martini glasses full of green crushed ice with one shrimp atop each, and set them on a buffet table, and the herd of waiters would grab a glass, deliver it, and carry off the empty plate. Did I mention a new, fresh glass of champagne with each course? Anyway, this went on, over and over. I stopped after my first champagne, but Tim drank both mine and his. I sure hope the senator is more efficient in his office than this. I'd never been to a fundraiser like this, and I have gone to a whole bunch of parties with dates who pay me.

They had started bringing desserts. I'd had a tiny round scoop of cheesecake, and Tim had his.

"You ready to get out of here?" Tim asked.

We kind of snuck off, caught an elevator to the seventh floor. He already had a key.

"You live here?"

I knew it was a dumb question, but he had a key.

"I live here tonight." He laughed. "I checked in earlier. I hope you like the room."

It was nice, but nothing could beat our penthouse suite in Cannes.

"I love it," I said. It had two bathrooms, a living room and a bedroom. Two bathrooms mean I can shower after, and it's not such an imposition on the client.

All the lights were on, and we were standing in the living room. Tim hugged and kissed me. I stepped out of my shoes beside the coffee table.

"Thanks for going to the party with me," he said. "Was it boring?"

"Not at all. All those important people. All those tiny plates."

"Did you see any familiar faces?"

"Hey, is that getting personal?" I stayed cool. I'm always cool.

"Good answer," he said, whatever that meant.

Tim poured himself white wine from an open bottle. I accepted a short pour. We raised our glasses and carried them to the bedroom. The white comforter on the bed was turned down, his and hers slippers were on a cotton floor mat, two Godiva chocolates and a long-stemmed red rose in a crystal vase was on each table. I don't know why the flower caught my attention.

"Can I get you ready?" I asked, setting my wine glass beside a vase of six beautiful roses on a round table close to the bed. Beige drapes. Beige lamps by the bed. Beige paneling halfway up the wall, then stark white wall above that. The floor was covered in beige carpet with a thick nubby plaid weave that was soft under my feet.

Tim chuckled. "Oh, I've been ready since the frozen peeled grape. I got it. I can't wait to get you," he said. "I've been savoring every time I look at you. You are very pretty, you know."

If he was in that big of a hurry, who am I to make him wait? In a heartbeat, I was out of my Dior dress, shoes. I beat him getting into the bed, both of us naked under that cloud of a comforter.

After we had sex, he talked a lot. He was a lawyer, divorced, or so he said, and had four kids, three girls and one boy. I didn't ask for ages or names, and he didn't tell me. He tried to go a second round. He couldn't. I tried to get him ready. He was just not getting hard. I told him that it was okay and blamed it on the gallon of champagne he'd slurped with dinner. I'm not sure he heard me, because he was out like a light. I enjoyed the jacuzzi tub in the marble bathroom. He was still zonked out when I came out of the shower. I tucked him in, took a cab at one and was home in twenty minutes.

Gabi was totally out. Maybe she was still a little jetlagged. I closed her door. She always leaves it open when I'm away. I went to my room and took about ten minutes to get in my bed. An early night. Heavenly.

My cell phone rang.

"You feel like doing a run downtown? Five hundred. Probably in and out in one hour."

"Going to take me thirty to get out of here. I got to get dressed."

"Thanks, Mona. Glad you're back. His name is Ronnie. Call me when you're ready to roll and I'll give you the details."

September 1985
Los Angeles, California
Gabi

I drove to the Los Angeles County jail to meet Robert Lopez. Never mind that he'd been paddling me in a canoe in Cannes half the night.

Sometimes it is difficult to have a private conversation with a client because the room gets packed, but today, the attorney room was not packed. A class action about to begin. This room was the only place where a jailed client could sit without a divider or a glass enclosure. The rules were that I could hand the client anything from my file as long as I raised it so the guard could see and nod his okay. No physical contact of any kind was allowed.

My ass was lucky to get a table that had an attached chair with a back instead of a metal table with attached swivel stool. This was better on my ass.

He was in an orange jumpsuit, familiar wear for my eyes. The guard uncuffed him, and Lopez sat down. Given he was in my head all night when I was sleeping with Prince Valium, I felt both very familiar and very awkward. This was our first real meeting.

He gulped air. "You're kind of young. Are you my public defender?"

I introduced myself, raised my business card for permission, and the guard nodded. I handed it to Lopez.

"Yes, I'm your lawyer, and I'm not as young as you might think."

"Yeah you are." He had a nice smile. "I need a good lawyer." He sighed deeply.

His sigh implied I was not the good lawyer he needed. He was better looking than the mug shot I had memorized. Better looking than his dream self on top of me.

"I'm a good lawyer," I said. "Let's discuss your case. The police report says you claim to have been in San Diego when the crime happened. The victim identified you from a police photograph. The District Attorney figured that was enough to file charges against you."

"Look, I'm innocent."

I smiled at him. "Innocent or not, tell me about San Diego."

He sighed for at least the third time since the interview started. He was not sighing for love of me.

"San Diego?" I repeated.

I spent two hours with Lopez. Once he got started, he talked and talked.

In San Diego, he claimed he had been incarcerated on a petty theft charge, accused of stealing a jacket and sunglasses from a parked convertible with its top down. He insisted he was in custody at the city jail.

"The district attorney didn't file charges. I was released the day after the burglary took place."

"How are you so sure?"

Sigh. "That's what I mean. You are too young for this."

"Stop playing games, Lopez. I'm all you have right now. Answer my question."

Sigh. "I was arraigned. You should know that. I got the copy from the PD that handled the arraignment."

He was either a con or a damn good liar.

I wanted to believe him.

I tried not to stare but I know I did, and he knew it.

He smiled.

I looked at my watch as I got in my car. It was too late to return to the office. I called Mona.

"Just leaving the county jail. Do you have a gig tonight?"

"Not yet. Early still. Why?"

"I thought you'd meet me, and we'd have a real meal."

"Where?"

"Do you mind driving to the Marina? Thinking about the Lobster House."

"Sounds delicious. What's your ETA?"

"I'm getting on the freeway. Probably forty-five minutes."

"Meet you there."

I wish Mona was a man, my partner for life. Wishful thinking. We both like men. We both prefer a real penis.

In the morning, I called Deputy District Attorney Henry Moss who was handling the Lopez case. I thought I would have to leave a message, but he answered. I told him who I was and who I was representing.

"I don't see anything in the police report about the arrest in San Diego. Am I missing something?"

"I didn't check the alibi. The victim identified him."

"Henry, the victim was injured. Her prognosis was death. Thank God she made it back, but you know how possible it is that she wasn't up to making an accurate id. What was her condition when she made the identification? It wasn't even a lineup, just a photograph."

"Gabi, I'm not going to try the case with you on the phone. The case is filed."

"Did you have an investigator check his alibi? Was he in San Diego at the city jail or not? Did you arrange for a lineup?"

"Detectives will handle the lineup. You have the right to be there."

"I know," I said. "You didn't give it to an investigator?"

"I already told you, I did not."

"Don't get pissed at my tone," I said. "Nothing personal."

"I know that, Gabi. We need to do lunch one day."

"Of course," I said. I always say that. "I may need a continuance."

"No sweat. Let me know."

Ten minutes later, I had the necessary approval to assign a private investigator to check out the alibi in San Diego. It was not as easy as making a phone call. I needed solid proof. I explained this to my private investigator, Mr. Harmon.

I barely made it on time to my next court appearance.

"Your Honor, we're ready for trial."

My client was Ruby Perez, a shop-lifting case filed as a felony because the merchandise was valued at more than two hundred dollars.

Judge Allison was a no-nonsense lady who had been on the bench for ages. I liked her, and I'd had cases in her court before.

"Counsel, have you discussed a possible disposition in this case with Mr. Bolton?"

Mr. Bolton was the deputy district attorney standing at the next table.

"I have your honor. He says he's not interested."

"Before we proceed to trial, I want the two of you to have a heart to heart and try and settle this matter in the interest of justice for all concerned."

I went into the hallway with Bolton. Ruby had been standing. She sat back down. She was out on bail, and in a bright red flowered dress and purple tennis shoes. Hard to miss.

"Petty theft, community service, that's what it will take," I said right off.

"Gabi, have you seen the evidence? Your client had six hundred dollars worth of clothes on, four dresses under her own clothes. She's a thief."

"She's twenty. Give me a break."

I'd locked horns with Bolton before. He was a good guy, but he was not always nice.

"Petty theft, two weekends in county jail and summary probation."

I countered. "Petty theft, she makes restitution for the items, and serves community service for six weekends cleaning the freeway, four hours each Saturday, and four hours each Sunday."

Bolton twisted. I smiled up at him. He wasn't much taller than me.

"Pretty please," I said. "Let's get rid of this."

Bolton agreed. He went back to court. I followed him to get Ruby to join me in the hallway. I gave her the scoop.

"You think that's a good deal?" she asked nervously.

I didn't know if she was just anxious, or simply not the sharpest tool in the shed. "What do you think? Right now, you got a felony. Petty theft is barely a misdemeanor."

She smiled but only a little. The smirk gave her away.

"I hope I don't get killed out there on the freeway. Why so many weekends?"

She was playing me. She knew it, and I knew it. I ignored her complaints.

The judge ordered her bail exonerated and gave her a three-minute scolding while Bolton and I exchanged looks. Ruby looked bored by it all. She was tough.

In the hallway again, I told her, "You have six months to pay three hundred restitution," I said.

"I didn't get the clothes. Why do I have to pay for them?"

"You only have to pay three hundred. The dresses were more than twice that."

Ruby looked me square in the eye. I could see how unjust she felt the justice. I could practically see her thoughts. If she had three hundred in the first place, she wouldn't have had to try stealing the dresses. She reminded me of me, only this girl had been shoplifting, not hooking. Which is worse? When the conversation was over, I was ready to go to my office. Our business today was done, but she was still standing there, looking awkward.

"Hey, Gabi, you got a ten spot? I got like no money for parking or gas."

"Bus is cheaper than a car," I said.

Ruby's chin went up defiantly. I got it. She needed to get home, and all I was offering was free advice. I remember being her age, and all I got from everybody was free advice. Tell me something I don't know, people.

I took a twenty from my wallet and handed it to her. My tough Ruby. She would have denied it, but her eyes moistened. I hugged her.

"Find something legal to do."

I held the hug for a while, maybe like a mom would do. She stepped back slowly, looking at me.

"I'll try," she said. "Hey, what size dress do you wear?"

I frowned at her. She put her hand on her hip, emphasizing the thirty pounds she had on me. Plus, we were eye to eye, her in her flats, and me in my tall heels. There was no way she could wear my clothes. My sedate, bland courtroom clothes. I was slow to catch on that she was kidding.

"Funny girl," I said. "I better not hear you pulling this prank again. Clothes aren't worth it. If it happens again, the judge you get won't be so lenient."

When had I turned into Aunt Isabel? Feeling a little embarrassed, I walked away. When I looked back, Ruby was standing where I had left her, waiting for me to turn around. She waved.

I waved back. My heart twisted a little.

I shut my door and called Macho from my office, but on my cell. It was pretty late in the day, and I figured if he was asleep, the machine would pick up. But he happened to be awake.

"Is Roger free? I could use a massage."

Now that I had a cash stash again, Macho told me to call Roger direct. I would have called him, but Sandra knocked on the door with paperwork I had to fill out right away.

On my way home, I called him.

"Hey, if you have a couple hours to sell me, I need a fuck like you would never believe. Are you up to it?"

"I love it when you talk dirty," he said. "What time?"

"Does nine work for you?"

"I'm open," he said.

"Deal. See you then."

It's great not coming to an empty apartment. I passed on dinner. I'd made no dinner plan, but if I changed my mind, Mona had Chinese for me in the fridge. Mona and I shot the breeze while she got ready for work. I took a long hot bath followed by a cold shower. An hour later, Roger arrived for my tune-up.

Just as I was a pro, Roger was a pro at what he did. I paid for service and got two hours of enchantment without having to give anything back. It was all for me, and no obligation. When he left, habit drove me to the bidet to douche and hit the shower. I thought how often I douched going way back to when I started with Rose in Hollywood. The latest articles frown on douching. They say it's bad for the vagina. Tough luck scientists. You can walk around with smelly pussy if you want. I'm staying squeaky clean.

My investigator got back to me with the skinny on Robert Lopez's alibi. By the time I finished reading the report, I was steaming. I had two court appearances before I could run over to the county jail. By the time I got to the jail, it was almost four. My temper had cooled a little.

I raised the copy of Harmon's report. The guard nodded.

"Read this."

He didn't even look at the report. He stared at me for a few seconds.

"You lied to me." I pushed the paper in front of him.

"I don't have my reading glasses. Read it to me." He pushed it back.

"You don't need reading glasses," I said. The way he said it, I knew he was lying.

I took my copy and read the two-page report aloud. It was lying on top of my legal pad. I'd taken no notes yet.

He interrupted me five times in two minutes. I was getting exasperated.

"If you are found guilty of these charges, you will do serious time in prison. Stop messing around. I might find a way to help you, but it can't be with lies."

I looked at him as harshly as I could. I was tired of his wasting my time. If he had been straight with me from the beginning, we'd be closer to wrapping up the case.

"You're beautiful," he said.

"What part of what I just said don't you believe?"

He spread his hands flat on the table and stared at them.

"I did get arrested in San Diego. I was released the day before the burglary, but I was not in Los Angeles the day or the night the burglary took place."

"Where were you?"

"Hitching a ride from San Diego."

"I need more than that."

Still, no notes on the legal pad.

"A girl named Pat picked me up. I was on the on ramp of the freeway, hitching. One thing led to another. I ended up with her all night in Oceanside. I swear I went to her house and spent the night with her."

"How did you get to Los Angeles and when, exactly."

"I hitched it from Oceanside the morning after the burglary."

"Where did she drop you off?"

"I don't remember. Somewhere in Boyle Heights on the five freeway."

"She dropped you off on the freeway?"

"No, she dropped me off at the off ramp to Cesar Chavez. That's where I got off."

The report noted his arrest date six days after the burglary in downtown Los Angeles on 7th & Grand on a charge of being drunk in public.

"Were you drunk in public?"

He shrugged and didn't answer. I was getting nowhere fast.

"Tell me about Pat."

"Who is Pat?"

"Listen Robert, if you want to dump me, I'll see what I can do about it. If that happens, you will get another PD. You may think the judge will appoint private counsel, but it won't happen."

"I was kidding," he said. "What about Pat? What do you want to know?"

"Tell me where she lives in Oceanside. She could be your ticket out of this."

"Get the judge to sign an order to release me, and I'll take you there."

I got up and snapped open my briefcase, shoved the legal pad in there, slammed it shut. I was entirely pissed enough to slam him in the forehead with the edge of my briefcase, but I happened to look up and notice the guard noticing me slamming around. He quirked an official eyebrow at me. I flashed him a smile, and glared at my client, who had to know I was fuming.

"No more jokes," Robert said.

I stared at him for a good minute before I sat down.

"Go on."

"When I left her house in the morning, I took her wallet with ninety-five dollars in it. When I got to Los Angeles, I walked in a post office on Cesar Chavez Boulevard, and I put her wallet and everything in an envelope. She had all sorts of identification. I kept the cash. She works at JPL, and she had another identification for the navy base. She told me her husband is on a ship somewhere. I wrote the name and address on her driver's license on the envelope."

I'm not used to clients copping to anything.

"How did you mail it?"

"I stood in line, gave it to the mailman at the counter and paid postage from the money I took from her wallet."

"Did you get a receipt?"

"If I did, I don't have it. I walked to a downtown liquor store and bought a bottle of whisky."

He was hard to read. When I first met him, I believed when

he said he was in jail when the burglary occurred. Why would he tell the truth now?

"Her last name?"

"Her name was Pat Smith."

"Fuck, give me a fucking break, Lopez."

He smiled.

"You made my day, Miss Public Defender. You're human."

"I need to send an investigator to get a statement from her," I said. I did not understand his cavalier attitude. He reminded me of Alex Rose. I was more human than that creep would ever know. Stealing a wallet from a woman who gave him a ride and let him stay overnight. Asshole.

"She may be mad at me about the wallet."

"Do you think?" I asked. "Anything else she should be mad at your for?"

"Can I speak frankly to you?"

"I'm your lawyer."

He considered me for a minute.

"I fucked Pat for hours, and she loved it."

The snide expression on his face made me glad I had Roger.

"I'm not your confessor, but in that case, she might not be mad at you. Tell me how to find this Pat. And give me her real last name if you know it."

"Pat Jones," he said.

He didn't remember the address, but her street was Margarita in Oceanside, less than ten minutes from the five freeway, though he couldn't remember which off ramp.

On my way home, I talked to Mona.

"I was worried. Where are you?"

"On the way now. I had to visit a client at the county jail. Got a late start."

"I'm leaving in fifteen. Two small pizzas just got here."

"Got it. Thanks."

"Want me to wake you when I get back?" Mona teased. "Or did you get enough from Roger?"

"He wiped me out, but it depends."

"You nasty girl," Mona said before we disconnected.

June 1990
Los Angeles
Mona

In Cannes there are many hotels, yet all of my dates were in two hotels. Los Angeles doesn't have many hotels, but certainly there are more than three or four. Macho's clients are upper class, and most of my dates were in the handful of high-end locations. One out of twenty dates might be in a private home. Tonight, I had a date in a home.

Macho said there would be no driver to pick me up. My map book guided me to the house in the hills of Trousdale Estates above Sunset Boulevard. I wound around and around the streets, the views becoming more spectacular and the streets narrower. Finally, I found the address though the house wasn't visible from the street. The address was on an illuminated plaque on a wall, and two gates hid the residence.

I pulled up to a metal framework and pushed the lit button, presuming it would open the gate. Nope. It was an intercom.

"Are you as pretty as your picture?" a voice asked.

The gates started to open inward.

"You can tell me in a few minutes," I said and drove in.

The house was a grand two-story, all lit up. I passed manicured grounds, fanciful topiary, and water features along the circular driveway, and everything was lit up like Disneyland. Four cars were parked along the curb, including a Ferrari in front of me. Before I was out of my car, a man came out the front door.

"Park where you are. That's fine," he said. "It's just us tonight."

I stepped out of the car, and I saw him. To me, he looked like a middle-aged movie star. He was maybe in his forties, dark hair with a sprinkle of gray. His features were sharp, squared, beautiful. I mean, he was tanned, and had that 'beautiful people' look. Maybe it was just the glow of the grandness of the house that rubbed off on him and made me think he was in the movies. He wasn't dressed fancy, just west coast casual, tee shirt, shorts, sandals.

I extended my hand for a shake, and he bypassed it, and smacked me on the lips.

"You are marvelous," he said. He was smiling like a loon.

"Thank you. You're too kind."

"We're going to have fun."

He walked me from my car to his massive front doors. They were giant, like the entrance to some ancient church in Cannes. I mean, the doors were easily twice as tall as me. One of them was standing open, revealing the house's colorful interior.

"Mitch, wait till you see what I have in store for you."

"Wrong," he said with gusto, taking my hand, walking fast. "It's what I have in store for you."

We passed through a marble foyer and a couple rooms to a

bar in a great big entertaining room, unlike a normal den, and more like an amusement park, only one that was inside a residence. I never saw machines like this in a private house. Coke machine, juke box, seven arcade games, and four slot machines with lights flashing just like in Vegas.

"What a fun room," I said. "Vegas shut down, and you bought it?"

He laughed. "Everyone loves this room. What can I get you to drink?"

"A coke is fine, thanks."

"I'm having a dynamite Merlot." He raised his glass and handed me one.

"Sure. Thanks."

He showed me around the room, introducing me to the machines. They were vintage collectibles, and they all worked.

He went to the bar and refilled the glasses..

"What do you want to do first?"

"Whatever you wish."

"I'd like to start in the bedroom where I can see your beautiful body."

"Let's do it, Mitch."

He handed me my glass of wine that was now half full again.

"The bedroom is this way," he said.

We went up a circular staircase. As we ascended, I tried not to gawk, but looked up at the huge chandelier hung from the second tier's ceiling. Brilliant light sparkled through crystals. I held my wine glass carefully so I wouldn't spill anything on the carpet. Massive paintings in gold leaf frames were leaning like soldiers against the wall all the way down the hall.

The bedroom was as huge as I expected, but there were no family pictures. I wondered if he lived alone or what? I did not ask.

I set my glass on the nightstand. I unbuttoned a single button, and my dress dropped to my ankles. He checked me out for two minutes, having me turn this way and that. I offered to fold down the blankets.

"No time," he said. "I need you right now."

I was under him in a flash. We connected, then he rolled me on top, still connected.

"Show me what you got for me," he said, laughing. His good humor was contagious.

"Let me see," he said, his eyes wide open, my face an inch from his.

"Okay," I said.

I sat up and tried slow and deep as I like it. It was worth a shot. He wanted it fast, fast, faster, like a piston. It was his party, so I was pumping up and down like a jack hammer. He was squealing, laughing, serious fucking. I never slowed for an hour until he exploded, pleading at last for me to stop. The laughter slowed but did not stop until he kissed me with such passion. I've never seen such a happy man. His cheeks were rosy from happiness, and he was just beaming. He wanted to keep playing around in the bed for a couple of hours. The smile never left his face.

Macho charged him two thousand dollars for four hours.

Mitch showed me the door after three hours and gave me a five hundred-dollar tip.

"I want you back," he said.

"Sure bet."

I called Macho soon as I was outside the gates of the house. My phone had great reception.

"Okay, done. Two thousand plus a tip."

"Can you handle another one at the Peninsula?"

"I can't. I didn't get to shower or douche. It went all too fast afterward for me to get a shot at the tub."

"Are you sure?"

"I can't go unless I'm clean. It's your own rule."

"Good girl. No worry. Go home, sending you kisses."

"Night Macho. Sending you hugs."

Gabi was sound asleep when I got there. I ran bubbles, got into the hot bath, and gave myself the works. I lit candles, used a bath pillow, turned on the radio, and grabbed one of my novels, enjoying the luxury. There's nothing as revitalizing or relaxing as a hot bath, and nothing on the clock to rush it. Before I got into the book, I could not resist wondering about Mitch, a charming dude, but a strange little puppy. He sparked my curiosity. Why was he so happy? Maybe I'd be that happy too if I were that rich. But his happiness seemed uncomplicated, joyful. I wondered if he was celebrating something in particular, and who shared that huge residence with him.

Did he live there alone?

Why all the cars?

Some hours after I went to sleep, the bed dipped to one side. I heard and felt Gabi slip under the covers. She didn't say anything, and she hung close to the other side of my bed. The room was dark, only the faintest of glows from the hallway nightlight.

"Come here you," I whispered.

"I'm sorry to wake you."

"You're not sorry. Come."

We hugged. We snuggled.

"You're so warm."

I wondered at her joining me. Gabi pushed to get her sleep. She worked long hours, and I know she'd had trouble getting her days and nights back in sync after Cannes.

"You're not working tomorrow?"

"Tomorrow is Saturday."

"It's already Saturday."

"Fun," Gabi said. "Let's sleep."

We've known each other five years and we're still like this.

Some married couples by now would be on either end of the mattress. There's magic with a woman and woman.

"G'nite Gabs," I said.

She didn't answer. Gabi was already asleep. It was my turn to pass out.

We were shorthanded in the PD office. Normally a senior to my grade handled a serious case, and I would play second chair. Although I have handled a whole lot of cases, I was getting more serious ones now. Experience is the thing. That's what's so great about starting in the public defender office or the district attorney office. It's like barber colleges where you can get a haircut for a dollar but the person cutting your hair doesn't have a license yet. I'm not saying that as a lawyer, I'm like a cheap haircut, just that I'm accumulating lots of great experience in my field.

My client, Rose Miner, was charged with assault with intent to commit great bodily harm. She was in custody awaiting trial and being held on bail of $100,000 dollars. Another PD had been representing her, but he left to join a law firm that swiped him away. His case load had been divided between a number of deputies. I ended up with Miner.

I had a fast introduction meeting with Rose behind the courtroom where inmates are held until their case is called. She was forty-one and looking rumpled in one of those regulation blue jumpsuits, no cuffs. Her hair was scraped back tight, showing four months of dark roots, and she had shadows under her eyes like she wasn't sleeping well. We didn't meet under the best of circumstances. It works like this: The deputy sheriff calls out the name, and we talk with the jail bars between us. It is so noisy we don't have to whisper. It's a zoo. There were multiple attorneys beside me, all in shouting matches with their respective clients, and the cage was full.

I told Rose her attorney had left the PD.

"I didn't like that man anyhow," Rose said, looking at my business card.

"I promise I will get in your case as fast as possible and get to trial. I know it's no picnic in county jail."

"What I need is good representation. I already been here four months. I can wait."

"Do you want me to get a new bail hearing? Can you make bail if bail is lower?"

"I can't make bail even if it was a dollar. Know what I mean?"

Rose's husband beat her up. The arrest pictures showed horrible bruising of her face. She made the mistake of not going at him with the kitchen knife right there and then. When he went to sleep, then she started stabbing him. The district attorney had put it in the record that her bruises were caused when her husband was defending himself.

I went back to the courtroom.

When Rose's case was called, I approached the counsel table. The deputy sheriff escorted Rose to stand next to me.

It was not the first time I had been before this judge, but formality dictated that I introduce myself when stepping in on this case. The deputy district attorney introduced himself and offered no objection or comment.

Judge Marion looked over the file.

"Counsel approach the bench please. Both of you."

The deputy DA looked puzzled.

"Are you handling this alone?" the judge asked in a very kind voice.

"Yes, your honor. We are on overload as you know."

"Don't take this the wrong way. I'm going to appoint private counsel to represent your client."

I looked at the DA real fast then focused on the judge who was in intimate distance of the DA and me. I think I hid my feelings well.

"No problem at all, your honor. I had hoped to be second chair on such an interesting case, but no one is available."

I went back to stand next to Rose. When I faced the bench, I noticed the judge smiling kindly at me.

"Rose Miner, I am appointing private counsel to represent you. The Public Defender office is swamped with cases at this time. Let's continue this until afternoon, at which time your appointed attorney can appear with you."

"This is good for you, Rose. Thank the judge," I whispered.

Rose thanked her. I smiled at Rose as the deputy walked her to the holding area.

I smiled at the deputy DA and split back to my office. I called my supervisor and gave him the scoop of the judge appointing private counsel.

"You'll get one soon enough," he said.

"No problem," I said. "It's a good move for the client."

I called Mr. Harmon who I'd asked to find the Jones lady in

Oceanside that my client claimed he was with the night of the crime in Los Angeles.

"Gabi, I am going to get it done, but not until next week. I am swamped. Yesterday I put in sixteen hours."

"Okay. Stay in touch," I said.

"Gabi, this client of yours lies like a house on fire that is not on fire."

"I know," I said.

I knew Harmon was pissed off about that wild goose chase when he went to San Diego to check on the alibi that Lopez was in custody on the night of the burglary, a lie.

I had never gone out to speak with a possible witness, but there was nothing in the rules that said I couldn't do it. We have a badge as identification, one I'd never used since I signed up to work here.

I got home earlier than usual for a Friday. I told Mona about my plans for Saturday morning. She was in front of a mirror putting on her face.

"You only have the name of the street and a name. Have you tried calling information to see if she's listed?"

"Good idea," I said, and used the house phone to call information.

"No listing," I said to Mona.

"I knew it."

"You didn't know it. Some people just use cells now."

Mona wouldn't let go. "We don't."

"Anyway, I'm going."

"I'll go with you."

"I'm going early. You need your sleep," I said.

I told Mona about getting kicked off the Rose Miner case.

"I wouldn't call that kicked off. You just got the case."

"I love you," I said.

"I know. Sounds like this Oceanside case is a big one too. Do you think this judge will do the same thing?"

"I don't think so, but anything can happen. I do have experience with burglaries. I can handle Lopez. Rose is a domestic violence case. If he did beat her like the pictures show, I can't blame her for going after him while he was sleeping."

"You dig being a lawyer, don't you?" Mona put eyeliner on one eye, flicked her gaze to me, then back to her reflection.

"I dig it, yeah."

"More than the other?"

"I dig everything I do," I said.

"You dug Cannes," Mona sung it out like a song lyric.

"You did too," I said.

"I have that mink coat I'll never use here in LA. Wonder if they'll take it back."

"You don't want to take it back. Someday you'll need it."

For dinner, I piled loads of cheese on buttered sourdough and put it in the toaster oven to get crisp and melty. When it was gold, I slid it next to the dill pickle on the salad plate I was using. Aunt Isabel had always sliced sandwiches into triangles, so it didn't feel done to me until I'd made a diagonal cut revealing all that cheesy goodness. I carried the plate into the den. The TV was on, but I was thumbing through our collection of CD movies.

I bit pickle first, then sandwich. Perfect.

"If you go to the bedroom to watch the movie, you'll end up going to sleep at an ungodly early time," Mona said, eyeing my plate.

"I'm staying right here until you come back tonight."

"No, you won't. You're going to Oceanside in the morning."

I held out the plate, and Mona carefully bit off the corner of one triangle.

"Did I mess up my lips?"

"Not at all," I said, offering her half of the sandwich, which she said she didn't want, then polished off.

I didn't put on a movie.

I went to my bedroom and put on a white cotton, sleeveless baby doll, turned down the sheets, and propped myself up to watch TV. I scrolled through the movies playing, but all I could think of was my coming trip to Oceanside.

If he's lying again, I'll find a way to drop out of the case. Fuck him.

I didn't hear Mona come in. I presume she didn't hear me when I left at nine in the morning.

I was wearing jeans, white tee shirt, and white tennis shoes. The weather was becoming typical California again, calling for me to put down the top of my Ferrari. When the top goes down, I put on my trusty bandana, so my hair doesn't look too crazy. When I get where I'm going, I always stash the bandana, and give myself a quick brush. If I didn't do that, the top down would give me a case of chronic bedhead.

I got on the Santa Monica Freeway off Robertson Boulevard headed south. Saturday traffic was a breeze. When I merged to the five freeway and drove thru East Los Angeles, I remembered City Terrace where I had lived with my aunt and cousins. I exited to hit the McDonald's drive thru. The sausage biscuit and black coffee reminded me of how I earned my first job with a hand job on the manager in his office.

An hour or so after I got back on the freeway, I saw the first exit for Oceanside. I took the second, filled up the tank and went inside to speak with the cashier. He was standing behind the counter behind his register. The counter was crowded with lighters, display boxes of dozens of kinds of candy and gum. Behind him was a brightly lit case where cigarettes were kept under lock and key. Light streamed in from the parking-lot side of the building which was entirely of glass. All the other walls were lined with refrigerator cases of drinks. There was a line from the door to the coffee island which shared space with a self-serve Slush machine agitating a grainy slush in an improbable shade of blue.

"I need to buy a map for Oceanside," I told the cashier.

The nametag on his bright red jacket said Tucker. I guessed him to be in his sixties. He wore granny glasses low on his nose, his hair and brows were gray, sparse on top, and he had a long gray ponytail.

"Don't have one with the streets correct. How can I help you? I've lived here all my life." He looked at me over the top of his glasses, wrinkling his very creased brow.

"I'm trying to locate Pat Jones. She lives on Margarita, but I don't have the address."

I could tell Tucker liked my look. I gave him an encouraging smile.

"You got business with Pat?"

I opened my eyes wide.

"Tucker, you know her?"

He cleared his throat. "That depends on what you want with her."

"I'm an attorney representing someone she may know. He says he was with her when a crime was committed in LA. I want to believe him, but I can't without Pat Jones."

I put my purse on the counter and pulled out a hundred.

"Tucker, I'm one of the good guys. Not a cop."

"I like your car," he said.

"Thanks. You wouldn't like it if you saw the monthly payments."

I always lied about the payments to strangers who admired the car.

I was tempted to show him my badge, but even though it clearly said I am not a peace officer, I didn't want to take the chance he would be scared off.

"Money is not necessary," he said.

"Tucker, take the money."

I pushed the bill across the counter and put my purse back over my shoulder.

The gas station was four minutes from the house.

I was having trouble believing that there was a Pat Jones who lived on Margarita and that I happened to stop at a convenience store where someone knew her.

"She be home," Tucker said. "She don't work Saturday or Sunday."

I parked on the curb in front of the light blue house.

I took off the bandana, ran a brush through my hair, and got out of the car. I was halfway to the house when the door opened. Tucker must have called her. A woman stepped out. She was pretty. Her pink crop top and shorts reveled a good figure and a nice tan. She smelled of cocoa butter and had a pair of big sunglasses pushed up to the top of her head. Her hair was a hundred different colors of gold in the sunlight, but inside it was just brown, and the ponytail made her seem younger. She was a couple of years older than me. Her light brown eyes were kind of gold, too. I wondered if I'd interrupted her sunbathing, but she never said.

"I knew that motherfucker was a crook," she said.

I extended my hand.

"My name is Gabi Guerrero." I pulled out my badge wallet, opened it and showed her the badge. "I'm a public defender in Los Angeles."

Pat Jones did not shake my hand. She didn't invite me in the house right away, but she did invite me in. She had a worried expression on her pretty face. After she stopped crying, I held her arm with one hand and patted her back with the other. I saw no neighbors, but if anyone had come out, they would have seen Pat Jones tearing up.

"I thought he would stick around a few days. He took off without a word."

"Is that why you're crying?"

"No. I don't know why. I'm just your run-of-the-mill navy-wife basketcase."

Her house was nice, a small two-story, neat as a pin. Her husband was attractive. I know this because there was a picture of him on the downstairs bathroom wall.

She offered me coffee.

We sat at her kitchen table. I took out my pad and pen to scribble down her words. She poured coffee for us both. I drank mine black. She added lots of cream and sugar and some kind of flavoring into hers and kept stirring. I didn't see her take a sip. She lit a cigarette and offered me one. I declined.

"I hope the smoke doesn't bother you."

"The smoke is no problem," I said. "Why did you pick him up?"

She gave me a funny look and took a seat at the table. "I never pick up any hitchhikers." Pat looked at her hands with an embarrassed expression on her face. The ember on the cigarette glowed as she sucked on it.

"He said he was hitchhiking," I said.

"I don't remember if his thumb was out. I passed him up then stopped, and he ran to the car."

"Why?"

She shrugged, blushing a little bit. "He's a looker."

I nodded.

"Ten minutes after he was in the car," she said, "his hand was up my skirt. Jack is in the Navy. He's not going to be back for nine months. The vibrator gets to be drag. No doubt you don't have that problem." She smiled for the first time.

"He told me he mailed you back your wallet with everything in it except the cash."

"I was furious at him. But he did send my wallet back. Everything is in that wallet. Driver's license, base id, credit cards, everything."

"Pat, if it turns out that he was with you when the crime was committed in Los Angeles, I will need to subpoena you. Will you cooperate?"

I drank the last of my coffee.

"Are you sure this smoke doesn't bother you?" she asked again.

"I'm okay with it," I said.

"I'll cooperate. Go easy on me. I can't miss more than a day of work. I'd prefer to give a written statement and not appear in court."

"You're good people," I said. "Can't lie to you. You will have to appear in court. First things first. Let's figure out the day and date he was here with you."

"It was a Tuesday. I go to AA on Tuesday and I missed that day. First time I ever missed."

I took my appointment book from my purse to check the calendar. I did not tell her the date the burglary occurred. I showed her the calendar.

"It was end of March," she said.

I paged back a month.

"Show me the last Tuesday in March," she said with certainty.

That was the date the burglary took place in Los Angeles. He could not be guilty of a crime in Los Angeles on the same night he was in Oceanside, unless he left Oceanside, committed the crime and returned to Oceanside. Anything is possible but I don't believe that's what happened.

"Are you absolutely sure he stayed the night?"

"He stayed the night. I ordered Dominoes after we had been rolling around in bed for hours. We nibbled pizza all night. We had pizza for breakfast as the sun came up. It was hell getting the stains out of my white sheets."

"Pat, can I get another cup and use your restroom?"

"I'll brew a fresh batch. Restroom is through that hallway," she pointed.

The bathroom was as neat as my own, only much smaller. I figured the master bathroom and bedroom were upstairs. A vase of plastic flowers and an air freshener was on the back of the toilet, a small carpet on the floor, and a matching shag covered the toilet lid. A squirt bottle of coconutty hand soap was by the faucet, a little bowl of soap shaped to look like shells, and a linen hand towel for visitors. I didn't use the hand towel. Aunt Isabel raised me better than that.

Pat Jones and I connected. She spent at least three hours with me. She told me a lot. She had been in AA for a year already. She had been drinking every day before and after work. Her supervisor had smelled liquor and gave her an ultimatum to clean up or find another job. She'd been dry for eleven months. She still kept liquor at the house because when her husband was around, he drank. She needed to see the liquor bottles and have the restraint not to touch.

I told her she was strong.

"The PD must pay you very well to afford that car you're driving."

I said, "My pay sucks." I didn't throw in the monthly payments lie.

We laughed.

Pat told me she made thirty dollars an hour working in software development at JPL. The Navy paid her husband much less than she made.

"His being a sailor comes with perks. I could stay cheap at base housing, but base housing gets old after a while. We got this house financed with no money down with a great low interest rate.

There is medical, shopping at any base. The tradeoff is not just chicken-shit pay. He's never home. For all I know, he has a family across the ocean."

I asked another question as she walked me to my car. "You don't have to tell me."

"Ask me."

"Do you mess around much like you did with Lopez?"

"Used to but not anymore, and never a hitchhiker."

We hugged like friends would do. I got in the car and she stood there with her cigarette as I tied on the bandana and drove away.

I made a U-turn and stopped at the sign across the street. She was still standing where I left her. I waved.

She waved back.

I passed the gas station where I had met Tucker but didn't stop.

"Thank you, Tucker," I said for my own ears.

I was home before three. When I walked in, Mona was in the bathroom brushing her teeth.

"Why didn't you wake me? I wanted to go."

She gave me a toothpaste kiss.

"You were dead asleep."

"Did you find her?"

I pulled my pad out of my purse. It was full of notes. Mona beamed like she had won something. She made a grab for it, and I stuffed it back inside.

"Tell me all about it."

"I'm starving. Want to have a late lunch?"

"I'm in. Give me five to put on my shoes."

I called the PD detective on his cell. I figured I would leave him a message, but I got him instead of his machine.

"Hey Detective," I said, and gave him a summary of what I

had learned. Mona sat on the couch tying her tennis shoes. She got the story as I told him.

"I told her you would be in touch right away to get a statement and serve her with a subpoena that I will have ready first thing Monday. You need to squeeze this in. Please."

"I'll pick up the subpoena Monday morning, and call her to arrange a meeting."

"You're the best," I said.

Mona and I headed to lunch at Canter's deli. We went inside, and the conversation was still on Pat Jones and everything I learned that I didn't share with the investigator.

"Pretty girl, three years older than me," I said.

"How pretty?"

"Very cute. Smart too, to be working computer software. She talks smart. I like her and I think she likes me."

"We could do a three-some," Mona suggested.

"We could but we're not," I said. "Silly girl." How stupid would I have to be to mix work and pleasure? That never went well.

"I was kidding. You don't like threesomes?"

Mona made fun, no matter what was on the table. The counter guy brought our food. Mona's Reuben was at least four inches high, stuffed with corned beef. I was sitting with my back to the wall of flakey pastries in the glass case.

"This dude Lopez must be a real looker."

"He's a looker and an asshole. Can't get over that he swiped her wallet."

"He sent the wallet back. He probably felt he needed the cash more than she did."

I bit into my hamburger with my eyes on Mona. Sipped my mocha shake as she peeled off the top layer of her sandwich and added a ton of mustard.

"What already?" she asked.

"I love you," I said. "You have an answer for everything."

Mona wiped mustard from a corner of her mouth and got busy with her Reuben on rye with a side of chips.

1990
Oceanside
Pat Jones

I told him how Jack would be away for nine more months. He said he would stay for a while. He said yes at least fifty times while he was kissing me and fucking me like few men have fucked me before. Yes, he said. Yes. Yes. We did it again at dawn, then I came out of the shower and he was gone, and so was my wallet. My purse was dumped out on the kitchen counter. He left the car. Left my purse. You don't call the cops because a hitchhiker that spent the night having consensual sex ran off with your wallet, cash and credit cards.

I freaked out, but I still had to go to work. A day or two later, I got this brown envelope in the mail. No note, nothing in it but my wallet, credit cards and ID. The postage stamp had a postal code but no city name. I could look it up but what for? When he first called collect from jail, I didn't have a clue who it was. I knew no one in jail. I never heard of Robert Lopez. I hung up on the operator twice in a row. Then it dawned on me. Robert.

I knew Robert. Robert the hitchhiker. Robert the thief. Robert the motherfucker. Big surprise. His last name wasn't son of a bitch. The man lies. I'd figured he'd lied about his first name. He kept calling. When I wanted him to call that first twenty-four hours to explain himself or apologize or promise to pay me back, he never did. Now he wanted me to talk to him. It doesn't work that way. But I was curious. I hadn't reported his crime. What was he arrested for? My curiosity got the better of me. I wasn't accepting the call because the sex had been so good.

"Operator, I'll accept the charges," I said.

"You know who this is?"

I recognized his voice.

"Yeah, the motherfucker who conned his way in my house, ate my food and pizza, used my shower and toilet, and split without a fucking word. I know who you are. Why're you calling me?"

"Babe, you left out what I did for you. Let's see, what was it you told me? You came, was it four or five times?"

A grown woman like me, a puppy. Every word he said pissed me off. Also, he turned me on.

He called me the next day, gave me his jail address, and in the morning, I bought a postal money order for one hundred dollars and sent it to him.

He promised the moon.

"Babe, I get out, I come over and take care of you until you throw me out."

"You're a liar."

"I didn't want to leave that morning. Sorry I didn't wake you."

"You're a liar," I said, every time he said that. "You snuck out like a thieving dog when I was in the shower."

"I know you're interested," he said, "or you would have stopped accepting my calls. I want you bad, Pat. I'm standing here at the jail payphone in my jumpsuit and I'm hard as a rock just hearing your voice."

"Tell me what you'd do to me if you were here right now."

We talked until someone made him hang up. He left me aroused. I couldn't get to the vibrator in my bedroom fast enough.

I love my job. Love the opportunity I have there. I can't drink just one drink or two glasses of wine. I'm an alcoholic but I'm not risking my job. Robert saw the liquor here. It's a big assortment for Jack and his friends that come over when he's on leave. Robert asked for a coke. He may have done it because I told him that I was in AA. I've had many men, but they are drinkers and pot-heads. If Robert wasn't a drunk, he'd be less threatening to my sobriety and to my job.

"I need you to help me beat this case I was busted for. I could be with you. Help me."

He wanted me to testify that he was with me Tuesday night in late March. I listened.

After he hung up, I checked the calendar. I'm a mathematician, a software developer, not a dumb ass. He was with me on Monday night, not Tuesday. I am a hungry woman that comes home to an empty bed every night, but am I hungry enough to be a fool? He never told me what crime he committed on Tuesday night.

On the next call, I told him, "I'm not lying. You were here Monday, not Tuesday."

"You're wrong Pat. Look at your calendar again. It was Tuesday, the 24th of March."

I disconnected the call.

Thirty minutes after I got home the next day, he called.

"It is possible that an investigator from the Public Defender office may come out to see you."

I wasn't lying for him, but I didn't tell him that again.

A day after his lawyer was here to see me, he called.

"Your lawyer visited," I said. "I thought you said it would be an investigator."

"The babe has spark. I told her your name and only the name of the street. When was she there?"

"Yesterday. So, happens she stopped at Tucker's Chevron and he told her where to find me. He called to warn me in case I didn't want to be here."

"What did she say?"

"She's sending an investigator for a statement and to serve me with a subpoena."

"You need to take a vacation. Oh baby, I'm going to fuck you for days."

I curled up on the sofa and let him tell me everything I wanted to hear. The puppy in me.

"So, you remembered it was Tuesday?"

"Yes, I got it straight. You were right. It was Tuesday."

Gabi had gotten home early enough that we ordered burgers for dinner. We thought we were going to eat together, so we'd set up for dinner in front of the TV to watch Pretty Woman. It had been out since February, but we hadn't had a chance to see it yet.

"How are you doing lovely lady?" Macho asked on the phone.

"I'm doing good. What you got?"

"Les from last week wants to see you again."

"He tips a thou, and I like him."

"I got you four hours, two thousand."

"Where and when?"

"Dinner at Peninsula. After, same place."

"Good. I'm going to pass on the burger I just ordered."

"Are you over the bad experience in Cannes?"

The day after it happened, I told Macho a dozen times I was over it. I've told him I'm over it every day since.

"I would have gone there and wiped everyone out if you had not been released."

"You're so sweet, Macho. I do love you."

"He asked you again about Cannes?" Gabi asked.

"He did. It happened in May, and here we are in July and he's still asking."

Gabi shook her head over it. I laughed.

"You still want a burger?"

"Nah," Gabi said, dialing the restaurant to cancel. She hung up. "I may do a grilled cheese here. Don't look at me like that. I like a grilled cheese. We still have sourdough and that good cheddar. I'll hold off on the movie, though. We should watch it together."

Dining at the Peninsula is sweet, but it's not as fancy as one would think. The food is good. I arrived at nine, right on time. Los Angeles is not a late dinner place, and that's fine with me. Les gawked at me like he was my boyfriend. He's cute. Can't be more than thirty-five.

Les is in video games, worth millions, lives in Beverly Hills but he apparently stays days and nights at this hotel. I never asked if he was married or not. That only matters if he has a wife who sticks a camera in the bedroom like Max's wife.

"Thanks for coming to see me again, Mona."

"Thanks for requesting me. I was flattered to no end when Macho told me."

Les smiled. He did have a nice smile. Freckles.

"What's your pleasure?" he asked as the waiter handed me a menu.

"You pick."

He ordered the Crab Louie as appetizer and twenty-month

aged steaks for us both. I stopped him there.

"The crab will be plenty," I said. I knew the night was ahead and I didn't want to be that full.

I am not much for champagne, but how do you say no to Cristal at a thousand a bottle in a place like this? We drank two glasses and he took the bottle with us to his suite. The restaurant was at the top of the building like his rooms.

It was the same suite I'd seen him in last week. Like Tim Wells did at the Century Plaza Hotel, Les kept rooms at the Peninsula. I'd been here many times before, different floor, different rooms, but this was my second time in this room at the Peninsula with Les. I loved this suite, with its gray carpet, curtains, and furniture, slate fireplace, white walls. The black glass dining table had some kind of big white flowers that smelled amazing. I wish I knew what they were. The bedroom had gray walls that were soothing, and a huge purple iris blooming in a glass full of black rocks.

We started off shoulder-to-shoulder on the gray sofa in the living room with the lights dimmed, and Cristal on the coffee table.

"I'll get glasses," I said, getting up to fetch them from the kitchen.

"Please," he said.

I poured twice as much in his glass than in mine. We clicked glasses. I wrapped my arm around him. It would be easy to get swept away over him. How neat would it be if he was really my boyfriend? I told myself to stop dreaming. Pretty Woman was just a movie, not real life.

"Les, what's your pleasure?" I asked, just as he had asked before dinner.

He grinned like I had made a joke.

"Can we start with a body to body massage. It will calm me."

"You got it."

He had no idea I'm a licensed massage therapist. Body to body massage is not what they taught us, but I'm good at it. I love doing Gabi, body to body.

"I'll go to the bathroom and get ready." I said. "Give me ten minutes."

"Take your time. I'm going to get a quick shower."

The main flow of my business is businessmen visiting Los Angeles, normally not tourists. For the most part, repeat customers are locals looking for escape or to pamper themselves. Since they can afford Macho's prices, they can afford a great hotel. With a repeat client, I learn what they like. Les likes me in my underwear. Because he requested a body to body massage, I took the chance today to be naked as he was. Last week, there had been no massage. No matter what he wants during the four hours he's buying, it will be easy to do. He's a total sweetheart and as easygoing as can be.

I found him propped up on three pillows, the duvet tossed to the foot. Music was playing, and he was naked.

"I have massage oil from a session a couple days ago," he said, pointing to the nightstand.

I picked up the bottle of Jojoba.

"Great. I was worried about what I was going to use."

He looked happy. When my panties fell to the floor, he was beaming.

July 1990
County Jail
Robert Lopez

PD Guerrero is a hot bitch. She stares at me like she wants some of what I got. I got plenty to give her, and maybe after I get out, I will. My days are numbered now that she has taken the bait. I had to run her around with the San Diego City jail story, but it was easy, like taking candy from a kid. I needed the time Guerrero was looking into San Diego to get Pat on board to back my alibi. Pat is hot, too. Pretty face, hot body, and she needs it so bad, she's like putty in my hands.

I got to get the fuck out of here.

Stupid me. I was drunk off my ass. I broke in the tiny match-book house without checking what was in there. Jack shit was in there. Not a thing worth taking. The old lady had twenty-two bucks and a whole lot of coins in her purse. What was I thinking? Why not a big house like I done before? No jewelry or anything. The old lady kept screaming. I didn't mean to hit her as hard as I did, but I had to shut her up. Good thing she didn't croak. No jury is going to believe the old lady after they hear Pat testify that I was with her that night. Everyone will figure the old lady is confused.

I hate this fucking county jail. I'm stuck in a cell with two bunks and five guys. I was ready to kick ass to get one of the bunks. Some of these guys are big, and they're all mean like junkyard dogs. I got to be cool. I ain't gonna catch a new beef in here. I'm on the floor with a blanket. Every time one of us has to use the toilet we all have to shuffle around to keep from getting pissed on. Fucking mess.

I should have stayed at Pat's house. She asked me to stay and I should have taken her up on it for the nine months till her old man gets back. I had it made when I was there. I'm a fucking fool.

Cannes
Gianna

At midnight in Cannes, it is three in the afternoon in Los Angeles. I call Mona many times, every day, different times, no answer. Maybe I have wrong number. I not get Gabi's number, stupid me. They get up at two in the afternoon here. Could be they are up late over there.

I am in my bed in my little house. The only light is one bulb by my bed so I can see to dial. It rings. Finally, Mona answer.

"Mona, it is me, Gianna in Cannes. Remember me?"

She laughs out loud. I picture my friend when she laughs loud in hotel restaurant, and everyone turns around to see, funny, pretty girl. She doing that laughing now. I laugh too. She is like pied piper with the laughing. You can not not join in.

I ask how is Gabi, then I say, "After you leave, Cannes still busy. No festival but still busy, busy for me. Guillermo give me good business. I have five thousand dollar saved. I want go see this Los Angeles you tell me so much about. The Hollywood sign on the hill. What you think?"

"I need to talk to Gabi, but yes, I'm sure it is okay."

"Mona, I stay in hotel, no bother you and Gabi. I only want to see you when I am there. I can be big tourist, see sights, carry camera, wear Los Angeles tee shirt."

Mona, she laughs at me. I laugh too. I see myself dress like China tourist here, camera on neck, asking strangers to take pictures in front of red carpet.

"You need a passport and a visa."

"I have passport. Travel agency where I price airplane ticket can get tourist visa for me. What you think, want to see me?"

July 1990
Los Angeles
Gabi

Her name was Elly Clark.

She was sixty-seven, retired, a widow living alone in her own home. She was the victim of my client Robert Lopez. Allegedly. He was alleged to have broken in her home and punched her face. She fell, struck her head on a trunk and ended up on the floor. For several days she was perched on the edge of death. The attending doctor did not give much hope of her pulling through.

Lucky for her and whoever broke in, she survived.

Until she didn't. I got a call from the deputy at the DA office that Elly had passed away two days ago. The autopsy report was not yet released, but the medical examiner believed she died of a heart attack unrelated to the injuries sustained during the burglary.

The DA had a problem with his case. Elly was the only witness, and she had identified Robert Lopez on a photo lineup as the person who attacked her. Police had dropped the ball on expediting a lineup after Elly was well enough to be taken to the police department.

"Henry, I sent you notice of a witness on subpoena that will state Lopez was in Oceanside on the night of the burglary. Witness is solid."

"I'll check it tomorrow and call you."

"You have no witness, no fingerprints, nothing to pin Lopez at the house."

"Gabi, I will call you tomorrow." The DA had been in a hurry to get off the phone.

I had the police pictures of Elly on her arrival at the hospital. Her face was bruised from the punch. The bump on her head was so big it distorted the shape of her face. I felt bad for the poor thing, and it is no wonder her id was mistaken. I drove home trying to leave the case behind at the office like most of my other cases. I believed Pat Jones, but even without Pat, the DA had no case.

In the morning, I did three plea bargains, three fewer cases to try. I was back in the office at ten thirty. Henry Moss left a message. I called him.

"I read Pat Jones's statement. Where did she come from?"

"If you read the statement, you know. She picked him up, took him home."

"You planned to use Jones to rebut the victim's identification of Lopez?"

"Henry, my job is to defend my client. I drove out to meet Pat Jones in person. I don't sell easy."

"I am pissed that Lopez is going to walk. If he didn't do it, the real guilty bastard is out there, and we're not going to catch him."

"The creep that did this will fall, sooner or later."

"You sold on this alibi? The way I see it, I don't need Pat Jones. What you got that you didn't give me on discovery? How do you want to handle this?"

I had nothing to add.

"Tear up Pat Jones's statement and dismiss the case for lack of evidence. Shit happens."

I drove to the county jail to meet with my client. My first glance at him when I got there, I felt something more than just my hormones. I did not trust this bastard for a second. The guy was a liar. It was the street in me that was suspicious. I told him what had happened and watched for an expression that would give me something. But I felt like Pat Jones was not lying. He was with her that night for the pizza, skipping AA. As bad as I felt about Lopez, I felt good about Pat.

"We don't need Pat to testify," I said.

Lopez did not smile. He did not look happy or excited. He looked like he was wondering why it took so long to get justice.

"When do I get out of here?"

"Court in the morning at nine. Judge will order your release."

I got up. He remained seated. At any moment, the guard would be there to get him on his feet.

"You did a fine job," he said. "Thank you. I had you all wrong. When I heard from Pat that you had driven out to Oceanside to find her, I couldn't believe it."

"Part of the job," I said. I wondered if he would go to Oceanside to be with Pat while her husband was away.

"You're one fine lady," he said, looking me over, and standing as the guard handcuffed his hands behind his back.

"Watch your mouth," I said. My street sense kicked in again.

On my way back to the office, I kept thinking how stupid the DA was to have filed the case before he had something more than a photo ID. Everything should have been set in stone.

I called Mona as I was driving in bumper-to-bumper traffic, finally heading home.

"It's that time of the month. We have seven days to kick back," she said, happy as happy.

"Cool," I said.

"I wish you could take off from work. How cool would that be?"

I laughed. Mona did most of the talking.

"Gianna called and wants to visit. I did not tell her she could stay with us," Mona said. "Matter of fact, she said she plans to stay in a hotel."

"If she stays in a hotel, how long is her money going to last?"

"You mean you'll let her stay with us?"

"As long as she sleeps in your bedroom, I don't care."

"You so nice," Mona said. "You're my hero."

"Let's go out to dinner," I said.

"I was hoping you'd say that. Food court at the Plaza?"

The Century Park Plaza, a very large outdoor mall, was primo and not far from home.

"Okay, give me ten when I get home and we're off," I said. "Maybe we can catch a show after dinner."

"Hurry, already."

I arrived for the Lopez hearing a half hour early to visit with him. The raunchy holding area behind the courtrooms is a gated cell with a steel bench for twelve and an open toilet. The cage is always standing room only, jammed with men, and more disgusting than you can imagine, even if you have a good imagination. The women's holding tank is just as bad, except they have a short metal divider around the toilet for privacy from the outside. No one gives a damn about the conditions except for those trapped inside.

"Morning, Robert," I said.

"Morning, Counselor," he said, an unusually respectful greeting for him. I smiled at that.

"This is it," I said.

"I'm sorry the lady died."

I nodded, straining to hear him over the din. I don't know how the deputy sheriffs handle it.

"You'll need to go back to county for your belongings. It will take hours to get released," I said. Between transporting a prisoner two miles back to the county jail, and processing the prisoner for release, it's two hours, easy.

"Yeah, I know. No difference. I waited this long already."
I nodded.

"Okay. See you in a little bit."

I returned to the courtroom, surprised that Pat Jones was not there. I know she was off the hook for the subpoena, but I figured she'd show to give him a ride back to her place or show support or something,

June 1990
Oceanside
Pat Jones

He called me at work to hurry over. Usually, he called after I got home from work. It wasn't even noon. He said the charges had been dropped, that I did not have to testify, and that he needed a ride to Oceanside to my house. I got this chill like I'm some inexperienced chick who hasn't been married for years.

I left work early, a first for me. I got to the county jail and waited in the line. It's crazy how they have so many windows and only one person doing anything. So, at the jail, even the people not in the jail have to wait until they get to a line marked on the floor and wait for them to call you. A sign says not to get past the line, and I heard at them yelling at people to back up an inch. After hearing them chew out people for touching the line, I was meek and quiet. The person at the counter told me Robert was being transported and that his release would not happen for nine hours. I was irritated. I could have stayed at work and taken my time. As ticked off as I was, what good would it be to complain? The deputy on duty was like an enlisted soldier with no authority. The deputy didn't tell me to hurry over. Robert did. He probably didn't know how long it took to get released.

I drove to a Denny's off the freeway, had a late lunch, read a free paper, and killed two hours before I returned to the jail. On my return and next excursion through the line, a different deputy looked up his name in the computer.

"He's in transit. He is getting released when he gets here. Figure five hours or longer."

I went outside. It wasn't a pretty day. It was arid and grey, and LA smelled like hot pavement, sweaty armpit, sushi gone bad, and sunscreen. They always blame it on the Santa Ana winds. It was more like being a piece of live toast in a convection oven. I opened my car door, damn near burned my hand, and the inside of my car blasted at me like a pizza oven. Change of plans. It was too hot to sit in the car. I took a seat in the jail lobby. I interrupted the boredom by going out to smoke, and watching people touch the line and get their heads bitten off. I found another free paper to read, finished it, and left it on a chair for the next poor slob. I'd burned my last cigarette, but that was good because it gave me a mission. I found a vending machine and bought a new pack of smokes. No one was paying attention to my standing and sitting. They all had their own fish to fry. Everyone in the waiting room here looked miserable. The only really happy faces were the people I passed on the sidewalk who were getting out. Maybe the people picking up were happy at some point, but not so much after the long wait.

Some of the guys looked at me with hot interest. I wasn't in anything special, just a light cotton sundress, kind of short, something that made enduring the heat a little easier. At work, I wore a jacket over it to make it look more professional. A few of the guys tried picking me up, but I shined them on. Guys getting out of jail might not be picky, but I know I'm not ugly. Men stare at me all the time, at work, at the store, everywhere I go. If I frequented clubs like I used to when I was drinking, I'd be getting laid all the time like I did then, and I never went without. I'm trapped in a way. I was doing this for Robert knowing that I would be having him stay for a while. I'll have someone there to come home to after work. Someone in my bed at night.

I sat down inside, staring at the plain gold band on my finger. I twisted it around, then tried to leave it alone. I don't even know if I feel guilty. I mean, am I supposed to believe that Jack is not fucking his brains out every time the ship docks somewhere? He's been in Tokyo for two months on this tour of duty so far. Is he just jacking off? Not a chance. He's surviving, doing what he has to do. Robert Lopez is my survival package until he splits or wears out his welcome. If he gets mean, he's out the door. I may need company but I'm not taking shit from anybody.

I stayed inside till I cooled off and went through my wallet. The lawyer's business card was in there. When I was smoking my next one, it occurred to me that she might know something, so I called her number.

"Public Defender's office. May I help you?"

I was about to disconnect but took a chance and asked for Gabi.

"This is the answering service. Is this an emergency?"

I knew if I said no, they would not try to contact her.

"Yes, it's an emergency. My name is Pat Jones. She has my number."

It was getting dark. I went inside. It was around half-past seven. Maybe it's just me, but it seemed like after dark, the crowd waiting for jail people got creepier. I didn't know her all that well, but I was glad when the lawyer called.

"Hey, Pat. Are you okay?"

"Sorry I said it was an emergency. I'm turning gray here, waiting for them to release Robert."

"The call is okay. I was going to get in touch, but I figured Robert would bring you up to date."

"He said I didn't have to testify, and he needed a ride to Oceanside. Here I am, been for hours. He hasn't been released."

"Oh, I'm sorry, Pat. It can take forever to get released from the county jail. They have a huge population. He should have told you how long it would be."

"I called to see if you knew what happened to the case. All I knew is that it got dismissed. I wasn't needed. What happened?"

"The witness was also the victim. She died."

"She died?" I stood up. I heard my voice get high and shrill.

"It was a little old lady. She'd been injured in the robbery, but her death was from a heart attack. Her death left the district attorney with no prints, no evidence, nothing. Case got dismissed."

"The victim died. Oh my God."

I sat down again.

"Coroner said it was not due to the beating she got during the burglary. It was heart failure."

"How old was the victim?"

"Senior citizen, retired, lived alone. It was a burglary."

"I see," I said. "Gabi, sorry I disturbed you."

"Not a problem. If you are taking him home, hide your wallet and car keys." Gabi laughed softly. I felt uncomfortable not to laugh, too.

"He won't find my wallet or car keys," I said.

I went back to the lobby. It was almost eleven at night. I got in the line again.

"I'm expecting Robert Lopez to be released. Where should I be waiting in order to see him when he comes out?"

The deputy told me to go outside, make a right and there were benches under a covered area where I could wait. I don't know why I didn't ask before. I moved to the new area. At least it was a change of scene. I saw the people getting released. There were more of them than there were people waiting. I guess everyone doesn't have someone to call, or they don't want anyone to know. Or their families don't want to deal with it. A lot of people were coming through a big metal door.

A few minutes past midnight, he came through.

He saw me. I got up and smiled, not sure how to act. He made it easy. He hugged me. I hugged him back.

"Thank you, Pat, for sticking by me. For believing me."

I wasn't so sure about believing him.

"I'm parked over here," I said, pointing to the parking lot.

We started walking.

"Did you wait long?" he asked. He put his arm around my waist.

"Doesn't matter. It was okay," I said.

"Can we stop and buy cigarettes? I'm dying for a smoke."

"I have two left," I said, reaching in my purse. We stood under a parking lamp and lit up, took a couple of drags, then started for the car again.

"We can get cigarettes when I gas up. Are you hungry? There's a Denny's close by."

"I'm starved. Let's eat something, but cigarettes first," he said, opening the driver's side for me.

I was about to start the car, and he said my name. He put his arm around me and kissed me hard on the lips. Too hard, but I didn't pull back. I was desperate to be held, loved. I know it's insane. I refused to consider my suspicions. I was that desperate.

By one in the morning, we were in the corner booth, eating the biggest breakfast on the menu.

"Are you sure it's okay for me to stay at your place? You got neighbors who might talk to your husband when he gets home.

Talk to me, Pat."

Robert smiled. I was dazzled by his smile, his handsomeness. He gave off this aura. Well, he needed a shave, and a bath, but I wasn't talking about that kind of aura.

"Fuck my neighbors. We don't socialize. We barely nod at each other. I've lived there four years and don't even know the names of the people next door."

"Okay, I'm all yours."

A rush passed through my body, like pure sexual heat. If I could bottle that feeling, I wouldn't need a man.

So far, so good.

He had not been lying about coming to Oceanside. We finished the food and got back in the car. He was being nice. More than nice. I was driving. He had my panties down to my knees, torn where he pulled them to shreds. His fingers were deep inside, about to cause me to have a heart attack and crash the car with us in it.

August 1990
Los Angeles
Gabi

I was in the den curled up on a wing chair. The television was on, sound low, some movie of the week. The Tiffany reading lamp gave good light for me to read this Sidney Sheldon title, *If Tomorrow Comes*. It was one of Mona's many books. Once upon a time she must have read a lot, but in the time we've been living together, I've never seen her read a book. Plenty of magazines. Maybe she had more reading time as a stewardess. All I knew was that Mona was working, and I was alone at four a.m. What else is new?

Our work-schedules are at opposite sides of the day.

My cell phone rang. I picked it up expecting it to be Mona. Who else would call at this time of the morning?

"Kylie, is this you?"

My heart just about leaped out of my chest. There was no

Kylie, of course. She was a Cannes name, a figment of imagination. No one should be calling here looking for Kylie.

"Who is this?"

"It's Robert Sphere. We met in Cannes. The old man from London."

Did I give him my number? I remembered him. I did not give him my name. The more I thought about it, the more certain I was that I didn't give my number.

"You're not an old man," I said with a laugh.

"You see, that's why I am calling you. You made me feel like a youngster."

"How nice of you to call. Where are you?"

"I'm in London, and you are in Los Angeles."

"I am," I said. "You are up early. It's about eight in the morning there."

"I'm an early riser."

"How did you get my number?"

"A little arm-twisting on my part. Please don't be angry."

"No, I'm not angry," I said. I was surprised Guillermo would give up a phone number to a client. I didn't know what to think.

"Guillermo didn't give me your number. It was Joe. G is on vacation."

"What can I do for you?"

"Are you free this coming Saturday?"

My silence was long enough that he caught my hesitation.

"Kylie, I know you are an attorney and that Cannes was no doubt an aberration. I'm calling for a date. Please don't take offense."

I was shocked and disturbed but didn't ask how he knew I was an attorney. He owned that yacht. He paid ten thousand dollars for a few hours with a hooker. He can afford to pay an investigator.

"Tell me about the date," I said.

"That night, I didn't believe you were in the business. I liked you right off. I'd like to see you again."

I folded the novel on the table. Sidney Sheldon could wait. I sat straight up in the chair and suddenly the reading light was bothering me.

"I'm flattered. Why me?"

"I just told you."

"How is Bilal?" I asked, remembering he had introduced us.

"I'm sure he's doing fine. I haven't talked to him since Cannes. What do you say? Want to fly to London for couple days?"

"I have a full calendar of court appearances," I said honestly. I wasn't still reeling in shock, but I hadn't figured out how I felt about his calling me.

"Gabi, what if you were ill?"

"I'm not."

I also didn't know yet how I felt hearing my real name out of his mouth. I had been doing a pretty good job at keeping the two sides of my life each in their own compartment. At least that's what I thought until this phone call. I was unpleasantly reminded of coming face to face with Max's lawyer in the halls of justice. I was walking a narrow tightrope.

I did not agree to visit him in London.

I agreed to think about it. I was going to devote some time to it. I could not do anything as quickly as he proposed. I had clients unable to make bail who were depending on me to move their case forward. I had clients out on bail that were not in a big hurry to get to trial because they were free. I couldn't just pretend I was sick and take off to London.

I hung up.

I picked up the book, but it just sat face down in my lap, not calling to me at all. I was not liking that Robert Sphere found me out, not because I didn't like him.

He was a session that I did in Cannes. He left me impressed.

Who wouldn't be impressed with a ship like his? My session with him ended that night. That he had my real name and my real detail was disturbing. What else did he know? Why would he go to all the trouble of tracking me down? It was a little terrifying, even though he was in London, and I'm across the Atlantic and on the other side of the country.

Keith and Rossi who gave me the suite to use when they departed early—they knew my name, because I gave it to them. They don't know I'm a lawyer. All they knew is that I took a bath in the huge tub in their suite, and I had sex as I was hired to do.

At six, I went to work with an early meeting and had a full day. I wasn't exaggerating about the full calendar. When I got home, I was tired, but Mona and I crossed paths. I told her about the call.

"You should have agreed to go. What's the big deal? Maybe he wants to marry you."

"Oh, please," I said. "We had one session, and it wasn't even romantic."

Mona laughed. "Anything is possible. I wish Bilal would invite me to fly to a distant land."

"You'd go?"

"For the right price, of course."

I had to laugh.

I used to have a little wooden desk under Mona's bedroom window to grow plants on, but my brown thumb and I had never gotten around to keeping plants alive. When Mona got the room, she got white paint and gold paint, and the next thing I knew, the plant table was a boudoir vanity with a puffy little gold stool decorated with a white feather boa. She had one of those little makeup mirrors on top, and filled the top drawer with makeup, and the side drawers with lingerie. That's where I found her sitting the day before Gianna arrived. I wanted to have a heart to heart with Mona.

"Here's what can't happen," I said. "Gianna is not going to work with Macho. If she does, she can't live here. You understand how risky that would be for me and my job."

"She's coming to visit. Don't worry about it. I promise not to get her worked up about sticking around and working with Macho. Besides, you know how he is. He says he takes on no new girls."

"That's what he said just before he hired you."

Mona got up from her makeup chair and put her arms around me.

"Don't be mad, please. She'll be sleeping in my room, and everything will be fine."

"I'm not mad. Just remember what I said about Gianna. I have no problem with her staying here, and she doesn't have to pay anything. You got that pretty girl?"

"Loud and clear, Captain."

Gianna arrived in the first week of September. She wanted to find a small monthly apartment, but with some encouragement from us, she agreed to stay at our apartment. I like her and so does Mona. That was enough reason to let her stay with us.

Mona picked her up at the airport. When I got home from the office, she was already there. She gave me a long hug, and kisses, and a gift.

"Gianna, you should not have bothered with the gift, really."

I opened the small box and found a bottle of Coco by Chanel.

"I love it," I said. "You are way too generous." I dabbed the inside of one wrist, rubbed my wrists together, and touched them behind my ears.

"I got one too," Mona said.

I gave her my just-ate-a-lemon face and stuck out my tongue.

Gianna was first to laugh.

"I told Gianna you're a lawyer and don't do here what you were doing in Cannes."

Gianna shrugged. "I wish I was advocate," she said in English "Maybe in next life."

The first night, we went to dinner at Matteo, an Italian restaurant with sky-high prices but Mona and I like it there. It has red booths, white linens, gold and white chandeliers, assorted lamps at the tables, and there's always a chance you'll see a celebrity there. Mona took off from work, so we didn't have to make it an early night.

"I pay, yes," Gianna said.

Mona insisted it was going to be her treat.

"You pay nothing," Mona said.

"No argument from me," I said. "You're the one with the big paying job."

The three of us split a bottle of wine and ended it there because drinking and driving, right? We ate heartily. I had the Gamberi e Cappesante Fra Diavolo, which is a fancy name for shrimp, scallops and a garlic tomato sauce that is not half as spicy as Aunt Isabel's. Mona always gets spaghetti and meatballs because they don't put garlic in it, and she didn't want to go anywhere off-gassing garlic. Gianna got a filet mignon in mushrooms and wine and loved it.

"You have good food in America," Gianna said.

Gianna was more beautiful than I remembered.

"Here is the plan," Mona said to Gianna. "During the day, you and I will hang out. When Gabi gets home, you two hang out."

"I'm warning you, Gianna, I'm a bore," I said. "All I do is work and sleep."

"I also boring," Gianna said. "Do not worry. I very appreciative you let me stay with you at your lovely apartment. I so glad I do not take you home to my casa, very tiny, very old."

Mona was a planner. Gianna's week was planned.

Tomorrow when I went to work, Mona's plan was to take Gianna to visit Universal Studios and the Universal Walk where they could have lunch. Then when I got off, we would visit Century City Plaza Mall to show Gianna an outdoor mall. We also planned other tourist days to take her to a regular indoor mall, drive around Hollywood, and drive around Rodeo Drive in Beverly Hills. If there's one thing LA has plenty of, it's touristy stuff.

September 1990
Los Angeles, California
Mona

The phone rang, waking me up. I had no idea the time of day thanks to the black-out shades plus black-out drapes that keep this room looking like midnight. I grabbed the phone without looking.

"Guess who wants a session with you?" Macho asked, skipping hello.

I swung my feet off the bed, walked over to the window, and pulled open the shades and drapes. The sky wasn't that bright, but it bored into my eyes like I was a vampire. I looked for Gianna who had spent the night with me, but she wasn't here.

"Good morning to you too." I guessed. "Les at the Peninsula?"

I put on a robe and walked out into the den. Gianna was on

the sofa frowning over an American newspaper. The frown disappeared when she saw me. She patted the couch beside her, then hopped up and ran into the kitchen. I sat down where she'd indicated, still talking with Macho.

"Not Les at the Peninsula. Want to try again?"

"Not really. Tell me who is it that wants my fine ass again?"

"Remember Max?"

I handle surprises pretty well. I didn't show it in my voice, but my heart bounced like a spring.

"My former employer in Dallas, Texas? The one with a wife named Lily who planted a camera in his plane's bedroom and recorded the action with him and Gabi, and after he left, the action between me and Gabi? That Max?"

Macho was laughing. I wasn't. The bitch wife was responsible for me being fired as Max's flight attendant.

"Yes, that Max. I knew he would surface eventually. You know he's retiring."

"I know. I read the paper. I watch the news. Why does he want me?"

Macho cleared his throat. "He called for Gabi. I told him she retired. He said he knew she's a lawyer in the public defender's office. His attorney told him so."

"How did he get around to me?"

"I asked Max the same question. Thank Tomas Lopez, his attorney. After you and Gabi settled with Max on the privacy issue and the video, Lopez figured you two were living together, and spilled the beans to Max. So Max asked about you."

"I worked for him for a long time," I said, my eyes focused on Gianna, but I was somewhere else.

"Five hundred an hour, four hours minimum. Are you in?"

I hesitated. What would Gabi say?

"What do you want to do?" Macho asked.

"Where and when?"

"Biltmore at ten."

"How do I know his wife doesn't have a spy camera in the room?"

"If she does, you could go for another fifty grand like before."

This was Macho's idea of a joke. I didn't find it funny. I still didn't laugh.

"If it happens again, it will be a hundred grand," I said.

When Macho hung up, I was able to focus on the room, and saw Gianna standing there with a steaming mug for me, and boggled eyes.

"Thanks," I said, accepting the coffee.

"What you do for hundred grand?" she asked.

"No, that was just talk. Five hundred an hour, four hour minimum."

I explained to Gianna, but she only had ears for what I was being paid. Her eyes opened wide. I knew she wanted in, but so far, she had not said anything.

When Gabi got home, I told her before her second foot was inside the apartment.

"Interesting," Gabi said. "I was curious why Tomas never made good on that lunch date he really wanted to make."

"Before Max asked for me, he asked for you. You want to do it?"

Gabi laughed at me. "You know I'm out of business. I can't do it. You go. I'm surprised he'd go to a hotel."

I too was surprised that Max had relaxed his guard so much. The Max I remembered would never have met up with a woman in a location as public as the Biltmore, or any hotel for that matter. His sessions with Gabi had been held in secret aboard his plane as it flew to Dallas, Texas.

She kicked off her shoes, and moved over to sit next to Gianna, and put her arm around her.

"I give you massage," Gianna said. "As long as you like. What do you say?"

"I love that plan," Gabi said.

We ordered Chinese fried rice, chow mein, dumplings, orange chicken, BBQ spareribs, and jalapeno beef. By the time the food arrived, I was out of the shower. We filled the kitchen with food, and ate at the dinette, all of us in robes. I lost my appetite. My stomach was full of anticipation, and I was too excited over this upcoming thing with Max, the thousand-dollar tipper. They tried getting me to eat more, but they both should have known better.

A valet opened my car door and gave me a claim ticket. I walked through the glass doors and was struck with the sheer size of the lobby. It echoes when you walk in, like a European church. I only took a few steps inside and was staring up at the elegantly decorated ceiling. An offensive-lineman-sized giant dressed in a suit and tie was in front of me when I finally looked straight ahead. It was one of those moments where you look at eye level for someone's face, then look up and up and even further up before you make eye contact. He was a really big guy.

"Mona, my name is Sly. I'll take you up." His voice was like a kettle drum.

"Okay," I said.

We walked through different sections of the hotel's ground floor, walking on marble, and red carpets, passing massive pillars, and each section had a different, more elaborate ceiling. I mean, glass skylights, artwork, intricate woodwork, frescoes like we saw in Cannes. My heart was racing, but not because of the architecture, even though there were fountains indoors, and who doesn't love fountains? Max was waiting upstairs for me. I used to fantasize about Max, but I'd never had sex with him.

In the elevator, Sly put a key in the panel and we zoomed nonstop to the penthouse. When the door opened, I stepped out to an enormous suite, windows floor to ceiling, facing West and

North, the room lights dimmed so I could see the city lights out-side.

Right in front of me with a big familiar smile was my former boss, Max.

"Mona, you're beautiful. Thank you for coming."

Max was as tall and big as I remembered him. He hugged me then kissed my lips.

"Hey, you never did that when I worked for you," I said.

"I should have."

"Is it safe here? I mean, any cameras we need to deal with?"

He chuckled but only a little.

"That's behind us, but I'm sorry about it, you losing your job, everything."

"It was a bad joke for me to bring it up," I said. "I'm sorry."

"It's okay."

"Maybe that's enough apologizing for both of us," I said, laughing through the awkwardness.

We smiled at each other. He was as beautiful and sexy as ever, and my body remembered how much I'd wanted him before.

"What can I get you to drink?"

"A coke or wine, any color."

Max was barefoot. His legs were lean, and heavily muscled from his athletic career. He was in tennis shorts and a button-down silk shirt that hung almost long enough to cover his shorts.

I was in Chanel, top to bottom.

"Make yourself comfortable," he said, handing me a glass of white wine.

"Max, thanks. Are you sure you don't mind?"

I smiled.

"Do it right here," he said, smiling.

I kicked off my five hundred-dollar heels.

By the time I was down to my underwear, Max had already

taken off his shirt. I saw the bulge pressing against his shorts. It was an impressive bulge, as Gabi had already told me. Hell, I'd seen it in living technicolor video with my own eyes.

The fewer clothes I had on, the more intense his expression got. He had beautiful teeth.

"You worked for me for so long, and I never made a pass. I must have been blind or out of my mind crazy."

"We can make up for it tonight," I said.

He dropped his shorts. No underwear.

"You're a turn-on. This is a fantasy come true for me," I said, eyes on his bat. I could tell he liked what he heard, but it was only the truth. "What's your pleasure, boss?"

He patted the arm of the sofa and I was there in a flash, bent over, his hands on my hips. He wasted no time. He was aggressive but gentle and didn't just shove it in. I was so wet that it didn't take long to suck him inside. He pulled my hips, and I gyrated my ass, pounding against him, a demanding rhythm, a pulsing moist cadence that took me over the top. To think I was being paid for this was incredible.

Between the time we left the living room for the bedroom, we drank a single glass of wine. I don't know how many he drank before I arrived, but that's all we'd had when we started round two on the bed with me on top. With a monster like him, on top is the best place to be, and he seemed to savor the position. Gabi had never told me he was a kisser. I know we didn't watch the whole thing, but I don't remember him kissing Gabi a lot in the video that recorded over two hours of them having sex. I remember seeing a lot of oral, a lot of sixty-nine.

His mouth tasted of wine. I loved the kisses, and each time I gave back with all the passion in me.

At midnight, we took a break in the living room.

"Let's order dinner," he said, looking over the room service menu.

"Sure," I said.

He had two more hours. I was glad I'd skipped the Chinese. And I had worked up an appetite.

"Room service will know you're with someone," I said.

"Don't worry about the small things," he said as he read off suggestions.

On the phone, he ordered a steak, two baked potatoes, two lobster tail cocktails, a carafe of coffee

"I want it alive. Rare, got it?"

He ordered me the French fries, salad, and the well-done hamburger I wanted. No lettuce, tomatoes, or onions on my burger. His refrigerator was stocked with drinks. I filled the cups with ice. When room service arrived with the food and to set up the dining room table, I stayed in the bedroom. They were quick. He pushed open the door, bowed grandly, and said, "Dinner is served."

He tossed me a sleeveless tee shirt from his open suitcase. I slipped into it. It came down almost to my knees and his top did not do much to cover my top, which was okay.

He ate in a gargantuan hotel robe that fit like the hotel knew him well. He talked about retiring. He had considered extending his contract another year, but he had a number of businesses that needed him, and just decided to retire.

I didn't ask what businesses. I didn't remember offhand what businesses he had outside of basketball. It didn't matter. I enjoyed dinner and the conversation.

It was inevitable that the topic of Gabi finally came up.

"I always knew she was smart lady, but I had no idea she was going to law school when we were dating."

"She's amazing."

"I'd like to see her," he said. "Think you could arrange it?"

"Max, you need to speak with Macho. All I can tell you is that she's out of the business."

"Mona, don't josh me. I know Guillermo in Cannes. It so happens I didn't make it to Cannes this year, but I talked to him. He said Macho sent two great chicks, and by his description, those two chicks were you and Gabi."

"Max don't put me on the spot. I can't speak for Gabi."

I never eat heavy when I'm on a session. There's no telling what is coming after. I ate some of the huge plateful of fries and nibbled at the burger. Max finished everything he'd ordered for himself and polished off what I didn't eat. With Max, food was fuel. He got me back in bed with a renewed appetite for sex and fucked the living daylights out of me. He got rough, not ugly rough, but penetrating rough. I handled it. It was not the first time I got a rough one.

At two, I used the bidet, showered and dressed.

"Max, if you want me to stay, you don't need to pay me the extra hours."

"I have an early start," he said. "If not, I'd ask you to stay the night."

I headed toward the door, and he bent down by the bed and picked up his shirt.

"You forgot something." He tossed it at me.

I caught it.

"Good catch," he said. "Consider a career—"

"In shirt-catching?" I laughed.

He took me by surprise and kissed me again until I was breathless, then walked me to the elevator door.

"This will take you down to the lobby direct," he said.

I tried giving him the shirt back. He put the envelope and shirt in my purse.

"I've got to see you again. I'd love it if you can do in call. That's less exposure for me."

I kissed him back. In-call means having the session at home, an impossibility. When Gabi was alone, she kept the bedroom I was in for in call, but she said it was rare when she had used it. She'd never allow it now because of her job.

In the lobby, I called Macho.

"Max is tucked in bed and happy."

"Good girl. Have a good night, Mona."

"You too," I said.

When I got home, Gabi was asleep. Gianna was in my bed, pretending to be asleep. In the bathroom, I took off my makeup and put on the shirt Max gave me. I took the envelope out of my purse and counted.

Two thousand for four hours and a thousand-dollar tip.

Gabi used to get the same. He was still a thousand-dollar tipper.

I would have given him the tip back for the memory I now had about fucking him. I had always wondered. Before tonight, the closest I'd ever been to seeing him naked was in the notorious video. He didn't mention it, but I'm sure he viewed that video and saw Gabi and me going at it for a couple of hours during her return trip to Los Angeles. I shudder with heat when I think of him watching us.

I slipped into bed.

"Did you have fun with the basketball player?" Gianna asked.

"A sweet evening is what it was."

"Tell me."

"I will if you massage my shoulders and neck."

"I massage you all you want. On your stomach, flat, no pillow."

I positioned myself. The comforter was pulled back.

Gianna has massaged Gabi and me before. I get more time because she sleeps with me. My opinion as a licensed massage therapist is that Gianna gives a great professional massage. She says she was never trained.

My neck and shoulders were getting Gianna's million-dollar treatment. I savored her hands on me.

"Mona, I am giving you therapy. Tell me details of tonight with ball player."

I pictured him as she worked me in near total darkness.

"This guy is a big dude. Big. Manly."

He has thousands of fans. Chicks by the thousands would spread for him, free, but he paid me to have sex with him.

Gianna was cuddly but I was used to Gabi. When Gabi and I talked in bed, she normally dropped off to sleep. Gianna was a different story. She and I both loved to talk. That messed with my sleep.

Gianna had already hit me on introducing her to Macho. I told her that he was not taking on anyone.

"That's what Guillermo told me for more than two years and then you and Gabi got him to put me on as a regular."

"That wasn't our decision," I said. "That was Guillermo."

I must have dropped off to sleep then, because that's the last thing I remember.

Gianna had gone out to buy food down the street. She likes fast food so much it makes me feel like a food snob. Who gets that excited over McDonalds fries? I'd been waiting for her to leave so I could have a minute alone with Gabi. After Gianna left, I went into the kitchen and found Gabi making coffee. I toasted an English muffin. She made scrambled eggs. I put the ranchero salsa on the table. She put the mugs out. I poured the coffee. We each took half of the muffin, topped it with egg, cheese, and tomatoes. There's not a whole bunch of room in the kitchen, so cooking together was almost like a dance. The dance was over, and we sat down.

"She's been asking me to introduce her to Macho."

Gabi gave me the old I-told-you-so look, then she just had to say it, too.

"I told you she would, even before she arrived."

"I know. I brush it off. She doesn't push it."

"If you want to introduce her, take her over there. Let her know if she hooks up with him, she has to move. If Macho wants her bad enough, he'll stake her."

"I'll wait until she pushes. Maybe she won't."

"She'll ask again. She's on fire to make money."

"You're right, as usual."

"She's a bolt of lightning."

"If she becomes one of Macho's models, it's two risks you don't need. If she gets busted, the word would get out that she's bunking with a public defender. That could hurt."

"It's funny, but true," Gabi said.

"I don't think it's funny," I said. "You and I, we know our way around here, but Gianna doesn't. Anything could go wrong. Anything. Anything at all."

"You've moved on from talking about Gianna," Gabi said, looking at me shrewdly.

I nodded. "Max asked me if I can do in house."

Gabi picked up her mug and cradled it between both hands, looking over the rim at me. "That means he wants to see you again."

I shook my head. "He wants in here to see you. He knows we live together. He asked if you were available before he asked me. If you want the gig, fucking is not a crime," I said. "I won't stand in the way of your thousand-buck tipper."

"Since when is it not a crime?" Gabi said, quirking her eyebrow at me.

"Who is going to know you get money for it?" I asked.

Gabi started laughing. "That was my logic in Cannes."

"You sound like you'd let him come over."

"It's not a random guy. It's Max. If you want him to come over, have him park in the underground garage and tell him how to take the elevator and come direct so no one sees him."

"You mean that?"

"I mean that for you, not for me."

I gave her a conspiratorial wink. I was really asking, but it seemed better to pretend to be kidding. "You want me to set you up for a date with him, no money?"

"No," Gabi said. "It's still a no."

"You sure?"

"I'm out of the play. Period."

"Got it," I said. "At least with Gianna here, you have company when I'm gone."

"She's great company, but I know she wants to get out more."

"She gets out during the day. She has it made," I said. "She's got us, a place to live free. I know she likes being with you."

"She says it to me all the time," Gabi said. "I know though, she has to be bored. I come home, eat and hit the sack. She probably feels tied down at night in this apartment. She's used to night work." Gabi finished her coffee and poured another cup. "Since it's Saturday, let's the three of us hit Santa Monica for brunch. As soon as Gianna's back."

An hour later, in jeans, sandals and sunglasses, we were at Loew's Hotel where they have a great brunch Saturday and Sunday, steps from the Santa Monica Beach boardwalk. We walked around the beach dodging kiddos on mopeds and listened to a guy playing an oboe. Gianna was wearing a huge black sunhat, and she took it off and passed the hat for the guy. In the restaurant, a ton of food was laid out buffet-style for fifty bucks each, champagne included. We ordered cokes. They should have given us a discount for not drinking, but they don't have any breaks.

It was my treat. At five hundred an hour, I can afford it.

When I met Guillermo, he was in French law enforcement, and I was a DEA agent. As he was my informant, I was able to pay him some good agency money for solid information he passed on to me. Drugs were a very big deal in France. We were in France, but the traffickers we were after were American. During a big bust we made, millions of dollars went missing and although there was absolutely no evidence of who got the dough, when I got back to the States along with four other agents who worked that case, I was offered a desk job in Oakland, California. After fourteen years with the DEA, the last ten years of which I spent in Morocco, France and other foreign countries, I quit.

From my days in Morocco, I knew Omar who had a modeling

agency, all high-end ladies. I always admired beautiful women. While in that part of the world, I used the services of Omar's models. Omar never spoke of sex, only modeling. He was simply an agent selling modeling hours. If the job went beyond modeling, there was no extra cost unless the lady got a tip. I never found a flaw in Omar's business strategy, and I am a person who looks for the cracks in everything.

The ladies Omar sent to me were well dressed, gorgeous and eager to do anything other than modeling.

After I quit the DEA, when I decided to open a model agency with high class women who were beautiful, pristine dressers with the style and panache to attend an event for any occasion, I was copying Omar.

I hate the word escort and never use it with a client. When a lady from my agency goes for a session, it is to keep the client company in public or private. A session could be taking photographs of the model or anything a model is expected to do, going out to dine, attending the horse races at Santa Anita or Hollywood Track, providing personal companionship aboard a domestic or international flight on a private plane, or whatever. Word of mouth snowballed. My client list grew. As a DEA agent, I had no experience in vice, but it's not rocket science. In fourteen years in the DEA, I was the never the brunt of a single entrapment case. In the years since, I've not had a single bust. I know my clients. I've spent years of cultivating special people who kept coming back for more.

As careful as I am of my clients, I am just as careful about the women under contract to my agency. I seldom take on someone new. As my models age, they find other careers, start families, or I have to retire them. I am very particular about who I take on.

Mona came over and introduced me to Gianna who had come over on a tourist visa and wanted to stay in the U.S. for good.

I knew she had experience, and that she was new to G's list. I said I would think about bringing her on board. She was certainly lovely enough and seemed uninhibited. I called Guillermo to see if he had a problem with me putting Gianna to work.

"I knew it was a bad idea to help her get the visa to go visit Gabi and Mona," Guillermo said, laughing on the phone.

I wanted a direct answer. "Do you have a problem or not?"

Guillermo took a few seconds to reply.

"She has no green card. She will be illegal after her visa runs out."

"Let me handle the particulars," I said. "Tell me if you have a problem. If you do, I will not take her on. Or, I can pay you for your loss."

"Go ahead," Guillermo said, "No money needed."

"I owe you one," I said.

I told Gabi, "I won't do it if you object."

"I don't own her or you. How can I have a problem?"

"This is a courtesy call," I said.

"I don't have a problem. You need to help her get a place of her own, though."

I had staked Gabi when she started with me, got her a place to live and funded her first round of clothes buying.

"I can do what is necessary. I like her. I assume you feel the same or you wouldn't have her living with you."

"I love her," Gabi said. "I wish she could stay but I can't afford the risk."

"No need to explain."

I nearly asked why she let Mona live there. Mona was out every night on sessions. Maybe two working models living there and going out every night increases her vulnerability. Her reasons are her business.

A few days later after I had made some tentative arrangements, I asked Gianna to come see me. Mona drove her over.

Both of them joined me in the spare bedroom I currently use

as my office. Gabi and Mona had rearranged my office a couple
of times, and I see no harm in it. Sometimes I use my dining room
table, but using the office made this feel a bit more official. My
desk faces the balcony, and the stool tucked under my desk rolls
any direction, but I was standing with my back to the view and
looking at Mona and Gianna. Mona was sitting on the sofa, and
Gianna was standing an arm's length from me.

"I am enamored of your country," Gianna said in French.

"Take off your clothes," I said, as I had said to Mona before
her, and Gabi before that. She didn't do a striptease as Mona had
once done, but undressed eagerly, just dropped the clothes where
she stood, not taking off her tennis shoes. I walked in a circle
around her. She was beautiful, slim-waisted, and round in the
right places. Her ass didn't come close to rivaling Mona's, but
then, no one's did. Her nipples perked upward. I'd seen her give
herself a little squeeze to help them along, not a bad move at all.
She had a little bit of an overbite, but it was sexy in a French way,
the same way her accent would make her seem exotic and inviting.
She stood confidently, a little bit of a challenge in her eye.

"You can dress," I said, and looked out the window for about
thirty seconds. When I turned around, she was clothed again, sitting beside Mona.

"I think I can keep you busy," I said. "I have rules about dressing, manners, all kinds of things. If you agree to it, I'll take you
on. It's going to cost you a bigger cut to me. I want forty percent.
If you do good for six months, I might cut that down. I am not
promising I will. You want the work?"

Gianna went from sitting placidly to clutching her hands, to
standing, to jumping up and down and squealing yes. Gianna was
gleeful.

"Thank you, Macho, I won't let you down."

She jumped at me and gave me a hug. I pushed her into the
sofa beside Mona and held my hands on her shoulders for a few

moments.

"There's more. You can't live with Gabi. She has an important job. Having Mona and you living there and going out every night is not going to work. I will help you lease an apartment. I will advance you money for clothes. You will wear nothing fake. No knock offs. You don't have to pay me back. The forty percent will cover it. Did I speak too fast? Is there anything you don't understand?"

I let go of her shoulders, pulled out the stool under my desk and sat on it.

"I understand. I understand everything. Macho, I am grateful. I will not disappoint you."

I don't smile often. I smiled. "I know you won't disappoint me."

"Believe me," Gianna said. "I will always be truthful and loyal to you."

Gianna was joyful, but beside her, Mona looked sadder and sadder. Mona's lips curled down.

"Why you look sad?"

"I hate to see her move. Maybe we can find an apartment in our building. What do you think?"

"That's up to her. I don't pay her rent. She will. With a nice place, I can send you clients who want in-call. I have a friend who handles immigration. I'll ask him to look at your matter and see what he can do get you legal before your tourist visa runs out."

Gianna jumped off the couch and launched herself at me again, knocking the stool into a two-meter slide until we rolled to a stop against the wall. She lay across my lap, hugged me as much she could with me sitting down. Her enthusiasm was, well, enthusiastic.

"Thank you. I so worry about overstaying visa."

"Do good by me. I'll be here for you. My lawyer is good."

I handed her two bundles of cash, ten thousand in total.

"Get a local cell phone. The French cell service will kill you here. You need to buy a couple of nice outfits. Build your wardrobe as you make money as Mona and Gabi did. Keep your closet filled with nice outfits. Do this, and I will give you plenty of business. Am I clear?"

Gianna was nodding fiercely. She said, "I clear. Thank you."

I waited a few seconds, and Gianna took the hint that it was time to stand up. She got off of me. As soon as I stood, Mona gave me a smooch. I have a soft spot for Mona, and thought about having the both of them, but my phone rang, reminding me that it was time to work.

"Mona, I'm counting on you to groom her, and let her know the rules. I don't have the time I used to have when I taught you myself. Take her by the photographer's studio for her photos tomorrow."

"Count on it," Mona said.

I was on the phone with an old client, Henry Burke when I let Paulo in. The lobby guard knew who worked for me. No need to call. I let him in.

Henry Burke was from Chicago. Another client called.

"Carlo, you can take my word for the lady I send, or I can send my runner with a photo album"

"Photos work good. I'll tip your runner."

Fifteen minutes later, Paulo was on his way to meet up with Carlo to show him a dozen models who were available. In a couple days, I would have photos of Gianna to add to the portfolio. By eight thirty I had booked eleven models. Business was predictable. By nine thirty I would be fully booked. I had enough work, I could have had a few more girls, but I don't want to spread myself too thin.

By the time Carlo decided, it was too late.

"I can send someone after her first session. It will be late."

"Macho, I'm here four nights. I'm tired anyway tonight. I like

Terry. Can we do that tomorrow?"

I got the details. Terry was Mona. All my models are beautiful. Mona is always one of the favorites. Mona checked in at two in the morning that she was done with her session.

"I have you booked four hours at JW Marriott tomorrow at nine. Two thousand."

"You so good to me," Mona said with that voice I liked so much. A lot of Gabi had rubbed off on her. Maybe that's one reason why she was a favorite of mine.

Two weeks after I gave Gianna ten G, she called to let me know she had passed her driver's license exam and driving test, had purchased a Honda, and got Allstate to sell her liability insurance. She leased an apartment in the same building Gabi was in, a one bedroom on a lower floor. She got approved with no credit check and gave no references because she didn't want to connect herself with Gabi or Mona. She put down on the application that she worked for Beverly Hills Models, my agency.

"I got a map book and know how to use it. When can I start working?"

"I have your photographs back. They look good. Tell me about your outfits?"

"I have three beautiful outfits, complete. Mona suggest buying for now, so they all summer clothes. One white, one black, one pastel, heels and accessories to match. Mona show me to make them all easy to take off. She give me pointers how to undress too."

"Did you have enough money?"

"I do. Thank you. I have some of my own money. It's okay. I ready. I know what to say and not say. I can do this, Macho. Please trust me, yes?"

"Okay, get ready," I said. "I will call you."

I'm going to miss Gianna when I'm home alone, again. I never
made a big deal, but I've been happy she was here. Nothing is
forever. Homer, Archie, that was nice while it lasted, then it was
over.

I didn't lose Mona. That's one good thing.

Gianna is not as busy like Mona. I think Macho is spacing out
the assignments. He's getting forty percent, a damn bunch of
money. You'd think he'd be burying her in sessions to make more
money for himself and recover his ten thousand quicker.

I was in bed watching television, a book in my hand when at
eight, I got a call on my cell.

"Want me to come over? I'm off tonight."

"Are you sure you want to be part of the boredom?"

"We can be bored together," she said.

"Come on down."

She came down, then we came together. It wasn't the first time we got it on. Like Mona, Gianna was aggressive and a fantastic lover. Afterwards, we sat up in bed, propped up on way too many pillows. I had a bunch.

"I know you need love," she said. "You so happy in Cannes."

"I don't look happy here?"

"You look happy in Cannes. When we eat brunch. When we out by pool."

My arm went over her shoulders like a pal would do. My eyes were on the television, but I was not paying attention to it.

"I'm happy," I said. "I love my job. I love helping people who have no money to hire a private lawyer. I love helping find justice."

"You need be happy when you come home. What I can do to make you happy?"

"You just did. I'm soaked."

Laughs.

"You want more?"

I turned to look at her, our faces inches apart. "You wouldn't," I dared her.

She grabbed me down there. Her hand was not big like a man's would have been, but she grabbed like a man would.

"Do it," I said. "Please do it."

When Mona kissed me, she was all into it. When Gianna kissed me, it was powerful. I crumbled like a weakling, and a weakling I'm not.

Another day at work. As it was a couple hours past noon, and as I hadn't had time to eat, Sandra had gone out to pick up taquitos, guac and Tamarindo Aguas Frescas from Cielito Lindo on Olvera street. It wasn't just for me, though. She often takes orders for all the PD. I just happened to be stealing a few minutes to eat when I got a call on cell.

"Can you talk?" Macho asked.

"If you don't mind listening to me chew," I said, swallowing the bit of taquito I had in my mouth. "Is something wrong? What are you doing awake at this hour? Is this urgent?"

"No trouble," Macho said. "It's Max. Max always calls me when he wants companionship. He doesn't wait until I'm up. Can you talk?"

"Shoot. What's up?" I took a big bite of chicken taquito and chased it with Tamarind water.

"Mona said it was okay to book a model session with her at your apartment as long as it was Max."

"Yeah. I agreed to that. So?"

"Now he's calling to see if he can see you."

I had this rush of heat blaze through my body. I flashed a vivid memory of the big guy on the bottom and me on top going to town. I had to gulp some more of my drink and talk with my mouth full of taquito to keep from sounding hot and bothered.

"I said okay for my roommate, not me."

"Are you sure?"

"You know I'm sure. I had this same discussion with Mona."

Macho turned grump.

"Doesn't make sense to me but okay."

He wasn't happy when he disconnected. I finished up a taquito.

It took about a minute of me sitting there with my mouth full, and my cell phone in hand before I started laughing. The best I can say is that I didn't spew a mouthful of lunch all over my desk, or snort Tamarindo water out of my nose. It's a good thing I was alone. I wasn't sure why I laughed. I didn't know what was funny. Maybe it was knowing that Max was hot for my bod. A star of his stature who could have anybody he wanted, and he was after me.

I would have called Mona, but that would make me late for my next appearance. I gulped down my food, dumped the paper refuse in the trash and grabbed my briefcase. Just before I made it out the main door of the PD office, Evelyn, the receptionist said, "Hey Gabi, your purse is totally over the top beautiful."

I faced her with a smile.

"Thanks. Isn't it the best knock-off ever?"

Of course it was no knock-off, but it's not like I could have gotten it on my salary. I blew her a kiss and backed through the door.

When I entered the apartment, still carrying my purse and briefcase, Mona appeared.

"Give me, let help you," she said, grabbing for my purse and briefcase.

She was excited.

"You said it was okay, and he's coming tonight."

I didn't tell her I knew and didn't mention Macho calling me.

"Does he know how to get up here from the garage?"

"He has the code to get in the underground, and the direct code for the elevator."

"Well then, good. What time?"

"Ten."

"I'll be asleep by then," I said.

"Oh, you won't be asleep."

"Just watch me," I said. "What's for dinner?"

"Are you upset?"

"No way that I'm upset. You hungry?"

"How about Chinese?"

"Deal. I'll buy," I said.

"I'll order," Mona said, beaming,

I knew why she was so happy. Max would fuck her like he hadn't fucked in weeks and pay her for it.

We ate in the kitchen. Mona ordered a spicy and mild version of beef, chicken, and shrimp dishes, fried rice, plain rice, and crab Rangoon. The to-go boxes were in the center of the table, and we shoveled food indiscriminately on paper plates, then attempted to use chopsticks. We would have leftovers for days, but that was one of the best things about Chinese take-out. After the boxes were safely stowed in the fridge, we nibbled ice cream for dessert.

"Use the living room so the big guy can stretch out before you show him the bedroom," I suggested, taking a spoonful and shoving the Neapolitan carton in front of Mona.

"Okay, he likes to get down right away." She dipped in her spoon.

"I know," I said. When we met on his plane, we were in bed before the plane was wheels up. The man wastes no time. "Have fun."

When he arrived, I was in bed, sleeping with Prince Valium. I managed to check out so fast that I didn't have to hear anything through the wall.

October 1990
Los Angeles
Max

I have a problem that's been around for years. I can't get
enough strange pussy. Don't matter that I have a hot-looking wife
and three kids. I'm a man. Playing ball may look like fun, but the
stress on and off the court is enormous. Don't get me wrong. I
love what I do, and I been reaping the fame and financial rewards
for years, and I'm grateful. Nevertheless, I need to blow off steam,
and I do that by getting laid by a stranger. I can't afford to lose
Lily or any product endorsements and getting caught fucking
around can do exactly that. Lily has caught me more than once,
but it never went public, so I only had to deal with her broken
heart and nothing on the business end.

I'm retiring this year. I'm in community redevelopment in Los

Angeles and back home in Dallas, multi-billion-dollar projects. I now have a reason to spend more time in Los Angeles, a city I've always wanted more of.

Mona used to be my flight attendant on my personal plane. She worked for me for years and I never touched her. I trusted her and my flight deck crew not only with my life, but also to keep my personal flings secret. I'd book a model to have sex with me while on my way somewhere on my plane. I can't count how many pussies I had on that bed while flying high, but one of them was Gabi, Mona's roommate. I don't just take, I give back. It's no fun if I'm the only one who gets pleasure.

I reached out my car window and punched in the parking lot gate code. I drove in the underground lot and parked in a guest spot steps from the elevator sign. Nice cars down here.

I took out my phone and dialed Mona. I had to do it more than once. Reception was terrible through the tons of cement, but I got through.

"I'm here, getting on elevator."

"Can't wait."

I had no idea how hot this girl was when she worked for me. How did I not notice? She has legs and an ass that will not quit, and she's fucking gorgeous.

I took out the piece of paper that had the code, read it, and entered the code on the elevator console pad. The door shut, and I was delivered quickly to the fifteenth floor. I got off and went to the right. The hallway was empty. I rang the bell.

Mona opened the door.

"Welcome big guy," she said.

We hugged. I'm too damn tall for a good hug, so I picked her up and cradled her. She squealed, laughed and hung on my neck.

"Where's the bed?"

She laughed and pointed to the bedroom door. Her scent overcame me. I felt myself get hard.

November 1990
Oceanside
Pat Jones

The first two weeks after I picked up Robert from the Los Angeles County Jail and brought him to home was like a honeymoon. I took off for a week, and we spent day and night in bed having sex in ways I'd never done before. After I went back to work, I could hardly wait to get home to be with him. He liked to cook. Nothing fancy. Nothing that required a cookbook. Hamburgers, steaks on the outdoor grill, warm-up of food he bought at Costco. I gave Robert the keys to my husband's jeep and money to grocery shop and get liquor. No point in keeping the jeep parked on the driveway with a cover on it.

I'd been wrong about him that first night he slept over and stole my wallet. He had me convinced he didn't drink, just because he wanted a coke the first night. He drinks. He tried to hide it for the first couple of days.

I tried to get him to stop drinking. It only agitates him.

The good thing is that I haven't missed an AA meeting, and I haven't had a drink. Seeing him drinking and drunk has been good in a way. It strengthens my resolve. Drunks are sickening. Seeing him fading out of consciousness actually turns my stomach, and his rages sure don't make me like him. The smell of alcohol in the house should be a temptation but thank God it hasn't shaken me over the line. He buys marijuana. I'm a chain smoker of Marlboro, but I don't mess with weed. Weed would lower my guard. It would be a gateway to drinking again. I love my job too much. I was warned last year about smelling like a bar at work, and that is never happening again.

His pattern is that he starts drinking, and then complains.

"You are no fucking fun!" It's like his mantra. I don't show it hurts me to hear it, but it does. I know that I am no fucking fun. He doesn't say that when I'm eating his cock for an hour at a time. He doesn't say that when we fuck. I love fellatio. I love to get fucked. When that is going on, he doesn't say I'm no fucking fun. But I say no to a drink, and suddenly, I'm queen of the buzz kills.

For two months we've been going downhill.

When I leave in the morning, he's already had a beer or two to get over his hangover. When I get home, he's either drunk or passed out already. Sometimes he's awake, watching television, the volume blasting. When he listens to music, it's the same loud volume. He needs the noise to get through his stupor. The heat I felt with him went down the toilet with a single flush. He's a bitter taste in my mouth that Listerine can't kill.

When he calls me a buzz-kill, I have a comeback. I agree.

"I'm a buzz-kill. You need to split and find your next hot sugar mama. I'll give you a thousand bucks to stake you someplace."

He laughed in my face.

"Make it ten thousand, and I'll consider it."

One morning before going to work, I refused to give him cash. He went ballistic. He followed me to my car, yelling at me. I gave him forty dollars to shut him up. When I got home the next day, I fixed dinner, and when he was passed out, I went into the hall closet in back of the utility door where Jack kept the house rifle and revolver. Firearms don't frighten me. When Jack was here, he taught me to shoot at an indoor firing range, and we went every week, made a night of it. Crazily enough, the gun range had a full-service barbecue restaurant that was pretty good. Since he'd been gone, I went at least once a month to stay polished. I have two handguns and a shotgun. One of the few things that my husband Jack and I have in common is how we like our guns. He kept them obsessively clean, and during happier days, we cleaned them together. I thought about turning a gun on my unwanted guest, but I just stared at my weapons, and shut the door. At least he hadn't discovered them.

The next day when I left for work, he followed me out again. I ignored his tantrum. While I was backing out of the driveway, he opened the car door, and dragged me out by my hair. I fell on to the driveway, got bruised up and skinned my knees. The car would have kept going into traffic if I hadn't thrown it in park. He grabbed my purse and swiped the cash I had in my wallet.

He left me where I'd fallen and went back in the house. I cried from anger. My hip hurt, both my knees were bleeding, soaking my slacks. I seriously thought of crashing the car, but I couldn't be sure doing so would end this ordeal.

At work, I checked in and went to the first aid department. I told the nurse I had slipped and fallen on my own driveway. Minor injuries, but both knees were bruised, the bleeding had stopped but caked up on my slacks. I had a bruise on my elbow. My ass had a bruise I didn't tell the nurse about.

I had two bowls of vegetable soup at the cafeteria and managed to finish the day.

After work, I stopped at the police department in Oceanside. The desk officer was busy on the phone. I saw a woman with a holstered gun and figured she was a plainclothes detective. Short hair. No make-up. Kind face. She was in conversation with a scruffy-looking person, maybe another desperate citizen like me. I had no idea if he was a criminal or a victim, and at that point, I really didn't care. I interrupted her.

"Excuse me. Can I talk to you for a minute? I'm having a problem at home."

She stopped talking to Mr. Scruffy.

"Desk officer will be done in a minute," she said.

All day I had been in pain from the injuries. I hated the bastard. I hated myself for being weak and stupid when I've never been like that until I got married to a sailor that I seldom saw, and I lived alone like a spinster and I ached with loneliness. I didn't cry but I felt it coming on. The dam was about to burst. I was seconds from exploding in tears all over the whole precinct. She saw the approaching melt-down.

"Come to my office," she said.

I followed her. Her name was on the desk. Sergeant Ann Marquez.

"Tell me what happened," she said.

I looked at the floor.

"I'm married. My husband is in the Navy. I'll cut to the chase. He's been gone too long. I took a man into my house to ease my loneliness, and now I'm afraid he might kill me if I stop giving him money to buy liquor and weed. I've asked him to leave. He said if I give him ten thousand dollars, he'll consider it. Help me, please. He scares me."

She was sympathetic, a good listener. She told me about filing charges.

"I don't want to file charges, Sergeant. I want him out of the house. Please help me with that."

"He's committed a crime," Ann Marquez said before we left the station. "The choice of filing charges is not up to you. The district attorney will decide. If we go with you, we're arresting him."

I'd been feeling a weight on my shoulders, but it was lifting. I agreed.

As I drove home, Sergeant Ann Marquez was in a patrol car following me, and following her, a patrol car with two officers.

I walked in the house with officers on both sides of me and behind me.

We walked into the living room. I didn't see him, but I said, "Robert, I'm here with the police. I want you out of the house."

No one said anything, including Robert. The officers looked at me.

"He's probably sleeping it off upstairs in the master bedroom," I said.

They didn't go straight upstairs. They checked the entire first floor and opened the door to the backyard to see if he was out there. He wasn't.

"You wait here," Sergeant Ann said. "We're going up."

"It's the room at the far end of the hallway," I said.

I waited at the foot of the stairs.

Fuck you Robert, I said inside my head.

It was eerily silent. I could hear traffic outside on the street. Some distant radio was playing. The floor creaked as they went upstairs. They were trying to be quiet, though I doubted Robert was in any condition to hear them coming, even if they were thumping around in army boots. I wanted to be there to see his fucking face, but I was stuck down here with nothing but my ears.

"Mr. Lopez, this is Sergeant Marquez. I'm coming in the room with two officers." I heard the sergeant speaking in a normal tone of voice.

"Snitch whore," I heard him slur, drunk and loud enough for me to easily make out the words from the first floor.

"We're coming in, guns drawn. Don't be stupid," one of the officers said.

Bang!

Bang!

Bang!

The noise was deafening. It jarred the house. It jarred me. I didn't know who had done the shooting, and I was scared because it was happening in my home.

"Put the gun down," an officer said.

Robert yelled something. I couldn't make out the words, other than that the tone was loud and venomous.

I heard another shot, then four rapid shots mixed with thumps and crashes and what sounded like body contact thumping around the walls and furniture. There was a lot of noise between shots, and things were happening up there, and I couldn't picture it. Like an idiot, I ran up the stairs toward the noise. It sounded like a brawl with way more than four people involved.

When I reached the bedroom, the door was open, and a heavy cloud of smoke hung in the middle of the room. It smelled like the range and a bar. I saw the two cops and Ann standing there, guns drawn. They holstered their weapons.

"Pat, go downstairs," Ann said. "You don't want to be here right now."

She tried to block my view, but I looked at the bed. Robert Lopez was lying face down, my own gun still in his relaxed hand.

By itself, my hand came up over my mouth. I don't know why. I didn't have a scream coming, but my heart was beating fast. I'd never pictured the handsome-faced black-hearted son of a bitch dead in my bed. I don't know what I felt except that my lungs weren't working, and I really wanted a drink.

One of the cops got on the radio requesting paramedics and

officer backup. "Suspect is wounded. Suspect may be dead.

He hadn't moved since I'd gotten here, and he definitely looked dead. I found myself exchanging glances with Ann and the two male officers. The dispatcher on the other end was a woman, and she sounded so calm, so matter of fact. An ambulance was on the way.

I looked at Robert so motionless in one of Jack's white tee shirts and a pair of brightly patterned jockey shorts Jack would not have been caught dead in. A bottle of bourbon was shattered on the floor. I did not know if the bloody crater in his back was where the bullet entered or exited. I'd never shot anything myself but the targets at the range, and I'd never seen the damage a bullet does to a person. This was too real. I remembered he'd beaten up that old lady. I had no tears for him. He probably planned to threaten me, maybe even shoot me with my own gun when I got home. What a motherfucker. If I hadn't gone to the police, I'd probably be the dead one. I still wanted a drink, but what I was feeling was close to relief.

There's no way I could keep this secret from Jack. What could I tell him?

I was still standing there with my hand over my mouth. I realized Ann was by my side and put my hand down.

"Are you sure you weren't hit with a stray bullet? One went through the door."

"I was downstairs when I heard the shots," I said. "I'm okay."

"I'll walk you down," she said.

"Sergeant, I'm okay. Can I get you water or coffee?"

They all wanted coffee, or maybe they just said it to get me out of the way. I was glad to have something to do and went down to the kitchen to start a pot of coffee. On the way, I looked out the living room window. I saw the neighbors I never see standing out on the sidewalk in front of my house. Two police cars and a shootout in my bedroom are pretty hard to ignore.

The ambulance and two more police cars arrived. I poured a lot of coffee and stayed downstairs out of the way. The coroner arrived. Sergeant Ann directed traffic inside my house. I've never had so many people there.

"Can I get you something?" I asked her. "A sandwich to go with the coffee?"

"Nothing, thank you," she said, taking a seat at my kitchen table. "Pat, do you have relatives here?"

"Nope. My parents and two brothers are in El Paso. The only friends I have are my fellow nerds at work. No family here at all." I thought of Tucker at the filling station and my friends at AA. I told her about them, not by name. "I do have some friends here."

"You should call someone," she suggested.

"I will."

"Is your marriage in trouble? Is that why you let this man to stay here?"

"Jack's absence sucks. I get lonely. I guess that's led to some bad decisions."

Ann nodded.

"Any children?"

"None. I love my job, and he likes being a sailor. Before we got married, we agreed that we wouldn't have children early on. Been on the pill for years. It might happen at some time in the future now that I'm on the wagon. But I don't know. Maybe Jack and me, we might be too selfish to have a kid. Are you a mother?"

"Yeah," Ann said. "It ain't easy with this job. Having a son made us closer. My husband is a chef who works nights, so he is home during the day. I only see him a couple hours a day, and barely see the kid, but I couldn't do it without him. He's a great dad, and he worries too much about me. Sometimes we fight like cats and dogs, but it works for us. I see him a hell of a lot more than you see your Jack."

She stopped talking abruptly, finished off her coffee, and

stood. I was surprised at the details of her life. I wasn't really expecting her to be a parent, much less to talk about it.

It took hours for the coroner to take the body away. I walked into the kitchen and rewashed a pile of clean cups and saucers so I wouldn't have to see them haul Robert away in a body bag. No sentiment—I just didn't want that memory in my house. I heard every creak and mumble while the paramedics navigated the gurney down the stairs and around corners. It was still several hours later that the homicide detectives wrapped it up.

"Are you going to be okay?" Ann asked. She looked tired.

"I'm fine. I'll sleep on the couch or in one of the two other bedrooms."

It was late, long after dark when she left. When I closed the front door and locked it, I saw there were still six people on the sidewalk.

I'd been downstairs while they were all here. For the first time, I went upstairs to the master bedroom. The stairs, hall and room were dark. I switched on the recessed ceiling light when I walked in and found that the bed was completely stripped. The linens were probably in an evidence bag somewhere. They could keep it as far as I'm concerned. I found five holes in the walls, plus a hole in the bedroom door. Before, I hadn't noticed the blood splatter on the walls, drapes, ceiling and carpet, but the bare mattress was remarkably untouched.

I brought down a pillow, sheet and blanket from the linen closet and bedded down on the sofa with my forty-five under the pillow, all dark except for the kitchen and living room nightlights, and my cigarette. I had trouble getting comfortable, but I stuck it out since neither spare bedroom was made up. In the morning I noticed a cigarette butt. I had gone to sleep with a cigarette in my hand.

I called work and requested three days off. When I hung up, Tucker from the Chevron called.

"You're a celebrity on the front page of the Oceanside News. Are you okay?"

"I'm good," I said. "I'll see you when I come in to fill up."

"Worried about you, kid."

I laughed softly. "I'm glad someone cares about me. Thanks, Tucker."

I got on the phone and made things happen. I called Laura, my housekeeper. She had read the paper. I assured her I was fine and yes it was true the man was dead and no longer at the house. She was going to come in the next day. I dumped my clothes in the closet and got Salvation Army to pick up everything in the master bedroom. They wanted to schedule me for another day, but I told them if they couldn't get it today, Goodwill would. I found an Oceanside painting contractor in the yellow pages and scheduled him to come out in the early afternoon.

"Are you good with patching drywall?"

"You'll never know there was any damage when I'm done," he said.

"Okay, Mr. Picasso, you need to come in tomorrow and be done by the following day. I need to get back to work."

We went back and forth but agreed. He liked the nickname.

"I read what happened," he said when I handed him a check as a deposit for the work. He was an older man and had showed up in white painter's overalls with stains from many painting jobs.

"I haven't. I don't get the paper," I said. "What did it say?"

"That you took a homeless person in and he turned on you, and when the police came, he started shooting at them."

"Yes, that's what happened."

"Aren't you afraid to be here alone?"

I still had a smile in me, and my contractor saw it.

"Afraid of what?"

He scratched his head. He didn't have much hair.

"What am I supposed to be afraid of? Being alone? I was already alone."

"Ghosts?"

"I don't believe in ghosts."

He smiled and headed to the door.

That night I slept upstairs in one of the bedrooms I'd never used before. The TV in there was an old one Jack had before we got married. I made up the bed and turned the television on to make sure it worked and left it on while I ordered Mexican.

The next morning, Laura arrived for her once a week session with my house. The painter and two helpers arrived about the same time as Laura and went right to work.

"Laura, I want everything in the house wiped down with bleach, especially the bathrooms, the stair bannister, everything. Be sure to wear gloves. Understand?"

"I understand."

I had already tried cleaning the blood spots on the walls in the bedroom even though I knew they were going to paint. I tossed the drapes, the vertical blinds and the area rug.

I was calling him Picasso, but the painting contractor was named Amos. While his crew patched, he showed me a book of color charts. For the walls, I went with a modern forest green, and white for the trim. He agreed to replace the bedroom door.

I drove to a furniture outlet in San Diego for bedside lamps and walnut nightstands, a wing reading chair and a reading lamp in brass, and a California king-sized bed with a red-tufted headboard. I thought the contrast would work with the new walls. Friday after work was the scheduled delivery. The painter would be done on Thursday and I would be back to work.

What would I tell Jack?

The truth.

I have months to decide what the explanation will be. If he wants a divorce, he wants a divorce. It's not like he's home anyway.

He has friends in Oceanside who probably read what happened. Would they contact him in Tokyo to tell him?

I took the easy way out. Laura had brought me the article cut out of the Oceanside paper. I folded it and put in an envelope along with a short note.

> Dear Jack,
> The article sounds worse than it was. I'm okay and unhurt. I hope you're doing well. I had the bedroom painted. I think you'll like it.
> Your wife,
> Pat

On the day I went back to work, I dropped the note off at the post office, knowing it might open up a shitstorm.

I went back to work, and no one said a thing. No one at work lived in Oceanside and the story wasn't important enough for the San Diego papers. Over the weekend, I bought new bedding, a couple of sheet sets, a fabulous duvet and shams to match for the master bedroom. The window blind company installed my new vertical blinds on Saturday. The drapes wouldn't be done for several weeks. The bed looked so beautiful I hesitated to mess it up on Sunday night, but I did it anyway.

I lay in that bed remembering Robert when he was nice, even though he was scheming all along. He played the part really well. Cooking, welcoming me home when I got there in the afternoon. Was it the booze that made him so horrible? Or was he hiding his true colors all along?

I had no doubt in my mind now that he had killed that woman. I could go to prison for giving that statement. Providence had been looking out for me, that I was not called to testify.

It was a cold evening, but the chills I felt were from the dread of getting in trouble for lying.

When Tuesday rolled around, I had a lot to say. I felt lucky that I had people to listen. A brief history here: my first week in AA, I went every night. I went to every meeting between home and work. It was anonymous, didn't mean anything, and I was doing it to save my job. Then something unexpected happened. I connected to the group in Oceanside, closest to my house. That was my meeting. After a year, these were my people. It was in a basement room at a small church. I think it served as a day care or kindergarten during school hours. Miniature tables and chairs were all lined up out of the way against the cinderblock walls papered with bright artwork, stick figures and crafts. Blue and red mats were piled high in the corner.

The dozen adult-sized folding chairs we were using were arranged in a circle. Eleven others and I were at the meeting. The chairperson put out a couple of extra chairs in case there were stragglers after we got started. Everyone there was from Oceanside. They were all just so normal and nice. None of them had ever pried or asked me to share more than I was willing to. All of them knew what had happened so I didn't have to explain. I was greeted with lots of hugs, welcoming and encouragement. Tucker was the last hug before I sat down next to him. The chair asked me to go first.

I gave them a reprise of what the article had said, that I'd let a homeless man stay with me, and things had gone bad from there. I told them how he'd demanded money, and wouldn't leave, and how after he got physical, shoving me down, and stealing from me, I'd had to appeal to the police. I told them that I hadn't seen it, but I'd been downstairs, and I'd heard everything. I mentioned the body, the blood, and shuddered, and shut my eyes.

"Did you drink?"

"I wanted to. I really wanted to, but no. I did not have a single drink, no."

The group applauded.

"I was tempted every day. Every day, I came in the house and smelled the booze. Every day I spent working, he had been drinking all day. But I never came close. I didn't smoke his weed either. After they took him away, I went to sleep on my couch. I could have burned to death. I went to sleep with a lit-up cigarette. I found the butt in the morning."

I got a lot of feedback from that.

Then someone asked, "Are you back to normal?"

"What is normal? I don't know what normal is. My mattress was fine, but I had all my bedroom stuff hauled off, and redid my bedroom. Is that normal? I come home to an empty house, yes, I've redone the room completely. Thank God I can afford it. It was not cheap. But now I don't have to sleep in a bed someone died on. I can live with the loneliness."

"Adopt a dog or a cat or both?

"I would but I don't have the heart to leave a pet at home all day while I'm at work."

Everyone was in favor of me adopting. "You'll be doing the animal a favor. They're lonely too."

"Worse than lonely. They're facing death."

"A pet would be happier alone at any home than alone in a shelter. No dog or cat would prefer the shelter to a home, or someone who comes home to them."

I went silent. I couldn't help picturing coming home to a dog or cat. It wasn't a bad picture. I've got a fenced-in back yard.

"I might check adoptions out," I said. "I love dogs, and I love cats."

"If I had a house, I'd adopt a dog in a heartbeat."

"Thanks for the suggestion. I'm excited about it. I mean the thank you, for real. I haven't been excited about anything in a long time."

When I'd first gotten to AA, I'd been above all this. I had just been going through the motions because I had to, but somewhere along the way, things started making sense. I looked around at the faces around me. These people had become friends. I'd really come a long way. The group clapped, and it was another person's turn to speak.

After the meeting, I always go home to emptiness. I've seriously thought about attending more than one meeting per week, just to fill the emptiness. AA has been a life saver for me. Since I've been attending, I vented my personal problems. I've heard their stories too.

It's good to know you're not alone.

November 1990
Los Angeles
Gianna

Macho is a total sweetheart. He reminds me of Guillermo. I like them both. I had my fifth session in as many nights. I left the apartment at seven-thirty for a meet at nine to give myself plenty of time in case I get lost. The Hilton Hotel in Beverly Hills is easy to find. I got there too early, so I went to the gift shop for a magazine to read in the lobby. I was in a strapless black and white flowered Christian Dior, black hose, hat, gloves, and shoulder wrap. I looked fucking elegant. In the outfit I was wearing, security will never peg me as a sex-for-pay girl. I felt confident, secure, unafraid and not shy.

Either Los Angeles is an early start city or maybe nine is not that early. In only a few months, I'd come a long way from working the streets of Cannes waving at cars passing by.

At nine on the dot, I rang the doorbell of room six hundred.

"Hello Edgar. My name is Gianna."

I didn't extend my hand for a handshake yet, nor did I just

take it on myself to plant a kiss on the client. First, I had to get a feel for him, a lesson from Mona. Macho had used my real name, but that was okay. Who knew me here, anyway?

"You are dazzling. Please come in," he said.

Edgar was fifty plus. I couldn't tell how fit he was under his robe, not that it mattered. I was here to serve.

"Can I kiss you?" I asked.

He opened his arms and I walked in them. I pulled away a little and kissed. He's not much taller than me. Macho had arranged a thousand for three hours. I know Mona makes more money than that but I'm not going to make any noise. After I pay Macho his four hundred, I would have six hundred dollars left. If I could make that every night, wouldn't that be wonderful? I was already better off here in America. It's not just the money. Even my place is so much nicer.

I accepted a glass of wine because he was drinking wine. We sat on a sofa, lights mostly off. I felt him all down my side where our bodies touched.

"What you want me to do to you, Edgar?"

I didn't know if it was my accent or what I said that made him laugh. A hearty laugh. He gently slapped my upper thigh above my stocking where my dress was hiked up. I was wearing a kind of silk stocking held up with a body adhesive Mona said was used in beauty pageants.

"I want it all," he said, setting his wine glass down on the coffee table. I did the same and he hugged me. The sofa was awkward and uncomfortable. I didn't want to rush him to the bed until he said so.

He said so.

He dropped his robe, revealing a body fitter than I'd expected. He had an older man's barrel chest, but his biceps were lovely. I reached over and touched the curves there, and my little gasp was real. He gave me a surprised, no, delighted smile. His boxer shorts stayed on as he sat on the edge of the turned-down bed.

"May I undress, Edgar?"

"Please leave your lingerie on," he said, looking at my stockings.

He propped pillows so he could sit up against them. I stepped out of my dress. The red silk thong I was wearing looked normal in front and was nothing but a string in back. The bra, panties and stockings were a set.

He reached under a pillow and pulled out a pair of cuffs.

"Are these for me or you?"

"For you if you are okay with it."

"You won't hurt me?"

"I will be gentle. I want to see you lying here on the bed."

He stood to position me on the bed. I was on my back, my arms above my head, and he moved me this way and that until he was satisfied with my position. He put a cuff in each of my hands, so I was holding them. He made no move to put them on me. He pulled an ottoman to the bed, sat on it, put the back of each of his hands as high between my legs as he could go, and slid his hands down from the inside of my thigh to my ankles, touching only with the back of his hand, not just touching my skin, but also pressing my legs wider apart.

"You're softer than the silk," he said.

He started with my feet. I giggled Kissing each toe tickled.

"You like it?"

"I love. Do you?" I said.

Edgar said, "You are breathtaking."

I cuffed myself.

"Do what you want to me. Don't hurt me."

"I would never hurt you."

His kisses were wet. He kissed and nibbled his way to my knees, then to my panties where his lips played my bits like a musical instrument. I was feeling notes and rhythms in me I didn't know it was possible to feel. He worked his way to my mouth, and except for the stockings, removing lingerie as he moved up. I could tell he wanted to feel the stocking silk against him. It was an effort to read his desires because I was bucking my hips with real pleasure. He had me steaming. I kept my eyes open; I didn't want him to think I was thinking of someone else. Then he was inside me, noisy and satisfied.

When he was spent, he took off the cuffs. I showered and retrieved my underwear from the mess we'd made of the sheets. I dressed. He gave me the thousand and then five hundred as a tip. I smothered him with kisses. Edgar got hard standing there.

I went down on my knees and did him.

We were six feet from the door. My thousand-dollar dress was short enough that I could kneel without damaging the material.

"You are delicious," he said. "Please stay the night. I'll give you another thousand."

Just then he burst into an orgasm. I left him tucked in bed.

I had figured I'd spend Thanksgiving Day with Aunt Isabel. I seldom saw family. My cousins were out of the house now but were going to be there for dinner.

Macho doesn't shut down shop, but business is slow around turkey day and Christmas. It was almost a sure thing that Mona and Gianna would come with me to spend the day eating and having family fun. Frankly, it's not fun. It's the right thing to do. I could take or leave the tradition of spending time with family on special days like Thanksgiving and Christmas, but it meant a lot to Aunt Isabel.

Two days before the fourth Thursday of November, Mona announced that her local high tech client wanted her to spend the day with him at the Peninsula. Macho offered Gianna a half-day date with a local looking for company at his Marina Del Rey apartment.

I let them both off easy and reported to my aunt that I would be coming alone.

I knew Gianna was working and so was Mona. I felt very unsettled, not so much over it being almost Thanksgiving, but just that it would be another night after I had worked all day, and then come home to be alone. Mona had dashed out the door. Dinner had been a bowl of noodle soup and a salad with a squeeze of lemon. I just couldn't get excited over it. I washed my dish, and put it away, and lay down in my bed, thumbing through the TV guide. A movie wasn't going to change my life, but it might take my mind off it being two nights till Thanksgiving dinner at Aunt Isabel's. And that's when I got an unexpected call from Rob Sphere. I recognized his voice right away.

"You should be on my shit list," I said, sitting up in bed. "You called me back in August. I really thought you were going to call me back."

I was teasing. I did not expect him to call back after I turned down his request for me to drop everything to see him in London. I got off the bed, pulled off my sweats, and put on a white silk negligee. I lay on top of my comforter, smoothing the silk against my skin, but I kept my voice all business.

"Sorry about that. I've been busy. You said you were also busy defending criminals who can't afford private counsel."

"Hey, that doesn't sound nice." I pointed one leg toward the ceiling, then the other.

He laughed. "I'm sorry, I speak that way. You know I'm a kitten at heart."

I didn't know Rob Sphere was a kitten. I did know he was generous, and I figured he was loaded to afford a ship everyone called a yacht. Yacht did not give credit where credit is due. It did not illustrate how big the ship was. The ship he'd built for his dead wife. I remembered the tragic story. I let my legs fall on the bed.

"Come see me," he said. "You can fly commercial, first class, or push it, and I'll send my plane for you if I have to."

"You are kidding of course. Thanksgiving is the day after to-morrow."

He laughed again.

"We don't have Thanksgiving in London. Come on, say yes."

"Why me?"

"Gabi, you asked that back in August. It's obvious why. I like you. I like having conversations with you. You're beautiful, and you are unique."

Next he was going to tell me I reminded him of his late wife, like Homer.

"Gabi?"

"I'm here."

"Are you at least tempted?"

"Where will I stay?" I blurted it out without thinking. Not where would I stay. I guess I decided.

"How much time you got?"

"If I push it, a week."

"I'm glad I called," he said. "I'm excited as all hell."

Actually, I felt good about it, too. I got off the bed and stood in front of the mirror. The silk gown looked good on me. At least being a lawyer hadn't chased the bloom off the rose. I did a sexy little dance, watching myself.

"Gabi, are you there? What are you doing?"

I laughed. I wasn't about to say dancing half naked in front of the mirror and wondering what he was wearing.

"I'm here. I'm excited you asked me."

"I have two homes in London. I think you'd like my favorite in Kensington Palace Gardens, an old and cozy relic with four service people living in a guest house year-round. We can relax like we're well off. What do you say?"

"Is this for real?"

"It's for real. Name your price."

That caught me off guard. I went from being really excited to a little deflated.

"Gabi, are you there?"

"If I take you up on this, it's not about money," I said. I lay flat on my back and stared at the ceiling.

"We can get to that when you're here."

"How do I get there?"

"I will have my assistant call you for passport details. She will arrange everything for you."

"Okay, sounds good. What if there's no seat?"

"In that case, I will send my plane for you. I will see you Thursday."

"Just like that?"

He laughed. "I am excited," he said. "I promise you will love London. You can shop your heart out, and it's on me."

"I thought we were going to stay home and pretend we were well off."

"We can do both."

I hung up the phone with a sense of disbelief. Was this what Cinderella felt like? I'm going to London.

Fuck. I had to call my aunt. At least I could put it off till morning. It was too late to call tonight.

I told Mona about it in the morning before breakfast.

"Unless he proposes marriage, charge him."

I laughed.

"I'm happy you're going," Mona said. "I'll be working and so will Gianna. You won't have to be sitting here eating turkey by yourself."

"Hey, you, I was going to my aunt's house. She was hella disappointed. I had to promise I'd come for dinner in December at least twice."

"You know what I mean," Mona said. "I remember Sphere, and his buddy Bilal that I spent the night with, and the yacht we were on. He called you after you turned him down. How sweet is that?"

"I can't remember the sex being so far out that he would want me to be with him in London him for a week."

"Stop trying to figure it out. I wish I was so lucky," Mona said.

His assistant got me a seat on a non-stop from LAX to Heathrow Airport, first class. I left Thursday afternoon and arrived at noon, London time, Friday. Sitting there with a lot of room to stretch out, I remembered my trip from New York to LAX when I met Homer. I had always worried that something about me put out the hooker vibe.

This was a new adventure in London to meet up with a stranger I had spent a couple of hours with in Cannes. It had been enough time to get him curious enough about me to seek out my secret—that I was a lawyer and not a full-time woman of the night. My round-trip ticket set Rob back over eleven thousand dollars, not counting the car service in Los Angeles and London. I've been with way too many rich clients, but I never had a client look me up like Rob did and personally invite me to fly six thousand miles to London to spend time with him.

I flew to Paris on a booking through Macho once, to meet up with a Saudi Arabian prince only to find out I was one of more than a dozen chicks at the hotel waiting to see if the prince was interested. I was paid ten thousand for being there. I had a prince at the Century Plaza Hotel, same circumstances. I got paid for being there, plus a Rolex watch, but didn't get to fuck the prince. Macho has sweet clients, powerful clients. Look at me still thinking about it.

November 1990
UK
Rob Sphere

Back in May, right after the Cannes festival ended, and I returned to London, Babs said, "Rob, in Los Angeles, she's not a hooker. She's a lawyer for the county public defender, representing clients who can't afford an attorney to represent them in criminal court," Babs said back in May, right after the Cannes festival ended, and I returned to London.

"I knew it."

"She came to Cannes to escort the rich and famous like you," Babs said.

"I should have spent more time with her in Cannes. The escorts I met after her were drones by comparison. I knew she was not doing what she was doing full time."

Babs was with me at the Kensington house awaiting Gabi's arrival. My Kensington house staff seemed happy to be hosting a visitor and me. When in London, I often stay in my other home, a penthouse in Knightsbridge. I have many assistants, but only one Babs. She is always close unless I am out on my yacht. When I told her that I had a friend from Los Angeles spending a week with me, she guessed who it was.

"Must be Gabi, the lawyer."

Kylie the hooker in Cannes had turned out to be Gabi the lawyer in Los Angeles, a fact sleuthed out by a private-eye Babs had engaged.

I remembered tearing off Gabi's clothes. Her laughter had been a turn on.

"What are you thinking about?" Babs asked. "You have this grin."

"I was thinking about the night I met Gabi. She's a handful.

"The driver called. They are ten minutes away. You seem excited. Is it because she's coming here, or is it the block of Microsoft that I confirmed this morning?" Babs asked.

"Good job on the stock, Babs."

Fifty thousand shares of Microsoft to add the stock I'd bought early on at twenty-six dollars. At every opportunity, I keep buying. Babs handles my portfolio with my broker.

Almost a month after Robert Lopez was shot, Jack called.

"I just got your letter. What the fuck is this article? Some homeless guy was shot in our bed? Matt said he heard it on the news, that a man was shot dead in our master bedroom. Is that true?"

"What a great way to start a conversation, Jack. You haven't called in months. You have my number, but it's not like the Navy lets me know where you are."

"Cut the crap. You know how hard it is to call on a cruise. Is it true?"

"Yes, it's true."

"What was he doing in my house?"

"You mean our house," I said. "Community property."

"What was he doing there?"

"I brought him home to keep me company. I needed to get fucked. What are you doing in Tokyo? Are you jacking off? Is that what you do? You haven't even asked me if I was hurt or if I'm okay." I started crying. "I came really close to getting shot. Did you know that? Do you even care?"

The line went dead.

Fuck you Jack.

I found two gorgeous female three-month-old black and white cats at the San Diego pound. I was excited to bring them home in two new pet carriers. I also bought a litter box and litter and the cat food recommended to me by the vet at the pound. They already had their shots.

I named them Boots and Nancy. At first, it was hard to tell them apart. They couldn't jump on the bed until I moved a chair close that they could use like a ladder. They slept with me right from the first night. I loved them right off. I wanted to stay home and be with them. It was crazy. No, not crazy, just crazy lonely, especially when I thought of Jack.

I knew he was right to be pissed, but he could have handled it better than he did. I should have handled it better too. I should have done better than sending the damn article. I know mail takes a month or longer. I should have called, but I was chicken-shit. It was shitty that he heard it from a friend who read the newspaper. If I had to do it again, I'm not sure I would have handled telling him differently.

Fuck the house. I make good money. A new house is within my reach. What happens next is up to Jack. I am not ashamed of what I've done. I told my friends at AA the same thing. I have a lot of feelings. I am pissed that I was stupid, soft, and ignorant. I was a lot of things, but ashamed is not one of them. Being lonely is no picnic. At least with Boots and Nancy, I'm not coming home to solitary confinement.

I want to be sorry that Robert died. I brought him home to be killed by police, eventually. Robert was a rotten human being, but he had a mother and father. For all I know, he had kids somewhere. For all I know, he had no one.

Robert, you killed that old lady in her house. I know you did. Eventually you would have died in the gas chamber anyway. Fuck you Robert Lopez. Rest in peace but fuck you.

Thoughts like this that can drive an alcoholic to drink. I didn't drink a drop of alcohol. It probably wasn't because of any great resolution on my part. It was because of the people I knew in AA. Their encouragement has made a huge difference in my life.

I smoke no weed. I am clean.

Not long after my fur babies had settled in, I had my first visit with a psychiatrist I found in the yellow pages. His office was fifteen minutes from my work in San Diego. A human being had been killed at my house, and I didn't care. I needed help.

He was a hot-looking man, at least to me. He was gentle, round-jawed and soft spoken, and the first session when I met him, he wore a sweater. I was not on a chaise like in the movies. I sat in a chair in his private office. He sat in a chair across from me. I liked that I could see his face as I talked to him. He was a little pudgy which made him seem approachable and had kind brown eyes. I wonder if his eyes will still be so kind after he hears all I have to say.

"Where do I start?" I asked him.

"Start in the beginning." His voice was low and pleasing and gentle.

"Can I smoke?"

"I prefer you don't."

"Okay, here goes. I was driving home one afternoon, and I spotted this man hitchhiking..."

My first major was business. Second semester, I switched to economics then third semester, I was back to business. Some colleges allow two majors but not mine. I wasn't sure what I wanted to do. At home I had no one steering me. My parents never went to college. My mum was a clerk at a major department store in London. My father was an electrician whose philosophy was why change if it works. Both were happy having a boss and wouldn't dream of going out on their own. That was never me. When other little girls dreamed of being Cinderella, I made believe that my mum owned her own clothing store, and that my dad's truck had the name of his electric business on it.

I worked at Harrods Department Store in London. Between that and my parent's savings, I got through four years of college.

When I decided to study law to become an advocate, I got a student loan to make it work. I remained at Harrods. Why change it if it works, right? I was shooting for the stars, but I had to finish school and get a license.

In my last year of law school, I was recruited by a scout looking for a new advocate who understood economics and the stock market.

"I'm too young. I don't know anything your employer would want me to know," I told the scout. He went away. Then one of Robert Sphere's assistants called for an appointment.

My meeting with Sphere was at an office in an old estate. Everything in his office looked like it had been there for the past hundred years. I mean, there were electric lights, but they looked like gas lights. His phone was inside a cabinet, but I didn't know that at the time. The windows had leaded glass, tiny triangles of old glass that distorted and softened the view to the outside. Persian rugs covered the floors. There were a lot of boat paintings, statues, and figurines. Instead of grilling me from his desk, he had chosen to have me come for afternoon tea served by a trio of maids from a tea cart while we sat at an Irish mahogany tea table with a scalloped edge, a birdcage base and cabriole legs. I was impressed by his table. He was impressed by my grades. We talked for two hours about subjects that were totally apart from the law. He wanted to know what I knew of the world in general.

"Do you care if you practice law or not?"

"Why become an advocate if I don't plan to practice law?"

"I'll put it another way. If you were making, say, fringe benefits plus one hundred thousand pounds a year, would you care if you were practicing law?"

"One hundred thousand for how long?"

"For a year. Twenty percent increase each year with a number of fringe benefits."

"What would I be doing?"

"You would be my special assistant. I will teach you what you need to know to be my assistant."

"Why me?"

"You're young, aggressive, and you don't have any bad habits you have to unlearn."

I was flattered that he had checked me out. I looked at him, liking the way he met my eyes directly.

"Also, you're beautiful."

Maybe I should have been offended, but that flattered me too.

I cleared my throat. "What fringe benefits?"

"A car, a living allowance, or the option of living wherever I am at the time, and rooms in my properties in London and else-where."

He had two houses in London and houses in other countries and had made it big investing in high tech companies.

I signed on for five years with an option to renegotiate a new agreement at the end of my term or split. If at any time within the five years I was dismissed, Robert would owe me for the time remaining.

My signing bonus was one hundred thousand British pound sterling.

When he heard the terms, my father said, "He wants to fuck you." My father speaks his mind.

My mum is the opposite. "You don't know this man. You got no right to talk that way."

I wasn't born yesterday. I didn't tell my parents that I agreed with my father, that Sphere was after my caboose. I finished my last year of school and prepared for my exam while working with Robert. I chose my car: a red BMW three series convertible. Two days later, I had it. The company would pay all upkeep, including gasoline. I moved into a furnished flat in Knightsbridge two blocks from Harrods. Both of these were written into my contract.

Gabi was stunning, a creamy-skinned blonde whose photos did not do her justice. The investigator's snapshots revealed an attractive young woman. In person, she was a ninety on a scale of fifty.

That's Rob's scale. He uses it for everything.

Rob gave her a hug, a couple kisses, and pulled back to admire how she looked. A houseman took charge of her mink. She looked perfectly put together and fresh, not like she'd been in those clothes since Los Angeles.

"You were right, Gabi. Gorbachev got the Nobel Prize."

She smiled and gave him a thumbs up.

"I thought about you," she said.

Gorbachev got the award in October, just a month ago. I didn't know what the thing between Rob and Gabi was. Maybe a thread from a conversation they had at an earlier time.

We agreed to meet back in the living room in one hour and we would discuss dinner plans. A houseman carried in Gabi's Louis Vuitton suitcase and she followed him to her room.

After she left, he said, "A keg of dynamite is what she is. What do you think?"

I said, "I'll tell you when I get to know her."

"Don't be hard on her."

"Not in a million years would I be hard on a friend of yours."

"I think we eat dinner here tonight."

"I'll arrange it," I said.

I excused myself and ran to the home office where I share a partnership desk with Rob when we are at this house. I called Martin, Rob's stockbroker. The market was already closed but Martin was always available on cell.

"Tomorrow we're looking at 100k of Apple at today's close or close to it. If Microsoft is steady, he wants 100k more. Call me to confirm."

"Have a good night, Babs," Martin said.

"You too."

I called Stella on staff here at this house and requested two female massage therapists at ten. I figured dinner would be done by eight. A massage at ten would be a good time.

I called Millie at the Noble Fir farm to order a tree. "It's been a year already. Can you believe it?" I said. "We're at Kensington. Any chance you can send a twenty-foot tree day after tomorrow?"

Rob always ordered a Christmas tree for this house and his penthouse, even when he was out of town. I thought it would be nice to have the tree here while Gabi was visiting.

Millie said she would make it happen. She would order it cut in the morning and trucked to London right away. I also ordered an eighteen-foot Fraser fir for the penthouse. Fraser firs last five weeks. The ceilings there are not as tall as here.

I planned to ask Gabi if she wanted to do anything special during her stay. Whatever she chose to do, I would arrange. I had cleared Rob's schedule. In the seven years I've known him, his lady visitors seldom stayed more than one night. Actually, in the past three years, since Priscilla died, I doubt one stayed even one night. Not that he was celibate—this was just Priscilla's home, and he had a care for her memory. His driver was on standby. I had a current list of the hottest shows, and contacts for the best seats at all the theatres. I only needed some direction. Rob had warned me not to plan anything unless Gabi gave me a green light. He didn't want her pushed into doing something she didn't care to do.

I wondered about this Gabi. Rob seemed mesmerized by her.

Thanksgiving Week 1990
Gabi

The guest room I was assigned is—as Rob would say—bloody brilliant. I'm sure the bedding is new. The furniture is from different periods, with no signs of wear and tear on the fabric. The shades and curtains are on remote control. The bathroom is enormous, and has a shower, bathtub, bidet, and jacuzzi. I desperately wanted to get in the tub, but with an hour to get downstairs, I settled for a shower. I rinsed in cold water to shock away the jet lag.

What kind of man sends five thousand four hundred miles for a call girl and puts her in a guest room fit for a fairy tale princess? Rob Sphere must be a nut case.

If I was here for the money, I would have arranged the price before I agreed. I got on the plane out of curiosity. I remembered Rob very well, but I could not figure out what got him to call me twice to invite me here.

Babs is a knockout. I bet she's a handful for him. On the

phone when I gave her my passport information for the plane ticket, she said she was his special assistant. Could be I have a dirty mind, and that's why I'm thinking her job includes looking after all of him.

My phone rang.

"Gabi, this is Babs. Rob wants to know if you are okay having dinner here."

"That's great. Of course, Babs. I'll wear casual."

"Casual works," Babs said with a little laugh. "What's your pleasure? Steak, lobster or chicken?"

"It all sounds wonderful, but I can do with a steak if the chef can do it well done. I hope your chef won't hate me for that."

"The chef will not hate you. His job is to please your taste buds. Is Porterhouse okay?"

"It is more than okay. You're making me hungry."

"There will be many sides to choose from," Babs said.

I have read about English food. I'm just glad she wasn't offering a choice of organ meats or blood sausage. Steak sounded wonderful. A good meal would stave off the jet lag, I hoped.

I wore flats, beige Dior wool slacks, and a matching cashmere sweater. The house was comfortable, but I was accustomed to warmer climes. I did a three-sixty in the three-way mirror in the bathroom, and I think I would have passed anyone's muster. Wool is less flattering than jeans, but wool is more appropriate here among the toffs. I stepped out into the hall, and a waiting girl smiled at me and led me to the dining room.

I was glad I was wearing flats. Their soft soles didn't make much sound as I made my way down several set of stairs, across a landing, and through numerous rooms, some with carpet, some with floors so polished that they looked like glass. Heels would have made a noisy clatter.

The dining room was straight out of Architectural Digest.

There was so much dark wood, it reminded me of his yacht. The main table had twenty chairs and reminded me of Homer's house. No place settings were on the long table. Next to it was a round burled table that I figured could accommodate ten, but there were only two high back chairs, and they both had fancy place settings, lace, napkins, gold chargers, and candlesticks placed strategically so they were not blocking the cross-table view.

All the seats at the long table reminded me of the orgy on Rob's yacht. Neither he nor I had spoken much of the public sex at the time. I didn't really know what he was into then or now. I mean, he hadn't participated in the orgy, and when we went below, he'd gotten into tearing off my clothes. I don't know which he was really into. I guess I'd find out soon. My wicked imagination put all the naked guests on the yacht sitting at the table, naked, and dining. I'm glad they were only in my imagination, because their actual presence would have complicated dinner. And I was hungry enough to eat a porterhouse.

"You look sensational, Gabi."

We hugged, looked at each other, and hugged again. I kissed his lips. A perfect kiss. Not wet. A peck.

"Babs told me you're hungry," he said.

"She spoke truth."

A server pulled the chair out for me, and another server did the same for Rob. I put my napkin on my lap wondering where Babs was. It took a few moments for it to sink in that she wasn't going to be eating with us.

"I'm starved."

"I dispensed with the before dinner drinks. Like sex, sometimes you best get with it right away."

I laughed. I glanced at the long table. "I keep picturing all your yacht guests sitting at that table." I couldn't help a little giggle. I didn't mention I was picturing them as I had last seen them, naked. "But I am glad it is just us."

He seemed pleased that I mentioned the yacht.

"Did you have fun on the yacht?"

"I loved it. I remember the clam chowder served in sourdough bowls. Creative and delicious."

"I love it, too," he said. "We could fly to Marseilles and take it out for a spin."

He made it sound so simple.

"Just like that?"

"Of course, just like that. Let me know if it is something you wish to do. What do you think about the invasion of Kuwait?"

The abrupt change of subject didn't quite throw me. I'd sort of expected another current event quiz. I ignored the servers bringing the food in and looked at him.

"My guess is that the U.S. is going in soon to liberate the country."

"You think that will happen?"

"I'm surprised we haven't already moved on it.

"I'm sure the Brits will join forces."

"I'm no war expert. Kuwait is tiny. I wouldn't be surprised if our troops can go in there and chase the invaders out."

"Kuwait has plenty of money. If the U.S. does it, they should pay you for it."

"Same goes for the Brits if your forces join us.'

The servers delivered the food. My steak had to be two pounds. The baked potato on my plate looked like a football. I let the server put on a chunk of butter, a round scoop of sour cream, a dipper of melted cheddar, and a thick coating of fresh snipped chives.

I took a steak knife and began on the steak.

Rob was plowing through his steak like he hadn't eaten in days, but still asked questions between bites.

"Gabi, you like keeping up with world affairs?"

"I get several newspapers at home, but sometimes I don't get to read them till the weekend. There are always magazines around the office, but they tend to be focused on local news, and American law. I read everything I can get my hands on. I read as much as my time allows."

"Babs is that way," he said. "She didn't predict Gorbachev would win the Nobel prize."

"Gorbachev did too much good not to be rewarded. He probably prevented decades more of war. How do you reward a person like Gorbachev? The Nobel Prize."

I dipped my steak into the liquid on the plate. It was like a combination of Worcestershire sauce, garlic, herbs, and au jus. Delicious. The steak was perfectly cooked.

"Are you up on the Hubble telescope launch?" I asked.

Rob ate. He talked with excitement. "Babs and I keep up with everything. World events influence what stock to buy or dump."

"So, you are into the stock market. I wondered what you did for a living." I said more than asked it. I was still working on the steak. I didn't think I was going to touch the potato.

"I thought I told you that," he said, looking up from his plate.

"No, I didn't know. When would you have told me?" I laughed.

"I'm in a lot of businesses, but my savvy with stocks has been rewarding."

"Impressive."

The table was too big for us to click glasses, but we raised our wine glasses every so often.

I finished the whole porterhouse. I did not touch the potato, impressive as it was. Rob's plate was so clean, a dog could not have licked it any cleaner.

The servers cleared the table and poured tea.

"Care for spotted dick?" Rob asked.

I laughed, realizing this was the dish. He had to know Americans would respond this way.

"What an offensive name for a pretty little bundt cake," I said.

"Actually, it's a current pudding." He accepted a slice, and some cream sauce poured over it.

"I've seen it. Never tried it." I declined a taste.

After dinner, we walked to a sitting room overlooking the well-lit grounds. The room lights were turned down low. A servant opened the drapes with a remote, revealing a pond, swimming pool and many tall trees.

"Your home is out of this world," I said. "What an idyllic setting."

"I like it. I don't spend as much time here as I would like. I have a penthouse flat in Knightsbridge. One day when we are out shopping, I'll take you there."

"Very nice," I said.

The room we were in was much like my bedroom here, furnished fully with antiques from many periods, but somehow working perfectly together. The floor was some kind of polished wood, but a large Persian rug covered all but the edge. I felt sure the artwork in the room was famous. The view was gorgeous, but the room was also gorgeous. I wanted to ask if his wife had done the decorating, but I felt it would be rude to mention her. I believe she passed away three years ago. I had seen her picture in different places in the house.

A servant came in, brought wine and glasses, and a dish with crackers and bonbons. I could not look at the food, but the wine was nice. He placed a crystal bell, serving dish and napkins on a table, poured two glasses half full, and left without a word.

We were alone, sipping wine. Rob was still talking of world affairs. He spoke at length about up and coming tech companies that he made investment in, in the UK, India and the United States. "Long shots," he said. "If just one comes in, the rewards will be fruitful."

It's not that he was boring, but I had had a long day. I suppressed a yawn, and asked, "What's the plan tonight Rob? Are we in separate bedrooms or what?"

"You want to get some rest. I'm fine with that," he said. "Jet lag is a bear. All the traveling I do, I have to fight the bear frequently."

"I'm good," I said.

"In that case, come visit me in my bedroom. I'm sure you'll love it."

"I'm excited. Show me."

I could not have told you the path we took to get there, except we went through several rooms, up at least two flights of stairs, maybe three, and walked down a long hall. Like many old buildings, the place was a maze.

His bedroom was elaborate and brand new. It looked newer than three years old, and I could only say that because I often looked at architectural magazines. I doubt it had been like this when his wife had passed. I guessed he and Babs had worked with a decorator. There were two bathrooms.

I thought the bathroom in my guest room was unbeatable, but the one he led me through topped it and then some. The wall-coverings were Asian, white and black high gloss satin-like cloth. An Asian-styled pedicure chair had its own corner, and a manicure table and two beautiful oriental chairs had their own corner. The bathtub was a huge marble and glass jacuzzi. A bidet and toilet were in separate glassed stalls, and there was room for a graceful chaise lounge big enough for two.It was spectacular.

"Do I have time to take a tub bath?"

"You bet. Take your time. I'll be at my desk in the bedroom." He moved close and kissed me on the lips.

"Are you sure it won't inconvenience you?"

"Gabi, Babs complains I'm a workaholic. I always have stacks of projects on my desk that I look into when I am supposed to be resting. Please make yourself at home. I want you to be as comfortable with me as I am with you here."

I kissed him back.

"I'll go grab some lingerie and be right back."

I had showered before dinner, but nothing compares to a hot bath. It wasn't just a bath. The tub itself was an experience. I felt like a princess as I stepped in the bubbly water. The jacuzzi experience reminded me in a way of Keith and Rossi in Cannes. The marble and glass aesthetic raised the bar, but I half expected Rob to join me, or come to watch. He didn't do that. He was still a mystery, and I needed to find out what makes him tick. That night on the yacht, he'd torn off the clothes he'd provided. Maybe that was his thing. It had been difficult to return the favor when he was wearing regular clothing. I waited a bit, but when he didn't come join me, I followed up with a quick shower to rinse off the soap, dried my hair and put on something sexy.

I walked out to the bedroom and found that he was at the far end of the room behind a desk with a desk lamp on. The lighting of the room was very controlled. One might even say staged. The bookshelves had lighting, the art had lighting, the bed had reading lamps. Lighting had very much been built into the room's decoration.

I was in gray silk pajamas. The shirt had no buttons and was worn over a bra that was more for looks than function. The drawstring pants were pretty, but something that could be pulled off easily. The outfit wasn't as fragile as the clothes he'd provided on the yacht, but he could tear them off easily, if that was his thing.

I approached two stuffed leather chairs at the foot of the bed with a table between them. They looked flawless and comfortable. The throws that were tossed over them looked too soft to be real. Four big candles burned on the table. If the lights were turned off, I pictured how the candles would enhance the ambiance. I was getting very excited about the night to come.

"Hello, Rob."

I heard his chair grate against the floor, and he stood.

"You look adorable," he said. "I am so happy you came to London to see me."

"I was happy you invited me. You've made me feel like a princess."

"You haven't seen anything yet," he said, coming close, and putting my hand to his lips.

He brushed my knuckles with his lips, turned my hand over very deliberately and kissed my palm.

I shut my eyes for a second as a shiver ran down my back. "No one has ever done that to me before," I said.

The turned down bed was five feet away. I could feel it calling. We were standing there looking at each other. He was in a black and white robe, embroidered in an oriental style with bits of red here and there. I could make out a pattern of black cranes flying across the cloth. Cranes are good luck. I remember reading that somewhere. I bet the robe looked fantastic hanging in the bathroom. It suited him.

His eyes flicked away from my face and ran over my body. I waited till he'd looked his fill before I took his hand with both of mine and kissed each fingertip, one-by-one, then licked each one. He tasted of lavender soap. His face was flushed and rosy.

"Gabi, can we get in bed?"

I left my pjs on the floor beside his robe, and we met, skin to skin on the bed. He was naked, and his hair was damp. The rascal had been in a shower while I was luxuriating in the tub.

I moved on top of him. We were both ready and he went right in. I leaned over so my face was up to his.

"Don't come, Rob. I want you to enjoy this."

"Yes," he said.

I didn't want to move too much, or he'd orgasm right away. I took his hands and guided them to my breasts. He took it from there. This was different from the yacht. I was wet, and we were desperately trying to make it last as long as possible. It started off leisurely, but then it moved through stages. I changed positions a couple of times to keep it going, but don't know how long it was. It could have been hours. We were both dripping with sweat, and it was getting intense. It wasn't about me, but I was on the brink. He said my name, and the way he said it, I took it to mean he was ready.

"I'm going to make you come. Are you ready?"

He gave me a grin and looked positively boyish.

"Yeah!"

I moved up and down him, with just the right friction, the right bit of squeeze and motion. He came to a massive overheated orgasm. So did I. It was practically an out of body experience. I stopped moving and caught my breath. I leaned over and rested my face on his right clavicle, my cheek against his neck. I started to laugh, the kind of laugh you do after an unbelievable orgasm.

"Tell me you liked it," I said.

He said nothing.

I raised my head to look at him. He was white as the sheet.

"Rob, talk to me. Talk to me."

Rob was out.

I ran to the bedroom door, opened it, and yelled out, "Help in the master bedroom!"

I ran back to the bed, picked up the house phone, dialed nine one one.

It didn't work. I wanted to cuss. I jerked open the end table the phone was resting on and found the London white pages. Emergency was nine-nine-nine. I dialed nine-nine-nine.

"The owner of the house is having a heart attack. Trace the call, I'm setting the phone down to give him CPR. Hurry."

I grabbed his robe that was on the floor and put it on. I was back on the bed on my knees, giving him mouth to mouth, lifting his arms, getting him in a better position. This was not the time to fucking panic. I did CPR.

Babs walked in wearing a robe over boy-cut shorts and a pajama tube top. Two household staff were following her.

"What is it?" Babs said, then she saw what it was.

I didn't answer. I kept the rhythm. Breathed for him.

"Oh my God," Babs said.

"I dialed nine-nine-nine," I said. "That phone."

My mouth went back to Rob.

It seemed like eternity before I heard the sirens. A medic tapped me to move out of the way.

I stepped back. My heart was racing. I was out of breath like I'd been running, and it seemed like it took forever before the medics had an AED on him. I found myself clinging to Babs, though we were strangers.

"I think you saved his life," Babs whispered to me. It wasn't like a confidence. It was more like that's all the sound she could make. She was white-knuckled and upset. So was I. But when they wheeled him out to the ambulance, Rob was breathing on his own.

"It's a good thing you did CPR on him," one of the medics said. "He would have died."

Babs and I separated and stood on our own two feet. She tapped me on the shoulder, like good job.

"Gabi, I'm going with him. I'll call you on your cell and bring you up to date."

"Are you sure you don't want me to go?"

"Positive," she said.

One of the staff handed Babs her purse, a pair of jeans and a shirt.

"Thanks Mary," she said.

I don't know if she'd asked for them or if Mary had just brought them on her own. Babs threw off the robe, jammed into her clothes and ran after the medics with her shoes and purse in hand.

Then I was alone in Rob's room. It felt very alone without him in it. And there was my negligee in the middle of the floor. And I was barely covered in this silk robe. There was no question the medics knew what had happened.

I picked up my lingerie, dressed. I went into Rob's bathroom, and hung his robe on a gold hook. It looked right there, just as I had known it would. My clothes were still in the bathroom from before when I took a bath, so I gathered them, and walked back to my bedroom. It was all very mechanical, like my brain didn't want to focus on what had just happened.

I sat in the bed and found myself crying. I didn't know exactly why I was crying. I don't know how much time had passed, but there was a knock on the door. Quickly I wiped my eyes and took a few deep breaths.

"Come in," I said. My voice sounded normal to me.

It was Mary again. Turns out, she was a kitchen helper, and she brought me a tray with tea and cookies.

"This will calm you miss," she said. "Thank you for saving Mr. Sphere."

At the foot of my bed, there were two chairs and a table, just like in Rob's room. Well, they were dainty and white lacy fabric where his were leather.

I felt my throat catch.

She put the tray on the table between the chairs, poured a cup and excused herself.

"Thank you very much, Mary" I said. "It is very thoughtful of you."

I sat down in one of the chairs and touched the throw. It was as soft as the one had looked in Rob's room. Before I picked up the cup, I was crying again.I had never had an experience any-where close to this. I was relieved that he'd been breathing when they hauled him away. I prayed they would keep him alive. When I was ready for the tea, it was cold, but cold is how I usually drink tea anyway. I had two cookies, water and went to bed with my cell phone on the nightstand.

At some time during the night, the door to the bedroom opened.

"Gabi, it's me, Babs. I wanted you to know that Robert is going to be fine. The doctors told me to come home and let him rest."

I sat up and turned on the bedside lamp.

Babs was standing beside the bed.

"Sit down," I said, patting the bed beside me. "Has this hap-pened before?"

"No," she said, still standing. "He has a son and daughter, both married with kids. They live in France. They're going to be here tomorrow. Normally they stay in this house."

"Babs, no problem. I'll leave right away."

"I can put you up in a hotel," Babs said. "Thank you for your understanding."

"Of course, I understand. If you can book me out, I prefer going home."

"Are you sure?"

"I'm positive."

"I would send you back in Rob's plane, but it's going to Paris in the morning to pick up his son and daughter to bring them to London."

"I can work on my reservation back," I said.

"No, I'm going to do it for you. Get some rest. If you leave by noon, it will be time enough."

"Okay. Let me know about the return ticket."

"I'll let you know in the morning." Babs leaned over to touch my face. "It would have been horrible to lose Rob like that, and so embarrassing for him if it ever got out."

"My lips are sealed," I said. "I'm so happy he made it."

Babs kissed me. "We owe you Gabi."

"You owe me nothing. Thank God CPR was a college requirement."

At ten in the morning, a hired driver picked me up at Robert's house and drove me to Heathrow Airport. I was booked on Virgin Atlantic Airlines first class direct to Los Angeles.

Babs walked me to the car and handed me an envelope.

"Gabi, this check was written before you arrived. Robert planned on giving this to you for coming over for the week. We owe you a lot more for what you did to save his life. He will be in touch with you."

"Babs, I don't want this check, doesn't matter how much it is. I'm delighted that Robert is okay and will be home soon. I enjoyed the trip out here and even though it sounds horrible, I loved being with Robert for the hours we spent together."

Babs hugged me.

"I know how hard you work, and how hard you worked to get through the schools you attended." She smiled a real smile. "I had you checked out. Take the check."

I didn't open the envelope until I was on the plane, savoring a glass of white wine. The check was payable to me. One hundred thousand U.S. dollars.

The female flight attendant saw me crying and asked me if I was okay.

"I'm fine," I said, "All good."

I closed my eyes, switched gears, and mentally went through my caseload back at the public defender's office.

Whether George Hatcher is traveling the globe as a consultant/strategist for lawyers in high profile wrongful death cases, running one of his many enterprises, or at home with Molly amid the birds and cats in California, he's always got his eye on the next project. He does a whole lot more than what is mentioned here.

A longer bio is on his website.

http//georgehatcher.com/bio/bio.html

www.ingramcontent.com/pod-product-compliance
Lightning Source LLC
Chambersburg PA
CBHW070924100726
47908CB00001B/93